A Little Light Magic

JOY NASH

LEISURE BOOKS  NEW YORK CITY

A LEISURE BOOK®

June 2009

Published by

Dorchester Publishing Co., Inc.
200 Madison Avenue
New York, NY 10016

ISBN 10: 0-505-52693-X
ISBN 13: 978-0-505-52693-9
E-ISBN: 978-1-4285-0679-4

The name "Leisure Books" and the stylized "L" with design are trademarks of Dorchester Publishing Co., Inc.

Printed in the United States of America.

10 9 8 7 6 5 4 3 2 1

Visit us on the web at www.dorchesterpub.com.

MIXING BUSINESS WITH PLEASURE

"Why switch contractors? I'll get you open on time, and you'll save money in the bargain."

The dream replayed in her mind. She stared at Nick's big hands, still wrapped around the end of the two-by-fours, and a wave of heat cascaded through her body. Her palms started to sweat, and she began to get desperate.

"You said you didn't even want the job when you first showed up. Why are you so anxious to do the work now?"

Nick caught Tori's gaze and held it a couple of heartbeats too long before he let it go. His lips twitched. "Let's just say I want to please the client."

"Oh." She felt as if she were on one of those boardwalk rides that lifted you a hundred feet into the air and dropped you into a free fall. "You do?"

"Yes, I do. Now could you open the door?"

"Wait a minute," she said. "I can't in good conscience let you work on my house without making a confession first."

"Sounds serious."

She couldn't quite look at him. "It is. The thing is, you didn't agree to do this job of your own free will. I cast a candle magic spell. It brought you here."

Other books by Joy Nash:

IMMORTALS: THE RECKONING (Anthology)
IMMORTALS: THE CROSSING
IMMORTALS: THE AWAKENING
DEEP MAGIC
THE GRAIL KING
CELTIC FIRE

This book is dedicated to the
wise female voices of my childhood:

Helen, Mary J., Elvira, Rose, Dolly,
Bert, Esther, Amelia, and Mary R.,

and most of all,
to my mother,
Verna Mae

Your words are silent now,
but never forgotten

I miss you, Mom.

Author's Note:

Absecon Island, New Jersey, is home to Atlantic City and the Downbeach communities of Ventnor, Margate, and Longport. While there's much on the island that's new and glitzy, if you know where to look, you can still find old treasures tucked away.

Tori's shop and Nick's house don't exist, but many of the places Nick and Tori visit in *A Little Light Magic* are real. If you're ever on the island, stop by and visit my personal ***Best of Absecon Island***.

The White House Sub Shop, 2301 Arctic Avenue, Atlantic City
An Atlantic City legend. Famous for Philly-style cheesesteaks and hoagies since 1946. Features Formica Bros. sub rolls.

Formica Bros. Bakery, 2310 Arctic Avenue, Atlantic City
Hand-crafted breads and pastry since 1919. Currently owned by the third generation descendant of the original founder. Sub rolls and cannoli to die for.

The Steel Pier, Atlantic City Boardwalk at Virginia Avenue
This historic amusement pier, once home to such acts as the High Diving Horse and Rex the Wonder Dog, was first opened in 1898. Despite an announcement that the pier would close "permanently" in October 2006, the Atlantic City landmark has remained open while redevelopment plans are being finalized.

Sack O' Subs, 5217 Ventnor Avenue, Ventnor
Cheesesteaks and subs by the Sacco family since 1969. Fantastic! Will ship your sub to anywhere in the country. Features Formica Bros. sub rolls.

Lucy the Elephant, 9200 Atlantic Avenue, Margate
This quirky six-story wooden elephant, built in 1881 to attract real estate investors to the island, has also done duty as a hotel and tavern. It's now a local history museum and a National Historic Landmark. The only elephant you can walk through and come out alive.

Margate Dairy Bar, 9510 Ventnor Avenue, Margate
Soft ice cream and Italian water ice since 1952. A *Philadelphia Magazine* "Best of the Shore" award winner. If you find yourself in town, you really don't want to miss it.

Ozzie's Luncheonette, 2401 Atlantic Avenue, Longport
Betty Boop rules in this 1950s throwback diner.

All the best!

Joy Nash

A Little Light Magic

Chapter One

It's tough being alone in the world,
with no family to turn to.

Nick Santangelo double-checked the address. Yep, he was in the right place, but he could hardly believe it. The little pink house was a mess—and that assessment was generous. The only thing it had going for it was its location, location, and location. And that, as they said in the business, was everything.

The property was half a block from the Jersey shore's quirkiest tourist attraction—a 128-year-old oversize wooden elephant affectionately known as Lucy. Luckily for the six-story pachyderm, she faced the ocean, not the neglected property tucked into the downscale alley behind her sizable derriere. His prospect was wedged between a dive bar and a tired summer rental that had surely seen its share of lost security deposits.

He paralleled his truck into a space a foot too short to be comfortable and got out to take a better look, leaving his keys in the ignition and the motor running. The place was twenty feet wide, tops, and maybe three times as deep. Peeling paint adorned the cracked stucco, and the sun shone through rips in a faded green awning. Some kind of formless music drifted through the open bay window. He peered through the dirty screen and made out the shape of a woman moving around inside.

According to Doris's notes, the owner, a Victoria Morgan, didn't want anything major. Just enough work to allow the front room to open as a retail shop. But she needed the job done ASAP, before the summer season got into full swing. Not much hope of that. Memorial Day had already come and gone.

He looked up, at shingles that were starting to curl. Now, a teardown and rebuild—that might interest him. But a code touch-up on a postage stamp? Why the hell was Doris wasting his time with this? His secretary knew better than that.

He scanned the prospect sheet attached to his clipboard and found his answer. The owner, Victoria Morgan, was the grandniece of Doris's recently deceased friend Millie Whittaker. He vaguely remembered Doris taking a day off to attend the funeral. Apparently, this Ms. Morgan had inherited the old Whittaker place and was in dire need of a contractor.

Dire need. Doris had underlined the words in red felt-tip and added three exclamation points.

Nick snorted. What was he, a freaking doctor?

He tossed the clipboard back into the truck. Lord knew he'd do as much for Doris as he would for his own mother, but the timing couldn't have been worse. He had three crews working overtime on the largest project Santangelo Construction had ever tackled—a job that had fallen behind schedule. No way could he fit this rehab in. Not even as a favor to the world's best office manager.

He checked his watch as he climbed the cracked concrete steps. Five twenty-nine. Right on time, and he couldn't wait long—there was a mountain of paper he had to move across his desk before tomorrow. Mentally, he plotted out his evening. Two minutes to explain he couldn't do the job, five to drive home and grab a sandwich, fifteen to get back to his office in Atlantic City.

He rapped on the frame of a battered screen door.

"Hello?"

No answer.

He pounded again, harder this time. "Hello?"

"What? Oh! Just a minute."

The door opened. "Hi," a breathless voice said. "Can I help you?"

Nick opened his mouth to answer, then took a good look at the woman standing in the doorway and shut it again.

She wasn't at all what he'd expected.

Not that he'd been expecting anything. But if he *had* been expecting something, it wouldn't have been a freckled pixie with wild black curls and streaks of silver paint smudged across her nose. Her eyes were green, her skin was flushed, and her full red lips drove every thought out of his head and straight to his groin.

Oh, man. This was not good.

Despite his best effort at nonchalance, his gaze flicked to her chest, and, Lord, that was a mistake, because she was wearing a stretchy scoop-necked tee with no bra. Her breasts were just the kind he liked—round and firm, not too big, not too small. Her highlighter green knit top stretched from peak to peak, distorting the lettering on the front.

DANCE AS IF NO ONE IS WATCHING.

Funny, dancing wasn't the activity that immediately sprang to mind.

Jesus. Why the hell had he left his clipboard in the truck? It would have come in handy right about now, positioned strategically in front of his belt buckle. . . .

The object of his unexpected lust tilted her head to one side and touched the tip of her tongue to her bottom lip. He nearly groaned out loud. She blinked up at him, one hand on her hip, the other holding a paintbrush dipped in silver paint. She came up only to his chin, but something about her seemed taller.

He floundered around for his lost professionalism. "Ms. Morgan?"

"Yes."

"I'm Nick Santangelo. From Santangelo Construction. You were expecting me?"

"Oh. Yes! Yes, I was. But not until five thirty."

He checked his watch. "It's five thirty-two."

"It is?" She looked genuinely shocked at the news. "I must've lost track of the time." She kicked a remnant of Sunday's *Press of Atlantic City* out of the path of the door. "Come in."

He stepped into a minefield of paint paraphernalia and moving boxes. The screen door slammed behind him, making him start. Broken. Well, why the hell not? Everything else in the house seemed to be, from the dented aluminum stepladder to the beat-up folding table, which was flanked by equally decrepit folding chairs that didn't match. A battered CD player—complete with duct-taped cord—was gurgling something that was probably supposed to be a clear mountain stream but sounded more like a running toilet.

Ms. Morgan circled her paintbrush at the walls. "What do you think of them?"

He guessed she meant the clouds. They covered all four walls of the twelve-by-twenty room, painted in billowing silver on a field of electric blue. Overhead, faceted crystals hung from the ceiling like stars.

What did he think of it? He looked at Ms. Morgan and entertained a few doubts about her sanity.

"Well?"

He cleared his throat. "It's . . . bright."

"Thanks. I thought so, too."

"Look, Ms. Morgan—"

"Call me Tori."

"Okay. Tori. I—"

She turned and started across the room, weaving between the boxes. "I don't really need much work done. It's just that the building inspector says I can't open Destiny's Gate in the front room while I live in the back without making a few fire code upgrades first." She bent at the waist to dip her brush into a can of paint. The zigzag hem of her skirt rose, giving Nick a glimpse of smooth skin and a Celtic-knot anklet tattoo.

With an effort, he refocused on a cloud. "Destiny's Gate?"

"That's what I'm calling my shop."

"Um . . . what do you plan to sell?"

She sidled back into his line of vision and started dabbing paint on the very cloud he'd been staring at. "Oh, tarot cards, crystals, runes, books." She paused. "I'll do divination, too. People need to know what the cosmos has in store for them."

"Divination? You mean like fortune-telling?"

"Some people call it that. I like to call it future sight."

"You're kidding, right?"

She frowned at him over her shoulder. "No. Why would I be?"

"Because you can't seriously think to sell that woo-woo stuff around here. Summer people come to Margate to take their kids to the beach, not to get their fortunes told. You'd be better off selling wave boards. Or Italian ice."

Her answering scowl sent him rocking back on his heels.

"Hey," he protested. "Don't go getting all mad. It's good advice. And it's free."

"Really."

"Yeah. If you want to tell fortunes, you should set up shop on the Ocean City boardwalk. That's where the tourists go when they're looking to throw away money."

"Throw away—Oh!"

Ms. Morgan—Tori—abandoned her cloud, her chest rising on a quick intake of breath. Nick tried not to look down, but, Jesus, it was a lost cause. She marched right up to him and halted so close he could practically feel her breasts in his hands.

A jab of her brush near his nose brought his attention back to her face.

"I'll have you know fortune-telling is a valuable art, not a waste of money! And I can't go anywhere else. I have to open Destiny's Gate here, in this house."

"You inherited the place recently, right?"

The light in her green eyes dimmed. "Yes. From my great-aunt. It's been a summer rental for the last seventeen years, since she moved into a nursing home."

"Well, maybe now that it's yours, you should think of selling. This close to the beach, you'd get a great price."

"But the new owners would tear the house down!"

"Well, yeah, obviously. The value's all in the land."

She shook her head. Nick was momentarily distracted by her glossy dark curls stroking and sifting over her shoulders. His palms started to itch.

"No," she was saying. "I can't let that happen. Aunt Millie left so much positive psychic energy in these walls."

Positive psychic energy?

She shot him a disgruntled look. "You know, I didn't ask your opinion."

"What?" Nick said. "I didn't say anything."

"You didn't have to. But it doesn't matter, because I'm not looking for your advice. I just want to hire you. And there's really not much work here. You can probably finish it in a day or two."

"Well, about that," he said. "I only stopped by to—"

"Do you want to see the list?" She moved closer and he caught her scent. Something old-fashioned and flowery. Calm. It seemed an odd choice for her. From what he could see, standing still wasn't something Tori Morgan knew how to do.

"I don't think—"

"Wait. It's around here somewhere."

Huh? A conversation with this woman shifted as quickly as sand in a storm. Bemused, he watched as she sank to the floor, her gauzy skirt swirling as she rifled through a stack of papers shoved into a cardboard box. Her paintbrush, seemingly forgotten in her left hand, dripped silver onto the floor.

"Here." He grabbed the brush before it could do any more damage. "Let me take that."

She blinked up at him, then frowned at the brush. "Oh. Thanks. I know I put the building inspector's list in here somewhere."

He set the brush in one of her four and a half open cans of silver paint. "Look, don't bother. I can't take your job anyway."

"What?"

She stood up so fast she nearly lost her balance. Nick caught her upper arm, then immediately wished he hadn't. Touching her wasn't the best idea. The urge to drag her flush against his body was entirely too urgent. What had gotten into him? He couldn't remember the last time he'd had such a sudden, overwhelming response to a woman.

She stared up at him with eyes the exact color of the ocean before a storm. She was so close now he could see that the green of her irises was touched with subtle flecks of blue. Her cheeks were flushed. And her lips . . .

". . . do it," she said breathlessly.

What? He stared down at her.

"You have to do it. You have to take my job."

Oh, right. The job.

Nick released her and took a step back. "Look, I'm sorry, but I'm afraid I won't be able to help you out. My company doesn't do small projects like this. Doris should have told you when you called."

"Oh, she did. But she also said you might be able to squeeze it in if I couldn't find anybody else."

"I'd really like to help, but I'm overextended as it is. I can't possibly take this on."

"But that's not right! The cards said that you'd help me."

"Cards? What cards?"

She pointed at the folding table. "The tarot. I did a reading after I talked to Doris. The outcome was favorable."

"I see," Nick said slowly, pacing toward the table. The cards spread out there weren't the regular playing kind, but some sort of fortune-telling cards.

"Favorable." He slanted her a glance. "But not, I take it, definite?"

She grimaced. "Well . . . no. Not exactly definite." She tapped the closest card. "I drew the Moon. That always denotes a time of uncertainty."

He smiled. "There you go, then. That proves I'm not your man."

She looked up just long enough to send him a scowl. "It does nothing of the kind. See this card? The Four of Wands foretells success in new ventures. I can't have success if I can't open. That means you're going to take the job."

"Uh-huh."

"And besides," she pressed on, "you're my last hope. My only hope! You can't even imagine how many contractors I've called. Not one will even give me an estimate before August. But when I looked into my crystal, I saw the work completed before the solstice."

Nick couldn't believe his ears. "You've got a crystal ball that tracks construction projects? You know, I could use one of those at the office."

"No," she said seriously. "It's not a ball. I can never get a good reading on a curved surface. I use a prism."

Nick shook his head. Time to go. Because, clearly, this woman had already left the building.

"Tell you what," he said, angling toward the door. "I'll ask around. Maybe one of my subcontractors will be interested."

He left before she could launch another protest, relieved to trade the whirling clouds and flashing crystals for the comforting solidity of his Dodge Ram four-by-four. Tori Morgan might turn him on like crazy, but no way was Nick going to follow his little head on this one.

Tarot cards. Positive psychic energy. Visions in crystals.

The woman was out of her freaking mind.

Tori hurled an extremely negative thought at the arrogant contractor's retreating back. She almost launched a can of paint after it. The broken screen door slammed on her last hope with all the finality of a shattered scrying mirror.

Well. Didn't that just suck the big lollipop?

She plopped down on a folding chair, then jumped up again when the broken leg gave way. Drumming her fingertips on the side of her thigh, she tried to figure out just where she'd gone wrong with the tarot reading. She'd been so sure Doris's boss would take the job.

Nick Santangelo certainly fit the image of the Knight of Swords, the card representing the immediate future. The Knight was dark and confident. Doris's boss had been that and more. Tori didn't think much of his attitude, but she had to admit the man was hot. He was in his midthirties, maybe, but not going soft like a lot of men his age were. His chest was solid, his hips lean. His tanned forearms were sprinkled with dark hair.

And he had very nice hands.

It was a thing with her—guys' hands. She always noticed them. Nick Santangelo's were large and capable, with long, graceful fingers. She puzzled over that for a bit. Hands like his belonged to an artist, not a tradesman.

He didn't wear a wedding ring.

She had no business noticing that. He wasn't her type at all.

But he'd been checking her out. No way she could have missed it. For a while there, his eyes had been glued to a point about eight inches below her chin. And she hadn't missed the look on his face when she'd explained about her crystal vision.

He thought she was a kook.

Not that she cared. Truth be told, she was used to it. A lot of people—okay, most people—didn't see life the way she did. Part of her was glad the man had turned down her job. He was entirely too appealing on a physical level, and she wasn't looking for a quick hookup. That was how things had started out with Colin—they'd hooked up, and before she knew it, pow! She was in love and changing herself to suit his moods.

She felt a twinge of pain in her midsection. She laid her hand over her stomach and blinked back tears. No, she wasn't looking for quick sex and all the heartache it brought.

But she *was* looking for a contractor. She couldn't open her shop without one. Too bad every Jersey man who knew how to use his nail gun was booked solid through September.

Maybe another tarot reading would shed some light?

Then she thought of the last Weird Zone tour she'd led with Colin before things went sour. They'd been camping with a group of vampire wannabes near a decrepit Louisiana bayou mansion. Weird Zone's local sources insisted the house was a vampire sanctuary. The whole thing turned out to be a hoax, but the trip into the swamp hadn't been a total loss. Tori had discovered a Cajun witch living in the mansion's gatehouse, and the old woman had taken a liking to her. She'd shown up at the campsite the morning Tori and Colin were packing the tents, insisting that Tori accept a gift: a bundle of seven hoodoo candle magic spell kits the witch had assembled and blessed herself.

The spells would keep their magic no more than a year, the witch had told Tori. Tori had promised to use them before their power faded. She'd given the old woman her sincere thanks and packed them away. That had been last September. Soon after, all the drama with Colin had begun, and the old witch and her gifts had slipped Tori's mind. Until she was packing for Aunt Millie's funeral and found them stashed in the bottom of her spare backpack.

In three months, the hoodoo mojo would be gone. So if Tori was going to use the old witch's gift, she'd better do it soon. And right now, with her money almost gone and her plans for the shop stalled, a little magic was just what she needed.

But where were the spell kits? Somewhere in the chaos she currently called home. Tori had spent nearly all her savings on merchandise for the shop, and as a result, boxes were everywhere—stacked in the front room, crammed into the dining room, shoveled into the smaller of the two tiny bedrooms.

She started hunting, and found the spells—and this had to be a good omen—in the first box she opened. There were seven gris-gris bags in all, each one a different color: green, red, orange, black, yellow, blue, and white. The handwritten tag on the white bag indicated the spell was to be used to call for help.

That seemed appropriate.

She unwound the twine holding the white bag closed. Inside she found a white candle about eight inches long, a small cotton pouch labeled, *Sugar*, and a scrap of rolled parchment. She rolled out the paper and bent her head over the spidery script.

> *Place the candle on a ceramic plate.*
> *Sprinkle sugar all around.*
> *Set the plate higher than your head.*
> *Light with a wooden match.*
> *Help will soon arrive.*

That didn't seem too difficult.

Miraculously, she found an old box of wooden matches in the kitchen. There was no shortage of chipped ceramic plates. But where to cast the spell? The stepladder was the only thing higher than her head, so she dragged it to the center of the front room and set the candle on top. She climbed three shaky rungs, matches in hand.

Help will soon arrive. . . .

Later, Tori figured this was the exact point in time where she screwed up the spell. When she lit the candle, she really should have been concentrating on the shop. The trouble was, she'd been in such a funk all day, missing Aunt Millie and trying not to dwell on how alone she was in the world now that her last living relative was dead and her relationship with Colin had gone up in flames. When the spell's instructions echoed in her head, her heart replied with one word.

Family.

She wanted a big one. She always had. She wanted a mother and father, grandparents, brothers and sisters, nieces and nephews, a collection of assorted cousins and in-laws. She wanted the kind of family that loved her because she'd been born to them.

Her wish was impossible, of course. She knew that. She'd

lost the family lottery the day she was born. The only way she'd get any kind of family now was if she started one of her own.

Her stomach started cramping again, and she almost let the tears come. But she'd cried a river since she'd miscarried, and she knew from experience that more tears wouldn't bring back what she'd lost.

Okay, so the white candle was about a foot over her head. It was leaning a little precariously, but she figured it'd be safe enough for a few minutes. She scraped the wooden match against the side of the matchbox. A plume of smoke rose with the sudden flame. She touched the wick. It crackled and caught.

She climbed back down the ladder and set the matches next to the tarot. The Knight of Swords, a dark-haired warrior in full armor, stared up at her. He rode a white horse. . . .

She heard a car stop outside. A second later, heavy footsteps thudded on the porch. She turned as the screen door banged open.

And she stared.

Because Nick Santangelo was back.

He scanned the room, brows knitted, his dark gaze uncertain until it settled unerringly on her. Suddenly, she felt restless. She told herself it was just stray energy from the spell.

He dragged a hand over his hair, rumpling the curls.

"Look," he said. "I was thinking—"

He stopped and gave a slight shake of his head, as if trying to clear it.

She could hardly breathe. "What were you thinking?"

"I was thinking I'd take your job after all."

He was out of his freaking mind.

Nick knew there was no other possible explanation. He'd been parked in his driveway, talking—okay, well, *shouting* might be a more apt description—at Thomas Southerland on his cell. Southerland had been busting Nick's ass for the delays on the Bayview job—delays caused by Southerland's endless parade of change orders. Nick had barely stopped himself from telling the Ivy League architect where he could shove his roll of blueprints. Teeth grinding, he'd snapped his phone closed.

And that was when things got weird.

Because for no good reason, he'd thrown his truck into reverse. Somehow, he must've backed out of his drive and made the turn onto Atlantic, because now he was standing in Tori Morgan's whacked-out witch shop, offering to take on a job he'd had no intention of touching with a fifty-foot tape measure.

"You'll work on my shop?"

Tori Morgan sounded stunned. But she wasn't looking at him. She was staring at her broken stepladder, which was now in the center of the room serving as an unsteady perch for a candle. A *lit* candle.

Jesus. Didn't she realize the place was a firetrap? And he didn't see a single smoke detector.

He jabbed a thumb at the ladder. "That's dangerous, you know."

"You have no idea," she replied. But she still didn't look at him.

He watched uneasily as she climbed three dented rungs and blew out the flame. "Did you find Brad Weinstein's list?"

"Brad Weinstein?"

"From the building inspector's office. You did speak to Brad, didn't you? Middle-aged guy, kind of balding?"

"Oh, right. I'd forgotten the man's name."

Why was Nick not surprised?

Tori sifted through her box of papers again. "Here it is."

He focused on Brad's dark scrawl. "This isn't a couple days' work. More like two weeks."

"That's some kind of contractor joke, right? Everything takes two weeks?"

"In this case, it's the truth." He was more annoyed than he should have been.

"Oh. Two weeks. Well, I suppose that's all right. As long as you're done before the solstice."

"And that would be . . . ?"

She blinked. "The first day of summer. Doesn't everyone know that?"

He shot her a look. "We have a problem, then. All my men are working overtime for the next month. I can't spare anyone for this project."

Her hopeful expression crumpled. "Oh."

He was surprised—and irritated—to feel a stab of guilt. "The date's that important to you?"

"Oh, yes."

"In that case, I'll tell you what. This isn't really that much work. I can do it myself. After hours. If I work every night, I should be able to get you open on time."

Christ. Had he really said that? What the hell was wrong with him? He didn't have time for this. He spent most of his evenings at the office as it was.

But Tori's face had lit up. Nick enjoyed her smile briefly before it faltered.

"After hours? You mean, like, at night?"

"Um, yeah, I guess. Till around eleven or so."

Night. A parade of interesting images marched through his brain, and none of them had to do with hanging dry-wall. He sent Tori Morgan a speculative look. Her color had risen, and she was looking everywhere but at him.

Nick started to smile. Maybe there'd be an upside to this job after all.

"You don't mind, do you?"

"I guess not," she said, still not meeting his eyes. Her hands were moving, as if searching for something to hold on to.

"Okay, then. I can start Monday afternoon. Five thirty. If that's okay with you."

She sighed. "I guess it'll have to be. How much will it cost?"

"What's your budget?"

She named a ridiculously low figure, and he didn't even care.

"I'll work with it." He tapped the paper in his hand. "Can I keep the list?"

Tori let out a breath. "Sure. Be my guest. Keep it."

Nick flashed her a grin.

"Okay, great. See you Monday."

Chapter Two

Women are the heart of any family.

The Santangelo women were arguing again.

Nick paused just inside his front door. The unrelenting rise and fall of feminine voices, more than anything else, told him he was home. He paused at the foyer table, dropping his wallet and emptying the change from his pocket into a jar he kept there for that purpose. He sometimes thought that if the women in his family ever stopped bickering, his house would collapse.

He didn't pay any particular attention until he realized they were talking about him.

"Come on, Mimi . . ." Leigh said to her grandmother.

Nick could hear the exasperation in his mother's reply. Rita enunciated each word slowly and clearly. "Leigh, forget it. Your father will never allow it. You know how he feels about Jason."

"He'll let me go if you say it's okay!"

Nonna's voice intruded, thin and pointed as a needle. "Where *is* Nicky? This chicken, it's shriveled like a prune."

Leigh's voice came again, wheedling. "But I have to go! I promised Jason I'd be there."

Jason again. Christ. Nick wished to God he'd never heard that kid's name. He started for the kitchen with angry strides, his blood pressure rising with each step.

Rita's voice rose. "Leigh, give it up already. Your father will never agree—"

He reached the doorway. "What won't I agree to?"

The conversation came to an abrupt halt as three pairs of eyes, belonging to three generations of Santangelo women, turned toward him.

Nick's right temple started to throb.

"What won't I agree to?" he repeated a little louder when no answer was forthcoming.

"Nothing," Leigh muttered. She grabbed a serving spoon and fork off the counter and turned to toss the salad.

"Nicky. At last." Nonna laid a hand on his arm. "*Grazie a Dio.* I was about to call the cops."

"I'm not that late, Nonna." He planted a kiss on his grandmother's withered cheek and allowed her to tug him to the head of the table. There was no way he was getting away with a quick sandwich now. He'd start World War III if he tried to get back to the office before Nonna's chicken was reduced to bones and gristle. And with Leigh's newest drama, whatever it was . . . *Damn.* He'd be lucky to get back to the office by nine.

Nonna forked chicken onto a serving plate while Rita pulled garlic bread from the oven. Nick, frowning, watched Leigh fling lettuce and tomatoes onto salad plates. If the waistband of his daughter's shorts were rolled down any farther, he'd be seeing parts of her he hadn't come face-to-face with since her diaper days. The thought made him slightly ill. *Goddamn it all to hell.* She hadn't dressed like that before *Jason.*

Leigh turned to place the salad on the table. Moodily, Nick watched her. A father didn't like to notice such things, but he could hardly deny the fact that Leigh had inherited her mother's bustline. Cindy's breasts had fried Nick's brain in high school, and he had no doubt that Leigh's assets were destroying a similar number of brain cells in Jason MacAllister's thick skull. If all this was God's idea of a sick joke, Nick wasn't laughing.

He stared down at his salad. *Christ.* He wasn't old enough for this. Damn it, he was only thirty-five. Other men his age were still changing diapers and coaching Little League. But Nick had been a horny, seventeen-year-old idiot when he'd gotten Cindy pregnant. Which was not a comforting thought, given Leigh's horny, seventeen-year-old idiot boyfriend. *Your father will never agree. . . .* Nick didn't know what Leigh's latest plea involved, but he was dead certain he wasn't going to like it.

Nonna presented Nick with a plate. "This chicken shoulda been eat a half hour ago. Don't blame me if it's ruined."

"I'm sure it's delicious, Nonna," Nick said, forking meat onto his plate. "You couldn't cook a bad meal if you tried."

A smile cracked Nonna's face. "You're a good boy, Nicky." She sank into her chair and bowed her head while he muttered grace.

"Amen." He took a piece of garlic bread and offered the basket to his mother.

Rita shook her head. "I'm on the Flat Belly diet. You know that, Nicky."

He eyed her enormous salad, sprinkled with sunflower seeds and topped with a naked chicken breast. "Don't you think you've lost enough weight, Ma? How much is it, now?"

"Thirty pounds. I've got another five to go."

Nonna snorted. "Stop with the diet already. You don't eat enough to keep a bird alive. A woman needs a little padding on her bones. You want my advice? Get rid of them hormone pills. They're making you *pazza*." She shook her head, but her tight gray curls didn't shake with it. "And all that exercise! *Santa* Madonna. No woman should lift weights."

"I think Mimi looks great," Leigh offered.

She was right, Nick realized. Rita did look great, but the weight she'd lost was only part of it. She'd also gotten contact lenses, dyed her hair, and acquired a bright, clingy wardrobe. He eyed her fingernails, done in red, with fake tips. Or maybe they were real. Who the hell knew? The effect of all the changes was unnerving. Aside from a few laugh lines, Nick's mother looked much the same as she had fifteen years ago.

Nick didn't like it. It made him feel like he'd gone back in time himself, to the year he'd turned twenty. The year Cindy had left him, the year his father had dropped dead. It was a year he didn't like to think about.

"And what was wrong with how your grandmother looked before?" Nonna demanded of Leigh. "She was fine. She don't need to starve. She's gonna get sick."

"I'm okay," Rita said through clenched teeth.

Nick knew better than to enter the estrogen-fueled debate. He kept his head down and ate. He was half-finished with his meal when Rita set her napkin down next to her barely touched plate. She rose, her chair scraping the tile.

"I've got to go," she said.

"Go?" Nick asked. "Go where?"

"Church."

He eyed her. "On a Thursday night?"

"I'm on the committee for the Fourth of July crab bake."

Leigh nearly choked on her Diet Coke. "What? No way. You swore you were blowing that off this year. You said—"

"Never mind what I said. Fiona Hennessey begged for my help."

"You've hated Fiona Hennessey since middle school," Nick pointed out.

"Yes, well, that's the very reason I couldn't say no when she begged."

Nonna was clearly displeased. "If Rita's going out, who's gonna drive me home? I can't sit around here all night. I need to watch that new *Survivor* show."

"Leigh can take you home," Rita told her.

"No, I'll do it," Nick said, dropping his napkin on the table. "I'm headed back to the office anyway."

Nonna waved a disapproving hand. "Office, office. Always that office. It's like you're married to that job. You work too much, Nicky. When you gonna get a new wife? I want to see a great-grandson before I die."

"Talk to Alex," Nick muttered. "Or Zach." Hell, even his youngest brother, Johnny, was more likely to fulfill that wish than Nick was. The very last thing Nick needed was another kid. Leigh had been more than enough to handle since day one. Another like her, and he'd have a stroke.

"Okay, then," Rita said. "Don't anybody wait up for me." She disappeared into the living room. A moment later, Nick heard the front door slam.

Leigh stood. "Nonna, you go ahead with Dad. I'll do the dishes."

Nick raised his brows at his daughter's sudden attack of domesticity. So she wanted him gone, did she? He wasn't about to let her off the hook so easily.

"*Grazie, carina,*" Nonna said. "Nicky, don't move. I'll be right back."

She disappeared in the direction of the bathroom, towing her handbag behind her. She'd carried the bag, a plain black patent-leather trapezoid with a big gold clasp and stiff, semicircular handles, ever since Nick could remember. The thing held the world.

Nick pushed his plate toward the center of the table, his eyes on his daughter. "So," he asked her. "What is it I'm not going to agree to?"

Leigh headed to the sink with a stack of plates. "If you're not going to agree to it, why bother talking about it?"

"Because I'm your father, that's why. What's up?"

She turned, still clutching the dishes. "Jason's having a graduation party. All the seniors are going."

"You're only a junior."

"Exactly! That's why I have to go."

"Aren't Jason's parents on a cruise?"

"Yes. But Beth is home from college. She'll be there."

"Jason's sister is what—twenty-one?"

"Yeah. She's an adult."

"Oh, right. An adult who'll buy the beer and disappear into her bedroom with her boyfriend. The next thing you know, you'll be with Jason in his bedroom."

"Oh!" Leigh's blue eyes flashed daggers at him. "That is so unfair."

Nick leaned back in his chair. Christ, but Leigh looked more and more like Cindy every day. The long, straight blonde hair, the blue eyes, the high cheekbones. And, of course, the figure.

About the only thing she'd gotten from Nick was her temper.

He sighed. "I don't want you to get hurt, honey."

"Jason wouldn't hurt me! He loves me."

Nick's temper flared. "Oh, come off it, Leigh. How many girls do you think he's told that one to?"

"One! Me. But you—Oh!"

She slammed the stack of dishes on the table. A soggy tomato flew off the top plate and struck Nick in the chest.

He jumped to his feet as it slithered down his shirt. "Jesus, Leigh!"

"God! You just won't understand! You never do. You won't even *try*!"

Nick tried to keep his reply calm, but didn't quite succeed. "I understand better than you think. And that's exactly why you are not going to an unchaperoned party with a muscle-bound lifeguard whose neck size is larger than his IQ."

"Jason's not dumb! He's going to Rutgers in the fall."

"That's right. He's leaving, Leigh. Do you really think he's going to spend his Saturday nights texting you? Get real. He's gonna find someone else. It's inevitable."

Leigh looked away, but not before Nick saw a shimmer of tears in her eyes.

"Ah, Christ, honey, I didn't mean . . ." He reached for her, but she took a quick step back and his fingers closed on air. She was always dodging him these days. He couldn't even remember the last time she'd let him touch her, let alone give her a hug, the way he had when she was little.

She hugged herself, blinking furiously at a point over his head.

Nick felt like kicking himself. Or better yet, kicking *Jason*.

"Look, honey, I'm just trying to protect you."

"Don't bother. I can take care of myself."

He ran a hand over his face. She couldn't take care of herself, not by a long shot, but there was nothing else he could say to her now that wouldn't make things worse.

"Look, I've got some work to do at the office after I drop Nonna off. I should be home by eleven. Will you be okay here alone?"

"Let's see . . . yeah, I think I can manage."

He ignored her tone. "I'll be back as soon as I can." He paused. "No visitors. Understood?"

Leigh's expression hardened. "Yes. Can I go now?"

Nonna chose that moment to reappear, her handbag clutched to her chest. Her knowing eyes darted first to Leigh, then to Nick.

"*Dio in cielo,*" she said. "I missed a fight."

Look before you leap.

Tori had heard that maxim about a zillion times from Aunt Millie, but she'd never really listened.

Maybe she should have.

She flung silver paint onto a cloud as she berated herself for fooling around with magic she didn't really understand. She really should have considered the consequences of lighting that candle before she struck the match. But who would've thought it would work so fast?

The brush slipped, smearing silver into blue. She frowned at the damage, then gave up. She'd fix it later, when she was calmer.

At least she had a contractor who would get her shop open before the solstice. The tarot had, as always, been right on the mark.

She collected her brushes and washed them out in the bathroom sink. The faucet leaked, which was annoying, but she had no idea how to fix it. She was sure that Nick Santangelo did. The thought only annoyed her further.

She couldn't get him out of her mind. But why? He certainly wasn't anything like Colin. Colin had a wiry kind of energy she'd loved, and an irreverence toward authority that she wholeheartedly shared. Nick? The man had a solid, conservative look about him. His pressed chinos and white golf shirt (complete with company logo embroidered on the left breast) made about as boring an outfit as she could imagine.

So why was her stomach doing backflips? She didn't want to know.

She tried to push him out of her thoughts. No luck. He filled her head as completely as he'd filled Aunt Millie's front room. He didn't belong in either place. He was too tall, too dark, too conventional. Too cynical. She thought of his curly hair and large, capable hands.

He was too sexy. Definitely too sexy.

He was too busy to do her job during the day.

And didn't she know what he was up to with that? How could she not? It had been written all over his face. He was a guy, after all.

He wanted sex.

To be honest, the idea was not without its appeal.

She gave the dripping faucet one last, savage yank. The last dribble of water just wouldn't stop, no matter how hard she twisted. The kitchen sink wasn't much better—the thing dripped night and day. There were a ton of other things wrong with Aunt Millie's house—light switches that didn't work, doors that stuck, a doorbell that didn't ring, a roof that leaked.

She wanted to fix them all, but the truth was she'd spent too much on merchandise for the store, and what savings were left had to cover the cost of the building inspector's list *and* pay the mortgage she'd inherited along with the house—not to mention her own living expenses. At least until money from the shop started coming in. Little luxuries like working faucets would have to wait.

She dumped the clean paintbrushes into an empty jar. Enough already. She'd go for a walk on the beach and do some tai chi. It was an exercise routine she'd started after her miscarriage, hoping it would help her painful periods. They'd always been bad, but since she lost the baby they hurt like no one's business. It was as if her body were reliving the trauma of losing that precious new life, over and over. Tai chi helped a little, if she did it every day. At least, she thought it did.

She walked the block and a half to the beach. The lifeguards had long since packed it in, leaving the wide stretch of sand nearly deserted. On the shore, a woman was building a sand castle with two little blonde girls. The younger one was just a toddler, still wobbly on her feet.

She was midcycle at the moment, not even close to her bad time of the month. But Tori's stomach twinged anyway. She pressed her palm to her belly and started walking the other way.

She headed up the beach past the rock jetty. Breakers pounded the black boulders, coughing sprays of white froth. She slowed at a break in the dunes. On the other side of the sculptured mound of sand and sea grass, she could just make out the house she used to call the Castle.

It was funny: She'd been back in town for a month, but she hadn't come to see it. She guessed she'd been afraid it would be gone, torn down like so many of the older houses on the island, to make way for something newer and bigger. But then, the Castle wasn't that old. It'd been completed just before Aunt Millie had her stroke. Tori had run down to the beach every day after school to watch it go up. It rose three stories high on the edge of the sand, each floor stepped back to form a terrace on the roof of the level below, all curved walls and wide windows.

It didn't look like a castle, really, except in her childish imagination. But she used to pretend it was her castle, and that she lived in it with her handsome knight and their dozen or so children. Her hero was slender and blond, with shining blue eyes and a soft expression. He kissed her hand and composed love poems in her honor.

She'd looked for that knight ever since she was twelve.

Now that she was thirty, she knew he didn't exist. If she wanted a castle, she was going to have to build one of her own. So she spread her legs in the warrior stance—a power pose. Arms lifted, she started her exercise routine, matching her breath and movement to the rhythm of the pounding surf.

She didn't know her knight was watching.

Tori Morgan was on the beach.

She was impossible to miss in that neon green T-shirt. Nick stood at his bedroom window and watched her do some kind of Asian exercise thing. Yoga, maybe? Her body stretched and swayed like grass on the dunes. The wind whipped her flimsy skirt against her legs. He kept his eye on her as he shrugged out of his tomato-spattered shirt and into a clean one.

She spread her stance wide, arms lifted. Even from a distance, her body intrigued him. She was supple and strong, slender for the most part—except for that beautiful round ass, which faced him now, taunting him as she bent at the waist toward the ocean and planted her hands in the sand.

His palms started itching.

He wasn't sure what lunacy had prompted him to take her job, but suddenly he was very glad that he had. It had been almost a year since he'd been involved with anyone, and celibacy was wearing thin. Tori struck him as the perfect incentive to get back in the game. She turned him on, and, as far as he could tell, she was unattached. She was a bit kooky, maybe, but that would probably work in his favor. In his experience, the free-spirited, flighty types weren't looking for long-term commitment, which suited him just fine. They could have some fun together. When it was over, they could both move on with no hard feelings.

He watched her straighten, then rotate and sink into a deep split. Her spine arched. Nick had a sudden, visceral image of Tori astride his body, arching her back in just that same way as he drove himself deep inside her.

By the time she'd finished her exercise and wandered to the water's edge, he was hard. He watched until she disappeared behind the dunes, then shoved his shirt into his pants and headed down the stairs. He paused on the second-floor landing, listening to the pulse of hip-hop from behind Leigh's closed door. He sighed. She was probably in there crying.

Some men—better men—would no doubt knock on the door and insist on a father-to-daughter talk. Nick, by contrast, took the coward's way out and continued down the stairs. He'd talk to Leigh tomorrow, after her emotional storm had blown itself out. It was always easier that way.

Nonna was waiting for him in the foyer, clutching her handbag to her chest and tapping her toe on the tile.

"What took you so long, Nicky? I coulda walked to Atlantic City by now."

It was almost true. Nonna had never learned to drive, and even now, at eighty-six, she walked everywhere.

"Sorry, Nonna."

"Were you talking to your daughter?" she demanded.

Nick escorted her out the door and into his truck. He settled Nonna and her handbag in the passenger seat. "Why bother? When it comes to Jason MacAllister, she doesn't listen to a single word I say."

"He's not such a bad boy. He reminds me of you at that age."

Nick felt his neck muscles tighten. "That's exactly why I don't like him. The last thing I want is for Leigh to end up like Cindy."

He rounded the hood and slid into the driver's seat. As he buckled his seat belt, Nonna said, "You got a beautiful daughter, Nicky. Do you wish she'd never been born?"

He put the truck in gear and eased onto the street before answering.

"Of course not. I just wish things had been different when Leigh was a baby."

Nonna clucked her agreement. "Madonna, but she was a feisty baby. She gave us a quite a time, didn't she?"

An understatement if Nick had ever heard one. A time? It'd been pure hell. Born six weeks early, Leigh had spent every night of her first year strapped to a sleep apnea monitor. When she stopped breathing, an alarm shrilled. Nick could count on one hand the number of nights the thing hadn't gone off in the first twelve months.

"I love Leigh more than anything in the world, Nonna."

"You're a good father, Nicky."

"I just want to avoid trouble, you know?"

"Trouble?" Nonna shrugged. "When it comes, it comes. What can you do?"

"You can get off the track before the train hits."

"It's the trains you don't see coming that hit hardest." Nonna patted his arm. "Don't worry so much. It's not healthy. Leigh will be fine. She's a good girl."

Even good girls get in trouble, Nick thought, but he didn't voice the sentiment. "I don't like leaving her alone while Ma's at her church meeting."

Nonna snorted. "Nicky, your mother's been going out every Thursday night for months now. If you think Rita's at Holy Mother church hall, your brain's gone soft."

Nick took his eyes off the road long enough to send his grandmother a questioning glance. "Yeah?"

"Yeah."

"If she's not at church, where is she?"

Nonna shrugged. "How should I know? Your mother don't tell me nothing."

Chapter Three

Nothing comes between daddy and his little girl.
Until she grows up and falls in love.

CrazyBoy69 was online.

Thank God. Leigh clicked Jason's screen name.

<Hey, there, hottie : -)>

The reply came immediately. <Hey, yourself>

<meet me 2nite?>

Leigh held her breath. Usually Jason asked *her* that. Sometimes she went; sometimes she didn't. They made out in one of the lifeguard stands, or behind the dunes. At least, that was all they'd done so far. She knew he wanted more.

<Time?>

Her fingers hesitated on the keys. If she went out before her dad got home, would he check on her when he got back?

After the fight they'd had at dinner, probably not. But Mimi'd be home at eleven, and sometimes she stopped in to say good night. The story about the church meeting was pure BS, of course. Dad might be too clueless to notice, but Mimi went out every Thursday, and Leigh knew for a fact she wasn't going to church.

Briefly, she wondered where Mimi was going. Mimi had always been more mother than grandmother to Leigh, since Leigh's own mother had left before she could remember. Mimi was about the same age as some of Leigh's friends' mothers, too, since the Santangelos tended to breed young. Which was why Rita insisted on being called "Mimi" rather than "Grandma."

But once the hot flashes started coming last year, it seemed Mimi had gotten less and less motherly every day. She used to be a mother hen, overweight and overprotective. Now she spent half her time exercising, the other half moody and distracted. She hardly even noticed Leigh anymore.

Leigh used to complain she needed space—well, now she had tons of it. Trouble was, she wasn't sure it was all good.

<?> Jason typed. <U still there?>

<:-) Meet me @ 12?>

Jason's reply took a little longer than Leigh would've liked. Who else could he be online with? She scanned her buddy list. ShoreCruiser—that was Matt. PinkAlien—Stacey. Angel42—Julia and BeachBum113—Kyle.

OneSexiLadi. Karla.

Shit.

Jason's reply finally popped up. <12 it is, babe ;-)>

Leigh stayed online for a while, chatting with everyone about nothing, all the while watching for Karla's screen name to go from black to gray. When it finally did, she shut down her computer and got out her sketchbook and doodled a bit. Usually, drawing calmed her down. But tonight it didn't seem to do the trick.

At eleven forty-five she rooted through the mess on her closet floor and found the knotted rope. She didn't need it to climb down off her balcony onto the patio below, since the stone piers supporting the upper terraces provided easy footholds. It was getting back up that was tricky.

Her hands shook as she clipped the rock climbing carabiner to the railing and tossed the free end of the rope over the side. Then she swung her legs over and shimmied down until her bare feet found a niche between the stones. From the lower terrace, it was a short jump off the seawall to the sand.

Jason waited in the lifeguard stand one block over. Leigh grabbed his hand and let him pull her up onto the bench beside him. God, he was strong. When he lifted her, she felt as if she weighed nothing. Talk of Jason's physique had always ruled the girls' locker room, but since he joined the Beach Patrol last year, his drool quotient had gone off the scale. And he was so cute, too, with blond, blond hair and dark, dark eyes.

They'd been going out since the spring dance. Leigh still couldn't shake the feeling she'd won the lottery. But there was a downside to dating the guy all the girls wanted. Her name was Karla.

Leigh beat back her insecurities and snuggled into Jason's side. He tipped her chin up for a kiss and made it last, holding her head and stroking his tongue across her lips and into her mouth. She sighed and just about melted. Jason was an incredible kisser. When he gave it his full attention, Leigh couldn't think about anything else.

She forced herself to break away before her head spun completely off her shoulders. "I didn't come out here for this."

He smiled against her cheek. "No? Then you got more than you bargained for."

She nuzzled his chin. He smelled of sunscreen. "Yeah."

"If not this, then what?"

"I need to tell you something."

He kissed her nose. "What?"

"My dad won't let me go to your graduation party."

She felt him stiffen. "You told him my folks were away."

"I didn't! He already knew."

Jason was silent a beat. Then, "So what if he doesn't want you to go? Come anyway."

"Oh, right. Like I could. He'd kill me."

"He doesn't need to know. Tell him you're staying overnight at Stacey's." Jason's voice turned teasing. "That way you won't have to worry about getting home before morning."

Leigh's heart started to pound. "What do you mean?"

"You know what I mean." Jason's hand slid into her open windbreaker. His palm cradled her breast while his thumb gently stroked its peak through her shirt. Her body responded, going into full meltdown mode.

"I want to spend a whole night with you, Leigh."

Lightning shot from her nipple to the place between her legs. *Oh, God.* She covered Jason's hand with her own, but whether she wanted to stop him or encourage him, she couldn't say.

"I . . . I don't like lying to him. You know that. I don't even like sneaking out here."

"You wouldn't have to lie if your dad didn't hate me. And I can't figure out why. He doesn't know me. He's barely even said two words to me."

"I know. It's not fair."

"Leigh, I want you at my party. It won't seem right if you're not there. I know we haven't been together long, but I've never felt like this before." He gave a rueful laugh, as if he couldn't quite believe he'd admitted it. "I love you, you know."

"I do. I love you, too."

They sat silently for a while, listening to the waves break on the shore. A lone gull flew overhead, its vague night shadow skimming the sand.

"Come to my party," Jason whispered. "For me. Will you?"

She could felt him withdraw a fraction for every second she remained silent. "Yeah," she whispered finally. "I'll be there."

He kissed her again, and the crazy fire he lit so easily sprang to life.

She shoved her misgivings into a dark corner of her brain and kissed him back.

Tori hated doctors.

One of her earliest memories involved a hospital waiting room. She was sitting on the floor, playing with one of those push-the-bead-along-the-wires toys. It was shiny and new; she'd never seen one before. She tried her best to look only at the beads, and not at the man who sat behind her, smelling of beer—her mother's latest boyfriend, Ed. A doctor materialized, saying her mother was lucky this time, but had to stay overnight. Ed muttered a single, sharp word. He took her home and she stayed out of his way until morning.

Another memory—she was about eleven in this one—involved another white-coated doctor in another hospital waiting room. Tori's mother wasn't so lucky that time. Tori stayed with a policewoman that night, until Aunt Millie came in the morning. But just a couple years later, another man in white broke the news that Aunt Millie's stroke meant she wouldn't be coming home ever again.

And that was why Tori hated doctors. And hospitals. She realized it was a shoot-the-messenger kind of thing, totally undeserved, but there it was. She would cross four lanes of traffic rather than meet someone in a lab coat on the sidewalk.

Nonetheless, here she was, in an OB-GYN waiting room, perched on the edge of her chair next to an enormously pregnant woman. She tried not to look, but her eyes kept drifting to the woman's round belly. She wanted to ask if she could put her hand on it and feel the baby, but of course, she didn't.

The woman had an older child, too. A cute, pudgy toddler who was playing with one of those push-the-bead-along-the-wires toy.

Tori looked away.

Looked up, actually. But that wasn't much better. Directly in front of her was a huge corkboard covered with photos of newborn babies with red, wrinkled faces and screwed-shut eyes. In some of the pictures, older children clutched the newborns on their laps, with a parent or two hovering nearby. In other photos, adoring grandparents beamed at the camera.

Families.

A nurse moved in front of her, blessedly blocking the view. "Victoria Morgan? The doctor will see you now."

Dr. Melissa Janssen was a petite woman with short hair and an even shorter smile. She briskly asked why Tori had come, even though she'd already told the nurse, who had duly noted it in the file currently open in the doctor's hand.

"It's my period," she said. "It hurts so much the first day I can hardly walk."

The doctor nodded. "Cramps?"

Right. Cramps. Tori proceeded to inform the doctor that *cramps* described her monthly torture about as accurately as, say, a pinprick described a knife wound in the gut. The doctor nodded and scribbled in the file.

Tori answered a slew of questions during the exam. Afterward, she found herself in the doctor's private office, eyeing the framed certificates above the desk. Just why did medical schools feel obliged to print up poster-size diplomas when a simple eight-by-ten would do just fine?

Dr. Janssen got right down to business. "In my opinion, you have a severe case of endometriosis."

Tori fiddled with her purse strap. "Is that a kind of cancer?" Because fear of cancer was the only thing that could have driven her into a doctor's office. She was terrified she was dying.

"No, not at all. It's the abnormal growth of endometrial cells outside the uterus."

Tori gave her a blank look.

"Sometimes, the lining of the uterus migrates into the body cavity, causing severe pain during menstruation."

"But it's not . . . serious?"

"Not life threatening, no. However, the condition often leads to infertility."

For a moment, Tori couldn't speak. Couldn't breathe, even. "Infertility?"

"That's right. The fallopian tubes become scarred, preventing conception."

"I . . . see. But . . . I'm not infertile! I was pregnant last year. I told the nurse."

The doctor consulted the nurse's notes. "That's a good sign. Your pregnancy ended in a miscarriage, I see?"

"Yes, that's right."

"Were there complications?"

Tori looked at her hands. "I bled so much, I ended up in

the emergency room. They did . . . some kind of procedure, I guess."

"Which most likely led to even more scar tissue, which may make it even more difficult to conceive in the future. You have options, though." The doctor paused. "Do you hope to have children at some point?"

"Yes."

"In that case, though I could prescribe hormone therapy, I'd rather do surgery, both for more extensive diagnostics and for treatment of the condition."

Surgery? In a hospital?

Tori's throat closed. Panic spiked and the room started to sway. She gripped the edge of the exam table.

"Ms. Morgan, are you all right?"

It took a moment for Tori to answer. "I . . . don't have insurance," she managed at last. "I . . . I couldn't possibly pay for surgery."

Dr. Janssen's frown deepened. She made a few notes in the file. "All right, then. If that's the case, we'll start you on hormone therapy right away. It's similar to taking birth control pills."

Tori's stomach cramped. "No. I can't take those. I tried once, and it was a disaster. I had horrible mood swings. All in the down direction. I cried night and day. I couldn't function." She tried to drag oxygen into her constricted lungs. "Isn't there anything else? Some diet I could follow? Special exercises?"

Dr. Janssen peered at Tori over her glasses. "While a good diet and exercise are always worthwhile, I'm afraid they won't cure your condition."

"There's got to be something besides drugs or surgery."

The doctor sighed. "I'm afraid the only natural treatment for endometriosis is pregnancy."

Pregnancy? Tori stared at her.

"Hormones again," she explained. "After nine months without a period, the endometrial masses shrink. Breast-feeding's beneficial, too." She consulted the file again. "But I see you're not married. Are you in a steady relationship? Maybe with the father of the baby you lost?"

"No. He and I . . . It didn't work out. I'm on my own now."

"So I'm guessing a baby isn't an option for you at this time."

"No," Tori whispered. "I guess it's not."

Chapter Four

A little brother is fun to play with, fun to reduce to tears,
and a good reason to beat up the neighborhood bully.
But sometimes, you just want to kill him.

Nick expelled a breath. This Bayview job was turning out to be a freaking pain in his ass. Today's fire was a feud between Nick's painting foreman and a carpentry subcontractor. Bill Arnett's drywall installers were behind schedule sanding the newly spackled wallboard. As a result, a half dozen painters were standing around on Nick's dime.

"Get some extra guys out here, pronto," Nick told Arnett. "I can't let the painting go another two days. How could you let this happen? Johnny gave you the new schedule weeks ago."

Arnett spit into a pile of drywall cuttings. "Your brother gave me nothing." He produced a crumpled paper. "This is the only schedule I got, and I'm on it."

Nick checked the dates. "This is the old schedule."

Arnett shrugged. The man looked like five miles of bad road and smelled like stale tobacco, but his work was decent and his prices were rock-bottom. "It's the only one I got."

Mentally, Nick consigned Johnny—his youngest brother and Bayview's project manager—to the lowest and most painful level of hell. But Nick should have expected this. A monkey humping a football was a prettier sight than Johnny running a construction site.

"Look," Nick told Arnett. "The owner and his candy-ass architect are breathing down my neck. You gotta get more men out here."

"No can do, Nick. They're all on that big casino job. If I'd known about this two weeks ago, I mighta been able to stall them. But now . . ." He shrugged. "It's not gonna happen."

Nick toyed with the idea of fratricide as he left the job site. A tempting thought, but it would upset the family to no end, plus Doris would quit, so it was pretty much a nonoption. Even so, he almost reconsidered when he arrived at his office and found Johnny in the waiting room, dressed in green surgical scrubs.

His brother's bare forearms rested on the low wall in front of Doris's desk, a quart-size Starbucks container perched precariously near his elbow. A barbed-wire tattoo peeked from beneath his sleeve, and two silver hoops glinted on one earlobe. Doris sat at her desk, spine straight, eyes on her computer monitor, but Nick would have bet money his secretary's wide smile had nothing to do with his accounts payable.

Johnny straightened as Nick entered the room. "Yo, bro. How're the dawgs at Bayview?"

"Rabid and foaming at the mouth. Why the hell didn't you give Bill Arnett the updated schedule?"

Johnny blinked. "I did. At least, I gave it to Rachel when I took her out to lunch."

"Rachel?"

"Arnett's receptionist. You know, the one who looks like Angelina Jolie?"

"Arnett said he didn't get it."

Johnny snorted. "That guy would lie to his own grandmother."

Nick suspected that was true. "Maybe, but that's not the point. Scheduling is your responsibility. You should've followed up, made sure Arnett was on top of things. This'll put us another two days behind. Three more and the penalty clause kicks in. We'll be giving back a chunk of our profit for every day this job drags on."

Johnny just shrugged.

"Why are you here, anyway?" Nick said. "You have a pre-construction meeting at Lighthouse Harbor at eleven."

Johnny plucked a stethoscope off Doris's desk and slung it around his neck, doctor-style. "Well, that's the thing, Nick. I can't make that meeting. You'll have to cover for me."

"What? Christ. I knew the doctor getup was bad news. What the fu—" Nick noticed Doris's raised eyebrows and cut himself just off. "What is it this time?"

Johnny flashed a smile that might have snowed Nick if he hadn't grown up with it. "Not sure yet, but my agent wants me in New York by two." He leaned toward Doris, glancing right and left as if scouting for eavesdroppers. "Rumor has it Franklinville General's looking to hire."

A radiant smile broke over Doris's face. "Oh, Johnny, you'd be perfect at FH! But . . ." Her eyes went round behind her tortoiseshell glasses. "Does that mean . . ."

Johnny's smile vanished, transformed into an expression normally reserved for funerals. "I'm afraid it does."

Nick could've sworn he saw tears jump into Doris's eyes.

"Poor Natalie!" she breathed. "And after all that dear girl's been through. And the baby, Johnny—what's she going to do about the baby?"

Johnny patted her hand. "Nat's a survivor, Doris. She'll make it."

Doris reached for a tissue. "I know. I know. It just seems so . . . so . . ." She blew her nose.

Nick looked from his brother to his secretary. "Um . . . am I missing something here?"

"It's my story," Doris said. "*Franklinville Hospital.* Dr. Marshall was shot by the drug dealers who broke into the hospital pharmacy. He's on life support."

"His wife is pregnant with their first child," Johnny put in. "It's a real tragedy. The whole town is in mourning."

Understanding dawned. "Christ. You're talking about a soap opera."

Doris nodded. "I know it's silly of me, but I get so caught up with the characters." She took off her glasses and wiped her eyes. "Poor Dr. Marshall. He reminds me of you, Nick. So dark and handsome. I was so hoping he'd pull through."

"Thanks," Nick said. "I think." He eyed his brother. "You have a soap opera audition?"

Johnny fiddled with the end of the stethoscope. "I'm hoping."

"Hoping."

"Yeah."

"How many other wannabe actors are hoping? A hundred? A thousand?"

Johnny scowled. "I know where you're going with this."

"You ought to. I'm paying you good money to handle this meeting at Lighthouse Harbor, and you're blowing it off for a cattle call that's going to come to nothing."

"Listen, you might not think I'm good enough to get the part, but—"

"Damn it, Johnny. It's got nothing to do with how good you are."

Johnny scooped up his coffee and headed for the door. "Doris says you're clear till two. Work with me on this one, Nick. I can't miss this audition. I'll make it up to you. You know I always do."

"Yeah, right. What about the takeoffs for the Carter bid? I need those numbers by tomorrow morning."

"You'll get them."

"Don't you have a comedy gig tonight?"

"Yeah. At eleven. So?"

Nick shook his head. "Do you sleep? Ever?"

"Sleep's overrated, big brother. So many more interesting things to do." Johnny glanced at Doris, then leaned toward Nick and dropped his voice to a whisper. "You should try some of them sometime. Might lighten you up."

"Johnny—"

But Johnny was already half out the door. "Bye, Doris," he called over his shoulder. "Say a novena for me, will you? I have a feeling this one's gonna break big."

"I certainly hope so, Johnny."

"See you tomorrow, love."

"I'll be here."

"Jesus," Nick said after he'd gone. "Do you have to encourage him?"

Doris tucked a strand of gray hair behind her ear. "Johnny's following his heart, Nick. You can't fault him for that. As wound up as the boy is today, he would have made a mess of the meeting with Mr. Peterson."

Nick sighed as he thumbed through his phone messages. He refused to set up voice mail, preferring to have Doris screen his calls.

"You're probably right about Johnny," he told Doris. "At least I can sweet-talk Peterson into pushing back our start date without coming off like a stand-up comic on his day job." Which was exactly what Johnny was.

He checked his watch before heading for his office. "Buzz me in half an hour. I don't want to be late for this one."

"Oh, Nick, wait—I almost forgot." Doris ripped another message slip off her pad. "Victoria Morgan just called. Such a nice girl."

Nick turned back to the reception desk. A nice girl. Not the first phrase that sprang to mind when Nick thought of Tori Morgan. And if he was going to be honest with himself, he *had* been thinking of her. He couldn't seem to get her out of his mind.

He put Tori's message on top of the others. "What did she want?"

"She didn't say. Are we taking her job?"

"We can't fit it into the schedule."

Doris frowned at him over the top of her glasses.

"All right, all right. If you have to know, it's not that much work, so I told her I'd help her out myself, after hours. Don't bother opening a file on it."

Doris beamed at him. "I knew you'd do it. You're a true knight."

Nick snorted. "Yeah, well, don't start polishing my armor just yet." He frowned at Tori's phone number as if it were a hidden code he should know how to read, but didn't. "Do you know her?"

Doris looked up from her computer screen. "Victoria?"

"Yeah."

"Her aunt Millie was one of my mother's closest friends. She took the poor girl in when she was orphaned."

"When was that?"

Doris glanced at the ceiling, brows drawing together. "It would be almost twenty years ago now. Victoria was ten or eleven at the time. She was such a pale, quiet little thing. She would jump if you said 'boo.'"

Nick had a hard time picturing it. "She's changed."

"Victoria lived with Millie for two years until the old dear had a stroke. Millie had to go to a nursing home. Since there weren't any other relatives to care for Victoria, the court took her." Doris's forehead wrinkled into a frown. "That would have been the year you graduated high school, I believe."

Right. That summer. The one between high school and what should have been Nick's freshman year at Notre Dame. The summer Cindy dropped the pregnancy bomb and shattered Nick's future. Sounded like that summer had been even worse for Tori.

"So she went into foster care at what, twelve, thirteen years old?" he asked Doris.

"About that. Bounced around quite a bit, from what I understand." Doris made a *tsk*ing sound. "Poor thing."

"What did she do when she got out?"

"I understand she worked for a tour company. Traveled all over the country. Millie loved to show off the postcards she sent. Victoria would visit when she could, of course. The poor dear was quite distressed at Millie's funeral. I gave her my number. When she called asking about a contractor to fix up Millie's old house, I knew you'd want to help."

Nick headed for his office. Help?

He could think of any number of things he wanted to do for Tori Morgan. But he doubted Doris would file any of them under the heading of *help*.

Chapter Five

Modern families come in many unexpected varieties.

Suddenly, babies were everywhere.

On the sidewalks, in the bank, at the grocery store. Apparently the entire state of New Jersey was bent on reckless reproduction. Tori couldn't walk twenty yards without bumping into a cooing newborn or a giggly toddler.

So when she walked into Healthy Eats and Treats, she really shouldn't have been surprised to see another one.

Eats was a health food store not far from Aunt Millie's. Tori had stopped in the week before and had been surprised to find out the owner was an old friend. Chelsea Froelich hadn't been afraid to be a little different, even in middle school. So it wasn't too much of a shock when Chelsea introduced her business partner and significant other, a tall, spiky-haired woman named Mags.

Tori thought Chelsea might have some advice about herbs or something she could take for her newly diagnosed condition. But when she saw her friend, all thoughts of alternative medicine flew right out of Tori's head.

Chelsea was holding a baby.

"Sitter didn't show," she explained, patting the little girl on her shoulder. The child kicked and twisted, making sounds halfway between a cry and a whine.

"She's yours?" Tori asked.

"Yeah. Lily's mine and Mag's."

"How old?"

"Six months. She's not normally this fussy. She's getting a tooth."

Tori gave the baby a sympathetic smile. Lily crammed her entire tiny fist into her mouth. Chelsea shifted her to the other shoulder and grimaced. "I'm lucky the store hasn't been too busy today."

"Where's Mags?"

"Running some errands. She'll be back soon. Did you stop by just to chat? Or can I get you something?"

Tori explained her problem. Chelsea turned thoughtful; then, bouncing Lily on her hip, she threaded her way through the store, pointing out items.

"Vitamin B is really important. Raspberry tea will tone your uterus. And yoga—"

"I already do tai chi," Tori said.

"That's good, too. But you know what'll really help? A vegan diet."

"You mean like no meat or dairy?"

"Yeah. And no refined crap, either. Like sugar or white flour. Cut out all that pollution, and your body will heal naturally."

Lily's whimpering worsened. Chelsea patted her back and sighed. "I just nursed her. I don't know what else to do. It's too early for her nap."

A woman came into the store, approaching Chelsea with a question about organic fruit. Lily opened her mouth and let out a screech, cutting off Chelsea's reply.

Chelsea sent Tori a pleading look. "Can you take her, Tori? Just for a couple minutes?" Before Tori could answer, she found Lily in her arms.

She froze. Lily must have been as startled as Tori was, because the baby's fussing abruptly stopped. The little girl looked up at Tori with huge brown eyes.

Tori's stomach tightened. Lily smelled like baby powder and freshly washed clothes. Tori walked with her toward the front of the store, away from Chelsea and her customer. Lily opened her mouth, and for a moment Tori was afraid she was gathering strength for another screech. Instead, the baby let out a big burp, then gave a wide grin.

It felt as if someone had tied a string around Tori's heart and started tugging. Lily settled her round cheek on Tori's shoulder and let out a sweet sigh. Tori's arms tightened around her. Her little body was soft and warm, and more solid than Tori had expected. Tori nuzzled her fuzzy hair and inhaled deeply. For a few precious seconds, she pretended the baby was the child she'd lost.

Tears crowded her eyes. The doctor's dire warning rang in her ears. *Endometriosis often leads to infertility. The only natural treatment is pregnancy.* But how could Tori get pregnant? She was manless.

But then again, so was Chelsea.

She looked down at Lily. Was she adopted? No, that couldn't be right. Chelsea had said she was nursing.

Chelsea, finished at last with her customer, hurried over. "Oh!" she said, smiling at her sleeping daughter. "She crashed. That's fantastic. Here, let me take her."

Tori relinquished the child. "She's an angel."

"Especially when she's sleeping," Chelsea said with a laugh. She eased Lily into a portable crib tucked behind the sales counter.

Tori hesitated. "Do you mind if I ask a personal question?"

Chelsea straightened and smiled. "No need. I'll ask it for you. You want to know who Lily's father is, right?"

"Unless you don't want to tell me."

"No, I don't mind. Everyone wants to know. It's simple. Mags and I used a donor."

"A sperm donor, you mean?"

"Exactly. There's a clinic not too far from here. We looked at all the profiles and picked the donor we thought we had the most in common with. Then we bought his sperm."

"And a doctor did the insemination?"

"No. Actually, we did it ourselves, at home. It wasn't hard."

Tori left Chelsea's in a daze. A baby. Without a man. Or

at least without one who dumped all his dirty laundry and emotional baggage on your head.

What a concept.

After visiting with Chelsea, Tori fell into an uncharacteristic funk. Holding Lily had felt so right. Now that Tori's arms were empty, they ached. She wanted a baby so badly, but the obstacles to her goal seemed like a high brick wall she would never scale. Tori wanted her baby to have the family she'd never had—a mother *and* a father, at the least. But there was no father in sight. Did she have the guts to go the route Chelsea had? Alone? After all, Chelsea wasn't alone; she had Mags. If Tori used a donor, she'd be a single mother. Just as her own mother had been.

That thought only deepened her depression. The mood lasted the entire weekend. At night, she was plagued by strange, vivid dreams. Finally, on Monday, she decided to search once again through her candle magic spell kits. Black was the color of reversal; the black bag contained a spell to counteract negativity.

Just what she needed.

The Cajun witch had included a black candle, a small mirror, and a vial of something called "banishing oil" in the kit. Bemused, Tori followed the instructions for anointing the candle with the oil, then lit the flame. After a brief meditation, she snuffed the candle while looking at the flame in the mirror, and sat back.

She didn't feel any different.

With a sigh, she went to the kitchen to make a cup of the raspberry tea Chelsea had recommended. As the water boiled, she contemplated the telephone. She'd called Nick Santangelo's office once last Friday and three times this morning, but he hadn't called back. Which meant he'd probably show up at five thirty, as scheduled.

What would he say when she told him she'd given her job to another contractor?

When it rained it poured, apparently. Friday morning, one

of the dozen contractors who had turned her down the week before had called to say he'd had a prospect fall through, and he'd be happy to do Tori's job after all. In broad daylight, no less. The man's price had been a bit high, and he wouldn't get her open by the solstice. On the other hand, he was everything Tori thought a contractor should be: middle-aged, balding, paunchy. Not exactly baby-daddy material. Not like Nick Santangelo.

So she'd called Nick's office right away to tell him he was off the hook. Because Nick definitely *was* baby-daddy material, especially in the eyes of a woman who wanted a baby as badly as Tori did.

But Nick hadn't called her back. Which had to explain the dreams she'd been having of him all weekend. She didn't normally dream of having sex with guys she barely knew. But now—whew! Her dreams about Nick Santangelo had been so raw, so hot—so completely mind-blowing—that Tori had awakened gasping and so turned on that her heart hadn't stopped pounding for a good ten minutes.

And then, in the light of day, she started thinking about going to bed with Nick just to get pregnant.

And that had scared her to death. Tori wanted a baby, yes, but she wasn't into casual sex, and she hoped she wasn't desperate enough to jump the bones of a man she barely knew, no matter that, judging from the hot looks he'd given her the other day, he was probably ready and willing. And even if she did sleep with her contractor, and conveniently wound up pregnant, what then? At first glance, Nick Santangelo didn't strike her as a casual-sperm-donor kind of guy. What if he decided he wanted custody? She could wind up in court fighting for her baby, and God knew she didn't have that kind of money. Of course, she could solve that problem by just not telling him about any pregnancy. But that notion struck her as the worst kind of deception. In fact, there was just no way to look at the situation without seeing *bad karma* written all over it. She was appalled she was even considering the idea, however hypothetically.

No, she could never trick a guy into getting her pregnant. That just wouldn't be right. Better to avoid temptation in the first place.

She'd forgotten to get Nick's cell phone number, and his office phone went over to voice mail on the weekend. So she'd called his office again first thing this morning. Doris told her he was out, and that he'd call her back when he got in. He hadn't. She'd called again, twice. He'd been in, Doris said, but had gone out for a meeting and couldn't be disturbed. Doris assured her he'd call back. He hadn't.

Didn't the man ever return his calls? Apparently not. Now he was due to arrive in an hour.

The screen door slammed.

Tori jumped, heart pounding. What the . . . ? She looked at the clock. It wasn't even five yet.

She wove through the boxes in what had once been Aunt Millie's dining room, and paused in the doorway leading to the front room. Nick Santangelo—looking too, too good in his white golf shirt, cargo shorts, and scuffed work boots—was standing in the front doorway, fiddling with the screen door.

Her dream replayed in vivid detail. Her breasts started tingling.

Then she remembered he hadn't had the decency to return any of her calls.

She scowled at him. "Don't you believe in knocking?"

He didn't look at her. "Don't you believe in locking your door?"

"Not during the day."

"Well, you should. Anyone could walk in without your knowing."

"I don't need to lock it. The door slams."

He didn't seem to catch her sarcasm. "That's because the closer's broken."

He fiddled some more, then shook his head. "Can't fix it; I'll have to pick up a new closer. Or better yet, a whole new door. Look, hold it for me, will you? I got a lot of stuff to bring in."

She crossed her arms. "What are you doing here?"

He gave her an odd look. "Starting your job, like I said. You're in a hurry, aren't you?"

"But . . . you weren't supposed to be here until five thirty."

"I left work early," he said with a shrug.

"I called you on Friday and three times again today. You didn't even call back."

"Yeah. Sorry about that. Had a rough few days. I have a job running overtime, and I was on site all weekend. Barely had time to breathe."

He walked out the door. The screen slammed behind him. Tori moved to the door. She couldn't help staring at his butt as he strode across the porch and down the three steps to his monstrous white pickup.

God, he looked good. No man had the right to be that sexy. It simply was not fair.

He turned as he banged the tailgate open. "What'd you want to tell me?"

He heaved a couple of two-by-fours out of the truck. Underneath, there was more lumber, several boxes, and a neat stack of wallboard.

She stepped out on the porch. "Wait a minute."

He paused at the bottom of the steps and frowned up at her, lumber balanced in his hands.

"What?"

"If you'd bothered to return my calls, you'd know that I no longer need your services."

"Why not?"

"I found someone else."

His dark eyes registered his surprise. "Like hell you did."

"It's true. And what's it matter to you, anyway? You didn't really want the job."

"Tori. Half of Home Depot is in my truck. Do I look like a guy who doesn't want your job?"

She couldn't meet his gaze. "You shouldn't have to work evenings."

"Aw, don't worry about that. I'm at the office most nights anyway. At least here I'll be working with my hands instead of shuffling paper." He shifted his grip on the studs. "You want to get that door?"

"No, I don't. I'm trying to tell you—I gave the job to another contractor."

His brows rose. "You couldn't have."

"Well, I did. Morrison Builders. I called them last week. Mr. Morrison called Friday and said he could fit me in."

"Andy Morrison? Forget it. He'll rob you blind. Open the door, Tori."

She didn't appreciate the caveman routine. Her hands went to her hips. "How do you know that? You have no idea what price we agreed on."

Nick lowered the leading end of his two-by-fours to the top step and heaved what could only be described as a long-suffering sigh.

"Okay, then. Let me guess."

She could almost see the numbers adding up in his head. He named a figure. "Am I close?"

She gaped at him. "Almost exactly! How did you know?"

"Easy. I priced your job, and I know Andy's markup. I also happen to know he's as busy as I am. I can't believe he can get you open by the twenty-first."

"Well . . . no. He can't even start for a couple weeks."

"So why the big switch? I'll get you open on time, and you'll save money in the bargain."

The dream replayed in her mind. She stared at Nick's big hands, still wrapped around the end of the two-by-fours, and a wave of heat cascaded through her body. Her palms started to sweat, and she began to get desperate.

"You said you didn't even want the job when you first showed up. Why are you so anxious to do the work now?"

Nick caught Tori's gaze and held it a couple of heartbeats too long before he let it go. His lips twitched. "Let's just say I want to please the client."

"Oh." She felt as if she were on one of those boardwalk rides that lifted you a hundred feet into the air and dropped you into a free fall. "You do?"

"Yes, I do. Now could you open the door?"

"Wait a minute," she said. "I can't in good conscience let you work on my house without making a confession first."

"Sounds serious."

She couldn't quite look at him. "It is. The thing is, you didn't agree to do this job of your own free will. I cast a candle magic spell. It brought you here."

He looked at her as if she'd suddenly sprouted two extra heads. "You wanna run that by me one more time?"

Tori twisted her fingers. "Well, last year I met an old witch who gave me a bundle of candle magic spell kits. After you turned down my job the other day, I lit one of the candles. And you came back and took the job."

"Tori. Just because you lit some candle hardly means that—"

"It was still burning when you got here. Don't you remember? You told me to put it out."

"I remember just fine. But you can't possibly expect me to believe that candle had anything to do with my taking this job. That's ridiculous." He sent a pointed look toward the door.

She sighed. Her goose was cooked, and she knew it. Well, she'd done her best to come clean. If Nick Santangelo didn't believe in what was obviously very strong magic, that was his problem. Mentally, she made a note to call Mr. Morrison and tell him she wouldn't be needing him after all.

"Tori. Open the damn door. This lumber's getting heavy." He caught her scowl and added, "Please?"

She shoved open the screen and held it while Nick passed through. "Such charm. Such politeness. What woman could resist?"

Nick found a clear spot for his lumber, then straightened.

His lips twitched, matching the amusement in his eyes. His smile was slow, and sexy, and beautiful. It sent a sweet, twisting sensation through her stomach.

"Look," he said. "I'm sorry. I'm a jerk. Ignore me. I had a rotten day, but I'll get over it."

He strode out the door. Tori followed. "Does your bad day have anything to do with why you're here early?"

"It's part of it."

"What happened?"

"Oh, just the usual bullshit."

His arms flexed as he hefted a bucket of tools from the truck bed. Tori tried not to notice his muscles, or his thick, dark eyelashes, or the tiny scar on his right cheekbone. She held the broken door while he unloaded the rest of his cargo. He had to stack the boxes against one wall to make room for all the lumber.

"This seems like an awful lot of stuff," she said doubtfully. "I didn't think there was that much work."

He mopped his forehead on the sleeve of his shirt. He was standing much too close, on the lone patch of floor not covered by boxes or building materials. She could feel his body heat and smell his sweat. The sweet feeling in her stomach spread downward.

He nodded at the wall between the front room and what used to be Aunt Millie's dining room. "I hate to tell you this, but you're going to have to paint the clouds on that wall all over again."

His words were a blast of cold air to her wayward libido. "What? No way. I worked on that mural for hours."

Nick dug into his back pocket and pulled out a folded sheet of yellow paper. The building inspector's list.

"You should've read this over more carefully before you started. You need a fire rating between the shop and your living space. That means installing fire-resistant wallboard."

"Can't you just put it on the other side?"

"Sorry. Doesn't work that way. It's gotta go on both sides.

And I'll have to build a fire separation in the attic, too. Is there an access panel?"

"In my bedroom."

He looked at her, and she felt her cheeks go blotchy. That was an annoying problem she had. When she blushed, it wasn't a seductive glow. It was an ugly red rash.

That blasted smile tugged the corners of his mouth again. "Your bedroom? Now that, I'd love to see."

"Then come on," she muttered. She brushed past him and nearly tripped over his massive toolbox.

His hand closed on her upper arm.

"Steady." He was so close, his breath tickled her neck.

Steady? How could she be steady with her biological clock ticking like a time bomb and that blasted dream playing over and over in her head?

She took a deep breath and led the object of her night fantasies into her bedroom, wishing she slept in the smaller of the two bedrooms—the one without the attic access panel. She wasn't sure she could handle having the flesh-and-blood Nick in the same room where she'd ravaged his dream twin.

He gave a low whistle as he ducked through the door. "Wow. Not big on neatness, are we?"

She shot him a nasty look. "It's not like I was expecting company."

"Hey, it's just an observation. I don't mind a messy bed." He studied her unmade futon a bit too thoroughly. "Though how you can sleep on that thing is beyond me. It's gotta be uncomfortable."

"I like it just fine." She kicked a pile of dirty laundry out of the way and wrenched open the closet door. "The attic access is in here."

Using a chair as an impromptu stepladder, Nick eased the ceiling panel off the frame. "No electric up here. Got a flashlight?"

"No."

He climbed down. "Never mind. There's one in my toolbox. Look, why don't you go back to doing whatever it was you were doing before I got here? I'll poke around for a bit and set up my schedule."

She wandered back into the kitchen, vaguely disturbed and vaguely excited. She was also suddenly aware of an embarrassing rumble in her stomach. It was nearly dinnertime; in an effort to detox, per Chelsea's instructions, she hadn't had anything but herbal tea since breakfast. That probably accounted for the dull ache in her head.

Opening the refrigerator, she contemplated the choices, then went in search of Nick. The man had to eat, right? It seemed rude not to ask if he wanted anything.

She found him frowning at the lock on her back door. "Something wrong?"

"This place needs more work than what's on your list. For one thing, this lock is broken."

"It is?" She took a closer look. "I didn't know."

He muttered something under his breath that sounded suspiciously like, "It figures."

"Leaving your doors unlocked during the day is one thing. You can't leave your back door open all night. I'll run over to the hardware store before it closes and pick something up."

"There's no rush. I've been here a month already, and nothing's happened."

"Yet. The season's just getting started, and there's more crime in the summer. This is asking for trouble."

He looked so serious she couldn't resist prodding him a bit. "That door's not completely unprotected, you know." She kept her expression carefully neutral. "There's a warding on it."

He fiddled some more with the lock. "A warding? What's that?"

"A spell of protection. It repels evil intentions. I guess you could call it a kind of magical dead bolt."

Nick's head jerked up. He stared, looking for all the world as if she'd whacked him upside the head with one of his two-by-fours.

She swallowed a laugh. Practical guys were so easy to tease.

"First the candle, now this. You can't seriously believe in magic," he said finally.

"Of course I do," she said loftily. She really had set a perimeter warding around the house, though it was meant to repel psychic attacks, not a physical one. "Not that it's any of your business."

"It becomes my business if I leave you with a broken lock and some deadbeat breaks in and attacks you. Christ, once you open the shop, you're going to have cash in here. What you really should get is an alarm system."

"Yes, but I—"

"—don't need one," he finished, looking disgusted. "You're nuts, you know that? Freaking nuts."

He started to laugh.

She'd been about to say she couldn't *afford* an alarm system, not that she didn't *need* one, but now that he looked so amused at her expense, she gave a huff and poked his chest.

"I'm not paying you to make fun of me, you know."

He chuckled. "Consider it a freebie."

Turning his back, he opened the door and strode into the postage-stamp backyard.

"What are you doing?"

"Proving your spell doesn't work." He came back in, making a big show of opening the door and stepping back into the hall. "There, see? Your magic is worthless."

"No, it's not!"

"Yes, it is. I got back in, didn't I?"

"That doesn't prove anything. You don't have evil intentions!"

He captured her gaze, his dark eyes dropping to her lips. His smile slowly faded. The intense expression that replaced it made her breath catch.

"You wouldn't say that if you knew what I was thinking," he muttered.

She blinked up at him. "I wouldn't?"

"No. Definitely not."

And then he kissed her.

Chapter Six

Never give the key to your house to anyone but family.

Nick kissed her.

He didn't plunge right in, though. He cruised into the kiss slowly, and Tori saw it coming a mile away. She had plenty of time to take evasive action.

But she didn't.

His lips were hot. Just like the rest of him. Her caution flew right out her open back door as she melted into him, wrapping her arms around his neck. He pressed her up against the faded wallpaper, a low groan rumbling in his throat.

Lust blew through her like a summer squall. It had been months since she'd been kissed, and she'd never been kissed like this. Nick devoured her like a starving man.

She tangled her fingers in his hair as he made love to her mouth, dipping and tasting and nibbling, awakening her body in ways she didn't want to think about. His hands stroked down her bare arms, halting at the sides of her breasts. She expected him to touch her more intimately, but, surprisingly, he kept his thumbs just clear of dangerous territory. It was as if he wanted to tell her he wasn't the kind of guy to cop a feel this early in the game.

And that only turned her on more.

He angled his head and teased her lips with his tongue. She matched his play, opening her lips on a sigh and tangling her tongue with his. He stroked into her mouth. The hard length of his erection pressed into her stomach.

Abruptly, sanity returned. *No, no, no!* This wasn't right.

She slid out of his embrace. He let her go. For a moment she just stood, arms wrapped around her torso, staring up at him. "What . . . what was that?" she asked.

He smiled a little. "Don't you know'?"

Her cheeks blotched. "But . . . we just met! We don't even know each other."

"I'd like to change that. We'd be great together. I can tell."

Something about his smooth tone irritated her.

"Does that line usually work for you? Because it's failing miserably right now, so you might want to rethink it for the next woman you maul."

He winced. "Ouch."

She rolled her eyes and headed past him down the hall.

Nick muttered something under his breath and followed.

"Look," he said, catching up to her in the kitchen. "I'm sorry. I don't know what got into me. I'm not usually this forward."

When she shot him a look, he held up both hands. "Okay. I admit it. Sometimes I am. But I really do like you, and I think you like me." He grinned. "At least, it seemed like you did back there."

"Hmph."

"Okay, okay. I'll behave. And I won't attack again until you give the go-ahead." He crossed his heart and gave his dratted slow smile. "Scout's honor."

She tried not to smile back, and failed. "You probably really were a Boy Scout."

He grinned. "Yep. And an altar boy, too. And it wasn't a line, you know. About us being good together." He backpedaled when her expression told him she wasn't buying it. "Well, not completely, anyway. Am I forgiven?"

She sighed. "Do I have a choice?"

"Nope," he said cheerfully. "I can be very persuasive."

"Lucky me." But she couldn't help laughing. "You know, what I wanted to ask you—before you started mauling me—

was, do you want dinner? I could make us something while you're working."

"Sounds good," he said. "What've you got?"

"I was thinking veggie burgers."

"Excuse me if I don't jump at that suggestion. What else is there?"

"Soy chili and mesclun salad." She'd stocked up on healthy choices from Chelsea's just that morning. "Or whole-wheat soy-cheese pizza. Oh, and Dreamy Rice for dessert."

"Dreamy Rice? What the hell is that?"

"A nondairy frozen dessert. You know, like ice cream, but vegetarian."

"Sounds horrendous. Don't tell me you're vegetarian."

"I'm vegan." As of a few days ago.

"What's that?"

"No meat, no dairy, no fish. I've cut out white flour and refined sugar, too."

He was clearly taken aback. "You don't eat any of that? What's left?"

"Vegetables, obviously. Fruits and whole grains. Tofu."

He shook his head. "No wonder you're so skinny."

"Skinny?" She blinked. "What are you, blind? My butt is huge."

Okay, so that wasn't something a woman usually pointed out to a man. But Nick's comment had caught her by surprise. She wasn't huge, but skinny? No way. It was clearly another one of his smooth player lines. No matter how sincere he'd sounded.

He raised his brows. "Do you really want to get into a discussion about your butt? Because if you do, you know, I wouldn't mind at all."

"You're impossible," she said with a half laugh.

"You'll get used to it. Tell you what. I'll run to the hardware store for a new lock. You shoot over to Sack o' Subs and get me a cheesesteak."

"Are you sure you don't want a veggie burger? It's a lot healthier."

"Positive. This is south Jersey. I was weaned on cheese-steaks." He plucked a twenty out of his wallet. "Fried onions and provolone. And a Diet Coke."

"The 'diet' part is completely meaningless," she informed him.

"You know, you're right." He grinned. "Better make it a regular Coke."

Sack o' Subs on Ventnor Avenue had been raising choles-terol levels at the Jersey shore for decades. It was a tunnel-like restaurant with a long stretch of Formica lunch counter on the right and a row of red vinyl-upholstered booths on the left. Signed photos of past Miss Americas and aging ca-sino stars beamed down from the mirrored walls.

White-capped cooks stood in full view behind the coun-ter, conjuring up Philly-style steak sandwiches on incredible Atlantic City sub rolls. The aroma of grease and onions satu-rated the air. It'd been seventeen years since Tori had been in the place, but it hadn't changed a bit. Even the hanging plastic geraniums were the same.

She relayed Nick's order, cringing at the thought of what all that animal fat would do to his arteries. And salivating at the thought of sinking her teeth into a cheesesteak of her own. But she didn't order one for herself. She was supposed to be vegan.

Nick was still at the hardware store when Tori got back. She climbed the steps to the porch, only to discover Nick had locked the front door. Which was pretty funny, really, considering the broken lock around back.

She hadn't thought to bring the house key with her. She turned, intending to head around to the back door, just as Nick pulled up in his truck. He joined her on the porch and unlocked the door.

"Hey," she said. "That's my key."

"Yeah. I found it on the floor. I thought it was your spare, but I guess that was too much to hope for, huh?"

She held out her hand. "I've only got one."

Nick handed it over. "Not anymore. I made myself a copy at the hardware store. That way you won't have to worry about being here to let me in. I hope you don't mind."

Did she? She supposed she should have been mad, but in reality, she wasn't. "Just don't surprise me in the shower," she quipped.

His slow smile started up. "Now, isn't that a thought?"

Oh, God. She should have kept her mouth shut. She could picture the scene all too clearly. Water sluicing down her body. A sound at the door. Footsteps. Nick pulling the shower curtain aside . . .

She looked up and found his dark eyes on her.

His regard spread through her body in a tingling wave. This situation was a slippery slope if she ever saw one. Flustered, she hurried inside and threw together a tofu-and-raw-veggie salad. Nick sat at the table and unrolled his cheesesteak from its white butcher paper. The aroma of steak and onions drifted through the kitchen.

Her salad suddenly looked a lot less appetizing. She sneaked a peek at the sub as she took the chair opposite Nick.

He paused with his sandwich in midair. "Want a bite?"

"Of course not."

"Could've fooled me. You look ready to take my hand off."

She picked up her fork and speared a righteous cube of tofu. Bland, but healthy. She forced it down.

"You sure you don't want a bite?"

She stabbed a carrot. "Quite sure."

"All right, but if you change your mind, let me know." He proceeded to inhale the foot-long sub. Tori soaked up peripheral grease fumes as she worked her way through her salad.

After dinner, Nick installed her new back door lock, set up a temporary workbench of sawhorses and plywood, then returned to the kitchen and sketched a quick floor plan of the house, with notes, in a small notebook he carried.

Tori watched his long, sexy fingers guide the felt-tip pen across the paper.

And she felt herself falling.

Chapter Seven

A grandmother crams her grandkids full of cookies, buys them stuff they're not supposed to have, and loves her little darlings like crazy. Sometimes, she's a little crazy herself.

Nick pulled out his checkbook and slapped it down on the counter. "How much do I owe you this month, Mr. Merino?"

Vittorio Merino was a genial old shopkeeper who ran a five-and-dime in the Ducktown section of Atlantic City. Twenty-five years ago, Mr. Merino had been a genial middle-aged shopkeeper and Nick had lived two blocks away, on the same street as the twin house Nonna now refused to vacate.

Mr. Merino thumbed his way through a spiral-bound notebook. Stopping at a column of numbers, he added the figures faster than Nick could've punched "2 + 2 =" into a calculator.

"One hundred seventy-eight dollars and thirty-three cents," he pronounced.

Nick looked up. "Seriously?"

"Yeah. She's coming in a lot. It's all I can do to keep up."

Nick swore softly as he wrote out the check. What was up? Nonna rarely stole more than fifty dollars' worth of merchandise in a month. "I appreciate this, Mr. Merino. I really do."

"*Nessun problema*, Nick. I know you're good for it. Maria's an old lady with a heart of gold. She's always taken care of my family, so I take care of her. But I gotta tell you, I'm worried about your grandmother. The last few times she was in, she complained my merchandise was getting cheap."

The old man sent Nick a meaningful look over the top of his bifocals. "I think she's looking to 'pick up' something outside my price range, *capisce?*"

Nick shoved his checkbook into his pocket. "No way. Nonna would never pick up stuff anywhere else."

Mr. Merino snorted. "I'm flattered, but you'd better watch her. Someplace else, they wouldn't be so understanding. Like at that new big-ass mart."

Nick felt a glimmer of apprehension. "No. That'll never happen. Nonna hates big stores."

"Just keep an eye on her, okay?"

"Sure thing, Mr. Merino."

Back in his truck, Nick didn't have time to contemplate the disturbing possibility of Nonna branching out with her shoplifting habit. His cell jangled the opening bars of the Notre Dame fight song just as he slid behind the wheel. He adjusted his headset.

"Santangelo here."

Joe D'Amico, the Bayview job-site foreman, answered. "Nicolo," he said. "Got a problem."

No shit, Nick thought as he eased into traffic. Joe never called when things were going well. "What's up?"

"That pretty-boy architect—what's his name?"

Nick's jaw clenched. "Southerland."

"Yeah, right. This Southerland, he's running around the job site like a chicken with its head up its ass. You got time to come pull it out?"

Nick gave his to-do list a mental run-through. No, he didn't have time. "I'll be there in ten."

He cut the connection, only to have the ring tone start right up again.

"Nicky," Nonna said. "I'm cooking meatballs tonight. You gonna be home for dinner?"

"No, Nonna, I'm sorry. I'm working late."

A beat of silence, then, "Who is she?"

Nick frowned at the phone. His grandmother was down-right spooky sometimes. "What do you mean, who is she?"

"I been talking to Johnny. He said he's been at the office every night this week and you haven't been there."

"So?"

"So, I figure you been out with a girl. That's good, Nicky. You need someone. Bring her to dinner."

Nick counted to ten before answering. Nonna knew perfectly well he didn't bring women home. Ever. At first it had been because he hadn't wanted Leigh to bond with a mother figure who wouldn't be sticking around. Now it was because he liked his life the way it was.

God only knew he didn't need another woman in the house. Especially not one like Tori Morgan. He liked her well enough, and the chemistry was definitely there, but a relationship between two people as different as he and Tori were was destined to be short-lived.

Which was only a plus, in his opinion.

"Tell you what," he told his grandmother. "You promise to stop picking up stuff at Mr. Merino's, and I'll tell you where I've been all week."

Silence. Then, "My doorbell's ringing."

"Nonna—"

"Listen, I gotta go. But, Nicky?"

"What?"

"Dinner's at six. Bring your girl."

Sure, Nick thought. *Just as soon as hell freezes over.*

Nick appeared on Tori's doorstep at five thirty on the dot, a hardware store bag in one hand and a grocery store bag in the other.

"Here," he said, handing her the grocery store bag.

"What's this?"

"Basic necessities."

He set the hardware store bag on his workbench and headed back out to his truck. Tori peered into the grocery bag. Tastykakes and Devil Dogs. About a billion calories' worth.

Thirty seconds later, Nick came back through the door

carrying two twelve-packs of Coke. The man had a serious sugar and caffeine habit.

"Make yourself at home," she said, watching him stash the Coke in the fridge. She crammed the Tastykakes into a cabinet next to her organic rice cakes.

"Thanks."

He popped the tab on a cola and took a long swig. He wore his usual white golf shirt, with the Santangelo Construction logo embroidered on the left side. Beige cargo shorts and tan work boots completed the uniform. To date, she hadn't seen him dressed in anything brighter. Did the guy even own any clothes in a color? Or a pattern?

She pictured his bedroom closet: a long, boring parade of white and tan.

Not that he didn't look great in white. He did. It set off his olive skin and dark hair beautifully. But he'd be even hotter in a purple-and-gold Indonesian batik camp shirt. She'd bought a few for the shop, and she thought she had one in his size. She'd have to search through the boxes in the spare bedroom.

Of course, he probably looked best wearing nothing at all.

No. Oh, no. She was so not going there.

Sure, Nick was hot and all—and, it seemed, willing—but Tori knew that if she were smart she'd keep her distance. She wanted a baby, desperately, and she just couldn't see herself with someone like Nick Santangelo long-term. Anything she started with him would just delay her ultimate goal of motherhood. She couldn't stop thinking of Dr. Janssen's advice about getting pregnant before it was too late. And about Chelsea getting pregnant without a man in sight. Maybe that really was the way to go. One baby in nine months. No drama, no complications.

So why wasn't she looking up frozen pops in the Yellow Pages?

"What did you get at the hardware store?" she asked Nick.

"A closer for your screen door." He found the recycling

bucket under the sink and pitched his empty Coke can into it.

"That wasn't on the building inspector's list."

"Maybe not, but the slamming's getting on my nerves. Don't worry; I'll get to the other stuff soon enough."

She watched him fix the screen door. Maybe she shouldn't have. Maybe she should have shut herself in her room, or gone out for a walk. But she didn't. She sat on a box and watched him. His hands were deft and sure. She felt her heart squeeze.

When he finished, the door closed with a soft whoosh.

"Where did you learn to do that?" she asked.

"I don't know." He slid her a glance as he adjusted the doohickey on the closer. "My dad, I guess. I used to help him when he worked around the house."

She felt a pang of envy. "You must be close to him."

"I was. But he died about fifteen years ago."

"Oh! I'm sorry."

He threw the broken closer in the empty five-gallon bucket he'd reserved for trash. "Don't be. At least I had him while I was growing up. That's more than some kids get."

He looked at her with an expression that was hard to read. "Doris told me both your parents died when you were young."

"Yes." She felt a familiar knot tighten in her stomach, as it always did when she talked about her family. "At least, my mother died when I was eleven. I never knew my father at all."

"It must have been rough on your mom, raising you alone."

"It was, I guess. She was only sixteen when she got pregnant. Her parents kicked her out. She caught a bus from Oklahoma to California and never saw them again."

"Is that where you grew up? California?" He collected the tools he'd been using and set them on his workbench.

"Yes. L.A., mostly." She picked up his tape measure, weighing it in one hand. "We never stayed anywhere long. Mom lived with whatever boyfriend she could sponge off of."

"That's a rotten life for a kid."

She slid the metal tape out of its housing and let it snap back again. "I used to wish my mother would give me up for adoption. Then, before I knew it, she was gone."

"How'd she die?"

"Heroin overdose. I called nine-one-one, but she died once they got her to the hospital."

"And you were only eleven?" His voice was tight. "No one took you away from her before it came to that? What about your grandparents? Didn't they even bother to find out what your life was like?"

He was angry, she realized. On her behalf. His concern touched a painful spot inside her. Slowly, she set the tape measure on the workbench. She walked to the screen door and stared out into the street.

"My grandparents were killed in a car crash the year before my mother died, though I didn't find that out until my mother was gone. Child services tracked down what was left of my family. One second cousin who didn't want me, and Aunt Millie, who did. She was my mother's aunt, actually, my grandmother's sister, but they were estranged. Aunt Millie didn't even know I existed until after my mother died."

She started when Nick's warm hand settled on the back of her neck. She stiffened, then felt herself relax into his touch.

"Your aunt must've been quite a woman to take in a little girl she'd never met," he said quietly.

She didn't answer. She couldn't. Not without tears.

Nick turned her around anyway, nudging her chin up with his fist until she met his gaze. "Hey." He ran his palm down her arm and caught her hand. "I didn't mean to upset you. Sorry I brought it up."

"It's all right." She looked down at their clasped hands. His was so much bigger than hers. A dark streak of grease ran over his knuckles.

"You're left-handed." She'd watched him working, but she'd only just realized it.

He smiled. "You noticed?"

"Yes." She looked up at him. "Left-handed people are very intuitive, you know."

He snorted. "That's a load of crap if I ever heard one. I don't have an intuitive bone in my body."

She turned his hand over. His palm was calloused and smudged with dirt. She was pretty good at reading palms, and now she studied his. "You have a long life line."

"Do I?" He sounded amused.

"Yes. And this . . ." She ran her finger across the top of his palm just below the fingers. "This is your head line. You're a careful thinker. You don't jump into anything."

"That's true enough, I suppose."

"And your love line . . ." She traced her finger over the line that ran from the base of his index finger to the middle of his wrist. Dangerous territory. She'd never seen a love line quite so . . .

"What?" he asked.

She looked up quickly. "Nothing."

"Oh, come on," he joked. "Just give it to me straight. What do you see? Erectile dysfunction? Premature ejaculation? Because if you do . . ."

A laugh bubbled up in her throat. Nick seemed to have no problem with poking fun at himself. It was a dangerously endearing trait. "No. Nothing that dire. Just the opposite, if you really want to know. You have a very strong . . . um"—she blushed—"drive."

He leaned close. "Really? Tell me more. I think I'm starting to believe."

"Well . . ." She placed her palm over his, comparing the shape of their hands. His fingers were so much longer, so much more graceful than hers. "You have a 'water' hand. Rectangular palm. Long fingers."

"Which means?"

"You're an artist. Emotions are more important than reason for you."

He chuckled. "Now, there's where your theory breaks down."

She forced herself to let his hand go. Truth be told, she was starting to feel a little light-headed.

"Palmistry never lies. But it's true there could be stronger influences at work, obscuring the palm reading. Like something in your birth chart, for example. What's your sign?"

He grinned. "Are you trying to pick me up?"

His hand glided up her arm, leaving a tingling path in its wake. Tori froze.

"Because if you are," he continued in his low, sexy voice, "my sign is anything you want it to be."

His hand settled on her shoulder, his fingers gently flexing.

She almost caved. She almost let him kiss her again. But just in time, she thought of Colin, and of Dr. Janssen, and of Chelsea and Lily.

And she moved out of reach.

The next day, Tori found herself driving over to the mainland with Chelsea.

"You really don't have to do this," she told her friend.

"Oh, it's no problem," Chelsea replied. Lily gurgled in her car seat. "Mags is covering the shop until three, and besides, the first visit can be a little intimidating."

She was talking about Tori's first visit to a sperm bank.

Tori had confided in Chelsea about her longing for a baby, and how the doctor had warned her that her pregnancy should be sooner rather than later. One thing led to another, the result being that Tori was now on her way to Choices, the same insemination clinic that Chelsea and Mags had used.

Tori reminded herself that the visit was purely informational. She was just checking out her options. But gazing at Lily's round little cheeks and sleepy smile, her empty arms ached, and her heart felt as if it were floating out of her chest.

She couldn't allow her chance to create a real family slip away.

Chelsea sped over the causeway leading to the mainland. Twenty minutes later, she pulled into the parking lot of a brick-and-glass office building. It looked . . . upscale.

Tori don't know why she should be surprised at that. She supposed that, in the back of her mind, she'd assumed a place where guys got paid to jerk off would be lurking in a skanky back alley. In contrast, the Choices facility was clean and sleek, with shiny glass doors and bright masses of impatiens planted on either side of the entrance.

"I'm not sure about this," she said. "It looks expensive."

"You'll drop a few hundred on the specimen," Chelsea said, "but if you do the insemination yourself, you save money. The syringe is a little tricky, but it's not like it's brain surgery or anything." She lifted Lily out of her car seat and plunked her into Tori's arms.

"To remind you why you're here," she said.

Lily was happy today—the tooth that had bothered her had erupted, and was visible as a white dash in her pink gums. Tori bounced the little girl's wriggling, cooing weight, as Chelsea took hold of her arm and dragged her up the walk and into the building.

The reception room looked like any doctor's office, with year-old magazines (none, as far as Tori could tell, were porn). The framed art prints on the walls depicted nondescript beach scenes. There were about a dozen chairs, but only one was occupied, by a young guy whose head snapped up when they entered.

He looked quickly away.

"Do you think he's a donor?" Tori whispered.

Chelsea looked over at the guy. He jerked to his feet and moved to a brochure display rack, where he snagged a pamphlet and pretended to read.

"Probably," she whispered back.

"He can't be twenty!" Tori said.

"They prefer young ones."

The nervous donor was called first. A woman in a white lab coat escorted him into the back. To a darkened room filled with back issues of *Penthouse*? Or would they have movies? Tori didn't want to know.

"You think he's doing it for the money?" she asked her friend.

"Don't think of it like that. In fact, it works best if you don't think of the donor at all. Just think of your baby."

Her baby.

She liked the sound of that. And holding Lily in her arms made the whole thing seem more real. She rocked the little girl and babbled some baby talk. Lily grinned, showing her new tooth.

A few minutes later, Tori left Chelsea and Lily in the waiting room and braved Dr. Brenner's office alone. The good doctor was tall, thin, and balding. He might have been a scarecrow dressed for Halloween. But his eyes were warm and friendly, and Tori was surprised to find herself liking him.

"We maintain the strictest confidentiality. Both for the donor and the recipient. But you'll receive a full medical history that goes back at least two generations." He paused. "Is there a partner involved?"

"No, I'm not married. Or even living with someone. That's not a problem, is it?"

"Not at all. A good percentage of our clients are single. I'm only asking because often a woman will choose a donor who looks like her partner. But since you're not in a relationship, you might consider choosing a donor with your own hair and eye color. That way the child will be more likely to look like you."

That sounded good.

"You'll fill out a detailed medical history, of course. That will help us eliminate any donors who may be genetically incompatible. Otherwise, you can have your pick of candidates from our database. We're affiliated with several sperm banks nationwide, so there's quite a selection." He turned his computer monitor toward her. "Let's do a search now."

He clicked his mouse and a series of questions appeared on the screen. "Race . . . Caucasian. Hair . . . black. Eyes . . ." He peered at her. "Yours are green, very unusual. An identical match would overly limit our search, so I'll just deselect brown. Let's see . . . complexion, fair. Ethnicity?"

"Irish," Tori said. "At least my mother was. I don't know about my father."

"I'll choose Anglo-Saxon. What education level do you prefer?"

"Excuse me?"

"Do you want your donor to have a college degree?"

"Oh!" Tori had barely made it through high school. It seemed snobbish to insist her child's father have a college diploma. "A high school graduate will be fine."

The doctor clicked the search button. A few seconds later, a list appeared.

"Twenty-six candidates," he announced. "Sperm from any of these donors is available immediately." He clicked again and a printer started spitting paper.

Tori left Choices with a bulging file. A medical questionnaire, a sample contract, release forms, a brochure outlining insemination options, and, of course, the all-important donor profiles. Once home, she spread all twenty-six donors on the kitchen table and considered each one.

It was worse than cruising a bar for a pickup. How could she choose her child's father from a few pages of cut-and-dried genealogical facts?

She needed a little deeper insight. Once again, she found herself sifting through the bag of candle magic spells.

Chapter Eight

Middle children often find themselves running interference between older and younger siblings, and between siblings and parents.

"You look like shit," Nick told his brother Alex as he slid across a duct-taped vinyl booth seat at their favorite Atlantic City diner. It was barely six thirty, but the early morning crowd was already out in force. The place reeked of coffee, bacon, and the occasional cigarette that hadn't been taken outside.

"Yeah, well, you look like a drowned rat," Alex said.

"I just got done swimming laps."

"Jesus. What time did you start?"

"Five."

"Christ. I'd never get up that early to exercise."

Nick examined his brother more closely. Get up? From what he could tell, Alex, an Atlantic City homicide detective, hadn't gone to bed the night before. "On a case?"

"Yeah." Alex took a long pull of coffee. "But it cracked early this morning, so I've got today to crash. What did you want to see me for, anyway?"

"It's Ma."

"What about her?"

"I'm not sure."

"Not sure? For that you're buying me breakfast?"

The waitress approached, pad and pen in hand. Nick ordered an omelet, hash browns, and coffee. Alex asked for more coffee.

"More caffeine? I thought you said you were headed to bed."

"Got paperwork to file first."

Nick eyed him. "You know, you haven't been by the house in ages. How's Sophie?"

"She's great. I'm getting her for a couple of weeks. Leslie's going to Bermuda with her new boyfriend. Think Leigh'll babysit if I can't get enough time off?"

"No problem. Leigh loves Sophie. And don't forget Ma and Nonna. Between the three of them, the kid won't know what hit her."

"Johnny said he'd take her to the boardwalk, but you know how he is."

Nick's jaw clenched. "Don't get me started on Johnny."

Alex snorted. "That bad, huh?"

"He ducked out on an important meeting for a soap opera audition."

"Really? Which show?"

"*Franklin Hospital*, or something like that."

"*Franklinville Hospital?*" Alex pulled a pen out of his shirt pocket and started doodling on his napkin. "Wow. That's big."

Nick set down his coffee cup. "Don't tell me you watch a freaking soap."

Alex colored a little. "I might've caught an episode or two in between cases." He fell silent as the waitress delivered Nick's breakfast. "Think he'll get it?"

Nick took a knife and fork to his omelet. "How the hell am I supposed to know?"

"Johnny's a good actor," Alex said, sketching a few more lines on his napkin.

"Doesn't make up for being a lousy contractor."

"He's only twenty-four. How good could he be?"

"I took over Santangelo Construction at twenty," Nick pointed out. "You entered the police academy at nineteen. Zach shipped out with the navy at eighteen."

Alex drained his second cup of coffee. "Johnny's not like the rest of us, Nick. He's—"

"Irresponsible."

"I was gonna say free-spirited. Give him a break. He just needs someone to keep his feet on the ground."

"Well, count me out of the running for that job. Damn it. I knew I should've said no when Ma asked me to hire him."

"Like you had a choice." Alex sketched a few more lines on his napkin.

Nick grunted and returned to his breakfast.

"So what's this about Ma?" Alex asked after a moment. "You know, come to think of it, she hasn't called me in . . . damn. Three weeks? Four? What gives?"

"She's not herself. She's distracted. Spacey." Nick put down his fork. "She's out every Thursday night and won't say where."

"So what?" Alex added a curl to his napkin doodle. "She's an adult. Maybe she's taking a class or something."

"Then why be so secretive? She even lied about it. Said she was going to a church meeting, but Nonna says she's not."

"But Nonna doesn't know where she's going?"

"No."

"What does Leigh think?"

Nick scowled and forked another bite of egg into his mouth.

Alex laughed. "Oh, so it's like that with Leigh, too, huh? Not talking?"

Nick swallowed his eggs. "Can we talk about Ma, please?"

"Sure." Alex added some shading to his drawing. "Where do you think she's going?"

"I think she's seeing someone."

Alex looked up. "A man, you mean?"

"No, freaking Rosie O'Donnell. Of course a man."

"You've gotta be kidding me," Alex said.

"I wish I were. But it fits. New clothes, a dye job, contact lenses. I even heard her singing in the shower, like she used to before Dad died. What else could it be?"

"Could be a lot of things," Alex said, shoving his napkin across the table.

Nick picked it up. His brother's doodle had morphed into a caricature of their waitress—all hips, breasts, and big hair. He couldn't suppress a grin.

"You'd better not let that waitress see this," he said. "Or I fear for your next cup of coffee."

Alex crumpled the napkin and plucked a fresh one from the holder.

"Ma out on a date," Alex said, chuckling as he started a new doodle. "You know, Nick, if it's true, I don't blame her for not telling you. She's probably afraid you'll give her Leigh's curfew."

Nick drained his coffee cup. "If Ma has a"—what the hell did you call a guy your mother dated?—"a boyfriend, I want to know. It could get out of hand. She could get hurt. She hasn't even gone out to dinner with a man since Dad died." He eyed Alex. "Look, do you think you could come over for dinner some Thursday night and tail her when she goes out? See where she goes? I know you're busy, but . . ."

Alex twisted his pen and slid it into his shirt pocket. "Never too busy to spy on my own mother."

Nick pulled out his wallet and dropped a couple bills next to his plate. "Thanks. It'll help me sleep at night."

"You worry too much. Ma's a grown woman. She's sensible. She can look out for herself."

"I'm just trying to keep things from getting crazy."

"As if that's possible." Alex slid out of the booth and handed his napkin to Nick.

The caricature was of Nick this time, dressed in medieval armor, driving an enormous bulldozer over a tiny house that looked suspiciously like his own.

He snorted. "Nice."

Alex answered him with a grin from their childhood. "I just draw it like I see it, big brother."

On Monday morning, Tori returned to Choices.

A spell involving a clove-studded yellow candle set in a bucket of sand had promised clarity of mind in making an important decision. Upon extinguishing the flame, Tori had managed to narrow the field of potential donors from twenty-six to seven without too much angst. Taking a deep breath, she now passed the pages to Dr. Brenner, and handed him a nonrefundable deposit.

In return, the doctor printed out expanded profiles of her finalists. Pages and pages for each potential father.

Tori brought the profiles home to read. She discovered each man's IQ, his blood type, his shoe size. His school grades. She flipped through his baby pictures.

She met his family. It wasn't exactly Sunday dinner with the folks, but pretty darn close. She read descriptions of his parents, siblings, and children, if he had any. Met his aunts and uncles. Grandparents. If anybody close to him was dead, she found out why. For living relatives, she got a chronicle of every ache and pain.

She didn't know anything about Nick Santangelo's family.

But why was she even thinking about that?

Eventually, she took the whole pile of papers over to Mags and Chelsea's. The three women went through the profiles one by one. Tori found herself looking for a reason to reject each candidate. One man was too heavy, the next too short. The third was a Republican.

"This guy looks promising," Chelsea said. "Twenty-four and in med school. Volunteers at a free clinic in his spare time."

"I don't know," Tori said, looking him over. "He likes country music. I don't think I could handle that."

"You're not looking to date him," Mags pointed out.

"No, just to have his baby! What if the kid takes after his father, and his father is a guy I would've hated?"

Mags snorted.

Chelsea sighed, flipping to the last of the seven. "This one's a Democrat, at least. A journalist."

"Black hair, green eyes, Irish—just like you, Tori," Mags read over Chelsea's shoulder. "Six feet tall, one eighty. Runs marathons. No family history of cancer or heart disease."

Tori's interest perked up. "He likes folk music and watches classic black-and-white movies," she read, stunned. "Oh! And he writes poetry." She stared at the picture of a handsome young man wearing jeans and a wild red print shirt.

He was perfect.

Chelsea turned the page. "He's gay. Does that bother you?"

"Really?" She looked over and saw it was true. *Sexual orientation: homosexual.* "No, I don't mind. It only figures. All the best men are gay."

"But you're not looking to date him," Mags reminded her. Again.

Tori looked first at Mags, then at Chelsea.

"No," she said, a smile spreading across her face. "I just want to have his baby."

"You know, Nonna, you really gotta stop with the shoplifting. I mean it this time."

Nick used the sternest voice he could muster. Which, granted, wasn't all that severe. Christ, the woman was eighty-six. She'd changed his diapers.

Nonna didn't answer.

Instead, she tipped the spout of her old-fashioned watering can, releasing a gentle rain on her garden. Nick stood in the center of Nonna's postage stamp–size back patio, eyeing this year's crop of tomato seedlings. The shoots marched like sparse soldiers along the garden wall. But he knew, come August, they'd be a tangled jungle, laden with bushels of ripe fruit.

"Mr. Merino told me you've been complaining about his merchandise," Nick said. "He's afraid you're gonna steal more expensive stuff somewhere else."

Nonna snorted. "Ah, Nicky, no one cares if an old lady picks something up once in a while."

"Mr. Merino doesn't care because I pay him."

Nonna set the watering can under the hose faucet. Nick cranked the tap, filling the can. Why Nonna couldn't water her tomatoes directly from the hose was one of life's little mysteries.

Another mystery was his grandmother's penchant for petty theft. You'd think a woman who hadn't missed Sunday Mass since the Kennedy administration would pay a little more attention to the Ten Commandments. But no, number seven—"Thou shalt not steal"—eluded her.

"Another shopkeeper won't be as understanding as Mr. Merino." Nick was starting to have a really bad feeling about this. "Just promise me you'll stick to Arctic Avenue Gifts, okay?"

He hefted the can and watered the next plant.

Nonna watched him. "Remember when you were little? You watered for me every Saturday."

"Yeah." Nick smiled. "You used to give me a quarter. I'd think I was rich."

"Those were the days. I miss them sometimes." Nonna's eyes grew misty, but only for a second. Then her shoulders lifted in an old-country shrug. "Ah, well, what can you do? Don't forget that one in the corner."

Nick gave the corner tomato a good shower.

"Stay for lunch, Nicolo."

"I'd like to, Nonna, but I can't. I've got a meeting."

"Another meeting. There's more to life than meetings, you know."

"Maybe, but the meetings pay for the rest of my life. Not to mention Ma's and Leigh's."

"I'm worried about you. You work too hard."

"I'm fine, Nonna."

"Ha. You ain't been fine since that wife of yours left you."

In the fifteen years since Cindy had left him and abandoned their daughter, Nick had never once heard Nonna refer to his ex by name. It was always "that wife of yours," or, less frequently, "Leigh's mother."

"You shouldn't be alone, Nicky."

"I'm not alone," he said. "I've got Ma and Leigh."

"You know what I mean."

He sighed. "I know you mean well, Nonna, but I like my life the way it is."

"Who you kidding? The way you live, it's only half a life. You're the kind of man who needs a woman. Like your grandfather." She made a gesture of annoyance. "He was another one who worked too hard."

Nick grunted.

"Don't take that attitude with me. You know I'm right. I'm tired of waiting for you to come to your senses."

The watering done, she took the empty can from Nick and set it in the corner. Turning, she wiped her hands on her apron.

"You know what I'm gonna do, Nicky? I'm gonna light a two-dollar candle at St. Michael's and pray you get married."

Nick laughed outright at that.

"Nonna," he said. "Please. Save your money."

Tori wondered if Nick would try to kiss her again.

Not that she wanted him to. In fact, now that she'd decided to get pregnant on her own, her life would be much simpler if she could keep her contractor at a professional distance. She'd already chosen Nick's polar opposite to be the father of her child. What would be the point in hooking up with a man whose donor profile she would've flat-out rejected?

Still, it would be nice if he'd at least try to kiss her. Just so she could turn him down.

But for the last week, Nick had been nothing but professional. He'd shown up every day at five thirty and kept his head down, working his way through the building inspector's list. The fire separation was almost done, the handrail on the porch steps didn't wobble, and she was the proud owner of a new emergency exit sign. But that wasn't all. Nick kept slipping in extras.

The bathroom faucet no longer dripped, the toilet no longer gurgled, and the electrical outlet in the front room had stopped spitting sparks. Even the annoying roof leak in the back hall was gone.

It was amazing. His big, sexy hands could fix anything.

It made her feel safe. And *that* made her feel anxious. She couldn't get used to him. He wasn't staying.

On Friday he showed up with a new CD player. He pitched the old one—duct-taped cord and all—into the Dumpster in the driveway. Tori barely managed to rescue her favorite New Age meditation CD. Only to have him crank up Bon Jovi, of all things.

Apparently, the two of them were worlds apart in music preference, too. No surprise there.

Tori sorted through a box of merchandise in the living room, but her gaze kept drifting to where Nick was working, just a few feet away. His shoulders flexed as he positioned the new fire door's metal frame in the opening he'd cut for it. Try as she might, she couldn't drag her eyes away. Nick was buff; that was all there was to it. There wasn't one soft thing about his body. She'd found that out firsthand when he'd kissed her.

He turned to get some kind of tool. His toolbox was an enormous affair with about a zillion separate compartments. A place for everything and everything in its place. What, was he afraid his wrenches would do the dirty with his screwdrivers when he wasn't looking? There were even little niches for screws, nuts, bolts, and washers. He had each and every fastener sorted by type and size.

The setup was so organized it was sick, that was what it was. That toolbox was clearly the product of a disturbed mind. She'd noticed that his truck was clean, too, inside and out. The man was pathologically neat.

She thought of her bedroom and winced.

The night was warm. Nick had been working an hour or so and his white shirt was already damp with sweat. His hair was rumpled, and he had streaks of dirt on his normally pristine khakis. Her fingers twitched. She wanted to touch him in the worst way.

Grimly, she plucked a paint scraper from his toolbox and headed toward the front door.

He shot her a look as she passed by. "Where're you going with that?"

"I thought I'd scrape the peeling paint around the front door."

"You don't have to. It's on my list."

Ah, yes. The List.

She'd found out that anything on the List was as good as done. Which was an interesting concept. Just this morning, she'd found herself fantasizing about stealing the List and adding *make love to Tori* in between *install door* and *sand spackle joints*.

But that was neither here nor there.

"I need to do something new," she told him. "I'm sick of taking inventory."

"Suit yourself."

She banged onto the porch. There was still a good bit of daylight left. She jabbed at the peeling paint. It was tough work, more tedious than she'd imagined. It took all of five minutes to decide paint scraping wasn't her thing.

But she kept at it anyway, sneaking glances at Nick through the screen. She watched as he set the tip of a long screw to the new door frame. Cradling his electric drill in his big hands, he drove the fastener home with decisive motion.

Suddenly, the air didn't seem to contain enough oxygen to keep Tori's lungs inflated.

Nick's long fingers dipped into the pouch at his waist. He fingered another screw, stroked it into position, and sank it into the jamb with one hard, deep thrust.

Then he did it again.

A trickle of sweat ran between her breasts. It was a warm night, and it had just gotten hotter.

Nick glanced at her. "How's the scraping going?"

"Fine," she said faintly. She scrambled for something else to say. "You know, you haven't sent me a bill yet."

He positioned another screw. "So?"

"So, I want to give you a deposit or something."

"Or something?" he said, chuckling.

Her cheeks blotched. "Money. I want to give you money. For all the stuff you've bought, at least."

He drilled another screw home. "It's funny. I've found that most clients don't volunteer to pay their bills early."

"You haven't even given me a final estimate yet. And you've been doing a lot of extra work. I don't know if I can afford it."

"Don't worry about it. We'll work something out in the end."

Door frame secure, he set his screw gun on the workbench and turned his attention to the new fire door propped against the wall. No use talking any more—Tori knew she wouldn't get another word out of him until he was finished. If there was one thing she'd learned about Nick Santangelo, it was that he focused his full attention on every task he undertook.

He was probably the same in bed. . . .

She set the edge of the scraper blade against a stubborn patch of paint and gave a hard thrust. It gouged the wood.

She couldn't deny it anymore: She had it bad for Nick Santangelo.

And it was only getting worse.

Chelsea and Mags stopped by around seven. Chelsea carried Lily; Mags carried a diaper bag big enough for a trek down the Appalachian Trail. Tori waved to them from the porch, glad to have an excuse to stop scraping paint.

"We wanted to see how Destiny's Gate was coming along," Chelsea said, peering into the shop, where Nick, finished with the door, was taping and spackling drywall.

She did a double take. "Is that your contractor?"

"I thought you weren't into men," Tori groused, keeping her voice low.

"He doesn't float my boat, but I'm hardly blind. That man's fine."

"Well, I don't see how it matters," Tori said dryly. "I'm not looking to *date* him."

Mags snorted. Tori invited her guests in to see the house. Honestly, she was glad they'd stopped by. Not only did the visit distract her from ogling Nick, but it would serve a greater purpose. Nick was a conservative guy—once he realized Chelsea and Mags were a couple, he'd probably make some ignorant remark. And that would put the chill on Tori's fantasies regarding her closed-minded contractor.

"The place looks great," Mags said. "And you can't beat the location, near Lucy the elephant. You'll get a lot of spill-over tourists." All the while she talked, she eyed Nick in a frank, man-to-man way.

Nick's gaze took in Mags's spiky red hair, tailored shirt, and narrow-leg jeans before moving on to Chelsea and her flowing, flowery skirt.

"These are my friends," Tori told him. "Chelsea Froelich and Mags Kotter. And their daughter, Lily."

He didn't so much as blink at the unconventional introduction. "Nick Santangelo." He set down his spackle tray, wiped his hands on a clean rag, and offered a hand to Mags. She shook it.

"Chelsea and Mags own Healthy Eats and Treats over on Ventnor Avenue," Tori said.

Nick replied that he knew the store but had never been inside. They made small talk for a couple minutes; then Lily started fussing.

"Time to go," Chelsea said. "We're taking Lily to the boardwalk."

Tori walked the family out to the porch. When she came back in, Nick had returned to his spackling.

She frowned at his back. "Well?"

He glanced her way. "Well, what?"

"No comments?"

"About your friends being lesbians?"

"Yes."

He shrugged and went back to work. "Not really."

"You're serious," Tori said. Imagine that.

"Sure, why?"

"You really don't care that my friends are lesbians?"

Nick worked the spackle on the tray, mixing and spreading. "Should I?" He sounded amused.

"Well, no, you shouldn't. But I thought you would."

"You know, that's not very flattering."

He was right. "Sorry."

"I could say something crude if it'd make you feel better. Let's see . . . how about, 'Think they'd let me watch?'"

Tori gave him a look.

He grinned. "Every guy's fantasy and all, you know."

She couldn't stop a half laugh from bubbling up her throat. "You know, you're really too full of it."

"Yeah, a couple of women have told me that before."

She watched him smooth a line of spackle down the wall. Her heart was suddenly beating way too fast.

"But what's with the baby?" he asked.

For one shocked instant, she thought Nick was asking about the sperm donor profile stashed in her dresser drawer. Then she realized he didn't know anything about that. He was talking about Lily.

"Did they adopt her?"

"No," Tori said slowly. "Lily is Chelsea's biological child."

"Really? Who's the father, then?"

It wasn't Tori's place to discuss Lily's parentage with a virtual stranger. She knew that. She should have made some vague comment. But for some reason, she wanted— needed—to hear Nick's reaction to the truth.

"They used donor sperm. Artificial insemination."

The truth didn't seem to faze him.

Chapter Nine

It's a rare teenager who follows all of her father's rules.

Leigh almost wished she'd stayed home instead of coming to Jason's graduation party. Karla had been underfoot all night, and she clearly had her eye on Leigh's hot boyfriend.

Leigh watched Karla sidle up to Jason, her fingers toying with the edge of the unbuttoned denim shirt he wore over a black T-shirt. Jason frowned, but he didn't move away, like Leigh thought he should. Encouraged, Karla eased in closer.

"Slut," Leigh muttered under her breath.

"If you don't like it, go over there," her friend Stacey said.

"Oh, like that wouldn't come off as desperate." Leigh eyed the half dozen newly graduated seniors laughing at the water's edge. Jason and Karla; Jason's friend Kyle; Stacey's boyfriend, Mike, and a couple of senior girls Leigh barely knew. Jason's sister, Beth, had taken off with her boyfriend after buying a case of beer for her brother's underage friends.

Everyone except Leigh had wanted to stop on a deserted stretch of bay beach to drink the first few bottles. It was a stupid idea, and Leigh had tried to tell everyone that, but no one was listening to her.

Okay, she told herself. *Calm down.* Karla might be touching Jason, but he wasn't looking at her. In fact, now he'd turned his back on her slightly, talking with Mike. He gestured with his beer bottle as they talked.

Leigh took a deep breath and counted to ten. Nothing to worry about. Really. A few minutes ago, Mike had had his arm around Leigh's shoulders and Jason hadn't gone all weird over it. She'd play this cool.

"Jason doesn't want Karla," Stacey said. "If he did, he'd have asked her out instead of you."

"Karla wants him. And she'd sleep with him in a freaking minute." Leigh was sure of that.

"You worry too much."

"Maybe."

Jason said something and everybody laughed.

Leigh shifted her weight in the sand. "We ought to get out of here, anyway. What if a cop drives by?"

If Leigh had been driving, she never would've stopped. But she'd given the keys to her Geo Tracker to Jason, since the guts of his 1986 Mustang were currently spewed all over his garage floor. He'd laughed when she'd told him underage drinking on a public beach was a bad idea. Just like Stacey, he said she worried too much.

And maybe that was true, but in this case, Leigh felt justified. There weren't many cars cruising the causeway at this hour, but if one of them turned out to be a cop, they were screwed.

She shoved her hands into the pockets of her jeans. She wasn't drinking—her dad would slaughter her if she did, and Uncle Alex would freak out on her, too. At least Jason had listened when she'd told him to put the soda in her car, and the beer in Mike's. Still, she didn't have a good feeling about this.

Karla's laugh was a bit too high and a lot too shrill.

"How many beers has she had tonight?" Leigh asked Stacey. "Six?"

"At least."

They both froze as the headlights of a passing car spilled over the edge of the highway and onto the sand.

"You're right," Stacey said when it passed and they were breathing again. "This is stupid. Let's see if we can get things moving."

She tugged Leigh toward the water. The sand was wet—

high tide had flooded the beach, wrapping around the low dunes to form deep pools in the hollows by the road. As Stacey and Leigh approached the knot of teenagers, Karla leaned into Jason, her breasts brushing his chest.

It was a move designed to make Jason take notice, and it worked. He looked down, his eyes widening.

Karla went for the kill. She crushed her boobs against his chest, linked her arms around his neck, and kissed him.

Jason didn't move. Was he stunned? Or enjoying himself?

"That's it," Leigh muttered. She marched across the sand and punched Jason's upper arm.

"Shit." His eyes widened, and he tried to shove Karla away. Not an easy task, since Karla had him in a death grip, and he had one hand on his beer. Somehow, he managed to peel Karla's arms from his neck without spilling the beer.

Karla swiveled and leaned back into his chest. "Oh! Leigh. Hi. I didn't see you there."

Leigh met Jason's gaze. "What do you think you're doing?"

Jason jerked away from Karla, made a grab for Leigh, and missed. "Nothing. I swear."

"It didn't look like 'nothing' to me! It looked like her tongue down your throat."

Karla smirked.

"Whoa," Mike said to no one in particular. "Lovers' quarrel. Could get ugly."

Leigh stomped in the direction of her car, then halted and shut her eyes briefly. *Damn it*. Jason had the key.

He caught up to her and grabbed her hand. He'd ditched his beer. "Leigh, wait. It's not my fault. You saw Karla. She was all over me."

"That's supposed to be an excuse?"

"It's heating up, boys and girls," Mike said, holding his beer bottle like a commentator's mike. "Should blow any minute. Ten, nine, eight—"

"Shut up, you jerk." Stacey grabbed Mike's arm and towed him toward the road. "Leave them alone and let's get out of here. You guys, too," she added to Kyle and the others, "before some cop stops and nails us." She plucked Mike's keys from his hand. "Get in. I'm driving."

Mike made a halfhearted swipe for his key ring, then gave up and staggered to the passenger's door. Kyle and the three girls piled into the back. *Thanks*, Leigh mouthed to Stacey. Stacey shrugged and climbed into the driver's seat.

Mike's taillights disappeared down the causeway. Leigh stood, arms wrapped around her waist, suddenly embarrassed. God, when would she ever learn how to play things cool? She'd come across like a clinging bitch.

Jason shrugged out of his denim shirt. "I didn't kiss her," he said, wrapping the shirt around Leigh's shoulders. It smelled like him. "Karla kissed me."

"There's a difference?" Leigh said, hating herself for sounding so vulnerable.

"Big difference," Jason said. "Come on." He tugged Leigh into his arms. "Don't be like this."

She felt herself relax against his chest. "Don't try to tell me you were too drunk to notice what she was doing. That was only your second beer, and you'd hardly taken a sip."

He took her hands and guided them to the back of his neck, locking them in an embrace. "Leigh. Don't you trust me?"

She looked up into his eyes. They were so dark, so serious. "I . . . I think so."

"You're the one I want, not Karla. Not anyone else." His hands wandered down her back and traced a line along the waistband of her low-rise jeans. "You're the one I love."

The bulge in his pants told Leigh he wasn't joking. At least not about the *wanting* part. It was the *loving* part she couldn't quite believe. Did Jason really love her? Would he love her even more if they had sex? Would he stop loving her if they didn't?

He bent his head and kissed her. "Ah, Leigh . . ."

She opened her mouth, letting him in, letting his hands explore until a passing car reminded her where they were.

"Not here," she said, pulling away.

He pulled out her car keys and gave her a smile that promised everything. "Okay," he said. "Let's go."

"Done scraping?" Nick asked as Tori entered the shop.

Tori was so done. Scraping paint was for the brain-dead. She'd been at it for hours, and to be perfectly honest, she wasn't dressed for it. Just before five, she'd changed into a sundress, a purple-and-orange gauzy thing, snug at the bust and loose around her thighs. If anyone had asked her if she'd worn it for Nick, she would've said no. But she would've been lying.

"Yes, I'm done." She plunked the paint scraper into his toolbox. In the wrong compartment, on purpose.

Nick frowned, but didn't call her on it.

"What about you?" she asked.

He checked his watch. "Yeah, I'm about set. The wall's almost done—I just need to sand the spackle joints and then paint. You'll have to take down all those hanging crystals tomorrow, by the way," he added, unbuckling his tool belt. "The spackle dust'll get all over them."

"Oh," she said. "I didn't think of that."

"I know." She could tell he was fighting a laugh. "You know, for a fortune-teller, you don't seem to think very far ahead. But don't worry; I'll help you hang them back up. Then you can repaint your clouds and start putting up your shelving. I've worked like a dog the past week so I could get done out here and get out of your way."

He started off in the direction of the kitchen. She trailed after him. "Is that why you've been so . . . quiet?"

He was washing his hands at the sink. "What do you mean, quiet?"

"I thought you might be mad at me."

"What for?" He snagged a dish towel and dried his hands.

She could tell he really didn't have a clue. "Because of last week," she explained, hot blotches creeping up her neck. "Because I . . . um, turned you down after that kiss."

He hung the towel on its hook and gave her that slow, sexy smile she was beginning to look forward to.

"You couldn't have turned me down. I haven't even started asking." He moved closer, close enough to touch her. "Yet. But believe me, Tori, when I do ask, we'll both know it."

He did touch her then, lightly on the cheek. His eyes were dark and steady. Intent. They stood there like that, gazes locked, as the moments around them stretched into eternity.

Tori looked away first. Then—because a little cool air sounded like a good idea—she opened the refrigerator door.

"Um . . . want a bottle of springwater?" She had a whole case. Chelsea had made her swear never to drink tap water again.

He exhaled. "No. No, thanks. I'll take a Coke."

"They're not very cold," she said, pulling a can out. "The refrigerator was weirding out this morning. Now everything's warm."

"I'll call someone to take a look at it."

"You don't have to. I'll do it. You've already done enough extra work."

"It's no big deal."

"Yes, it is. And I'm really worried that I won't be able to afford it all. But how am I supposed to know, when you haven't given me a price, or a bill, or anything yet?"

She could feel his hesitation. "We'll work it out once your shop is open for business."

She took a water bottle from the fridge. "But you've already spent so much money."

"I can carry it."

"You know, I'm sure most contractors don't work this way."

He shrugged. "I'm not most contractors."

"I can't afford it," she repeated. She tried to unscrew the cap off the water, but her palms were damp and the thing wouldn't budge.

"Here." Nick took the bottle and opened it. "You can afford bottled springwater, but not a lock on your back door? Or new fuses in your electric box?"

"I'm trying to be healthy." She took a swig.

He popped the tab on his Coke. "You look healthy enough to me."

They sipped their drinks in companionable silence. Tori was well aware that Nick had taken his cue from her, backing off when she'd shied away from the heat building between them. He didn't seem to take offense, didn't press for more. She marveled at that. There was nothing awkward between them now; they were just . . . comfortable together.

As soon as that thought came, she started feeling *un*comfortable. She'd been attracted to Nick from the beginning. When had she started liking him so much, too?

He was the one who broke the silence. "Doris told me you worked as a tour guide."

She blinked. "Yes, I did. I was with Weird Zone Tours for the past eight years."

He leaned on the counter and took a long pull on his Coke. "Weird Zone Tours? I'm guessing that's not like American Express."

"Hardly. Weird Zone specializes in tours to sites of paranormal activity."

"Like?"

"Well, the vampire tour of New Orleans was popular. And there was an antebellum mansion in Biloxi that was haunted by Civil War ghosts. Out west we did a Native American spirituality tour on the Navajo and Hopi reservations, and a weeklong hike to the vortices around Sedona."

"Sounds interesting." He finished the Coke and pitched the bottle into the recycling bucket. "I've never been out west."

"You're from New Jersey?"

"Born and raised in Atlantic City."

"You must have family nearby, then."

"Yeah, the usual assortment of relatives."

She became aware that he was watching her closely. His gaze kept returning to her lips. A restless feeling stirred low in her belly. Was he planning to make a move?

But he didn't. "What made you want to wander all over creation?" he asked instead.

The question surprised her. It wasn't the kind of thing most people asked. She set her bottle on the table. Picked it up again. Moved a step toward the window.

Nick looked like he wanted to reach out and pull her back.

"Well, I was used to a wandering kind of life. My mother and I moved pretty often. After Aunt Millie's stroke, I lived in foster homes. Seven of them in five years. I guess I don't know how to stay put."

"Sounds like a tough childhood."

"It could have been a lot worse. I wasn't mistreated or abused or anything like that." She threw her bottle into recycling and wet a sponge at the faucet. She pushed it along the counter, not really seeing what she was doing.

Nick came up behind her. "Tori. Do you ever stand still?"

There were dirty dishes in the sink. She plugged the drain and turned on the water. "No. There's something safe about movement."

"And yet you came back here to stay." He ran his hands up and down her bare upper arms, then started a slow, deep massage of her shoulders. "Why was that?"

His fingers were magic. She let out a moan, her head dropping forward. "I . . . broke up with my boyfriend about six months ago," she heard herself say. "He still works for Weird Zone. We used to lead tours together."

"So you gave up a job you liked because of him?"

"No, that wasn't it. Not exactly. I was tired of living out of a backpack. I wanted . . . I'd wanted us to quit, put down roots, but he didn't want to."

The other thing Colin hadn't wanted was the child Tori had been carrying. His own flesh and blood. But she didn't tell that to Nick.

"And then your aunt died and left you this place," Nick said.

"Exactly. This house is the only real home I ever had, even if it was only for two years."

He was still massaging her shoulders, pressing his thumbs deeply into the tense muscles at the base of her neck. Little by little, her body relaxed. Her guard lowered.

He eased forward, nestling her bottom between his thighs. She realized with a start that he was aroused. Hugely. Her body flooded with heat. She should have moved away, but she didn't.

He kissed the top of her head. Nipped at her earlobe. Nuzzled her neck.

She felt herself falling.

"When I walked back into this house after so long," she murmured, "it seemed like I . . . belonged. It'd been a long time since I'd felt that way. I was so glad Aunt Millie had never sold it."

Nick didn't reply. He moved his hands down her back, pressing, kneading all the tension from her muscles. She leaned forward, bracing her forearms on the kitchen counter, giving him better access.

"That's . . ." She drew a deep breath. "God, I can't describe it. It's incredible. Blissful." She melted into an exhale. "Don't stop."

His breath caressed her ear. "Don't worry. I won't."

He ran a fingertip over her upper back, tracing the thin straps of her sundress and bra. His other hand covered her breast, stroking her nipple to a hard peak through the gauzy fabric. She shivered and covered his hand with her own.

Should she stop him? Let him stay the night? Tendrils of aching lust unfurled inside her. Her limbs were turning to jelly. She had the strangest feeling that it had to be all or nothing with Nick. She wasn't sure there could be any middle ground.

He kissed her neck, just below the ear. "You feel it, too, don't you?"

She didn't pretend not to know what he was talking about. "Yes."

His smile was soft on her skin. "I felt it the first minute I saw you, standing at your door, silver paint smeared across your nose." He turned her in his arms and took her mouth in a long, drugging kiss. After what seemed like forever, he eased away and caught her gaze.

"I'm asking now," he said softly.

She wasn't sure of her answer. Her hands settled on his shoulders, not pushing him away, but not pulling him closer, either. She thought of the donor she'd selected, the man she'd decided would be the father of her child. It was insane, but she felt as if she were cheating on the anonymous guy. Or cheating on Nick, by not telling him about his frozen rival. Which, of course, made absolutely no sense at all.

Nick caged her with his body, his hands cupping the edge of the counter on either side of her hips. Her hand slid to his forearm. She teased his bare skin, stroking in circles on the light covering of hair.

"Tori . . ." His voice was rough, his breathing ragged. The muscles in his arms flexed. His lips brushed her forehead, her cheeks. The scent of him, spicy and male, enveloped her.

"Please don't tell me to back off," he whispered. "Please tell me you want this as much as I do."

She searched his eyes. They were so dark, so beautiful, so vulnerable. He was afraid, she realized. Afraid she'd turn him down. That, more than anything else, made her do what she did next.

Chapter Ten

*A single parent is on call twenty-four hours a day,
seven days a week.*

If Tori hadn't been so crazed with lust, she might've remembered Aunt Millie's maxim: Look before you leap. Right. As it was, she couldn't even remember her own name.

She didn't know what it was about her and Nick. Maybe it was a pheromone thing. Or his unassuming confidence, or how he poked fun at himself. Or maybe the way he'd moved into her house and started fixing things.

Whatever it was, she was hooked. She wanted—needed—to be closer to him, and it had nothing at all to do with wanting a baby.

She looped her arms around his neck and kissed him.

His lips moved on hers, gently at first, then with increasing urgency. He nibbled and kissed his way from her neck to her shoulder, pushing the strap of her sundress down her arm. The stretchy bodice didn't have a zipper, so it was easy for him to slide it to her waist in one smooth glide.

His hips pressed forward, trapping her between his body and the kitchen counter. Her bra, a barely-there pullover thing, didn't have a hook. He ran his hands over it, but didn't tug it over her head, as she thought he might.

Was all this a mistake? It didn't feel like one. It felt incredibly right. Nick's tongue tasting her mouth. His calloused palm stroking up her bare leg.

He moved back far enough to look at her. His hands

shook slightly as he rolled the top of her dress down to her hip bones.

His voice nearly cracked. "God help me, your belly button is pierced."

His hand closed on her breast, his thumb grazing her nipple through her bra. She felt the touch zing all the way to her toes.

She wanted to slow down, catch her breath, but he didn't let her. He toyed with both nipples at once, doubling the blissful torture. Somehow, she found the hem of his shirt and dragged it up. He ducked and shrugged his shoulders, helping her. The garment slid into a white puddle on the floor.

His bare chest—it was the first time she'd seen it—was amazing. She spread her palms on his tanned skin. He was nothing but hard muscle. She kissed him there, dragging her tongue. He tasted salty, like the ocean. But he felt warm and solid, like the shore.

She explored his body, teasing her fingers through the curly hair on his chest, scraping one fingernail gently over his flat nipple. He caged her again, gripping the edge of the counter on either side of her hips. His skin was damp with the exertion of his evening's work and his rising ardor. Heat and musk radiated from him in waves.

She touched him everywhere; she wanted to learn every muscle and line. She kissed a white scar on his shoulder, smoothed her thumb over a birthmark on his arm. He held himself perfectly still while she played, but she could tell by the roughening cadence of his breath and the way his arms trembled that she affected him deeply. The knowledge turned her on like crazy.

She reached for his belt.

He stopped her. "Wait."

She looked up, a question in her eyes. He held her gaze as he slid his fingers under the elastic of her bra. He tugged it up, over her breasts, over her shoulders and head. Then, with a neat, efficient twist, he tangled her hands behind her back.

His hot gaze raked over her. She jerked her wrists; the bra held.

He gave her his slow, sexy smile.

She nearly melted into a puddle on the floor.

"Let me go." She tried to lever her butt away from the counter, but his hips held her pinned in place.

"In a minute. I want to look at you first."

His gaze dipped to her bare breasts. He looked his fill, taking his time about it. Tori shivered. Standing there, trapped, while he looked and looked and looked was very likely the most erotic moment of her life.

"Finally," he murmured. "You've stopped moving."

"I didn't have much of a choice."

He touched her. He ran his hands lightly over her collarbone, her breasts, her stomach.

"You're beautiful, you know."

"I'm not. My breasts are too—"

He silenced her with a kiss. "They're perfect. Don't say they're not."

She watched as he palmed her breasts, lifting and squeezing, his expression reverent. She felt like a goddess, bound as a sacrifice on his altar. He bent his head and worshiped one breast, then the other.

His tongue was like velvet. She moaned and moved her hips against him. His lips trailed down her torso to her navel. At the same time, he lifted her skirt, bunching it at her waist with the top half of her dress.

His eyes went dark as he took in her pink panties.

"Nice."

"Glad you like them." She tried for sassy, though she was feeling anything but. What she was feeling was . . . needy, aching, and desperate. And so, so empty.

He slid one hand behind her knees, the other beneath her bottom, lifting her onto the counter beside the sink. Easing her legs open, he stepped between them.

His gaze dropped. Another intimate inspection. His hand followed, and he stroked her through her panties. She shuddered. Then he slid his fingers under the elastic, and touched her skin-to-skin.

And, God, it was good.

She tried to free her arms. "Nick. Please. I want . . . I want to touch you, too."

He cradled her face in his hands, threading his fingers through her hair. Separating the curls, he spread them over her shoulders.

A small smile touched his lips. "I love your hair, you know that? It's so curly and wild. Every time I look at you I want to touch it." He toyed with the end of one curl, using it to dust her cheek and nose. Then his lips moved in for a slow, wet kiss.

She closed her eyes. It was the only thing she could do to control her onslaught of emotion. A tingling like a thousand stars spread through her, the sensation heightened by the helpless feeling of having her wrists caught. She squirmed on the counter, trying to rub against him with her hips, but he held himself just far enough away to elude her.

Spurred to creativity, she leaned forward and touched him with the only part of her body he didn't have control of—her mouth.

He inhaled sharply, and held himself still as she rained kisses over his chest, his throat, his shoulders. She kissed his jaw, rubbing like a cat against his day-old growth of beard. She bit his neck and he groaned.

His hands began moving again, smoothing over her body, touching, teasing. Nick loved like she'd known he would— slow and steady. Not a glimmer of haste. He was completely and utterly focused, as if she were the center of his universe. And for those few, sweet moments, maybe she was.

He dropped to his knees and licked a circle around her navel. His tongue explored, hot and wet across her belly. Moving lower, he suckled her through her panties, using his teeth to lightly nip the silky fabric.

Her hips arched; she gasped. He must have been anticipating the movement, because in a flash he slid her panties over her hips, down her legs, and onto the floor. His dark eyes smoldered with an almost pained expression as he gazed between her spread legs.

"Christ," he said.

She twisted her wrists and this time managed to yank herself free. One wrist still trailing her bra, she threaded her fingers in his hair and pulled him up for a kiss.

"My God, you're hot," he murmured against her lips. "I knew you would be. I've been dreaming of this every damn night since I met you."

"You have?"

"Yeah."

She took a breath and breathed a confession. "So have I."

He drew back and smiled at her. It was just a brief flash of teeth, but she could tell she'd pleased him enormously. She shook the bra off her wrist and ran her hands over his shoulders and arms. Leaning close, she inhaled his unique scent of salt air, soap, and sawdust.

He was so unlike any man she'd been with. So unlike Colin. Colin, it seemed to her now, had been an overgrown, hyperactive adolescent. He hadn't wanted anything to interfere with his fun or his freedom—not Tori, not the child they'd created together. He'd been glad when Tori had miscarried. Glad! That had hurt perhaps worst of all.

But Nick . . . he might not be many years older than Colin, but he was light-years ahead in maturity. He was a serious worker, a business owner. Watching him day after day, Tori could tell that Nick, unlike Colin, wasn't a man who ran from his problems.

It made what they were doing now seem all the more real. As if this were truly *life*, and all Tori's previous sexual experience had just been juvenile playacting. The notion scared her no end. What was she getting into here? A part of her urged caution, told her she needed more information before continuing on this breakneck course, but Nick's kisses had turned almost brutal, and her body was beyond caring.

She wanted him. It was as simple as that.

Her hands went to his belt and fumbled there, working the leather through the buckle with trembling fingers. Nick held himself still, watching as she undid the button on his pants. His huge erection strained against the zipper, and she had trouble easing the pull over it. She gave a disbelieving gasp as the zipper teeth parted, but it wasn't because of what he was packing.

No, it was his underwear that had her staring.

"Red silk boxers?" She couldn't believe it. "I would've bet money on tighty whities."

His lips twitched. "What can I say? I have hidden depths."

She laughed. "Apparently."

He left her briefly to untie his work boots. He dropped his khakis and boxers in one smooth, heart-stoppingly sexy motion. His body was a work of art. His chest was tanned and dusted with dark, springy hair. His stomach was flat, his hips lean, his thighs long and sinewy. His erection jutted toward her, hard and proud.

Her breath evaporated. She couldn't seem to catch another one. He stepped close and she took his length in her hands and stroked.

His smile vanished, transformed into a grimace. He flexed his hips, then eased away with a whispered curse.

He positioned her hands on the edge of the counter, on either side of her hips. "Hold on." He curled her fingers over the edge. "Just like this. And don't move, or everything will be over before it's started."

"Too late for that," she said, but she did as he asked. Nick stepped between her legs and skimmed the tips of her breasts with his fingers. They puckered.

"Ah, Tori. I could look at you all night."

It wasn't a line. He wasn't playing her. The hoarseness of his voice, the vulnerable flash in his eyes—no way could he be faking this. At least, that was what she fervently hoped.

He bent his head and gently bit one nipple, using his teeth to tug on the tight nub. Her legs convulsed, unable to close, the inside of her thighs pressing on the outside of his.

The sensation sent streaks of fire shooting through her belly.

"Condom," she gasped.

"Got one in the pocket of my shorts," he murmured against her breast.

He did? "Should I be flattered?"

"Yes. Definitely."

She reached for him; he caught her hand and guided it back to the counter. "Stay still for once. No moving. Not until I say."

"Bossy," she breathed as his mouth closed again on her nipple.

She felt his amusement. Clamping her legs around his hips, she wriggled forward until her bottom perched on the very edge of the counter. His hot breath fanned her stomach, swirled past her navel. Her skirt had fallen over her legs. He gathered the folds and bunched them at her midriff. Then her legs were on his shoulders and his mouth was hot and alive between her legs.

She cried out. Nick's name, she thought, though she couldn't have said for sure—the sound didn't quite register in her fevered brain. She tried to think, tried to breathe, as he continued his erotic onslaught. She felt her climax mounting. Just as she thought she'd fly over the edge, he left her.

She anchored her fingers in his hair and tugged. "Come back."

"When I'm ready." He blew a cool stream of air across her heated skin.

She shivered. "Touch me again."

He caught her gaze, gripped her thighs, and blew another puff. She wiggled her butt and tried to use her legs to urge him closer. He didn't allow her to get far.

"Sadist," she accused.

He laughed. "Please. You're loving this."

"God. I'd have to be dead not to."

His gaze raked over her body. He wrapped her legs

around his waist. Their eyes met as he touched her intimately, right where she needed him most. His eyes were dark and watchful.

She gripped his arms and moaned. "Faster."

He increased the tempo. "Come for me, Tori."

"I want you inside. . . ."

"No. Now. I want to watch."

She arched her hips. Her bare bottom slid past the edge of the counter. But she didn't fall. Nick's palms slid under her, lifting, supporting.

He set her back on the counter, urging her to open even wider than before. He slid in one finger, then two. She floated on the relentless tide of his urgency, was helpless as it pulled her under. She surfaced, only to hang, suspended, for what seemed like an unbearable slice of eternity.

The tide broke.

Her body convulsed. She clung to Nick, gasping, as a stunning climax washed through her.

"Oh, yeah." Nick's fingers pulsed.

He didn't let up. He went on and on until he'd wrung every drop of pleasure from her body. Until she slumped forward, limp and sated, in his arms.

He covered her with kisses—her lips, her forehead, her nose—as his warm hands smoothed over her damp skin. She pressed her forehead to his and shuddered.

"That was . . ." A shaky laugh escaped her. "My God. I don't know what it was."

"It was you." His voice shook. "It was all you."

Her breath caught. She looked up, into his eyes. What she saw there made her heart contract.

All at once she felt empty again. She wanted him inside her. Needed him inside her. To fill all the lonely places in her soul.

"Nick, I—"

A faint electronic melody interrupted.

Instantly, he stiffened. "Shit."

Her head came up. The melody, vaguely familiar, sounded

again. Disoriented, she searched for the sound. It was coming from the front room.

"My cell phone." His voice was tight.

She kissed the corner of his mouth. "Let it ring."

"I can't. No one calls me at this hour of the night unless it's bad news."

Deftly, he unhooked her arms from his neck. He snagged his boxers and shorts as he strode swiftly out the kitchen door.

She slid off the counter, rubbing her arms against a sudden chill. Her dress was a wrinkled disaster. She smoothed down the skirt and tugged up the top as best she could. By the time she joined Nick, he was half-dressed, pants on, but hanging open. The cell was pressed to his ear.

Was she imagining it, or had his shoulders hunched ever so slightly when she walked into the room?

"Calm down. Just tell me what's the matter," he was saying into the phone. He glanced at Tori as she entered, then away, his expression closed.

Her stomach cramped.

It only got worse when Nick gave her his back and moved to the bay window, the absolute farthest point in the room from where she stood.

"Aw, honey, don't cry. Look, just hold on. I'll be there in five minutes."

Honey? Don't cry? Just who was he talking to?

He snapped the phone closed and laid it on the windowsill while he pulled up his zipper and buckled his belt. She could tell the phone call had affected him deeply; his jaw was clenched so tight she thought it might crack.

She crossed her arms, hugging herself. "Trouble?"

He looked up, startled at the sound of her voice, as if he'd forgotten she was in the room. "Yeah. A family emergency. Nothing too serious, but I've gotta go right away. I'm sorry."

"I could come with you—"

"No," he said sharply. Then, in a more normal tone, "No. There's no need." He pocketed his cell and strode back to the kitchen. Tori followed, leaning against the door frame as he shrugged into his shirt.

Her gaze drifted to the counter, where just a few minutes ago, the Earth had moved. Now it'd come to a screeching halt. Her afterglow was shot to hell.

"I'll be here tomorrow," Nick was saying. "About two."

She barely heard him.

"Hey." He touched her cheek. "That's not a tear, is it?"

She shook her head as another fell. "I wish you didn't have to go."

His hand dropped. "I have to take care of this."

I thought you were going to take care of me.

The thought popped into her head before she could censor it. It wasn't often she slipped back into the needy child she'd once been, but the orgasm had ripped the protective lid off her emotions. Right now she felt exposed, raw, and so very, very vulnerable.

He gave her a quick kiss. "Look, don't cry. Please. I'll see you tomorrow."

Then he was gone.

The glare of his headlights arced through the bay window. Tori stood still for a long time after they faded, staring at her reflection in the darkened glass.

Don't cry. Nick had said the same thing to his one a.m. caller.

A family emergency, he'd said.

Nick had a family. Well, of course he did. Everyone did, it seemed. Everyone except Tori.

But did Nick have a wife?

Oh, God. It couldn't be.

She didn't want him to be that kind of guy. But she couldn't help wondering. She'd never come right out and asked if he was married. He didn't wear a ring, but some men didn't, especially guys who worked with their hands. And the caller had definitely been a woman. She could tell by his tone of voice that he hadn't been talking to a man.

If not a wife, then maybe a serious girlfriend? One he was cheating on? That was almost as bad.

No. Nick couldn't be attached. Tori's instincts told her he was just too honest to screw around on someone. But the fact remained that there was a woman who thought nothing of calling him on his cell phone after midnight. It might have been a sister, she supposed. Or even his mother, though his tone had seemed a bit too intimate for that.

But if the call hadn't been from a wife or lover, why hadn't he just told her who was on the line?

She tried to stop the flow of miserable, obsessive thoughts. She tried to believe in Nick, but in her vulnerable postorgasm state it was hard for Tori to maintain her bravado. Ugly emotions she hadn't felt since that last terrible fight with Colin threatened to drown her.

She'd known Nick for only a little more than a week. Was he a player picking up some action? Or did he feel something more, as she did? She bounced between the two extremes, unable to reconcile either with what she knew of him.

Which was, she realized now, very little. She knew he could handle a power saw. She knew his diet was just short of lethal, and that he had the worst taste in music. She knew his slow, sexy smile melted her bones, and his hands on her body were enough to make her go up in flames.

In short—what did she really know about Nick Santangelo?

Next to nothing.

Nick's raging hard-on was a distant memory by the time he reached Leigh. The cops were already there. An ambulance, too. Jesus, even though he'd spoken to her five minutes before, his heart just about stopped when he saw those red and blue flashing lights. The rescue vehicles provided the only illumination on an otherwise empty stretch of bay causeway.

The bottom had dropped out of his gut the instant his phone had rung, and he'd yet to get full control over his emotions. Leigh had told him she wasn't hurt, but seeing those ambulance lights caused a familiar wave of raw, paralyzing terror. He remembered other nights, other ambulances, all too well. He could hear his mother's voice, trembling beneath its calm, relaying their address to the 911 dispatcher. His mind and lungs had gone numb each time he'd frantically worked on Leigh's tiny body, willing her lungs to start working again.

Nick knew, with a bone-deep certainty, that if he hadn't been trained in emergency medical rescue—thanks to his high school stint with the Beach Patrol—Leigh wouldn't be here now. But damn it, he couldn't protect her every minute of the night anymore. She was seventeen. And all they did these days was fight.

By the time he'd pulled onto the shoulder behind the accident scene, his hands were shaking so badly he could hardly put his truck in park.

Leigh's Tracker was just visible. It had swerved off the road, plowed through a clump of sea grass, and landed headfirst in a tidal pool. Her car was pitched at an awkward angle, the front wheels submerged, water seeping into the passenger compartment. Thank God the canvas top had been down, providing an easy means of escape. And she wasn't hurt.

It could have been worse. Much worse.

He spotted her standing near the back of the ambulance, her clothes and hair soaked, clutching a thin blanket around her shoulders. He jumped out of the truck and made a beeline toward her.

Halfway there, he jerked to a halt. Jason MacAllister was hovering at her elbow. Jason's shirt and jeans were as wet and sandy as Leigh's. Clearly, he'd been in the car with her.

Shit.

Nick's blood pressure rocketed, nearly exploding out the top of his skull. He forced himself to breathe, to unclench his fists. *Goddamn it.* Leigh hadn't so much as blinked when she'd told him she'd be spending the night at Stacey's. But he should've known something was up. He should've remembered tonight was Jason's graduation party.

He started moving again, more slowly than before. When he reached his daughter's side, he did his best to ignore her boyfriend. Because he knew if he so much as looked at Jason, he'd have to beat the kid to a bloody pulp. And with the cops nearby, that probably wasn't the best idea.

But then Leigh looked up at Nick, her eyes wide and brimming with tears. Just like that, his anger evaporated, leaving his insides hollow and hurting. God, he loved her so much. If he ever lost her, he'd die. It was that simple.

Her hair clung to her neck like blonde seaweed. Tears etched trails through the dirt on her cheeks. She looked so young. So fragile, especially when a cool breeze blew a shiver through her. Nick reached for her, anchoring her to his body in a reflexive gesture from her childhood. A gesture from a time when he hadn't thought twice about hugging her.

For once, she didn't pull away. She pressed her face into his shirt, sniffling. Nick felt cold, his stomach sick. What if he'd arrived to find her broken body sprawled on the pavement? What if, after all those nights he'd kept her alive by the sheer force of his will, it had come to that?

His arms tightened. He felt her tremble and knew she was trying to hold back her tears.

The police officer greeted him, nodding toward the Tracker. "You're the owner of this vehicle?"

He met the man's gaze over the top of Leigh's head. "Yes. I'm Leigh's father. What happened?"

"The young lady here says she swerved to avoid an oncoming car. She lost control of the vehicle on the curve."

"Another car? Where is it? Where's the driver?"

"The other car didn't stop," Leigh said, her voice muffled by his shirt.

Nick looked down at her. She didn't look up. He glanced over at Jason, but the kid was looking at his feet.

Ah, hell.

The policeman droned on. Both teenagers had passed a

breath test. There was no alcohol or drugs in the car. There were no injuries other than minor scrapes and bruises; the paramedics saw no reason to take either Leigh or Jason to the hospital. But Nick should call a towing service. . . .

When the officer finally returned to his cruiser to complete his paperwork, Nick eased back and looked at Leigh.

"Are you really okay, honey?"

She blinked back another round of tears. "Yes. I'm fine." She sniffed. "I'm sorry about the car, Daddy."

Daddy. When was the last time she'd called him that?

Jason inched closer, causing Nick's muffled anger to spike. He turned on the kid. "What the hell do you mean, putting my daughter in danger like this?"

"I . . ." Jason opened his mouth, then shut it again.

"It wasn't Jason's fault," Leigh put in quickly. "The other car—"

Nick glanced toward the patrol car, fighting to keep his voice low. "Do you think I believe that load of crap? About another car? About you being behind the wheel? Don't bullshit me, Leigh. I know you weren't driving."

"But . . . I was."

Right. And Nick was the pope.

Nick glared at Jason. The kid wisely took a step back. "And you. What were you doing instead of watching the road? Drooling all over my daughter?"

"Sir, I—"

"There was another car," Leigh cut in. "And it didn't have its lights on. It came right at us! I think the driver was drunk." She slipped out of Nick's arms and stepped in front of Jason, as if to protect him.

Jesus.

"Leigh," Jason said, trying to move her aside. "Let me talk to your father."

She ignored him. "We didn't see the other car, Daddy, not until it was on top of us. It's a miracle Jason even managed to avoid—" Abruptly, she shut her mouth.

Nick watched guilt flash through her eyes. "I knew it," he

said evenly. "Damn it, Leigh, you know you're the only one who's supposed to drive that car."

"I know, but I didn't think that—"

"Yeah, I can believe you didn't think. Just like you didn't think I'd find out you aren't spending the night at Stacey's."

"I was going to sleep at Stacey's, I swear! I went to pick her up at Jason's—"

"Jason's graduation party. The one I said you couldn't go to. Damn it, Leigh—"

He cut himself off as a violent shudder racked Leigh's body. By the light of the headlights, he could see that her lips were turning blue. And her breathing didn't sound good.

"Get in the truck," he ordered.

She hesitated. "What about Jason?"

"Jason can walk back to town. Or bum a ride from the cop. I don't care."

Leigh opened her mouth to argue, but Jason touched her arm. "Don't worry about me, babe. Go with your father and get warmed up. I'll get home fine."

She looked up at him and their gazes locked. Some unspoken communication passed between them. Nick saw the silent rapport and felt ill. Leigh thought she was in love with this kid. Had she slept with him? The very thought made him want to punch something.

"In the truck. Now."

Lips pressed tight, she stomped to the truck and climbed into the passenger's seat. He hovered behind her, leaning across her to turn the key in the ignition and flip the heater on.

The rise and fall of her breathing still didn't sound right. "Do you need your inhaler?"

"No," she muttered. "I don't. It's underwater, anyway."

"You've got another one at the house, right?"

"Yeah, sure." She hugged herself, scowling, looking past him through the open door.

Nick turned to find Jason watching. He slammed the door

and took three long strides toward the kid. "I'm warning you, MacAllister. Stay away from her."

Jason met his gaze without flinching. "Mr. Santangelo, I . . ."

Whatever Jason wanted to say, Nick didn't want to hear it. He turned on his heel and strode toward the police cruiser. After wrapping things up with the cop, he returned to the truck to find Leigh shivering.

Reaching behind the seat, he fished out an old sweatshirt. "Here. Take off that wet shirt and put this on."

She stared at her. "You want me to change here, in the truck? No way."

"I'm going to shut this door and turn around. It's dark. No one's going to see you. I want this dry shirt on you in under ten seconds. I'm not having you get sick on top of everything else."

"I won't get sick. I'm fine."

He threw the sweatshirt on her lap. "Damn it, Leigh. Could you please not argue with me for once?"

She glared at him, and for three long seconds he was sure she was going to throw the shirt back at him. Then she sighed. "Fine."

Nick got out of the truck and strode a short distance away. Why did everything between Leigh and him have to be so damn hard? No matter how he tried, she always gave him that look that said it wasn't enough. That *he* wasn't enough. Maybe it was because he'd been gone too much when she was small. Maybe he'd left her to Nonna and Rita too often after Cindy left. But damn it, what else could he have done? He'd been little more than a kid himself, and after his father had died so suddenly, it had been up to him to keep a roof over all their heads. He'd worked like a dog, day and night. How many nights had he come home after she'd gone to bed? Too many to count. Sometimes, when she'd been little, he'd just stand by her bed and watch her sleep for a while. Before he quite knew what had happened, Leigh'd been in middle school. Then in high school.

He'd done his best. It wasn't like he'd been an absentee father. He'd been there for her as much as he could, given the circumstances. He'd taught her how to roller-skate, how to swim, how to ride a two-wheeler. He'd even coached her softball team one season, and taken her to a father-daughter dance. Had it been enough? He didn't know, and now it was too late. He returned to the car. Leigh had put on his sweatshirt. It just about swallowed her up.

He put the truck in gear and pulled off the shoulder.

"Don't you need to call someone about my car?" she said in a small voice.

"It's not going anywhere. I'll call when we get home."

She scrunched down in the seat. "Okay, so maybe I lied about Jason driving, but, Dad, there really was another car. It swerved onto our side of the road and almost hit us! We didn't crash because we were fooling around."

Nick kept his mouth shut. He wanted to believe her; he really did. A few months ago, before Jason appeared on the scene, he would have believed her unconditionally. But now . . .

No. He just didn't trust her anymore.

Later, after Leigh had stomped off to her room and slammed the door, Nick shut himself in his bathroom and threw up in the toilet. It was always like this. Rock solid and calm in a crisis, he fell apart once the danger had passed and he was alone.

Stomach emptied, he turned on the tap with a shaking hand and splashed water on his face, still torturing himself with what-ifs. What if Leigh hadn't been wearing her seat belt? What if she'd been thrown from the car? She could've broken her neck.

He leaned on the vanity, arms rigid and trembling. There'd been too many times like this—and not all in that first, horrible year of Leigh's life. There'd been the time she'd gotten hit in the head with a softball. The day she'd gotten lost at the mall. And all the times her asthma had sent her to the emergency room, her lips turning blue.

He bowed his head. Dragged in a raw breath. His throat burned and his eyes felt like someone had rubbed sand in them. He swallowed a couple of times, trying his best to bury the fear somewhere dark and deep.

But the tears came anyway.

Chapter Eleven

*Single parents can have difficulty keeping their
love lives and home lives separate.*

"*Please* tell me you didn't sleep with him."

"No," Tori hedged, not quite able to meet Chelsea's troubled gaze. "Not sleep, no."

Chelsea shifted Lily in her arms. "Oh, Tori. You had sex with him, didn't you?"

"No! At least, not completely. Not all the way."

Her friend sighed and looked around the half-finished shop, as if wisdom lay boxed up with Tori's unpacked merchandise.

"But you went too far," Chelsea said quietly. "Farther than you should have. Tori, it hasn't even been six months since you and Colin split up. And like you said, you hardly know Nick. Even if it turns out he doesn't have a wife or girlfriend, do you really think you can handle another physical relationship so soon? With everything else you've got going on in your life?"

Tori knew her friend was referring to her medical problems, and her decision to have a baby as soon as possible.

"No," she admitted. "Probably not. And really, he's not even my type. There's no way we could have a future together. So that phone call shouldn't bother me at all."

"Is he coming over to work today?"

"I guess. At least, he hasn't called to cancel, and I'm pretty sure he would if he wasn't going to show." Nick was nothing if not dependable. It was Saturday, and he'd told her he'd arrive at two. "He should be here in an hour."

"Then don't you be here. Come with me and Lily to the beach. You need to put some space between you and that man."

So that was what Tori did. She went to the beach, then changed at Chelsea's house and went out to dinner with her and Mags, and then back to their house to watch TV. By the time she got home, it was midnight and Nick had come and gone. She looked for a note, but he hadn't left one.

It hurt, but she tried her best to ignore the pain. For the next few nights, she managed to invent reason after reason she had to leave the house just before Nick arrived. There was a movie she wanted to see. Shopping she needed to do. She babysat Lily so Chelsea and Mags could enjoy a child-free dinner. When she did see Nick, briefly, he watched her with a wary look. She didn't ask about the phone call, and he didn't volunteer an explanation. They spoke only about the progress on the shop. It was as if that searing intimacy they'd shared in the kitchen had set their relationship back a giant step, rather than moving it forward.

She tried her best to think of him as just a contractor. For a few days, it almost worked. She was busy scouring thrift shops for usable shelving and cabinets. In a couple of stores, she came across some secondhand baby furniture. She stopped to check the prices.

She wanted so much to be pregnant again. She wondered what it would be like, feeling the baby kick. She'd been eleven weeks along when she'd miscarried, too early to feel any movement. She tried to imagine the sensation, but it was kind of like a virgin imagining sex. You had to experience it to understand. And she wanted to. More than anything.

But she couldn't quite bring herself to go back to Choices.

Toward midweek, she thought she'd succeeded in distancing herself from Nick enough to handle an entire evening at home alone with him. She had work to do in the shop, and he was working in the attic now. She figured there was no reason for their paths to cross more than briefly.

She figured wrong.

She was mopping the kitchen when he cornered her. She'd been trying to banish the spackle dust left over from his sanding the new walls. It was everywhere—who'd have thought the stuff could seep under doors, around plastic tarps, into every crevice of a wood floor? For the last several days, she'd swept, wiped, mopped, and swept some more, and she still hadn't gotten it all up.

She was mopping under the table when he entered the room. She was so intent on cleaning one elusive corner of the floor that she didn't even hear him come in. He didn't say anything, just sneaked up behind her and pressed his lips to her neck.

Her mop clattered to the floor. She froze. Without a word, he turned her around, backed her up against the wall, and proceeded to kiss her senseless.

Her mind blanked. Her body, however, had no problem taking over. She kissed him back. Entwined her arms around his neck. Pressed her body against him.

After a while, he broke the kiss and let her gulp some air.

She looked up at him, dazed. "What . . . what do you think you're doing?"

His expression was unreadable. "I finally managed to get close enough to you to do that. Why have you been trying so hard to avoid me these past few days?"

"I wasn't. I'm just . . . busy." It was a lame lie, and they both knew it.

He didn't call her on it. "You've been running around too much. Take a rest."

She tried to wriggle out of his arms. "I don't like resting."

The corner of his mouth lifted. "I've noticed."

She tried to wriggle away again. His arms tightened around her.

And it felt good.

Too good.

Nick's chest was broad and strong; his embrace was solid and somehow comforting, even after the past week of awkwardness. She sighed. Another minute in his arms, and she'd melt in a puddle at his feet.

She couldn't let that happen. She pushed at his chest, but it was like trying to move one of the boulders in the rock jetty on the beach. "Let me go. I've got work to do. I need to repaint my cloud mural. Set up my shelves. Unpack—"

He nuzzled beneath her ear, insinuating one finger under the scoop neckline of her peasant blouse and tugging it off her shoulder. "You know, you should think about joining a union. Then you'd get regular breaks."

"Would I?"

"Yep." His teeth found bare skin and gave a playful nip. "You're definitely due for a break right now. How about we pick up where we left off Friday night?"

She couldn't believe her ears. "You've got to be kidding."

He frowned. "Why?"

She huffed. "As if you don't know."

He put a little distance between them, his gaze turning wary. "I don't. I have no idea why you've been giving me the cold shoulder. Why don't you tell me?"

"God. Men." She marched past him, out of the kitchen and through the shop. She didn't stop until she reached the porch. The new screen door hissed gently shut. How annoying. She would have given anything for the old door's satisfying slam.

Nick was right behind her. "Tori, come off it. What's the matter?"

She gripped the porch railing. "Nick, I think you've done enough work for today. Why don't you leave early?"

"Jesus, Tori—"

She marched back into the house.

Nick swore and came after her. He dogged her steps all the way back to the kitchen.

She grabbed her teapot. "Please leave."

He propped one hip against the counter. "No."

She turned to the sink and gave the faucet a savage twist.

"You might want to go easy on that," he said, watching her. "I just fixed it."

She shut off the water. Sure enough, no drips.

For some reason, that got her even madder. "When did you do that?"

"A couple nights ago, while you were out."

"Well, I didn't ask you to."

"I didn't do it for you. I did it for my own sanity. The dripping was driving me nuts."

"I told you, I can't afford all this extra work."

"Don't worry about it."

She closed her eyes and counted to ten. "I don't take charity, Nick."

He studied her a moment. "Are you going to tell me what's got you so upset? Or am I supposed to guess?"

She stared at him. "How can you not know?"

"I'm a guy. We're idiots. You have to spell it out for us."

She drew a breath. "All right. Who called you Friday night? When we were . . ." She couldn't finish.

He straightened, understanding dawning. "That's what this is all about? That phone call?"

"It was after midnight, Nick. And it was a woman who called. I could tell."

"Oh, for Pete's—"

"Who was it, Nick? I could tell you were close to her. Was it . . ." She drew air into her lungs. "Was it your wife?"

His jaw dropped. "My what?"

Her belly cramped. "Well, was it?"

His features hardened. "That's why you've been giving me the cold shoulder? That's what you think of me? That I'm the kind of man who cheats on his *wife*?"

"But . . . that's just the problem! I don't know what kind of man you are. I don't know you at all. It's only been a couple weeks and already we've . . ." She made a vague, helpless gesture toward the kitchen counter. The site of the orgasm.

"But then you left so abruptly," she whispered. "With no

explanation at all. And all I could think was how little I really know about you."

He was pissed. She could tell by the way he'd gone completely and utterly still. She realized it was the first time she'd seen him really angry.

His voice, when he finally spoke, was flat. "You don't know me? Well, here's a clue. If I was married, I wouldn't screw a client in her kitchen."

Ouch. That hurt. And he seemed genuinely appalled that she should think so little of him. Still . . .

"Who called you that night, Nick? I'm sorry, but I really need to know."

He was silent for a moment. Then he let out a sigh, and she watched his anger drain away as if someone had pulled a plug on it. "I'm sorry, too. I know should have told you more that night." He hesitated. "It was my daughter on the phone, Tori."

She'd run through all kinds of possible explanations, but this was one that hadn't been on her list at all. She was stunned.

"You have a daughter?" The image of a little girl with Nick's dark eyes and curls popped into her mind.

"Yeah, I do. She was upset, and she knows she can call me anytime, so—"

Tori lost another chunk of her heart, right then and there. Nick was a father. She was sure he was a wonderful one.

"You don't have to explain. I'm sorry. I shouldn't have doubted you. You gave me no reason to—"

"I'm not a player, Tori. I wouldn't do that to you. I have a daughter, but don't have a wife. I've been divorced for a while now."

"What happened?"

"Things didn't work out."

Okay, so that covered a lot of territory. She met his gaze, silently urging more.

He exhaled. "The only reason Cindy and I got married was because she got pregnant. Business was in a slump, and

I was working like a dog to keep afloat. She hated that. She hated clipping coupons, hated counting every penny." He paused. "She was mad the baby ruined her figure, and she didn't like being tied down with an infant." He rubbed a hand over his face. "And that about covers it, I guess. I wasn't what she really wanted."

"She left you?"

"Yeah. For another man. A casino manager, actually. She went with him when he got transferred to Vegas and she hasn't been back since. Not once. Not even to visit her own daughter."

His voice was completely devoid of emotion. That told her a lot. "You loved her."

He shrugged. "I got over it."

She touched his forearm. "Thank you for telling me."

His expression was strained. Wary. For all his teasing and flirting, she could tell Nick hated talking about his problems. He was a very private person.

Maybe she was starting to know him better than she'd thought.

"I don't have a girlfriend, either," he said.

"You must date." Jersey women weren't blind, after all.

He rubbed the back of his neck. "Sometimes. Not for the past year, though. It's been busy at work. If I'm not home, I'm at the office."

"You like your work, don't you?"

He grimaced. "Not the paperwork. But I like building things." He gave a rueful smile. "I started a long time ago, with sand castles."

Tori had no trouble at all picturing six-year-old Nick fortifying his castle against the coming tide.

She smiled. "You're good at what you do."

"Doesn't stop my clients from complaining," he quipped with a grin, and the last threads of tension between them vanished as if they'd never been.

He took her hand, wove his fingers through hers.

"Come on," he said, tugging her toward the door. "I'm

hungry, and we both need a break. Let's get out of here and find some dinner."

"Dad hasn't cooled off a bit," Leigh told Jason. "He's being a total jerk." She scowled across the picnic table at the Lucy-the-elephant snack bar. "He even told me I couldn't see you anymore."

Jason swallowed a hunk of his hot dog. "It won't last. He'll come around."

"I'm practically eighteen, but he thinks I'm still a baby." She jabbed a curly fry into her ketchup.

"Leigh, chill. Nothing your dad says or does is gonna stop us from seeing each other." He leaned across the snack bar table and kissed the corner of her mouth.

"There," he said, smiling.

"What?"

"You had ketchup on your face. It's gone now."

"Oh."

He went back to his hot dog. Leigh watched him eat. He'd worked on the beach today and still had traces of white zinc on his nose. With his red bathing suit, white muscleman tee, and sneakers with no socks, he looked yummier than her burger and fries.

And he was *hers*. For as long as she could keep him. Every hour she was stuck at home, Karla would be circling like a buzzard, getting closer and closer.

"He still doesn't believe me about the other car," she said. "He thinks you went off the road because we were fooling around."

"We were fooling around, a little."

"We kissed, but it had nothing to do with that other car running us off the road. My dad's out of his mind."

"He hates me," Jason said, "and I don't even know why. You'd think we'd get along. Wasn't he a lifeguard once, too?"

"Yeah." Leigh twisted her napkin until it tore. "I think . . . I think he's afraid you'll get me pregnant. Like him and my mom, back when they were in high school."

"Hey." Jason's fingers brushed her chin, urging her to meet his gaze. "You know I wouldn't let that happen. When we make love, everything's gonna be perfect."

When we make love.

As if she'd already agreed to do it . . .

Jason's dark eyes went darker, more intense. He didn't look away. *God.* Whenever he looked at her like that, a hot, restless feeling made her want to squirm. The tips of her breasts tingled. Something fierce and inevitable unfurled in her stomach.

He caught her hand. Bringing it to his lips, he kissed her fingers. "You do trust me, don't you, Leigh?"

If he'd asked her whether she loved him, she'd have answered yes right away. But trust him? That was a different thing entirely. Jason had always been one of the popular kids. Leigh hadn't ever been—at least, not before he'd noticed her. Sure, she was his girlfriend right now, but there were a ton of other girls who wanted him. Girls who would have sex with him in an instant.

Like Karla.

A gull landed on a nearby picnic table, lifted its wings, and squawked at Leigh's fries. Jason shooed the bird away, but the intense moment was lost. He stood and threw his trash in the garbage. Leigh's shoulders relaxed. Thank God he wasn't going to press her for an answer.

Yet.

She dumped her fries and what was left of her burger in the trash. "Walk me home?"

"What about your dad?"

"He's not there. He hasn't come in before midnight all week. He's working late. He's got some big job."

Jason laced his fingers with hers. When they reached the corner, Leigh turned toward home, but Jason's tug on her hand had her looking back. "What?"

"Isn't that your dad's truck?"

Leigh followed Jason's line of vision. Yep, her Dad's white pickup was parked halfway up a small street that opened onto Atlantic, in front of a tiny pink bungalow. There was a trash Dumpster in the driveway. "Yeah, it is."

"Doesn't look like a big job," Jason commented.

"No," Leigh said slowly. "What could he possibly be doing there?"

"Renovating that little house?"

"I doubt it. He doesn't do small rehabs like that." She stared for another moment, then shrugged and turned toward home. "Maybe it's not Dad's truck. Come on. I talked Mimi into letting me go out, but she made me promise to be home by seven."

"Wait a sec. Someone's coming out on the porch. Hell, Leigh, it *is* your dad." He gave a low whistle. "And he's with someone."

She looked back. It was her dad, all right, tugging a dark-haired woman by the hand. From this distance it was hard to tell, but Leigh thought she might be pretty. She couldn't believe it. And it got worse. Working? She didn't think so. Not when he was crowding the woman into a corner of the porch rail and kissing her. It wasn't a quick kiss, either. It was deep, and long, and probably involved tongues.

"Oh, gross," Leigh gasped, just as Jason said, "Whoa. Your dad's got a babe."

The woman's arms snaked around Leigh's dad's neck. His hands were on her waist, pulling her flush against his body.

"Sweet," Jason said, grinning.

"Oh. My. God," Leigh said. "He lied to me! He said he was working late."

Jason slung his arm over Leigh's shoulders. "Well, babe, at least now you know what he's been working on."

Chapter Twelve

*The oldest child in a big family learns to respect
the rules at an early age. And never forgets them.*

"How can you eat that . . . that . . . heart attack on a bun?"

Tori shoved a fork into her salad, but her gaze kept drifting to Nick's cheesesteak. A large Coke sat on the table near his elbow. It had to be the unhealthiest meal ever invented. She half expected him to keel over right in front of her.

But, God, it smelled good.

Aunt Millie used to feed Tori cheesesteaks. She used to say Tori needed fattening up. She grimaced. She didn't need fattening up now—a sub roll smothered with fried steak and cheese would go straight to her butt, which God knew was big enough as it was. But Nick, damn him, bit into the zillion fat calories without the least show of remorse.

"A guy's gotta die of something," he said.

She fought the urge to lean across the table and lick his lips. "Surely you can think of a more creative way to kill yourself."

He took a swig of his soda before answering. "Hey, I'm not a total loss. I work out almost every day."

Her gaze wandered from his mouth to his chest. She had no trouble remembering what he looked like with his shirt off. And after that kiss on the porch, she didn't need any reminders about what it felt like to be in his arms, either. Of course he worked out.

"What do you do?" she asked. "Lift weights?"

"Yeah. That and swim."

"In the ocean?"

"Used to. Now it's mostly at a health club."

"Oh." She toyed with her iceberg lettuce, trying to ignore the aroma radiating from Nick's sub roll.

He caught her eye. "Want a bite?"

Yes. "No." She attacked a perfectly innocent cherry tomato with her fork. "I'm vegan, remember?"

"Yeah, so you said."

"No animal products."

"Well, have some garlic knots, at least. That salad doesn't look like enough to keep you breathing for a day." He waved to the waitress and ordered a dozen.

"I've cut out white flour, too." Chelsea had been particularly adamant about that.

Nick snorted. When the waitress delivered the plate, he picked up a plump knot of baked pizza dough dripping with olive oil. Holding it between his thumb and forefinger, he leaned forward and brushed it against her bottom lip.

"Just one," he said. "For me."

Tori hardly even wavered before she caved.

The salty, garlicky knot tasted like heaven. Her eyelids shut as she chewed. After a long, ecstatic moment, she swallowed and opened her eyes again.

Nick was looking at her oddly.

He pushed the plate across the table. "Here. Have another one. Hell, have them all. You looked like you were about to freaking come right there on the table."

Her cheeks blotched. "God. You are so crude. How do you ever manage to get a date?"

"I have my ways." His gaze shifted to her mouth.

She licked the last bit of oil from her bottom lip. Nick's eyes went dark. Suddenly, the table between them seemed very flimsy.

He leaned across it.

His lips touched hers. Her heart pounded; her blood hummed in her veins. Her brain turned to organic oatmeal.

A heartbeat later, he pulled back. She couldn't stifle her gasp of protest.

He did his slow smile. "Hold that thought."

"I . . . I wasn't thinking anything."

"Liar." Grinning, he signaled to the waitress for the check. "Done with your salad?"

"Yes."

"Then come on." He dropped a five on the table for the tip and grabbed her hand.

"Where to?" she asked as he paid for their meal at the register.

"The Dairy Bar."

"Soft ice cream?" Wow, that sounded better than sex. Well, maybe not better than sex with *Nick*. Except . . .

"I can't eat ice cream."

He sent her a skeptical look. "Why the hell not? It's not meat."

"But it's not vegan. It's full of animal fat. And I'm not sup-posed to eat sugar, either." Another one of Chelsea's rules.

But she let him drag her there anyway.

The Dairy Bar was a tiny corner ice-cream stand done in funky turquoise-and-pink decor, a lovingly restored relic from the fifties. It was a popular place, judging from the small crowd gathered at the walk-up windows. Parents with kids. A cluster of teenagers. A few chatty middle-aged women. Quite a few senior citizens. Tori remembered coming here with Aunt Millie, way back when. Tori used to sit at one of the picnic tables and lick her cone as slowly as she could, trying to make it last forever.

It never did.

"I can't believe this place is still here," she said. "That no one's torn it down to build condos."

Nick steered her into line behind an elderly couple. "You want vanilla or chocolate?"

"I told you, I don't want one at all. You go ahead, though."

He ordered a large vanilla cone. Stepping away from the

stand, he locked eyes with Tori and took a long lick, dragging his tongue across the white swirl.

She sucked in a breath.

"Here." He held the cone a tantalizing inch from her lips. "Have a taste."

She couldn't stop herself. Her tongue snaked out. Licked. It was icy-smooth, a sweet dream. Her eyelids fluttered shut as the sugar rush washed over her.

When she opened her eyes, Nick said, "God, Tori. Do that again."

"No. One lick was enough."

"Not hardly." Bringing the cone to his lips, he licked the furrow her tongue had made in the ice cream, twirling the cone in a slow circle. She watched, mesmerized.

She wanted to feel it on her own skin. Nick's tongue, not the ice cream.

Oh, heck. Maybe the ice cream, too.

A sudden, vivid image sprang into her mind: Nick painting her naked body with alternating stripes of chocolate and vanilla soft-serve. Then licking the ice cream off with sure, strong strokes.

She shivered.

Nick did his slow smile. "Another lick?"

"Um . . . I'd better not."

"Oh, come on." He waggled his brows. "You know you want it."

Pure mirth flashed in Tori's green eyes. Her husky laugh came an instant later. Nick grinned like a teenager on his first date. It had been a long time since he'd been with a woman who really seemed to appreciate his personal brand of warped humor.

"You are so bad," she said, still laughing. Her hand closed on his wrist, pushing the cone away from her face.

Her touch affected him more than he wanted to admit. What was it about this woman? She made him feel like a kid. He wanted to tease her, make her laugh, laugh with her.

At the same time, he wanted to hold her, and keep her safe from everything except him.

"I can be a lot badder." He moved the cone toward her face, despite the resistance of her hand wrapped around his wrist. He painted her lips white.

She licked it off, the pink tip of her tongue sweeping the cream into her mouth.

Christ.

He smeared her lips with more soft-serve. Dear Lord, he was getting hard, right here on the sidewalk. He should back off. Now. But he couldn't make himself do it.

She licked her lips again. The cone cracked in his fist. He couldn't take much more of this. Not in public, anyway.

Her eyes fluttered shut, her lips parting on a sigh. His brain hazed with lust. He slid the tip of the ice cream swirl between her lips. Her grip on his wrist tightened, but she didn't push him away. Instead, she moved his hand back and forth, guiding the cone in and out and in again. And again.

Jesus, Mary, and Joseph.

She looked up at him, green eyes dancing. The pink tip of her tongue licked ice cream from her lips in slow motion. That was when he realized she was teasing him. On purpose.

If he'd been hard before, he was a damn steel rebar now.

He shoved the cone into her hands. "Here. Take it. Get rid of it. Fast. Unless you want me to perform an indecent act on you right here on the sidewalk, in front of all these little kids."

Tori's eyes sparkled. "You're the one who insisted I needed ice cream."

"Yeah. What was I thinking?"

She just smiled and took another lingering lick.

Nick sucked in a breath. "Let's go back to your place."

"No," she said, a speculative gleam in her eyes. "Let's go to the beach."

"The beach? Now? It's getting dark."

"All the more reason. I love the beach at night. When I

lived with Aunt Millie I used to sneak out after she was asleep."

"How old were you then?"

"Eleven."

Nick frowned. Leigh had done the same damn thing when she was that age, and he'd grounded her for a month. "Eleven's too young to be wandering alone on the beach at night. You're lucky you didn't get hurt."

"I never thought about that. The ocean called me. I used to sit in the lifeguard stand and watch the moon on the waves."

She licked more ice cream, and his brain blanked.

"Can we go?" she asked.

"Okay, sure." He'd have agreed to anything just about then. He'd much rather go straight back to her place, but a moonlit walk on the beach didn't sound so bad.

It'd be a great prelude to sex.

Tori walked with Nick the few blocks to the beach. They left their shoes at the bottom of the wooden access stair that breached the seawall. When they reached the ocean's edge, Tori splashed in until the water was up to her knees. It was surprisingly warm. Nick followed, wrapping his arms around her from behind.

Her bottom nestled between his thighs. She felt him harden against her lower back as a gentle blanket of night descended around them. The crash of the surf blocked the noise from the street, creating a cocoon of intimacy.

She wasn't a fool. She knew what all this flirting was leading up to. And right then and there, she decided to go with it, even though it was probably a bad idea. Her plan was to have a baby, not start a relationship. But her treacherous mind couldn't help wondering if Nick's little daughter would like a younger brother or sister.

Dangerous musings, she knew. They'd only just met. Even if somehow things moved along in the direction of commitment, it would take months, probably a year or two to get to the point where they were married and talking about kids. And according to the doctor, Tori just didn't have that kind of time.

A wave rolled in, splashing their legs. It receded quickly, at an angle to the shoreline, a strong undertow sucking the sand from around Tori's feet. She pushed her doubts away and settled back in Nick's arms. This was just one night. She didn't have to let it mean anything.

He nuzzled her neck, sending tingles zinging through her body. "So am I forgiven for last week? Honestly, at the time, I didn't stop to think how the phone call might sound to you."

"I shouldn't have shut you out afterward. I should've just asked you the next day what it was all about."

"It just about killed me to leave you that night, you know. I think my balls are still blue."

"Aw, you poor thing." She twisted in his arms, a smile on her lips. Then, because the crashing surf felt so inviting, she said, "Let's go in."

"My thoughts exactly." He turned them both toward the street.

"No! Not 'go in' like in 'go home.' I meant, let's go in the water."

He stopped and peered down at her. "What are you, nuts? It's dark."

"So? That'll just make it more fun." She slipped out of his embrace and waded out deeper.

He grabbed for her; she danced out of reach.

"Tori! Come back here! You don't even have a suit on."

The water was up to her waist now. She spun so the next breaker crashed against her back. The wave hit Nick front-on, soaking him to the hips.

"Come on, Tori. Cut it out. This isn't a good idea."

"Why not?"

"It's dark and the tide's going out. There's an undertow. It doesn't take much to—"

"You worry too much, you know that?"

"It's not a case of worrying. It's a case of not being stupid." Another wave crashed. "Shit. My pants are soaked."

She moved back to him, laughing, and slipped her fingers into the waistband of his shorts. "Take them off, then."

He blocked her quest to loosen his belt buckle. "I'll be more than happy to," he said. "At your place."

"Just a quick swim first."

"No."

She let go and backed out of his reach. "Fine. I'll go in by myself, then."

"Damn it." He made another grab for her.

She ducked, falling back into the water with a laugh. "It feels great," she called.

Nick waded in to his waist. "That's not funny, Tori. Get back here."

She felt giddy. "Come and get me!"

She flung her arms wide. A wave broke over her shoulders and head. Nick called again, but she ignored him and turned to dive under the next breaker. It was a big one, and it dragged her under, churning overhead. Tori was a good swimmer; she knew better than to fight the turbulence. She held her breath and stayed under until the water calmed.

She surfaced to Nick's frantic shout. "Tori!"

He was looking where she'd been; she was now about ten yards down the beach. She waved. "Over here!"

He slogged to her side. "That's it."

He grabbed her arm, hauled her out of the water, and dumped her on the sand. The impact of her butt hitting the beach had her gasping for breath.

She stared up at him. "What'd you do that for?"

"That was a goddamned dangerous stunt."

She scrambled to her feet. "No, it wasn't. I'm a very strong swimmer."

"So are a lot of people who drown." He shoved his fists into his soggy pockets.

That was when she realized his hands were shaking. "You're serious? You were really worried?"

He scowled. "I'd worry about anyone dumb enough to swim in the ocean at night. I used to be with the Beach Patrol, you know."

No, she didn't know, but somehow, she wasn't surprised. He was exactly the lifeguard type. "In Margate?"

"Atlantic City. For a couple years when I was in high school." He stared at her for a long moment, then sighed and held out his hand. "Come on. Let's go in and get dried off."

She took it and they started walking toward the street. "How long ago was that? I mean, how old are you? I don't even know."

He glanced at her. "Thirty-five. You're what, about twenty-nine?"

"Thirty."

"You look younger."

She slipped her arm around his waist. "Thanks. And thanks for what you did on the beach."

"What? Chewing you out?"

"Worrying about me." She paused. "For being my knight in shining armor."

He plucked at his wet clothes. "More like knight in soggy shirt."

"Close enough." She leaned into him, and his arm tightened around her. They came to a halt in the darkness behind the dunes. Silence stretched between them, louder than the pounding surf. Just a few steps away, a streetlight cast a soft glow on the sand, but here, in the shadows, it was so dark she couldn't see the expression in his eyes.

But she knew what he wanted.

She touched his face. "Kiss me, Nick."

He didn't need coaxing. He gathered her in his arms, pulling her into the heat of his body. His mouth found hers. They were both soaked, but she hardly cared. His lips were delicious. Her hands skimmed his shoulders, his arms, his hips. He was warm and solid. He wanted her, and she wanted him, too, and that felt good. It felt right.

Her hands wandered to the button on his shorts. She

worked it free and tugged the zipper down. He deepened their kiss, his hot tongue stroking into her mouth. Her fingers slipped through the fly on his boxers and closed on his erection. He inhaled sharply. She stroked the velvet length of him, once, twice.

He caught her hand and tugged it away. "Your place," he said, nipping a trail down her neck.

Instead of answering, she pressed her hips against him.

He groaned. "Baby, you're killing me. I want you so bad."

"Then have me." She tugged him farther into the shadows. "Right here."

He laughed a little, as though she were joking.

She licked a line down his salty neck and nibbled his shoulder. "I mean it. Let's do it here. I've always wanted to make love on a beach."

He shifted. "You're nuts."

She laughed. "I know." She kissed her way down his body. When she got to his navel, she dropped to her knees.

She felt the pressure of his hands on her shoulders, holding her at arm's length. "No. This is crazy. Someone might see us."

"Who? No one's around."

He shifted his grip to her upper arms and hauled her to her feet. "Tori. I'm not gonna have sex on the beach."

"Why not?"

"For starters, it's illegal."

"It's exciting."

"It's too sandy."

She kissed his jaw. "It's supposed to be sandy. It's a beach."

"I don't have a condom."

"We can do something else, then."

She dropped back to her knees, her hands on the back of his thighs for balance. The whole scene had her hot. The ocean, the night air—and yes, even the possibility of discovery. Maybe especially that. She'd loved doing it outdoors with Colin, before things went sour. She'd had some of her best times naked under the sky.

Moisture gathered between her thighs as she quickly un-zipped Nick's fly. He was hard; her lips sought the tip of his erection.

He jerked backward. "No. Not here."

His sudden movement sent her pitching forward into his legs. She fell against him, and he lost his footing in the soft sand. They went down in a tangle of limbs.

She laughed at the absurdity of it all. She wriggled onto his chest and kissed him, her tongue deep in his mouth, her body rubbing him like a cat. She straddled him, loving the feel of his hard body between her thighs.

He grabbed her waist. "Tori. Come on. Quit it."

She pulled up the hem of his sand-encrusted shirt and kissed his flat stomach. "No."

"Tori—" The drone of a motor cut him off. "Shit."

With an abrupt motion he rolled, taking Tori with him. She landed on her back in the sand, breathless.

The droning got louder.

"Lie still," he hissed, shielding her with his body.

"What is it?" she whispered.

"Police. They patrol the beach on ATVs at night. Just pray he doesn't look over here."

She lay motionless beneath him, heart pounding, loving the feel of his weight anchoring her to the cool sand. The cop's appearance hadn't splashed cold water on her libido—just the opposite. She was hotter than ever.

Headlights flashed over the sand, then receded.

Nick started to breathe again. After a moment, he sat up, pulling Tori with him.

"Shit. That was close."

She pulled him down for a kiss. "And now he's gone and it'll be ages before he comes back. . . ."

"Forget it."

"But—"

"Tori, I said no."

The anger in his voice finally got through. Her lust cooled a bit, and she fell silent.

He stood and started swatting at the wet sand on his shirt and pants. It was a hopeless task. She rose more slowly, suddenly chilled by the night air. But unlike before, she didn't snuggle under Nick's arm. In fact, she stayed a step or two behind him during the whole awkward trek back to her house.

The sinking feeling in her gut kept going down and down and down.

"Look," he said when they reached her porch, "it's not like I was turning you down back there."

"No?" She stared at his chest. He tried to hold her, but her crossed arms kept them apart.

"Aw, Tori, come on."

"Will you be working tomorrow?" Her voice sounded distant, even to her own ears.

He exhaled sharply. "Don't tell me you're pissed again." His tone was flat. "Just because I don't want to screw on a public beach?"

Her shoulders slumped. "It's not that, really."

"Then what?"

Good question. She tried to puzzle out why she felt so rejected. Because Nick hadn't wanted to ravish her in the sand? Even she could tell she was overreacting, but that didn't make his attitude hurt any less. She and Nick were polar opposites. Why did she imagine a little lust could get around that? They had no future together.

Chelsea was right, she thought wearily. It was too soon after Colin for Tori to be letting herself care this much about any man. Especially one she'd just met. She was on the rebound, trying to take shortcuts. She was trying so hard to pretend Nick was a comfortable, long-term lover, but he wasn't that. He was someone she was just beginning to know, and the more time they spent together, the more potholes appeared in the road of any future relationship. It would take a long time to reconcile their basic differences and make some kind of commitment—if they actually could. She thought of the baby she wanted so badly. How long would it be before she could even think of discussing children with Nick? Months? Years? *Ever?*

"I . . ." She swallowed, her throat suddenly tight and burning. "I'm sorry. I'm just really tired tonight. I'm going to crash early." She backed out of his arms. "I hope you don't mind."

His eyes were sober. "Tori, I . . ."

She turned away, fumbling in the pocket of her shorts. After a few seconds, she gave up and leaned against the door frame. "I forgot my key."

"No problem," Nick said, unzipping a pocket on his cargo shorts. "I've got the spare."

For some reason, Tori's already low-flying mood took a nosedive.

"Of course you do," she said.

Chapter Thirteen

*Family lies come in many varieties: little white. Big ugly.
Keep-the-peace. Don't-worry-Mom. Family is just too
damn close to trust with the truth.*

"Hi, Dad."

Shit. Leigh was the last person Nick wanted to see after that
scene with Tori. But there she was, sitting at the bottom of the
stairs in the dark foyer, even though it was almost midnight.

"Hi, yourself," he said. "You waiting up for me?"

"Yeah."

Her oversize T-shirt nearly swallowed her body, making
her look like the little girl she'd once been. The one who
used to hide behind the door, giggling, when he came home
from work.

God, he missed that. He hadn't realized how much until
that very moment.

"What happened to you? You're all wet."

He racked his brain for a plausible explanation. "Defective sprinkler head on the Bayview job." He hoped it was too
dark for her to see all the sand and realize he was feeding her
a load of BS.

"Bayview, huh? That's where you were tonight?"

"Yeah." The lie stuck in his throat. "We're working double
shifts and weekends, trying to wrap things up."

"How much longer till it's done?"

"A couple weeks. Tell you what," he added, forcing enthusiasm. "When you start working at the office next week, I'll
take you out to see it. You used to love going out to job sites
when you were young."

Leigh looked down at her painted toenails. "You know, Dad, I was thinking about that. Maybe I don't want to work at the office this summer."

"But you've worked there the last three years. Doris is counting on you."

"Yeah, I know. But Stacey got this great job busing tables at one of the casino restaurants. She said they're still hiring. The tips are fantastic."

Nick nearly choked. His daughter hauling dirty dishes in a casino? Getting ogled by low-life gamblers? "Absolutely not."

"Dad. A lot of kids from school have summer jobs at the casinos."

"You don't. And you're not going to. You're working for me this summer, as usual."

"But it's so boring filing contracts and answering phones!"

"Boring pays the bills. Including, I might add, the repairs on the car your boyfriend pitched into the marsh."

Leigh's angry glare hit him right between the eyes. "That accident wasn't Jason's fault! The other car swerved into our lane. We would've crashed if Jason hadn't gone off the road."

"Ah, yes, the mysterious other car. The jury's still out on that one, Leigh."

She stood, her hand gripping the stair rail. "You still don't believe me?"

"Why should I? You lied about staying at Stacey's. You lied about being behind the wheel."

"Oh! *I* lied, did I? You're a fine one to talk."

Nick started. "What the hell's that supposed to mean?"

"You're so smart. You figure it out." She turned and stomped up the steps.

Nick stood dripping in the foyer, staring up after her.

Tori was repainting her cloud mural on the morning after the beach fiasco with Nick, trying to ignore the twisting sense of loss in her stomach. Instead, she focused her thoughts on pregnancy. She didn't have the luxury of waiting for a good, steady relationship with a man before she took the motherhood plunge. She'd decided to call Dr. Brenner and tell him she'd chosen the gay journalist/poet/Democrat to be the father of her child. And if that felt a little weird, she calmed her nerves with a mental picture of Lily.

But it was so hard to stop thinking of Nick.

Someone rang her newly rewired doorbell. Tori's paintbrush paused. A pretty teenager with blonde hair, blue eyes, and a lush Barbie-doll figure stood on the porch.

"Sorry," Tori called. "I'm not open until next week."

"Oh, I don't want to shop." The girl opened the screen door a crack. "I just saw your 'Coming Soon' sign and wanted to talk. Can I come in?"

Tori put down her brush and smiled. "Sure."

"I'm Leigh," the girl said, stepping through the door.

"Nice to meet you, Leigh. I'm Tori."

Leigh looked around, taking in the unfinished mural, the hanging crystals, the empty shelves, and the full boxes.

"Wow. Too cool. You're painting the walls yourself?"

"Yes."

She looked through the new fire door, which Tori had left propped open. "You live here, too?"

"Yes," she said again, a little taken aback by the girl's curiosity.

"We're practically neighbors, then," she said with a smile. "I live a few blocks up the street."

"Are you in town for the summer?"

She shook her head, scattering her long blonde hair over her shoulders. "Believe it or not, I'm one of the ten people who live in Margate year-round." She gave the room another look. "Did you do all the renovations on this place yourself?"

"No. The city required me to hire a licensed contractor."

"Oh. Where is he?"

"On a bigger, better day job. He's doing mine on the side, after hours."

"Working late, huh?"

"Yes." Tori felt her cheeks go blotchy. She hoped Leigh didn't notice.

The girl peered at her. "What are you going to sell here?"

"Oh, New Age merchandise, mostly. Tarot cards, crystals, runes. I'll probably tell fortunes, too."

Leigh's startled expression kind of reminded Tori of Nick's face when she'd told him the same thing. "Fortune-telling? No kidding? Think you'll have a lot of customers?"

"I hope so. But so far you're the only person who's stopped by. Of course, my big sign's not up yet. That might have something to do with it."

"You should advertise in the newspaper."

Tori grimaced. "I called the Atlantic City paper, but you'd need a magnifying glass to read the ad I could afford."

"Take out an ad in the *Downbeach Wave*. It's a community newspaper. I bet it's way cheaper than the *Press*."

It was an idea. "Do you think that would help?"

"Sure. Everyone reads the *Wave*. They give it out free all over town." She gave a sidelong glance. "You know, I could make up an ad for you. Something really catchy."

"You do artwork?"

"Yeah. I took a computer graphics class last semester. I can do whatever you want."

Tori thought it over. With everything else going on, she hadn't thought much about advertising. "How much would you charge?"

"Oh, maybe fifty dollars for me, plus whatever the paper's fee is. I'll take care of everything."

Sounded good. "Okay. But I'll need to see the ad before you submit it to the paper."

"No problem there. What're you calling this place?"

"Destiny's Gate."

"Cool. I'll do something heavenly, with clouds." Leigh smiled. "You'll love it."

The next day, Tori visited Chelsea and told her she'd decided to go through with the donor insemination.

"What about your contractor?" Chelsea asked, too casually.

"What about him?" Tori countered, trying to sound equally casual. She mashed Lily's organic carrots with a Peter Rabbit fork.

"Oh, come on, Tori. What's the deal?"

She popped a spoonful of carrots into Lily's mouth. The baby grimaced and spit them out.

"I'm attracted to Nick, sure. What hetero woman wouldn't be? But he and I are so different. And you're right: I'm still on the rebound from Colin." She managed to spoon another dose of carrots into Lily. "I'm not ready for a man, Chelsea, but I'm more than ready for a baby. I don't see any reason to wait."

Chelsea put some cut-up pieces of banana on Lily's high chair tray. "I think you're making the right decision. It can be dangerous for a woman to arrange her life around a man."

"Don't I know it," Tori muttered, coaxing another spoonful of carrots past Lily's lips. The baby made a face. Tori did an airplane sound, swooping the spoon in for a landing on Lily's tongue.

Chelsea's expression was solemn. "Colin really did a number on you, didn't he?"

Tori chewed her lower lip. "I got pregnant, Chelse. It was an accident, but I was so happy about it. But Colin didn't want the baby. He didn't want his own child—the one we'd made together." Her stomach tightened in a cramp. "He wanted me to have an abortion."

Chelsea's breath escaped in a gasp. "Did you?"

"Colin was sure that I would. I always went along with whatever he wanted. But I just couldn't."

She watched Lily squeeze a banana chunk in her chubby fist. Yellow pulp escaped from between her plump fingers. "How could I get rid of my own child? I couldn't. I told Colin I was having the baby, no matter what. The very next night, I found him in bed with one of our tour clients."

"Oh, God."

"I went ballistic on him. It was almost funny. Five years together without a single fight, and I made up for it all in one night. I screamed. Threw things. I even tried to hit him, but he grabbed me. I had bruises on my wrists for a week." Reliving that scene caused Tori's pulse to kick up. The knot of pain in her stomach tightened.

Chelsea's eyes went wide, and even Lily picked up on Tori's distress. The baby's mouth opened wide, and she didn't even protest when Tori scooped in more carrots.

"It was the hormones," Chelsea said. "They can make you insane. Mags and I fought like bitches when I was carrying Lily."

Tori tried to laugh, but her stomach had cramped up so much she couldn't manage a deep enough breath. "Colin was so pissed. He told me . . ."

He'd told her he didn't love her. "He told me he didn't care what I did, but that he didn't want anything to do with the baby and I'd have to take him to court and prove the kid was his before he'd give me a dime for support. The cramps . . . they started the next day. My first prenatal visit was to the emergency room. I miscarried." She closed her eyes on a tide of grief. "It was as if the baby knew she wasn't wanted."

"It was a girl?"

"I never knew, really. They didn't tell me. But I think of her as a girl."

Sudden white-hot pain sliced through Tori's gut. Her stomach spasmed hard. She dropped Lily's spoon and bent over double in her chair, gasping.

Chelsea sprang to her side. "Oh, my God! What is it? Are you sick? Should I call a doctor?"

"No. No doctors." The pain wasn't new. She'd had it every month since the miscarriage. "Just help me get home."

Chapter Fourteen

Blood is more than twice as thick as water.
Which is why we're more than doubly pissed
when a relative lets us down.

Nick climbed the wooden steps to the temporary job trailer at Lighthouse Harbor. Work was due to start next week, but there was no chance in hell his men would be off the Bayview job in time. He'd set up a meeting with the owner's project manager, hoping to finagle a few days' grace. His hand was on the doorknob when his cell rang.

He checked the number and cursed. Joe D'Amico, calling from Bayview.

"Santangelo here."

"Nicolo," Nick's job super said. "Got a problem."

Nick sighed. "Joe. What is it this time?"

"You know them fancy cabinets? For behind the bar in the clubhouse?"

"Yeah. They're supposed to be delivered today. Don't tell me they didn't come."

"Oh, they came, all right. But the flunkies who took them outta the truck dropped one off the tailgate."

Christ. "How bad is it?"

"It's a busted mess. Can't fix it. Need another one."

Shit. Another delay. That job was bleeding dollars. "I'll call the millwork shop right away," he told Joe, but he knew he didn't have the time to make the call before his meeting.

He punched the speed dial for Johnny's number. Maybe his brother could be useful for once.

Voice mail answered. "Yo, dawg, can't talk now. You know what to do at the beep."

Hell. Nick called his office. "Doris, is Johnny there?"

"Why, no, Nick, he's not. He won't be in until two. He needed a new set of head shots."

Nick fought the urge to punch something. "He's getting his picture taken? Right now?"

"That's right, Nick. It's for his second *Franklinville Hospital* audition. They called him back. Isn't it exciting?"

"A riot," Nick said. "It's a freaking riot."

Please, somebody shoot me.

It was the only coherent thought Tori could muster. Her period had hit her like a freight train doing two hundred miles per hour, downhill. She sloshed down a double dose of the painkillers Dr. Janssen had prescribed, curled into a ball on her futon, and tried to sleep. It was no use. It felt as though someone were taking a butcher knife to her gut.

Since she'd lost the baby, each month was worse than the one before. She squeezed her eyes shut and tried a yoga breathing thing. It was supposed to release her pain to the universe. It didn't do squat.

She hated this. Hated feeling helpless. Hated that she was alone with all this pain.

And then . . . she wasn't alone.

Nick was there, his weight compressing the futon, his hand warm and sure on her forehead. He brushed the hair from her eyes.

"What are you doing here?" she whispered.

"It's five thirty. I knocked, but you didn't answer, so I let myself in. What's wrong, baby? Are you sick? You don't feel like you have a fever."

The concern in his voice caused a tear to run down her cheek. "No, it's . . ." She trailed off, embarrassed. She'd been practically naked with the man, but that didn't mean she knew him well enough to discuss her *period.*

Another wave of pain spasmed her midsection. She clutched her belly and swallowed a groan.

"What?" Nick's brow furrowed. "Is it your stomach? Food poisoning, maybe? You want me to call your doctor?"

"No. I'll be fine. It's not . . . food poisoning. I get this all the time."

"Jesus. How often?"

She grimaced. "Once a month, like clockwork."

Understanding dawned. "You've got your period."

God. She wanted to die. *Die.*

She rolled over and buried her face in the pillow. "Go away. Leave me alone. Take the night off."

But he didn't. What he did was settle down on her futon, his back propped up against the wall, and gathered her into his arms. He held her there, his hand rubbing circles on her back. She buried her face in his shirt. It smelled like fabric softener.

"Is it always like this?" he asked.

"Not usually quite this bad."

"Did you take something?"

"Yes."

"What can I do for you?"

"Nothing. I just have to wait it out." She lifted her head only high enough to meet his gaze. "But I don't think I can deal with all the hammering tonight. You might as well go home."

"Like hell I will." He eased her onto her side on the futon and started kneading the tight muscles in her lower back. "Does this help?"

It did. More than she wanted to admit. The pain receded a bit. Was it the pills? Or Nick? Probably a combination of the two.

After a while he got up and left the room. She heard him rattling around in the kitchen. When he returned, she rolled onto her back and looked at him.

"Here." He handed her a bundle of kitchen towels. They were damp and warm, and bundled in plastic wrap. "I heated them in the microwave. Not pretty, I know, but it's the best heat pack I could come up with on short notice."

"I . . . don't understand."

"Damp heat's good for cramps." He pressed the towels against her belly and held them there. "It helps the muscles relax."

"How do you know that?"

"My ex had a rough time with her period, too. Nothing like this, though. Have you seen a doctor?"

"Yes."

"And?"

She told me to have a baby. "She said I needed surgery."

"Jesus. When are you going to have it done?"

"Never. I can't."

"Why not?"

She bit her lip. She didn't want to go into it, but the concern in Nick's eyes made her want to explain. "My mother spent a lot of time in hospitals, because of her drug habit. I hate them. I can't even walk in the door of a hospital without getting all light-headed and woozy. I could never go in for surgery."

"But if the alternative is being like this . . ."

Her stomach muscles, which had begun to relax, cramped again. "Please," she whispered, sweat breaking out on her forehead. "Can we not talk about this now?"

He leaned over and kissed the top of her head. "Sure. Anything you want."

They didn't talk much after that. Nick just held her, surrounding her with his warmth. When a spasm came, he massaged her it until it faded. He didn't touch her intimately, or even kiss her on the lips. He did kiss the top of her head again, though, and for some reason, that made her want to cry.

Eventually her ragged breathing began to match the steady rise and fall of his chest. Her body relaxed—if not completely, at least enough to make her drowsy. The pain faded to a dull ache.

She must have fallen asleep, because she didn't remember him leaving. But when she woke up the next morning, he was gone.

Chapter Fifteen

Teenagers will tell complete strangers things they wouldn't dream of telling their own family.

Tori was more than a little embarrassed when Nick showed up for work the next day.

"I'm sorry I was such a pain last night," she said. "You really didn't have to stay with me."

"It was no trouble." His dark eyes studied her. "You still look a little pale. How're you feeling?"

"I'm okay. The first day is the worst. By the end of the week I'll be back to normal."

"Did you call your doctor?"

She hadn't, and she didn't want to talk about it, so she changed the subject.

"I had some shelving delivered today, but when I ordered it, I didn't realize I'd have to put it together. Do you think you could help me?"

"Sure."

They spent the next few hours assembling the shelves together. That had to be the very last activity that should have made Tori think of sex, but every time Nick drove a screw into a hole, she felt an answering twinge low in her belly that had nothing to do with last night's pain. Once they got the shelving put together, Nick set up her secondhand cash register on the glass-fronted counter she'd bought at a bankruptcy sale.

It felt so right working alongside Nick. Every once in a while his arm would brush hers, or he'd lay a hand on her shoulder. Or she'd touch his arm to get his attention. It was as if they were lovers, even though their spat on the beach had ruined what might have been their first time. But he didn't make a move on her, didn't pull her into his arms for a kiss. Was it because it was her time of the month? Or because he'd seen her curled up on her bed, looking like a reject from a horror movie?

Finally, he retreated to the attic to work on the fire barrier, the last item on the building inspector's list. After that came the final city inspection, and Destiny's Gate could open for business. And there would be nothing left to keep Nick here.

Except Tori.

She wondered if that would be enough.

Leigh stopped by on Sunday afternoon. "Your ad's done," she said.

"Already?"

"Yeah. It has to be in by tomorrow morning for the next issue." She slid a color print from a manila envelope.

Tori blinked down at the image of a silver portal floating on fluffy pink clouds. The words *Destiny's Gate* arched across the top of the page. At the bottom was a description of the shop, the hours of operation, and her grand-opening date. A map inset showed the location.

"I love it," she said.

Leigh grinned. "Great. I'll just need a check for the paper." She told Tori the amount. "You can pay my fee later."

Tori went to find her checkbook. It took her a few minutes to locate it under the stack of parenting magazines Chelsea had loaned her. When she returned to the shop, she found Leigh gazing at the divination merchandise, which was unpacked and spread all over the floor. Cards, runes, crystals, mirrors, astrological charts—you name it. If it told the future, it was there.

"Do you really know how to use this stuff?" Leigh asked.

"I know the basics on most of them, but the tarot is my

favorite." Then, because Leigh looked so intrigued, Tori added, "Would you like me to do a reading for you?"

Leigh's eyes widened. "You mean like tell my fortune?"

"Yes."

She hesitated. "I don't know . . . it seems kind of creepy, you know? What if something bad's about to happen? I'm not sure I'd want to know."

"It's not like that," Tori said, picking up a deck. "The cards won't tell you that at, say, seven o'clock tomorrow morning lightning will strike. What you do is ask a question and the cards provide guidance. Here, shuffle the deck and I'll show you."

Leigh took the cards and mixed them up a bit. "Now what?"

"Do you have a question? Something that's bothering you?"

She sighed. "Jason."

"Your boyfriend?"

"How'd you know that?"

"Lucky guess," Tori said, smiling. "Women almost always have a man on their mind." Herself included. "What do you want to ask about Jason?"

"If he loves me, I guess."

"Has he told you he does?"

"Yeah, but . . ."

Tori studied the girl. "Why don't you believe him?"

Another shrug.

She took the cards and fanned them facedown on the counter. "Okay. We'll start simple. Just choose one."

Leigh touched several cards before deciding. Finally, she flipped one over.

"The Lovers," Tori said. "That's very positive."

Leigh didn't look convinced. She set the card with the others, then touched a small box of body jewelry. She fingered a crystal belly-button stud.

"I got my belly button pierced last month." Leigh said, glancing at Tori, then looking away just as quickly. "My dad just about had a heart attack."

Tori chuckled. "So he's the old-fashioned type?"

"The worst. Overprotective, too. And he hates my boyfriend."

"I'm sure he just wants what's best for you."

"I guess." She glanced up from under her eyelashes. "But I don't see Dad all that much. He works late every night. When he does come home, all he does is get in my face."

"Have you talked to your mother about it?"

Leigh shrugged and turned her attention to a box of books without answering. She selected a volume on astrology, flipped through it, then put it back.

"You know," she said. "I was thinking . . ."

An odd sense of déjà vu flashed through Tori. There was something familiar about Leigh, but for the life of her, she couldn't put a finger on what it was.

"I'm out of school for the summer and I need a job. But I don't have a car, so I need something I can walk to. Are you hiring?"

"I haven't thought about it."

"Well, you'll need help, right? I mean, what if you have to go out or something? You can't just close up shop."

"I guess you're right."

"Will you hire me, then? Please say yes."

Tori smiled at her hopeful expression. "I couldn't pay you much."

"Minimum wage is fine."

It was a stretch, at least until money started coming in, but Leigh was right—it would be hard for one woman to run a shop completely on her own.

"All right. Consider yourself hired. But I'm warning you, I don't know the first thing about having an employee. There have to be tax papers or something to fill out."

"Oh, don't worry," Leigh said, and again that weird sense of déjà vu hazed through Tori's senses. "I worked for my dad a couple of summers. I know just what forms you need. I'll download them off the Internet and bring them my first day."

"When can you start?"

"When will your renovations be done?"

"Wednesday," Tori said.

"Okay. I'll see you then."

Nick stared at the utter chaos that was Tori's shop.

She'd been busy today. Open boxes and packing peanuts littered the floor, interspersed with some of the world's most bizarre merchandise. Oils, incense, bowls, and cauldrons. Statues of dragons and fairies. Jewelry featuring stars, moons, and spirals. A jeweled, blunt-bladed dagger. Books and CDs—but probably nothing he'd ever want to read or listen to. Bright gauzy dresses were piled on the floor like heaps of wildflowers.

And then there were the attitude T-shirts. *Worship me like the goddess I am. Surrender, Dorothy. Don't mess with PMS.*

He grinned. Tori was a trip. One he was definitely enjoying. He'd never met anyone quite like her. She was tough and funny and sassy, but there was a softness about her, too. A shadow of vulnerability that appeared in her sea green eyes, a remnant, he guessed, from her rotten childhood. When he saw that sadness there, all he wanted to do was soothe it away. He wanted to make sure no one ever hurt her again.

Christ. He hadn't felt this way since Cindy, and that was a long time ago. Was it about time for him to feel something again? Not exactly love, at least not yet, but something that might grow into it if he nurtured the feeling? Maybe Nonna was right. Maybe he was the kind of guy who needed to share his life with someone. He wasn't talking marriage, not this early in the game, but maybe in a year or two, if things worked out . . .

He imagined taking Tori home to dinner. Introducing her to everyone. They'd be surprised, to say the least. Tori wasn't his usual type. But then again, Nick didn't bring his usual type home.

He was falling, no doubt about it. Was it real? Or just an

intense case of lust? Maybe he'd stick around long enough to find out. There'd be no rush this time, not like eighteen years ago, when Cindy had exploded the pregnancy bomb and shattered Nick's carefully laid career plans. No, this time he'd do things right. Take things slow.

Very slow.

He picked his way between the shelves he and Tori had assembled. Man, it had been tough getting that job done without jumping her bones. But he'd kept his head down and his hands busy, because he knew she had her heart set on opening before the first official day of summer.

He could hear her now, rustling around in one of the bedrooms, humming some New Age thing that didn't really lend itself to singing along. He was about to call out to her, let her know he'd arrived, when he nearly tripped over a stack of books she'd left on the floor.

The one on top was called *Fingerpainting on Mars*.

Bemused, he picked it up. He couldn't believe some of the crap she was into. The one underneath wasn't much better. *Ghosts from Coast to Coast*. Right. *Abacomancy Made Easy* came next. He opened that one. *What the hell?* Now, this had to be a joke. No one could possibly be wacky enough to believe you could read the future in random dust patterns.

One last book. He picked it up and nearly choked.

Sacred Sex: The Path to Spiritual Ecstasy.

Okay, now. Finally, something New Age he could get into. The title curled in gold across the crimson leather cover, where a sepia drawing showed a nude man and woman engaged in a sex act. All the interesting spots on their bodies were artfully blurred. A ghostly image of the Taj Mahal floated behind them.

The subtitle under the illustration read: *Secrets of the Kama Sutra and Other Ancient Texts*.

Curiosity raging, Nick cradled the spine in one hand and flipped the book open. The drawing on the flyleaf was so graphic it made the one on the cover look like it had been lifted from a church bulletin. The artwork, he noted, was very good. His eye appreciated the delicacy of the inked lines, even as another body part stirred in response to the subject matter.

He sent a glance toward the bedroom and turned the page.

Another drawing, more explicit than the last. These new lovers were standing, the woman's legs wrapped around the man's hips. As if the visual weren't graphic enough, a paragraph at the bottom gave a name to the position—Suspended Congress—and some "how to" instructions.

Not necessary, as far as Nick was concerned. He needed no advice at all on how to "suspend" Tori.

The object of his flaming fantasies chose that exact instant to glide into the front room. She was all retro sixties today, decked out in a tie-dyed T-shirt and cutoff jeans shorts. A tantalizing slice of midriff showed off a green crystal belly-button stud.

And no bra today, either. He supposed that was a sixties thing, too.

Jesus.

"Oh!" she said, stopping short when she saw him. "You're early. I didn't hear you come in." She glanced at the book. "What are you read—Oh!"

Her cheeks went blotchy.

He lifted the book and gave her a slow smile.

Oh, God. Nick had found her Kama Sutra.

Tori's lips parted on a quick intake of breath. Her breasts tightened and suddenly the cotton of her tee felt rough on her nipples.

"Um . . . that's not supposed to be out here. I mean, it's not for sale."

Amusement—and something a lot hotter—flashed in his eyes. "You mean it's part of your private library? I think I'm glad to hear that."

Her face was blazing. "You know, the Kama Sutra is a sacred text. It's not a porn magazine."

"If you say so. Though I can't see it going over big in church on Sunday morning." He made a show of turning a page and bending his head over the next illustration. He gave a low whistle. "But I could certainly get into *this* on a Saturday night."

"Very funny." She held out her hand. "Okay, you've had your fun. Now give me that."

He looked up in mock outrage. "Excuse me? No way. I'm not done reading it yet."

"You are not reading it."

"Sure I am." His gaze dropped back to the page. "'The Rising Position.'" He turned the book around so she could see. "Ever try that one?"

"None of your business." She made a grab for the book.

He held it just out of her reach, lips twitching. "Oh, so you *have* tried it." His voice lowered. "Guess what? So have I."

"Hmph." But she couldn't stop her own smile.

He laughed and turned the page. "Now here's something called the Yawning Position. The woman has to be freaking double-jointed for that one. . . ." On the next page, "'The Lotus.' Hmmm. Can't say I've tried it." He flashed her a grin. "Yet."

A laugh bubbled up in her throat. "Making plans, are we?"

His gaze turned hot. "Maybe. But there are so many possibilities, it's damn hard to decide where to start. 'Splitting of a Bamboo . . . Fixing of a Nail . . .' Now, those look tough. They might take some practice, but I think we can manage them. You're pretty flexible, aren't you? You do that yoga stuff, right?"

She was laughing outright now.

"Hey, look! Here's the Congress of a Cow and Bull. That's one of my favorite positions." He winked. "But I always thought it was called doggy style."

Tori laughed and made another grab for the book. "You are so—"

"Whoa, careful! This is a sacred book! You wouldn't want to rip it."

He flipped to the next page, and his brows shot up. "Hello! Now, this one . . . You know, I'm not even sure this is physically possible." He turned the illustration toward Tori. "What d'you think?"

"I think you're crude and irreverent," she said when she managed to stop laughing.

"Yep. Turns you on, doesn't it?"

"No, it does not!"

"Liar," he said without heat. He closed the book and offered it to her. "Here you go. Thanks for the very . . . um . . . *stimulating* reading material."

She reached for the book. Nick, the fiend, waited until her fingers brushed the cover, then grabbed her wrist with his other hand and hauled her up against his chest.

The Kama Sutra fell with a thud.

She didn't even care.

Because Nick was kissing her. He cradled the back of her head in his big hand and captured her mouth, stroking and teasing with his tongue. Slowly. Thoroughly. She made a sound in her throat and all but inhaled him.

His hands followed the curve of her spine to her bottom and squeezed. Deftly, he maneuvered her past the bookshelves and through the open door to her living quarters.

He pressed her up against a bare patch of wall in her sitting room, pinning her in place with his hips as he kissed a line from the corner of her mouth to her ear. He swirled his tongue around the delicate shell. Blew gently.

She shuddered, her head lolling to one side. He kissed his way down her neck, pausing every now and then to nip with his teeth. His hand brushed the side of her breast. She arched toward him and he flicked the peak with his thumb.

"You're not wearing a bra," he said thickly.

"No."

He teased her through the thin cotton. She tilted her hips. He was rock hard; she was aching for him. She rubbed against him, wishing their clothes were already gone.

Then a thought hit her hard, and she broke away with a gasp. "Oh, God! We can't do this! We don't have time!"

"Sure we do. Give me twenty minutes. Hell, give me ten. Five, even. I want to show you what I dream about every night."

"You dream of me?" The thought made her giddy.

"Are you crazy? Trust me: We're going to be fantastic together. You know that, don't you?"

"Yes." She gasped as he did something very clever between her legs with his fingers. "But not right now—"

"No buts, Tori. No thinking at all. Just feel. I know you want this as much as I do."

Before she could answer, he bent his head and sucked her nipple, and the fabric covering it, into his mouth. Lust sliced through her belly. She gripped his head as he suckled ruthlessly, his tongue moistening the cotton and rubbing it against her tender skin. She moaned again, deeper this time. Liquid heat, like hot honey, poured through her.

Her fingers tangled in his hair. He found the hem of her shirt and tugged it up. His palm skated over her abdomen, rising to cup one bare breast. He teased one nipple beneath her shirt while continuing his torture of the other through the wet fabric.

The pleasure was intense, but it didn't quite obliterate her rising panic. "No, Nick. Stop! We can't."

"Aw, come on, Tori. I'm dying here. Take pity on me." He straightened, lifting her away from the wall and turning her toward the bedroom. "You'll thank me afterward. I promise."

"No, I won't! The—"

The doorbell cut off her protest. The screen door rattled. "Yo!" a man's voice yelled.

Nick's head came up. "Christ. Who the hell is that?"

"That's what I've been trying to tell you! It's the man from the sign shop. You should know. You made the appointment."

"Christ," he said again. He ran a hand over his face. "I

forgot. Shit. I never forget stuff like that." He cursed again, then looked at his watch. "Wasn't he supposed to be here an hour ago?"

"Yes, but he called and said he'd be late."

"Hey! Anyone in there?"

"Just a minute," Tori called out, heading for the shop.

Nick caught her by the arm. "Hold on."

She sighed. "Nick, he's waiting. I've got to go let him in."

His eyes flicked to her chest, his lips lifting. "Not like that, I hope."

"Like what?" She looked down.

And saw a perfectly round, wet circle of T-shirt, obscenely plastered to her erect left nipple.

"Oh, my God."

"Go change," Nick said, chuckling. "I'll take care of the sign guy."

Ninety minutes later, Tori was standing on the sidewalk with Nick and the sign guy, admiring her new sign. Sparkling silver letters spelled out DESTINY'S GATE on an indigo background. The sign hung in the peak above the front door, set off perfectly by the pink stucco.

"It's wonderful," she told the installer. "What do I owe you?"

"I'll send the bill to Nick here. He's got an account."

"That's not necessary. I'll write you a check."

She didn't like the way he exchanged a glance with Nick before answering.

"No need. Too late to cash it today, anyway." He moved off to load his tools into his van.

She frowned after him as he drove away. "Let me see the paperwork," she told Nick. "I'll write the check out to you."

"Don't worry. We'll square it away later."

She narrowed her eyes at him. "You know, this job is almost done and you haven't sent a single bill."

He shrugged. "Been busy getting the work done."

"Well, I don't like it. I'm calling Doris tomorrow and asking her for the full invoice."

He looked at her for a second, then suddenly grinned. "You know, I've never had a client beg for a bill before. It's kinda sexy." His voice dipped. "Bet I could make you beg for something else."

Honestly, the man had an ego the size of the Atlantic Ocean. And a one-track mind. "That is so unromantic."

He laughed. "Can't say anyone's ever accused me of being romantic."

She shook her head, exasperated. "Will everything really be done by the time the building inspector gets here, do you think?"

"Should be. There's not much left to do now that the sign's up."

She started to smile. "So my candle magic worked. I'm going to open on time. On the solstice."

Nick snorted. "Magic had nothing to do with it."

"It certainly did," she said. "But don't think I haven't noticed how hard you worked to meet my deadline. Thank you so much."

He brushed the hair off her shoulder and nibbled her neck. "Thank me inside, Tori."

Chapter Sixteen

Sometimes, family is the last thing on a guy's mind.

"All right," Tori whispered.

Nick locked the front door before leading her through the shop and into the sitting room. He eased her onto the first cushioned surface he could find—a threadbare sofa she'd picked up at Goodwill. He followed her down, kissing her. She looped her arms around his neck and kissed him back.

The stubble on his chin intrigued her. She turned her head and nuzzled his jaw, loving the sandpapery feel of it. It was so male. His thumbs found her breasts and circled. He avoided her nipples at first, but when she arched in encouragement, he caught them between his fingers through the silky blouse that had replaced her wet tie-dyed tee.

Liquid fire streaked through her, igniting every cell in her body. She clutched his shoulders and pressed her hips forward. She could feel how urgent his arousal was. She loved that she had done that to him.

He took her taut nipple in his teeth, catching her shirt in the process.

"Here," she said, reaching for the buttons. "Let me get out of this."

He rumbled a laugh. "Eager, huh?"

"You are so conceited! If you have to know, I just don't want to ruin another shirt."

She watched his face as she slipped off the blouse.

His dark gaze flicked to her breasts. "God, you're beautiful."

She let herself believe it. He certainly seemed to. He nibbled and licked as if she were the finest feast. She threaded her fingers through his hair and let exquisite sensations wash over her. Her eyes fluttered closed.

He suckled one breast, then the other, then went down on his knees on the floor. He tugged her upright, positioning her bottom on the edge of the sofa, easing her legs open, and moving between them. He bent his head and his tongue found her navel. He licked a circle around it, then sucked on the crystal stud. His hands spanned her waist, the rough pads of his thumbs stroking the bare skin just above the waistband of her shorts.

She moved against him, her body undulating. She desperately wanted him to unsnap her shorts and slide them over her hips. But he didn't seem to be in a hurry.

He cupped the mound of her sex, rubbing the faded denim against her hidden nub. She moaned with the intensity of it, closing her eyes and riding the wave of pleasure to a needy plateau.

"That's it," he coaxed. "Make another sexy sound. I love when you do that." His fingers continued teasing between her legs.

Another helpless sound escaped her throat.

"Yeah," he whispered. "Just like that."

He looked up at her with an almost reverent expression. She felt like some kind of treasure. He unsnapped her shorts and touched her more intimately. Only her panties separated his fingers from her exquisitely sensitive skin. She moaned again, arching toward his soft words of praise. Whatever he wanted, her body wanted to give it to him. Was she losing herself? Maybe so. She'd forgotten the future. Forgotten her plans to be a single mother. All she wanted was Nick, here and now.

He bit her hip gently, just above her panties, sucking a little before he let go. Her nerves tingled. He gave another nip, then another, working his way up her body to the side of her breast, creating a long path of stinging delight. She clung to him, awash with pleasure and tingling pain.

The love bites continued all the way to her shoulder. "A Line of Jewels," he murmured in her ear.

She was so dazed it took a couple seconds for the words to sink in. "That's . . . that's from the Kama Sutra."

He gave her his slow smile. "Yeah."

She blushed. "So what else did you learn from my book?"

"Well, now, I'm glad you asked." His teeth tugged at her earlobe. "I'd love to show you. Not here, though." He slid his arms under her. An instant later, she was in the air, clutching his shoulders.

"I can walk, you know."

"And your point is?" He moved unerringly toward her bedroom, sidestepping boxes as he went.

She smiled against his chest. "Nothing."

Being carried felt ridiculous—and wonderful. He nudged the bedroom door open with his shoulder, took two strides across the room, and lowered her onto her futon.

"I don't know how you sleep on this thing." He stretched out beside her on rumpled sheets. "It's worse than camping out."

"It's good for your back."

"*Your* back, maybe." He tugged her shorts over her legs, taking her panties with them. "Not mine."

She lay naked under his dark gaze, arms raised over her head. He was still fully clothed. A stream of light from the window painted her breasts and stomach. He looked at her, not speaking, for what seemed an eternity.

"Take off your shirt," she urged. "I want to see you."

He obliged, tugging the garment over his head in one smooth motion, muscles flexing. The white cotton slid down his arm to land partly on the sheets, partly on her bare stomach. He whisked it over the side of the bed, then covered her with his body.

She touched his chest, teasing the springy curls of dark hair, running her hands over his shoulders, touching the hard line of his collarbone. She splayed her fingers on his back. His skin was hot, as if he had some kind of internal furnace running full tilt. A faint sheen of moisture quickened the glide of her skin over his.

She wanted this—wanted him—so badly. She reached for his belt, but he shifted out of reach, forcing her to raise her shoulders off the bed. When she did, he caught her waist and flipped her smoothly onto her stomach.

Stunned by the unexpected move, she pushed herself up on her hands and knees, legs splayed, laughing. "What are you doing?"

He nudged her legs apart. "Right now? Enjoying the view."

She craned her neck and met his gaze. The intense expression in his dark eyes made her shiver.

He ran one hand down her back, then lower, over the curve of her bottom. He stroked one finger along the crease of skin at the top of her thigh, then between her legs. She shifted encouragingly.

But he didn't go where she wanted him to. Instead, his hand moved to the outside of her hip. She dropped her head and groaned.

Nick chuckled. "Ready so soon?"

"Ha. Like you're not."

"You got that right." He did more interesting things between her legs. Then, abruptly, he brought his hand back to neutral territory.

"You're a tease," she gasped. She tried to turn over, but he caged her with his body, keeping her on her hands and knees.

His khaki-clad erection bulged against her bottom. His bare chest slid over her back, hair tickling and teasing. Damp skin clung to hers; musky-hot scent surrounded her. He was breathing fast, almost as fast as she was.

She wriggled her bottom. At the same time, she tried to work her hands out from under his. He responded by shifting both her hands to one of his, and his head to nip her shoulder. A sharp current raced through her. His now-free hand slid around to her breasts. His clever fingers found their goal.

"Oh, please. Nick—"

"Shhh." He nipped her neck, then soothed with his tongue, tightening the frenzy inside her. "I love how you taste."

"I want to turn over. I want to touch you."

He didn't answer, just slid his hand down over her stomach and into her curls, teasing again. She arched her back and rocked her hips, trying to break him. "Nick, I think—"

"Let me think. You feel." The tempo of his fingers quickened. She dropped her forehead to the bed and let the waves of arousal wash over her. His mouth was on her back, raining kisses up and down her spin. One finger, then two, slipped inside her.

"God, I love you like this," he whispered. "You're so sexy."

"Let me turn around. I need to kiss you." She twisted her head and managed to brush her lips along his jaw.

He released her then, easing her onto her back and claiming her lips, tasting, his tongue dancing with erotic rhythm. She fumbled with his belt. She wanted him as naked as she was.

He knelt upright, watching her with an almost pained expression as she tugged down his zipper and slid his boxers over his hips. Blue silk this time, with little silver emblems that looked like stars. They reminded her of her shop.

She watched his eyes as she touched him. They flared dark. She wrapped her legs around his thighs and let herself fall back on the bed. His balance was hampered by his shorts; he couldn't help but follow her down. She laughed as he disentangled their limbs and stripped off the rest of his clothes. Then he was back, his gloriously naked body stretched out over hers.

The sensation of his weight, his sweat-slicked skin sliding and catching on hers, the rasp of his stubble scraping her breasts, blended into one long, dizzying caress. His erection lay hot and insistent against her thigh. She slid her hand over his shaft and lifted her hips, ready to guide him inside.

"Wait." He eased out of her grip, turning away as he rooted through her sheets.

"Now," she said, urging him back.

He came willingly, a smile tugging at his lips. He caught her hand and pressed something into her palm.

A condom.

"Oh. I forgot." She rolled it on him, trying desperately not to think about how much she didn't want to be using one.

"No need for you to remember." He stretched out over her again. "I told you I'd do the thinking, remember?"

She gasped as he entered her. It was just a slight invasion at first, stretching but not filling. She wanted more. She angled her hips to give him better access, but instead of surging forward, he withdrew almost completely.

He began a slow rhythm, easing in and out. His strokes were maddeningly gentle.

She gripped his hips and tried to pull him in. "Harder."

"You're a menace," he said. "You know that? You want it to be all over in thirty seconds? Relax, or my ego's going to be toast."

"Right. Like that would ever happen."

He grinned and entered her again, sliding in deep, but without the force she craved. On the next thrust, she anchored her hands on his hips and tried to pull him in.

He laughed and tugged her hands over her head. He held them there as he rocked at that leisurely, frustrating pace.

"Stop teasing," she gasped as he left her again.

"Ah, come on." He returned on an unhurried glide, then retreated just as slowly. "It was your book. I thought you'd enjoy it."

She blinked up at him, confused. "What?"

"Eight," he counted. He thrust in, then out. "Nine. Get ready." He released her hands, bracing his arms on either side of her head.

Oh. That book.

He plunged deep and hard on ten, lifting her hips right off the bed. A sweet burst of bliss exploded in her body. She clutched Nick's shoulders as he left her again. But when she arched to welcome a second satisfying plunge, all she got was more teasing.

"One," he said.

She glared up at him. "When did you ever find the time to read the chapter on tantra?"

He dropped to his elbows and pressed his forehead against hers. "Two. While you were bonding with the sign guy." His hips flexed. "Three. Ninety Strokes to Ecstasy. This rhythm is supposed to make me last all night."

Her hips twisted beneath him. "Nick. I can't take this all night. Don't do this to me."

He only chuckled.

"Faster," she said, panting. "It's supposed to get faster with each cycle."

"Four. Did I ever tell you how impatient you are? Impatient *and* demanding?"

He picked up the pace, but not by much.

"You like it," she whispered, echoing his own words.

He grinned. "Six. You're right. I do like it. I like you, Tori. A lot."

He kissed her nose, her cheek, her chin. She arched beneath him, trying to get the most out of each thrust. It was like being adrift on the ocean, rising and falling on each small swell, waiting for the big one to hit. Nick was her raft, her anchor, the only solid refuge in a sea of pleasure.

She wrapped her arms around his neck and kissed him. He was trembling, his arms rigid against the mattress.

"Eight," he said.

She nipped his lower lip and arched her hips. He groaned and thrust deeply, twice this time, harder than before, bringing the pattern full circle. It drove her close the edge, but not quite over.

He started the next cycle.

She moaned her frustration. "I'll go crazy if this lasts much longer."

"I want you crazy," he murmured against her mouth. His shallow thrusts were quick and steady now. Only seven this time, followed by three gloriously deep thrusts. "I want to watch you go insane. Come for me, Tori."

"Soon," she gasped, clinging to him as the next cycle began. Six shallow, four deep. Faster than before. The sweet, wet sound of their bodies blended with the rhythm of Nick's thrusts. Sensations scattered—she felt his body, slick with sweat. Heard his gasps. She shivered as the hair on his chest abraded her skin.

The rhythm quickened and she forgot to count. Almost all the thrusts were deep now, only two, then one, gentle moves separating the stronger ones. The peak rushed at her.

"I'm . . . Oh, *Nick*."

She pulled him into her, hard, at the same moment he dove. She rose on a tsunami swell of pleasure. A million sparkling fragments shattered, tossing her high. Her anchor was Nick, his body, his scent, his feel. *Him*. His arms wrapped tight, clenching as his own orgasm hit.

"Tori . . ." Her name rasped in his throat. His mouth sought hers and he kissed her, deeply, as a shudder rippled through him.

And as the bliss receded, her heart's last defenses washed away like a castle in the sand.

They ate midnight Chinese takeout in her kitchen.

"Have you ever thought about remarrying?" she asked as she spooned Szechuan tofu over her brown rice.

As soon as the words were out, she wanted to bite off her tongue. She wasn't an idiot. She *knew* marriage wasn't something a guy wanted to talk about right after having sex with a woman for the first time. But sex with Nick had left her feeling so lazy and comfortable, it had just slipped out.

Nick went very still. Tori wanted to crawl under the table and die.

"No," he said quietly. "Not really."

"Sorry," she said quickly. "Forget I even mentioned it. It was a rude question."

He studied her. "You have to understand, Tori. My first marriage was hell."

"Weren't there any . . . good parts at all?"

"The good parts happened before the wedding." A cynical note had crept into his voice. "Afterward . . . well, let's just say I think there's something about marriage that makes people a little insane. It's like all of a sudden, you can't see the other person. All you see is what you need from them. All they see is what they need from you. And nine times out of ten, no one gets what they need."

His words hit home, brutally. Wasn't she already doing that? Thinking of Nick in terms of her needs, rather than wondering about his?

He stood and started clearing the table, stowing the leftovers in the refrigerator. "I gotta be honest with you. I like you a lot. But if you're looking for marriage, I can't promise I'll be your best bet. I don't know if I'll ever be ready for that level of commitment again."

She backtracked wildly, in full damage-control mode. "I wasn't trying to put you on the spot. I'm not looking for marriage. I just ended one long-term relationship. I'm not going to be ready for another one for a long time."

He turned, one hand still on the open refrigerator door, studying her. "So you really don't mind keeping things light? Taking things slow?"

"I was going to suggest the same thing," she lied.

"That's great." Nick's relief was painfully evident. He shut the fridge. "So we'll keep things cool. Just concentrate on having fun. Avoid all the messy emotional stuff."

Way too late for that, she thought.

Chapter Seventeen

Beware. The middle of a family fight is a
dangerous place for an outsider to be.

"Bad move," said Chelsea, shaking her head. "I thought you were through putting a man's needs first."

"I was. I mean, I am," Tori said, pushing Lily a little harder on the playground baby swing. She'd stopped at Chelsea's to rehash her weekend with Nick. And to admit she was rethinking the whole sperm donor thing.

"Tori, be honest. This definitely qualifies as putting Nick's needs before yours. Didn't you learn anything from Colin?"

"Nick isn't Colin. In fact, he's nothing like Colin."

"That's right. Colin was your lover for five years. Nick is a guy you just met. One weekend of great sex does not make a relationship."

"It's a start." Tori pushed the baby swing again. It was red plastic, shaped like an airplane, making Lily look like an infant Amelia Earhart. "He makes me laugh. We're good together." When she ignored their basic differences. She pushed that thought away. "We can build on that. He wants to take things further."

Chelsea cleared her throat. "While he's playing it cool and keeping it light?"

"He's divorced," she protested. "Gun-shy. You can't expect him to jump right into this."

Chelsea's brow furrowed. "Does he have kids?"

"Yes. A daughter. She was the one who called him on his

cell phone that night. She was upset, and he dropped everything to go to her."

"Well, that's a good sign, I suppose. He's a responsible father. How old is the girl?"

"I don't know. School age, I think. Nick's only thirty-five himself."

"You haven't met her? What about the rest of his family? Parents? Brothers and sisters?"

"His father's dead, but I don't know about anybody else. He doesn't talk about his family much."

"You didn't ask him? About his daughter? About his family?"

Tori studied the sandy dirt beneath the swing and sighed.

"I guess I haven't. Maybe I've been . . . afraid to. I don't tend to ask people about their families. It's not like I have anything to tell in return."

Chelsea touched her arm. "Oh, Tori, honey, I'm sorry." She was silent for a moment, watching Lily swing up and back. Then, "Where does he live?"

Tori blinked when she realized she didn't know that, either. "His office is in Atlantic City," she offered. When Chelsea frowned, she added, "What is this, the Spanish Inquisition?"

"I'm just concerned about you. Did he ask you out for next weekend, at least?"

Tori had an answer for that, thank God. "Actually, he asked me out for tomorrow night. I'm getting my last city inspection in the morning. He said we'd celebrate my grand opening."

Chelsea made a noncommittal sound.

Tori sighed. "You don't like Nick, do you?"

"No, that's not it. How should I know if I like him? I only met him once. He seemed nice enough. Polite. I didn't get any bad vibes from him about me and Mags."

Lily's airplane swung toward Tori. She pushed it, sending Lily swooping into the air, giggling with baby laughter.

"I know I'm making some compromises," Tori admitted. "And I know Nick and I are very different. But when I'm with him, I feel . . . I don't know how to describe it." She shrugged. "Safe, I guess."

Chelsea studied her. "Safe enough to forget about having a baby? Maybe for good?"

Her gut clenched.

"You could think about having the surgery, I suppose. That would buy you more time to see if things develop with Nick. Have you considered that?"

The cramp in her belly cranked tighter, as if someone were tightening a tourniquet around her midsection. Surgery. Her head swam. Her vision filled with red blotches.

"I . . . don't know," she said, trying to breathe through the panic. "I'd . . . have to think about it."

She was nowhere near ready for the building inspector.

It was midmorning, and she'd been up since five, stocking shelves. She was kneeling on the floor, unwinding a stone goddess from bubble wrap, when the *Downbeach Wave* landed on the carpet beside her.

"I picked it up with my coffee," Nick said. "I didn't know you took out an ad."

"Oh!" She nearly lost hold of the statue. "What page is it on?"

Nick dropped into a crouch at her side, forearms resting on his thighs. "Seven."

She'd spent the night thinking of Chelsea's warnings, but now, confronted by Nick's spicy aftershave, every cautious thought she'd had evaporated. She felt dizzy. A flash of memory —hot sex and easy laughter—had her gripping the newspaper so hard it crumpled.

She sneaked a look at Nick. He was wearing a white button-down shirt and neatly pressed beige chinos. He looked crisp and clean, every inch the professional. But she'd bet it wouldn't take much to pull him down and give him a few wrinkles.

"Whoa," Nick said, steadying her with a hand on her elbow. "I can see what you're thinking. No time for that now."

Her cheeks went blotchy.

He brushed her ear with his lips. "Later," he whispered. "Later we'll do whatever you want."

"Hmmm."

Chuckling, he liberated the *Wave* from her fingers and flipped the pages. Not too many hours before, Nick had been naked in her bed. Now long sleeves, neatly buttoned at the cuffs, covered his tanned forearms. But she knew her teasing, coaxing lover was right there, below the surface.

The other night, he'd taken her to an obscenely expensive restaurant—the kind with no prices on the menu. She'd worn a flowing gold Celtic-style dress with a lace-up bodice. He'd looked like sin on Earth in gray dress slacks, a black collarless shirt, and a leather jacket. She'd felt like a princess. But not the virginal kind.

"I wish I knew exactly what's going on in that mysterious brain of yours," Nick said, his lips just a breath away from her ear. "It looks like something I could get into."

"Maybe," she teased, hiding a smile.

He cupped the back of her head with one hand and kissed her hard. "That's to tide me over until tonight." Releasing her, he shook out the newspaper. "Right now, look at your ad."

She took the paper and examined Leigh's half-page spread. "This is great."

"Yeah, it is. Did you do the artwork?"

"No. A local girl stopped by and suggested it. Do you think it'll bring in customers?"

"Can't hurt," he said, rising. "Sorry I didn't think of it myself." He offered her his hand.

She took it, letting him pull her to her feet. His fingers and palm were rough with calluses. All she could think of was how his hands felt on her breasts.

Amusement registered in Nick's dark eyes. "You're getting that look again. Keep it up and it'll go to my head."

"I hope so."

He laughed. "Come on. I couldn't have been that good."

"Which time?"

He swooped in for another kiss. "Doesn't matter. The next time is always better. I'd like to drag you back to that god-awful futon and give you a preview, but"—he checked his watch—"Weinstein'll be here in five minutes."

"So soon?" She picked up the goddess she'd been unwrapping and set her on the shelf. She was a fertility goddess, enormously pregnant. Tori's thumb stroked the statue's round belly, and the thrill of Nick's presence dimmed a bit. "I don't have all my merchandise set out yet."

"No worries. The man's coming to look at fire protection, not statues of naked fat ladies."

She sent him reproving look. "She not fat; she's pregnant. She's a goddess."

He grinned. "I never said she wasn't."

She shook her head, but really, it was hard to stay mad at Nick, even when he insulted her merchandise. She looked around the shop. She couldn't have gotten this far without him. Then again, there were a lot of full boxes that might've been emptied this morning if they hadn't been spending so much time in bed.

"Something smells good in here," he commented. His gaze fell on the orange candle she'd left on the counter after the flame had gone out. The scent of the cinnamon oil she'd rubbed on it was still strong.

He snorted, clearly amused. "Don't tell me that's more magic."

She gave him a repressive look. "Orange is the color of success in business. I cast the spell this morning."

"Well, hope it helps." He glanced at the door and checked his watch again. "Nine thirty."

"Oh, my God. The inspector will be here any second, and there's still so much I have to do! It's a good thing I have help coming later."

"You do? Who?"

"The girl who did my ad. She asked for a summer job."

"Can you afford it? Maybe you should wait a couple weeks and see how you do."

"It should be okay. I'm only paying her minimum wage."

Nick wrestled a couple of empty boxes into the spare bedroom while Tori gazed down at the fertility goddess. She was so round. So full of life. Serene and secure in her womanhood. She smoothed a hand over her own flat stomach. The fertile days of her cycle were less than two weeks away, and after that last conversation with Chelsea, she was wondering if giving up on the insemination was the right thing to do.

For a brief moment, she imagined carrying Nick's child. Then Nick's assessment of marriage entered her thoughts and she pushed the notion of his child away.

A car pulled up out front. "That's the building inspector," Nick said, returning from the back. "Don't worry about a thing."

Tori greeted Mr. Weinstein and shook his hand. Nick inquired after the inspector's wife and made small talk about deep-sea fishing, which, apparently, was the building inspector's passionate hobby.

Tori trailed after the men, trying not to wring her hands as the inspector prodded smoke detectors, peered at exit lights, and scrutinized the tag on the fire extinguisher. Finally, Nick escorted him down the back hall, heading for the attic access in Tori's bedroom. Tori stayed out front and tried to decide which box to unpack next.

"Hey," a girl's voice said.

Tori looked up to find Leigh coming through the door. "You're early," she said with a smile.

"I thought you might need extra help today."

"Desperately," Tori agreed.

Leigh was a teenaged summer breeze, her straight blonde hair loose, her cropped red baby-doll top revealing a flash of silver in her navel. She dropped the manila folder she was carrying on the sales counter.

"Wow. Everything looks fantastic. Totally cool."

"The ad looks great, too," Tori told her.

"Thanks." Leigh tapped the folder. "My paperwork's here. All the forms you need for Social Security and the IRS. I can take care of sending them in. All you need to do is sign."

"I really appreciate it. I don't know the first thing about that kind of stuff."

"It's no big deal. Just boring. Do you have a bookkeeping system yet? I can set it up for you." She looked around. "Where's your computer?"

"Um, I don't have one."

Leigh looked at Tori as if she'd crawled out of the primordial soup. "You're kidding me. You *can't* not have a computer. Even my great-grandmother has one. She only plays solitaire, but still."

"I need one, I know. But it's another thing I don't know much about." The only computer she'd ever used was Colin's laptop, for e-mail and Web surfing. The thought of accounting software was more than daunting. "Plus it'll be an expense. I'll need to see what's left of my bank account after I pay my contractor."

Leigh turned to scrutinize the aromatherapy display. "Is that his pickup truck outside?"

"Yes. He's in the attic with the building inspector." Something in Leigh's tone made Tori look at her more closely. "Why do you ask?"

She sniffed the patchouli tester. "No reason. You know, my boyfriend could get you a cheap computer. He rebuilds old ones."

"He must be smart, then."

"Oh, he is, but he's not all obnoxious about it, like some guys."

"He sounds wonderful."

Leigh's cheeks flushed. "He wants to meet you. He'll probably stop over after work. He's a lifeguard," she added shyly.

Male voices drifted from the back. "When's Ms. Morgan planning to open for business?" Tori heard the inspector ask.

"Tomorrow," Nick answered. "As long as you give your okay today."

"Shouldn't be a problem. Everything's taken care of."

Leigh's gaze flicked to the open fire door, then back to Tori. "So. What do you want me to do first?"

Tori frowned. The energy in the room had changed, but she couldn't quite put her finger on how or why.

"How about the Native American display?" She led Leigh to a bare tree branch set in a bucket of sand. "You can hang the dream catchers."

Leigh went down on her knees and started sorting through a box of decorated hoops just as Nick and the building inspector entered the room. Mr. Weinstein paused in the open doorway, eyeing the chunk of wood Tori had wedged under the fire door.

"You do realize this fire door must stay closed during business hours, Ms. Morgan."

"Of course," Tori said, trying not to wring her hands. "Nick told me that." What else had she forgotten? She sent him a worried glance, but he pitched back a reassuring smile.

"You can open for business as soon as the paperwork's complete," Mr. Weinstein said. "Congratulations, Ms. Morgan." He moved off to the sales counter with his clipboard.

Nick tapped Tori's nose with one finger. "Almost there," he said, smiling down at her. "By this time tomorrow, you'll be—"

He broke off abruptly as his gaze drifted past her shoulder.

"Shit." His curse was barely audible, but there was a wealth of emotion in it.

That negative energy Tori had felt earlier seemed to thicken. She turned and followed Nick's gaze directly to Leigh.

"What's wrong?" she whispered.

He didn't answer. Tori would have pressed him, but Mr.

Weinstein returned with a question about emergency lighting packs. Nick pivoted, giving her his back as he answered in terse sentences.

Finally, her occupancy certificate was in hand. "Zoning tells me your use permit's in order, too," the inspector said. "You can open for business at any time."

"Thank you."

Tori walked the inspector to the door, but her attention remained focused on Nick and Leigh. Nick was staring at Leigh's back. The girl's shoulders were rigid. Slowly, she rose to her feet and turned.

Tori shut the door behind Mr. Weinstein. The strike of the latch seemed to bring Nick to life.

"Just what do you think you're doing here?"

Leigh glared at him. "Working."

"Like hell you are," Nick muttered.

"Like hell I am," Leigh shot back.

Tori gaped.

"Don't you take that tone with me, young lady. Go out to my truck. Now." Nick's eyes cut to Tori, then back to Leigh. "We'll discuss this at home."

"Nick. Leigh," Tori managed. "What's going on?"

She might as well have been an astral projection for all the attention the two paid her. They glared at each other with identical obstinate expressions, arms crossed and shoulders hunched in exactly the same way.

Oh, God.

"I'm almost eighteen," Leigh said. "I'll work where I want."

"Wrong answer, Leigh. You'll work where I say."

"Forget it, Dad."

Tori had known Nick had a daughter. And she'd known Leigh reminded her of someone. She should have put two and two together. But she'd never considered it, because Leigh . . . well, she was practically a grown woman. And Nick was only thirty-five. *God.* He must not have been much older than Leigh was now when she was born.

And he clearly hadn't known his daughter had come to Tori's looking for a job. But Leigh had known her father was working here. She'd asked enough questions about Tori's contractor. The teenager had played her. But why?

"I am *not* working at Santangelo Construction this summer," Leigh was saying.

"Goddamn it, yes, you are. Doris needs you."

"She doesn't. You just want her to keep tabs on me."

"Can you blame me? After you lied about Jason's party?"

Leigh went deathly still. "Jason doesn't have anything to do with this. I told you I wanted to work in the casino with Stacey, and you said no."

"Leave Stacey out of this. *Stacey* didn't let her boyfriend wreck her car. *Stacey* didn't lie to me. You, on the other hand—"

"It wasn't Jason's fault! The other car didn't have its lights on!"

"Don't go there, Leigh," Nick warned.

The girl stomped her foot. "I told you the truth, but do you believe me? No. I tell you I want to choose my own summer job, and what do you say? No. You want to bury me in a closet at your office. Well, forget it. You don't want me to work at the casino? Fine. I'm working here with Tori."

Nick scowled. "Absolutely not."

Tori cleared her throat. "Um, Nick . . . ?"

He swung his head around. "You stay out of this."

She gave a little gasp of disbelief. "Excuse me? Stay out of it? I don't think so. This is my shop, you know."

"And this is my daughter. Just when were you planning to tell me you'd hired her?"

"Tell you?" Tori's voice lurched up an octave. "How could I have told you? I didn't know Leigh was your daughter!"

He eyed her disbelievingly. "You must have seen her last name when she filled out the paperwork."

Tori snatched up Leigh's manila folder. Sure enough, on the top form, next to *Name*, she'd printed, *Leigh Marie Santangelo*.

Tori relaxed a little. At least Leigh hadn't been planning to totally scam her.

"Leigh downloaded the IRS forms. This is the first I've seen them. I knew you had a daughter, but you never told me how old she was. I thought she'd be younger." Tori met Nick's gaze. "Why don't you want Leigh to work here?"

Nick took a step back. "I . . ." He glanced at Leigh and fell silent.

His cell rang.

"God*damn* it," he said, tearing the phone from his belt. He flipped it open so hard it was a wonder the hinge didn't snap. "Santangelo here."

Leigh rolled her eyes and turned away.

Nick's expression, already dark, turned downright thunderous as he listened to the caller. "No. Don't do anything. Just stall them. I'll be there in fifteen minutes."

"Problem?" Tori asked.

"The usual bullshit." He leveled a steady glance at Leigh. "Get in the truck. I'll drop you at home on my way."

A couple beats of silence ensued.

"No, thanks," Leigh said finally. "I've got work to do here."

For a second or two, it looked as if Nick would argue. Then he made a sound of disgust and strode out the door without saying a word. His truck engine sprang to life, then faded away.

Tori let out a long breath into the dead silence that followed. She thought Leigh did the same. She eyed the girl, wondering what crisis had prompted her to call her father in the middle of the night two weeks earlier. But she didn't dare ask. If she did, Leigh might wonder what Tori and Nick had been doing when she'd called.

Tori crossed her arms. "So. You want to tell me what that scene was about?"

"Not really. But I guess I should."

"Let me start. You knew your father was doing my renovation. You didn't tell him I'd hired you. You came early because you wanted him to find you here. You knew he'd get mad. Am I right so far?"

Leigh nodded, then sighed. "You're mad at me, too, right?"

"No," Tori said. And it was the truth. How could she be angry when Leigh's eyes held the same blend of vulnerability and defiance Tori remembered so well from her own teenage years?

"I do want some answers, though." She paused. "How about a drink first?"

"Sure," Leigh said warily. "You got any Coke?"

Tori laughed. Nick had just stashed a case in the pantry the day before. "You know, I should've guessed you two were related. You're a lot alike."

"That's what everyone says," Leigh groused, trailing Tori into the kitchen. "I don't see it, myself. I mean, I don't look anything like him."

That was true enough. "You must look like your mother."

"Yeah. I don't remember her, though. She left town before I turned two."

"I'm sorry."

"Dad got rid of most of her pictures, but Mimi saved a couple, so I know what she looked like."

"Mimi?"

"My grandmother. She was only thirty-eight when I was born. She didn't want to be called Grandma, so she made up Mimi."

Tori grabbed a can of Coke from the fridge and handed it to Leigh. "Your father was young when you were born."

"Eighteen. He got my mom pregnant while they were in high school."

"But you're not in touch with her now?"

Leigh took a swig of her soda. "She sends birthday cards. Most years, anyway."

It wasn't hard to hear the hurt in her voice. "It must've been hard growing up without a mother."

Leigh shrugged. "My grandmother lives with us. And my great-grandmother practically lives with us, she's over so much. And I had Alex, Zach, and Johnny looking after me, too."

Tori gave her a blank look.

"My dad's younger brothers. Didn't he tell you about them?"

"I guess not."

She filled Tori in. "Dad's the oldest. Uncle Alex is next. He's a police detective in Atlantic City. He's divorced and has a little girl named Sophie. Then there's Uncle Zach. He's in the navy."

Leigh took a breath and a sip of Coke. "Then there's Johnny. He's only twenty-four, so I don't call him 'uncle.' He works for Dad, but he wants to be an actor."

Tori's brain was spinning. All that family, and Nick had never mentioned any of them, even in passing. "Do you all see one another often?"

"Oh, all the time. Well, except for Uncle Zach, of course. Nonna's real mad Dad's been working late so much. He hasn't been home for dinner in weeks."

"So he told you all about working on my shop?"

"Are you kidding? He didn't say a word. We thought he was at the office. He even told me flat out that he was on another job."

Tori shut her eyes briefly. Chelsea would have a field day with that little bit of information.

Leigh caught her expression. "Don't take it personally. Dad never tells us about his dates. But then I saw—" She cut herself off abruptly.

"What?"

Leigh flushed, then said in a rush, "Jason and I saw him kissing you on your porch last week." She took a sudden interest in the nutritional information on the side of her soda can.

"Oh." Tori couldn't honestly think of anything else to say.

"So I, you know, had to come over and check you out."

"And? What did you decide?"

Leigh looked up. "Truthfully? I can't believe he's with you. You're great, and your shop is seriously cool. And Dad—well, let's just say he's not into anything too unconventional." She gave an embarrassed laugh. "I'm still a little wigged out about it all. No offense, but you're just not his usual type."

"And what type is that?" Tori couldn't stop herself from asking.

"From what Johnny's told me? Tall, blonde, and anorexic."

"Wonderful," Tori muttered. She paced to the window. "Why didn't you just tell me who you were when you first showed up?"

"I was going to tell you today. I swear. You saw the paperwork."

Tori sighed. "I think you should go now. I've got to get back to setting up the shop."

"But what about my job?"

"You're kidding, right?"

"No! I really want to work here."

"But your dad wants you to work in his office."

"I'm not going to." Leigh got up, found the recycling bucket under the sink, and pitched her empty can into it.

Just like her father, Tori thought.

"Look," Leigh said, "don't worry about Dad. He's got a wicked bad temper, but it blows itself out pretty fast. He'll let me work here. Besides," she added, "you need me. What if you have to go out in the middle of the day? You can't just close up shop and lose business."

You need me. Tori wasn't so sure she needed to get in the middle of Nick's disagreement with his daughter, but one look at Leigh's raised chin told Tori Leigh wouldn't give in to her father's demands so easily. The girl was stubborn.

Another trait she shared with Nick.

"Can I keep the job? Please?"

Tori couldn't find it in her heart to turn her away. "All right. You can work here—*if* you can convince your father to agree to it."

"Done," said Leigh. "And, Tori?"

"What?"

"You won't be sorry. I promise."

Chapter Eighteen

*Meddling and matchmaking are
time-honored family traditions.*

It was clear to Nick, even from halfway across the Bayview condominium's lobby, that his superintendent was right: Thomas Southerland's head *was* firmly stuck in his ass.

The Ivy League architect slapped at the spackle dust marring his black trousers, then frowned and slapped again. And again. Each time, the cloud of white powder around him expanded. Finally, after one particularly futile smack, Southerland assumed the long-suffering expression of a tortured saint.

Which was entirely appropriate, given that Fred Dalton, Nick's electrical subcontractor, was glowering at the architect as if the architect were a demon straight out of hell.

Jesus. Nick needed this aggravation like he needed a hole in a condom. Especially coming fresh from the run-in with Leigh at Tori's.

Leigh and Tori. He rubbed the sudden spike of pain between his eyes. His daughter and his lover. Together. Talking about what, exactly? Him?

Hell.

"Yo, Nick," Dalton called. "Come here and tell Southerland this here chandelier is just like what's ordered in the specs."

"It is not," Southerland said succinctly. "My specifications call for a different chandelier entirely. A fact I'm sure Nick knows."

"It's the same damn thing," Dalton said. "This one's made by a different manufacturer, is all."

Nick's blood pressure rose. A different manufacturer? What was this about? Dalton knew there weren't any substitutions on Nick's jobs.

"The fixture you installed is smaller, has less wattage, and the color is a shade off," Southerland said. "The entire design aesthetic of the space is disrupted! And there was no change order submitted."

"I put in my change order. Gave it to Nick here," Dalton said.

Nick frowned. "I don't remember seeing it."

"Ah, well, I mighta handed it to Johnny. He signed off on it. I got a copy right here."

After a bit of searching, Dalton produced the incriminating document. Sure enough, Johnny had scrawled his signature across the bottom. The space left for the architect's signature was glaringly blank.

Johnny. Nick's weakest link.

Nick was going to murder him.

"This change order isn't valid," Southerland said. "Not without my signature. I want that chandelier replaced."

"We're behind schedule as it is," Nick said. "Ordering a new fixture will push us back a couple weeks at least. That's assuming we can even get it by then."

"Not my problem," Southerland said, moving off.

Nick let out a stream of profanities. Profit on this job was disappearing faster than dollar chips off a craps table. And all because Johnny couldn't give his day job half the attention he gave his moonlighting stand-up act. If it had been anyone else, Nick would've fired him.

"Take it down," Nick told Dalton. "Get the right one up there as quickly as you can."

"You got it, Nick. Course, there'll be a restocking fee for the old one."

"Just send me the bill."

Nick's cell rang. Briefly, he entertained a fantasy in which he pulverized the thing with a sledgehammer.

Then he sighed and checked the caller ID.

Tori. *Ah, hell.* He had the vague feeling that he'd done something wrong, but damn it, why should he feel guilty? Just because he hadn't told Tori much about Leigh? Because he hadn't wanted to introduce Tori to his family, at least not yet? He'd known her for only a couple of weeks, for chrissakes. He wasn't ready for her to be in that part of his life.

If he didn't answer on the next ring, she'd go over to voice mail. Briefly, he considered it, then sighed and flipped open the phone.

"Hey, Tori, what's up?" His tone was sharper than he'd intended.

She hesitated. "I just wondered if everything was all right on your job. You left so abruptly."

"Yeah, it's okay. Just another fire to put out."

Another pause. "Well, I was thinking, instead of going out tonight like we'd planned, would you rather just eat here? Or maybe I could come over to your house?"

Nick cleared his throat. Why did it feel as if a noose were tightening around it? "Um, Tori, I think I'm going to have to cancel for tonight. There's a ton of work I've put on hold the last few weeks, and it's all about to hit the fan. I'm sorry, but I'm gonna have to work late tonight."

"Oh." The line was silent for a couple beats. Then, "No problem. I really don't have time to go out, anyway. There's a lot more merchandise to get out on the shelves."

He swallowed. "Right. Well, good luck tomorrow. I'll call you later, okay?"

"Okay." She cut the connection.

"Nicolo."

Nick looked up to find Joe D'Amico standing in front of him. "Dalton told me—" Joe caught sight of Nick's expression. His eyes dropped to the cell phone, still open in Nick's hand. "Bad news?"

"Nah." Nick snapped the phone shut. "Just the usual bullshit."

Tori waited for Nick's call that night, but it never came. The next morning, when Leigh showed up for work, she told Tori her dad hadn't gotten home until after midnight.

Okay, so he'd had to work late. No biggie. He'd probably been neglecting his more profitable clients while he worked on Tori's shop. She knew how much his business meant to him. Canceling dinner had nothing to do with her.

So why did it feel like a rejection?

At least her candle magic spell for success seemed to be working. The instant Tori turned her sign from CLOSED to OPEN, two women passing by on their way to the beach stopped in. They both made purchases. Tori exchanged a smile with Leigh, who was still arranging the last of the merchandise.

Steady business continued all morning. The cash register sang, and Tori was elated. This was actually going to work. She was going to be a successful entrepreneur.

Around three in the afternoon, during a lull in traffic, a round-shouldered, gray-haired old lady appeared in the doorway. She pushed open the screen and stomped into the shop, head bowed as if she were walking into a stiff wind.

An enormous black leather handbag swung on her arm.

Leigh's eyes widened. "Nonna? What are you doing here?"

"What d'ya think? I came to meet your father's girlfriend." The old woman advanced. Halting in front of the sales counter, she looked Tori up and down. "So. You're the girl Nicky's been hiding."

Leigh sent Tori an apologetic glance. "Um . . . Tori, this is Nonna. My great-grandmother. I hope you don't mind, but I told her about you. Nonna, this is Tori."

"Hmph."

Tori smiled. "How do you do?"

Nonna's bright eyes searched Tori's. What the old woman

expected to find, Tori didn't know, but her examination produced the same queasy feeling Tori remembered from high school algebra.

"You don't look Italian," Nonna said finally. She plunked her big handbag down on the counter.

Leigh rolled her eyes.

"I'm not Italian," Tori told Nonna. "I'm half Irish."

"Hmph. Can you cook?"

"Um . . . a little, I guess." This was the oddest interrogation Tori had ever undergone.

Nonna frowned, then sighed and gave a dismissive wave of her hand. "Ah, well, you can learn to cook. The important thing is, do you love my grandson?"

Leigh almost choked. "Nonna! I can*not* believe you asked Tori that."

"Well?" Nonna demanded. "Do you?"

Tori picked up a necklace a customer had left on the counter and rehung it on its display. "Well . . . it's a bit too early to say, don't you think? I've only known Nick for a couple weeks."

"*Fa niente.* Don't mean nothing. Nicky's grandfather proposed after two weeks."

And what could Tori say to that? She plucked a pentacle necklace from the rack and exchanged it with a crescent moon pendant from another hook.

Leigh rounded the counter. "Nonna, did you come here just to embarrass Tori, or is there some other point to your visit?"

"I came to ask her to dinner," Nonna said, looking over the bracelet display. She fingered one with seven colored stones, each one representing a different chakra center. "This is nice," she said.

"Dinner?" Tori said. "I'm not sure. . . ." Somehow, she thought it should be Nick who first invited her to his house. Not his grandmother.

"Tori would love to come," Leigh said. "What're we having?"

"Spaghetti, meatballs, and a green salad." Nonna draped the chakra bracelet over her wrinkled wrist, admiring it.

"Tori's a vegetarian, but that'll work. She can just skip the meatballs."

Tori tried to infiltrate the conversation. "I really wouldn't want to impose."

"Oh, it's no problem," Leigh said. "Nonna always cooks enough for an army."

Tori hesitated. Sure, she wanted to meet the rest of his family, but the awkward phone conversation she'd had with Nick the day before had left her stomach in knots. Chelsea was right: Tori wasn't ready for relationship drama. What if she went to dinner at Nick's and he wasn't happy to see her there?

"I don't know. . . ."

Leigh shot Tori a shrewd look. "Will Dad be home for dinner?"

"Nah." Nonna fingered the chakra stones as if they were beads on a rosary. "Your father's working late."

"Good," Leigh said. "The less I see of him, the better."

The old woman's dark eyes narrowed on her. "Madonna! Is that any way for a girl to talk about her father?"

"Sorry," Leigh mumbled, "but it's the truth."

Nonna made a gesture of disgust. "Kids these days."

She hefted her handbag off the counter. "Ah, well. What can you do?" She pointed her index finger at Leigh. "Be home at six. Bring her with you."

She turned and stomped out of the store. Leigh went after her and helped her down the porch stair.

"Sorry about that," Leigh said when she returned. "Nonna can be a little tough on the uninitiated."

"I didn't mind." Tori's gaze swept over the counter, and she frowned. "Do you see that chakra bracelet your great-grandmother was looking at? She forgot to put it back on the display, but I don't see it anywhere."

Leigh inhaled sharply. "Oh, no." She grimaced. "Um . . . I

don't think Nonna forgot to put it back, Tori. I think she's still got it."

Tori blinked. "What are you saying? You can't possibly think your grandmother stole my bracelet."

"Yeah," Leigh said with a sigh. "That's exactly what I think."

Chapter Nineteen

When you're the youngest sibling in a big family,
it can be tough getting the attention you deserve.
But you do what you can.

"*This* is your house?" Tori asked Leigh. She felt a little light-headed looking at it.

"Cool, huh?"

"Very," she agreed faintly. She could not believe it. Nick lived in the Castle. *Her* castle. It wasn't possible.

Leigh grinned. "I'll give you the grand tour after dinner."

Was Nick's bedroom on that tour? Tori tried to squelch the thought, but once it floated into her mind, it dropped anchor and stayed. Thoughts of Nick's bedroom led to thoughts of Nick's bed. Thoughts of Nick's bed led to thoughts of . . .

No. She wasn't going there. Nick's grandmother was in that house, for Pete's sake. How could she possibly look the woman in the eye while she pictured her grandson naked?

Leigh led the way through the foyer and into a high-ceilinged living room. Tori took in gleaming white walls, polished oak, and plush carpet. She was admiring a seascape when a giggling missile shot out from behind a buttery leather sofa and slammed into Leigh's legs.

"Sophie!" Leigh staggered under the impact, but recovered to haul a little girl into her arms. She kissed her soundly. "You're here!"

"Daddy and Uncle Johnny are here, too." Sophie said, brown curls bouncing.

"That's great. Look, Sophie, I have a new friend for you to meet. This is Tori. She's Uncle Nicky's friend, too."

Uncle Nicky? Tori smiled. Now, that was a facet of Nick's life she'd never contemplated.

Sophie grinned. "Hi, Tori. I'm five." She held up five fingers.

"That's a good age to be," Tori told her. "Fits all on one hand."

Nick's niece had soft brown eyes and a sprinkle of freckles. With her legs wrapped around Leigh's waist, she looked like a cute, clinging monkey.

Leigh carried Sophie toward the back of the house. "Come on," she said over her shoulder. "Back here."

The dining room was huge, with a large table that had surely seen hundreds of family dinners. At the moment, two men sprawled in chairs on opposite sides of the table. One, dressed in jeans and a dress shirt open at the collar, stood as Tori and Leigh entered. With his wide shoulders, slim hips, and dark good looks, the man could have passed for Nick's twin, though his hair was shorter and his aura more intense than his older brother's.

"Daddy!" Sophie cried. "Look! Leigh has a new friend!"

"That's nice, baby," the man said easily. He nodded to Tori, his sharp eyes seeming to take in all of her with one swift glance. "Hi. I'm Alex."

"Alex is the police detective," Leigh put in.

"Yeah, he keeps the streets safe for the rest of us deadbeats." The second, younger brother smiled, eyes twinkling. He lounged, loose-limbed and comfortable in a too-large T-shirt and ripped knee-length jeans shorts.

Leigh rolled her eyes. "This is Johnny," she told Tori. "You know, the one I told you about?"

Johnny sat up abruptly. "Not sure I like the sound of that." He winked at Tori. "Should I be worried?"

"Maybe," Tori said with a laugh. Johnny didn't resemble his brothers at all, either in features or demeanor. His longish hair was pin straight and streaked blond, and his eyes were so blue they were startling. He sported sideburns, a five-days-without-a-razor beard, two silver hoop earrings in one ear, and a barbed-wire tattoo on his left biceps. His build was slimmer than his brothers', and he lacked their classic good looks.

But no woman, Tori guessed, would ever call Johnny unattractive. Especially when he flashed his thousand-watt grin.

Which he turned, full force, on Tori.

She couldn't help grinning back.

Standing, Johnny held out his arms to Leigh and Sophie. "Come on, girls. Give Uncle Johnny a hug."

Leigh obliged, squashing Sophie between them. Sophie giggled.

"What, no girlfriend tonight?" Leigh asked Johnny as she stepped out of his arms.

He shrugged. "What can I say? They've all wised up. No one'll have me. Hmm . . ." He leaned toward Sophie, brushing her ear. "Whatcha got there, cutie?"

With a flick of his wrist, he produced a shiny quarter. "You should keep these in your purse."

Sophie, giggling, grabbed his hand. "Lemme see!"

"Here you go."

Leigh carried Sophie around the end of the table and kissed Alex. "Hey, stranger. Can't believe you finally made some time for us."

"Someone's gotta keep tabs on you."

"Nah, that's my job," Johnny joked.

Tori shifted, smoothing her skirt with her palms. She felt like a pigeon in a flock of seagulls. It was a familiar feeling—one she'd had for five years in foster care. She was used to being with families she didn't belong to. And she hated it. Being on the outer edge of intimate family banter reminded her all too sharply of what she'd never had. It was like watching a movie in a foreign language that she wanted desperately to understand, but didn't speak a word of.

Maybe she shouldn't have come.

Leigh must have seen Tori glance at the door, because she

immediately dumped Sophie into Alex's lap and came back around the table to Tori's side. "Tori's just opened a shop near Lucy the elephant."

Johnny's sparkling gaze was clearly curious. "Ah, yes, Nick's mystery woman."

"Hardly a mystery," Tori replied. She felt her neck heat up. "He just took care of a few changes so I could open a shop in the front of the house and live in the back."

Johnny's brows went up. "But that's exactly what's so mysterious. Here my uptight, workaholic brother starts ducking out of the office promptly at five, and hell hasn't even frozen over yet. You can't imagine how shocked I was when I found out that Nick—who hasn't done a job as small as yours in five years, let alone with his own hands—was doing work on the side." He winked. "But now that I see how pretty the client is, I have to say I understand perfectly."

Tori turned redder. "Leigh said you work for Santangelo Construction, too?"

Johnny laughed. "Try to, anyway."

Just then, an attractive middle-aged woman appeared in the kitchen doorway at the end of the room, wiping her hands on a dish towel. She smiled. "Hello, dear," she said to Tori. "I'm Rita, Nick's mother."

"It's very nice to meet you," Tori said. "You have a lovely home."

"Notice she didn't comment on your two sons' lovely manners," Johnny said.

"Speak for yourself," Alex told him, amused.

Nonna emerged from the kitchen, carrying a gravy boat filled with spaghetti sauce. "About time you all got here. Dinner's getting cold. Johnny, take this, will you? I gotta get the meatballs."

Johnny took the gravy boat. "Have I told you yet how beautiful you look tonight, Nonna?"

Nonna narrowed her eyes at him. "You know, that mouth's gonna get you in trouble one of these days."

"It already has," Alex said dryly. "More than once."

"Johnny, be a doll and open the wine," Rita said as Johnny put the gravy boat on the table. "Tori, do sit down."

Tori obeyed, sinking into the chair Johnny held out for her. It was the one next to his own. Tori watched as he expertly inserted the corkscrew into the cork and twisted it free.

He presented it to her with a flourish. "*S'il vous plaît*, mademoiselle."

Sophie, ensconced in her father's lap, giggled. "He calls me Mad Mosel, too. He said it's because I'm crazy."

Tori met Johnny's eyes. They were dancing, drawing her into his joke. She smiled, feeling a little less like the outsider she was.

She took the cork and sniffed it. "Excellent, monsieur."

Johnny made a show of shaking out a paper napkin and draping it over one arm. Tori laughed. The napkin, sprinkled with a pattern of tiny blue flowers, made the gesture beyond ridiculous. Bowing deeply, he splashed some wine into Tori's glass, then lifted it and held it out to her.

She tried to take it from him, but he didn't release the stem. Instead, her fingers covered his as he tilted the glass to her lips.

The wine slid over her tongue.

She caught his gaze again. It was warm and teasing. Conspiratorial. She could tell Johnny shared Nick's warped sense of humor. He gave it a polished twist, but the result was the same. They both liked to poke fun at themselves, putting their companions at ease. Tori sat back in her chair and felt herself relax.

Dinner flew by, with everyone talking at once. Tori struggled to take it all in. She learned Johnny worked nights as a stand-up comic and Nonna liked to play the quarter slots at the casinos. Rita wondered if Zach, the brother in the navy, had gotten the package she'd sent him. After dinner, Alex pulled Sophie onto his lap and drew funny faces on a napkin while Johnny told clean versions of his nightclub jokes.

"It's not this fun when Dad's home," Leigh confided as she and Tori cleared the table. "He and Uncle Johnny don't get along."

"I can't imagine anyone not getting along with Johnny."

"Dad thinks he's irresponsible. He misses work to go for auditions in New York City."

"Auditions for what?"

"Acting jobs. Commercials, mostly."

"Has he had any luck?"

"Some," Leigh said. "Nothing big yet. But he might have a shot at a part on *Franklinville Hospital.*"

"The soap opera?"

"Yeah."

"I'm impressed." Tori stacked the dishes in the sink and ran the water.

"You don't have to do those," Rita said, coming up behind her.

"I don't mind," Tori told her. And she didn't. There was something very appealing about being in a kitchen surrounded by women cleaning up, while the men talked sports in the next room. The stove was warm, the air smelled of garlic, and an intimate rumble of voices filled her ears.

"Tori and I'll do the dishes," Leigh told Rita. "She can wash and I'll load."

Tori plunged her hands into the soapy water and smiled. She almost felt as though she belonged.

Nonna shooed Leigh and Tori out of the kitchen before they were finished. Apparently, Nonna wanted to finish cleaning up herself, her way. Tori and Leigh trooped back into the dining room, where Rita told Tori how nice it was to have her there, then promptly excused herself, saying she had a meeting to attend at her church.

That announcement elicited a scowl from Leigh, but Tori didn't have a chance to ask the girl why. Rita had barely left the room when Alex rose and kissed his daughter, who was apparently staying to sleep over with Leigh. He gave his good-byes to the rest of the room, and followed his mother out the door.

"Well," Tori said once he'd gone, "I guess I'll call it a night, too."

Sophie's lower lip started to jut. "No," she commanded. "Stay."

Johnny laughed. "That's not polite, sweetie." He turned his blue eyes and smile on Tori. "But I do share my niece's sentiment."

"Yes, stay for a while, Tori," Leigh pleaded. "It's still early."

"All right," Tori found herself saying. Truth was, she didn't want to leave. This was Nick's home, after all, a door into a facet of his personality and his life that had suddenly swung open. She was insatiably curious.

Sophie took her hand and tugged her into the family room. It was a comfortable, lived-in space with dark wood paneling. The furniture was older and more forgiving than the living room's.

A tall bookshelf sported a jumble of framed family photographs. Tori wandered over to it. Each shot was a happy moment frozen in time. Some scenes were posed, others candid and bursting with movement. There were photos of the whole family, of course, but Tori's eyes gravitated to the ones featuring Nick.

Tori picked out his baby picture immediately—his eyes and his smile hadn't changed at all. In another he stood stiffly in a First Communion suit, hands folded. As a teenager, she noted, he'd been on a varsity swim team; there was a shot of him accepting a huge trophy. Another photo of Nick in a cap and gown, and another with Nick holding a toddler that had to be Leigh.

There was no wedding picture, of course.

Tori went farther back in time and picked up a family portrait from Nick's childhood. Nick, Zach, and Alex, all dark-haired and serious, stood in the background. Nick, as the oldest, was the tallest, the other dark heads stepping down like stairs. A younger Rita and a man who looked like a mature version of his three older sons sat in front of the boys. A startlingly blond baby perched on Rita's lap, laughing and waving his chubby fist.

"My brothers used to tell me I was adopted," Johnny commented. Tori started. She hadn't realized he'd come up behind her. "Either that, or the mailman's kid."

She met his laughing eyes. "Did you believe them?"

"Well, not the bit about the mailman. Ma and Pop were too much in love for that. But I did believe the adoption story for a few years." He laughed. "Still do, sometimes."

Tori replaced the photo on the shelf. It must have been bliss growing up in a family with a mother *and* a father, ones who actually loved each other, too. She stifled a sigh as she turned from the photos to examine the rest of the room. A computer setup and a large desk spread with blueprints filled one entire wall. Nick's desk.

The wall above it was filled with framed artwork. Pencil drawings of the beach and the boardwalk. A watercolor of Lucy the elephant, another of a seagull perched on a weathered piling. Several more, all original. Some had clearly been done by a child's hand, others by a more mature artist.

The largest drawing was an ink-and-watercolor rendering of the Santangelo home. It was a two-dimensional architectural drawing, the lines drawn crisply with the aid of a straight edge. The artist must have had incredible patience, Tori thought, to capture the house in such detail.

"I did most of those," Leigh said, following Tori's gaze. She'd picked up Sophie and was balancing her on one hip. "Except the one of the house. That one's Dad's."

Tori was surprised. "I didn't know your dad was an artist."

"He's not. At least not anymore. He drew that before I was born. Before the house was built, even."

"Before it was built? I don't understand."

Johnny leaned a hip on Nick's desk. "Nick wanted to be an architect. He designed this house as a high school project. Our father had just bought the land for a new house,

and he liked Nick's design so much he had his architect
work with Nick to draw up the plans."

"But I don't understand," Tori said. "If Nick wanted to be
an architect, and has so much talent, why didn't he become
one?"

Johnny glanced at Leigh. "He . . . um . . . never went to college. He went to work for my dad right out of high school."

Tori took one look at Leigh's pained expression and immediately wanted to bite her tongue. Leigh had been born
when Nick was only eighteen; her unplanned arrival had
obviously caused a drastic change in his life plans. But Tori
couldn't imagine Nick resenting his daughter for being born.
He just wasn't that kind of man.

Tori didn't know what to say. The moment stretched into
awkwardness. Finally, Sophie broke the tension by leaning
sideways in Leigh's embrace and grabbing Tori's arm.

"You wanna play a game?"

Tori smiled down at her. "Sure. What should we play?"

Johnny jumped up, rummaging through a cabinet.
"Cards," he said, producing a deck. "We'll all play."

"What's the game?" Leigh asked, taking a seat at a game
table set up in a corner of the room as her uncle rippled
the deck accordion-style.

"Blackjack." Johnny plunked a rack of poker chips on
the table and sat down opposite Nick's daughter. "I've been
tutoring Sophie, you know. She's a whiz."

"You're teaching a five-year-old how to gamble?" Tori ex-
claimed, appalled.

Johnny grinned. "She's got to learn sometime. Besides, it
helps with her math. Sophie can add and subtract all the
other preschoolers into the ground."

"Be on my team, Tori," Sophie begged.

"Okay." She took an empty seat. Sophie slid out of Leigh's
arms and onto her lap, wriggling to get comfortable. She
was warm and sweet, and her weight felt good. Tori's chest
contracted as she tightened her arm around the girl's tiny
waist.

"You smell good," Leigh said, sniffing. "What is it?"

"Lavender soap," Tori told her.

"I like it. Will you give me some?"

"Sure, if you want."

Nonna arrived from the kitchen at that moment. Her eyes lit up. She surprised Tori by settling into the remaining chair.

"Just a couple hands. Then Johnny here has to drive me home. I gotta watch that crime scene show."

Johnny gave everyone one hundred dollars in chips, then dealt the first hand. The pile of chips Tori shared with Sophie grew rapidly—mainly, Tori suspected, because Johnny and Leigh were throwing each round to their niece. Their obvious affection for the girl made Tori smile. Sophie bounced in her lap, thrilled every time a new chip landed in front of her. Counting them carefully, she built them into towers and knocked them down while Johnny kept the cards and jokes coming.

"Okay," he said finally, "last hand. Nonna's getting antsy."

Nonna peered at her watch. "I don't wanna miss my show."

"Don't worry," Johnny said. "I'll get you there in time if I have to run every light from here to Atlantic City."

"Don't you dare," Nonna said, frowning. "I'll get Alex to write you a ticket."

"Alex doesn't give out speeding tickets," Leigh said.

"He got police friends, don't he?" Nonna retorted.

Johnny leaned sideways, his lips a fraction of an inch from Tori's ear. "See what I have to put up with?" he said in a stage whisper. "My own grandmother, siccing the cops on me."

"You poor baby," Tori whispered back, just as loudly, meeting his laughing gaze.

"Better keep Johnny out of it," a voice called from the living room. "Nonna, I won't be long here. I'll drop you off on my way back to the office."

Tori's heart stuttered.

Nick's tall form appeared in the doorway. "I just stopped home to—" He halted abruptly, his dark eyes widening as they collided with her gaze.

"Tori."

Johnny straightened. Tori's pulse sped up. She searched Nick's face for some sign that he was pleased to see her. His expression was completely unreadable.

She gave him a tentative smile.

Sophie slid off Tori's lap and ran to him. "Uncle Nicky!"

Nick lifted his niece easily, the smile he hadn't offered Tori softening his features at once. "Hi, squirt."

"You wanna play cards with us, Uncle Nicky?"

"I can't," he said, carrying her to his desk. He hunted around and picked up a flash drive. "I'm not staying, honey. I just came to get something I forgot."

He set Sophie on her feet. "Ready to leave now, Nonna?"

"Just gotta get my handbag," Nonna said, pushing to her feet and heading for the door.

"Aren't you going to ask how Tori's first day went?" Leigh asked Nick, indignation plain in her voice.

He eyed her. "You worked there today?"

"Yes."

"I didn't give you my permission."

Tori looked at Leigh, aghast. "You told me—"

"Mimi said I could work at Tori's today," Leigh put in quickly. Her chin went up as she turned back to her father. "After all, *you* weren't home to discuss it."

"Just great," Nick muttered. His dark gaze cut to Tori. "So, how'd it go?"

"All right," Tori said carefully, trying to ignore the tightening in her stomach.

Nonna returned with her enormous black bag. Tori eyed it, wondering if, as Leigh insisted, Nonna had stashed the chakra bracelet from the shop inside. It didn't seem possible.

"Yeah, I'm good to go," Nonna said.

Nick escorted Nonna out the door with little more than a scant nod to the room as he left.

"Well," said Johnny. He collected the cards and chips. "That was fun. As usual. You can always rely on my big brother to liven things up."

His tone was carefully light, but Tori didn't miss the sharp edge to it.

She stood. "It's getting late. I'd better get going, too."

Johnny looked up. "Did you drive over?"

"No," Leigh told him. "We walked over together from the shop. It's only a few blocks."

"I'll walk Tori home, then," he said.

"You don't have to do that," Tori protested. "I'll be fine."

"I know." He flashed her an easy grin. "But I'm going to walk you home anyway."

Chapter Twenty

No one knows you like family. Fortunately.

Nick ran three red lights on his way to Atlantic City.

His knuckles went white on the steering wheel as his mind flashed an image of his first sight of Tori with Johnny. *Christ.* Johnny'd practically had his tongue in Tori's ear. And it sure as hell hadn't looked like she minded. She'd been laughing, the way all women did with Johnny, her inky lashes fluttering over her sea green eyes.

Nick felt scooped out and scoured raw. He'd broken his date with Tori and tried to brush her into the background of his life. He'd told himself it was because he didn't like the way she'd taken front and center in his thoughts. And he'd almost believed it. But now, after seeing Johnny putting the moves on her . . . *Damn it.*

He tried to tell himself he'd be just as pissed if Johnny had hit on any of Nick's old girlfriends. But that was a bald-faced lie, and he knew it.

"Your new girlfriend's a cutie," Nonna said.

Nick repositioned his death grip on the steering wheel. "She's just a friend."

"Oh, no. I seen you with friends, Nicky. You smile, you laugh, you charm. Tonight, your face looks like someone's squeezing your cojones."

"Nonna!" Nick was appalled.

She gave a snort. "That girl ain't no *friend*, Nicky. You're under her skirt."

He nearly plowed into the car in front of him. "Jesus, Nonna."

"Don't get me wrong. I'm glad for you. It's been too long since that wife of yours left you."

"I've hardly been celibate all that time. I've dated plenty of women." *Hell*. What kind of conversation was this for a man to be having with his grandmother?

Nonna's hand waved. "Is that what you call what you've been doing all these years? Dating? Come on, Nicky. A man brings a date home to his family. You never brought a woman home before today."

"I didn't bring Tori home," Nick pointed out grimly. "Leigh did."

"Well, however she got there, I like her. Even if she ain't Italian." She patted his arm. "Don't let this one get away."

He exhaled. "It's not like it's a fishing trip, Nonna."

"And you should make sure you look nice for her," Nonna said, ignoring his comment. She turned in her seat and squinted, forefinger pressed to one cheek. "You know, you always dress so boring."

He glanced down at his white Santangelo Construction golf shirt. "What's wrong with the way I dress?"

"Too . . . blah. You need some color to keep a nice girl like that one."

"Forget it," Nick muttered.

"Hmmm . . ." Nonna unsnapped her handbag. "Lemme see. I think I got just the thing."

Nick's apprehension rose as a panoply of items spilled from Nonna's black bag. Change purse, pillbox, hair spray. A soap opera magazine with the headline, "*Franklinville Hospital* Tragedy: Will Dr. Marshall Survive?"

"It's in here somewhere," she muttered.

Nick took his hand off the steering wheel long enough to rub a sudden pain above one eye. "Please tell me whatever it is you're looking for came from Mr. Merino's store," he said wearily, "and not from somewhere else."

Nonna's hand plunged into the bag's gaping maw. "Old

man Merino's stuff is gettin' too cheap for me. I stopped at that new men's store in one of them Trump casinos yesterday. Ah," she said finally, brightening. "Got it."

"It" was a truly hideous pink-and-yellow necktie. Real silk, clearly, and Nick thought he saw the flash of a designer tag.

"Did you steal that thing?" he demanded. "From a *casino*, for chrissakes?"

"I mighta picked it up while I was there."

Nick bit off a curse. "Nonna! You can't just waltz into a casino boutique and steal things. Do you know what would happen if you got caught?"

"Ah, they won't do nothing to an old lady like me. Besides, I put enough money in their slots to pay for a hundred ties."

"That's not the point."

"Ah, Nicky. You worry too much."

"Just quit it, okay? Quit the shoplifting."

She waved the tie under his nose. "What do you think? Nice, ain't it?"

"Nonna," Nick said, keeping his hands on the wheel and his eyes on the road, "that is, without a doubt, the ugliest article of clothing I have ever seen in my entire life."

"Well, I'm giving it to you," Nonna said happily. "A man can always use a snazzy tie."

"So, just what is it you see in my brother?" Johnny asked Tori.

She stopped, letting her bare toes sink into the cool, damp sand as she swung her sandals in her hand. Johnny had insisted they walk the three blocks south on the beach rather than on the street.

It was dark on the beach, and she couldn't gauge the tone of his expression. "That's kind of a personal question, don't you think?"

Johnny had left his shoes at the house. Now he moved closer to the ocean and stepped into the end run of a wave. "I'm a personal kind of guy."

She shifted her sandals to her left hand, following him. A wave rushed her, flattening out as it splashed her ankles, and sent a shock up her legs.

"Nick renovated my house," she said, as if what had gone on between them could be categorized as a simple business arrangement. "He helped me out when I couldn't find anyone else. And he didn't ask for any money up front. In fact, he hasn't even sent me my first bill yet."

"Nick didn't charge you?" She could hear the surprise in his voice.

"Not yet."

"I don't believe it. Nick is never late with an invoice." Johnny scooped up a clamshell and tossed it into the waves. "Of course," he mused, picking up another shell, "you aren't his usual kind of client."

She didn't like the way he said it. "And just what do you mean by that?"

He exhaled. "Your project's not on the company books. Did you know that? I did a little snooping after Leigh told me about you. Doris said Nick told him not to open a file on your job."

"But . . . I saw delivery slips on some of the materials. They said Santangelo Construction."

"Nick reimbursed the company personally. I know, because Doris showed me the deposits."

She stepped back as another wave hit. Nick had paid for her job out of his own pocket? That couldn't be right.

"What're you saying? That Nick isn't planning to charge me at all? That's not true. I told him I won't take charity."

Johnny sent her a sidelong glance. "I doubt he's thinking of you as charity."

"What other way can he mean it?"

Johnny's eyes were fixed on the sea. "Tori. I know my brother. Nick's a guy who likes to keep his balance sheets even. I probably shouldn't be butting into this, but I like you. I saw how you looked at him tonight, and I saw how pissed he was to see you there with all of us. There's something you gotta know about Nick. He never brings women he's dating home for dinner. He breaks up with them before it ever gets that serious."

A hollow, uneasy feeling took up residence in Tori's gut. "What makes you think I want things to get serious?"

He glanced at her, then resumed his walk up the beach. "I'd put money on it, Tori," he said quietly. "And I'd win. You're the family type. I can tell."

She swallowed the sudden lump in her throat.

"Do you know," he continued, "it's been fifteen years since Nick's wife left him, and in all that time he hasn't had a single serious relationship. Not one. And it's not because women haven't chased him."

Tori felt small. "He loved his wife that much?"

"Cindy? Hell, no. Nick married her because she was pregnant and it was the"—he made quotation marks in the air—"'right thing' to do. But it turned out to be dead wrong. I was only nine when they split up, but even I could tell he could barely stand her by then."

Tori's stomach cramp eased a little. "I don't understand. What does Nick's love life have to do with the money I owe him?"

Johnny came to a halt. Tori stopped, too. He looked down at the sand and kicked it.

"How can I explain this without getting you pissed at me?" His head came up, and for once, his smile was nonexistent. "Okay, I'll give it a shot. Nick's an uptight bastard on the outside, but underneath he's a great guy, with the biggest heart. He'd do anything for anyone, but what he'd never do is take anything from anyone. He doesn't like to be in debt."

"So?"

"So the reason Nick won't charge you for the work is because it's his contribution to your relationship. So he won't need to put in an emotional investment."

The humid air was thick in Tori's lungs. "That sounds like some very shaky armchair psychology."

"Well, I did spend a couple years as a psych major." He touched her arm. "Look. I'm sorry. Maybe I shouldn't have said anything. Forget it."

But his words had a ring of truth to them she didn't want to accept, and she just couldn't let them stand. "So you think . . . what? That Nick did my work in exchange for . . . for sex?"

Johnny's silence was answer enough.

Tori groped for a lifeline in the dark. "I . . . I just can't believe that, Johnny. Nick's an honest, caring man. He'd never cheapen what we have together that way. There has to be another explanation."

Johnny opened his mouth, then shut it and just looked at her.

"Shit," he said. "I'm too late. You're already in love with him."

"You can't stay," Leigh told Jason, leaning over the seawall at the edge of the patio. "Dad could be home any minute."

"I don't care." Jason's voice was low and husky, as if there were more inside than he was willing to let escape. He stood on the beach, five feet below, looking up at her. It made Leigh feel like Juliet. Except she was sure Jason was way hotter than Romeo.

"Come on down. Or let me up. I won't stay long. The second I hear him drive up, I'm outta here."

Leigh hesitated. "Okay. Come up. But just for a minute."

Jason's muscles flexed as he hoisted himself over the seawall. When he reached for her, her arms went around his neck as if they belonged there.

He nuzzled just below her ear. "Why didn't you call me earlier?"

"Sophie took forever to get to sleep."

"I would've come over and helped you babysit."

"You couldn't have! She might've said something to Dad about your being here."

He lifted his head, seeking her eyes. Even in the dim

light, she could tell his expression was troubled. "Maybe I should talk to your dad. You know, man-to-man. Tell him how much you mean to me."

"I . . . don't think that's a good idea."

Correction: It was the worst idea. Her dad would freak if he knew how serious she and Jason were. He'd lock her in her room and grind the key into dust.

Frustration laced Jason's voice. "Leigh, I'm sick of sneaking around to see you."

"I'll talk to him again. He can't stay mad forever."

Jason pressed his forehead to hers and sighed. "All right. But I doubt it will do much good. He hates me."

Leigh didn't deny it. Jason tugged her to a lounge chair, easing back and pulling her atop him. She sprawled on his chest, her legs stretched along his, their hips sliding together. She felt the bulge under his shorts. His hands moved to her buttocks, shifting her until her most sensitive spot pressed against his rock-hard erection. A jolt of desire nearly cleaved her in two.

He covered her gasping mouth hungrily. One hand slipped under her shirt. A second later, her bra was unhooked and he was touching her. His hips moved with an urgent rhythm, building the yearning inside until she thought she would go insane.

"God, I love you, Leigh. I think about you all the time." His tongue found her ear, making her shudder.

"I love you, too."

"When can we be together?"

The word drifted through the sensual haze. "Together?"

"I want to make love to you."

Oh, God. Right now, she wanted that, too, but . . . "I don't know," she whispered.

Jason's hands moved on her, making her forget her own name. He kissed her again, slow and wet and deep. Even so, a small, anxious knot shivered in her stomach.

It's nothing, she told herself. *Just a little stage fright.*

"I'm working at Tori's every day," she whispered. "And

babysitting Sophie most nights, since her mom's on vacation. I don't know when—"

"Come after everyone's asleep."

It was a possibility. Leigh hesitated. "When?"

"Fourth of July. My parents are going to Maryland for the weekend, and Beth will be out all night with her boyfriend. We'll have the house to ourselves."

"But . . . that's so soon." *Too soon.*

"I know. I can hardly wait."

She laid her cheek on his chest while apprehension ate its way through her gut.

He smoothed a strand of hair from her face. "Ah, babe, don't be nervous. You know I love you. I just want to show you how much." He kissed the top of her head, hesitating. "Please?"

The pounding sound of the surf blended with the beat of Jason's heart against her cheek. *Love's like the tide*, she thought. *Relentless. Inevitable.*

She made her decision. "Okay. I'll be there."

Chapter Twenty-one

A baby changes everything.

"What'd you find out?" Nick asked Alex as he sank into a chair at Formica Bros. Italian bakery on Arctic Avenue, carrying a cup of coffee and a *sfogliatelle* as big as his hand.

Alex, having just refilled his own cup at the coffee bar, slid into the seat opposite. "You'll never guess."

"Try me."

"Ma's not having an affair."

Relief washed through Nick. "Thank God. What's she doing, then?"

Alex took a gulp of coffee. "I trailed her to a music studio in Northfield. She's taking voice lessons. Jazz and blues, to be specific."

"Voice lessons?" Nick frowned into his own coffee. "So why is that such a deep, dark secret?"

Alex shrugged. "Don't know."

"Maybe she's having an affair with the instructor."

"The instructor's a woman."

"Oh." Then, "I don't get it."

"What's to get? You know Ma's got a great voice. She's sung in the church choir forever. Maybe she wants to expand her repertoire."

"Maybe," Nick said, trying to puzzle it out. "But why wouldn't she just say so?"

"Why don't you just ask her?"

"I did," said Nick. "All she said was not to worry."

"There you go, then." Alex slid a pen from his shirt pocket and started doodling on a napkin. "You know, I met Tori last night. She's cute."

Nick snorted. *Cute* wasn't quite the word he associated with Tori, but then again, he'd seen sides of Tori that Alex never would. "That's what Nonna said."

Alex drew a few more lines on his napkin. "You two serious?"

"I barely know her." Nick took a bite of his *sfogliatelle*.

"I'm only asking because Johnny was really into her last night. You might've thought he was onstage, he was trying so hard to impress her." Alex looked up from his drawing long enough to send Nick a pointed look. "She seemed to like him, too."

Nick set down his pastry, his appetite suddenly sucked into the empty hole at the bottom of his stomach. "Johnny flirts with women all the time. Doesn't mean anything."

Alex shoved his napkin across the table. He'd drawn a woman with curly hair leaning over a balcony railing. A man with two hoop earrings and an arm tattoo was climbing up an arbor to join her.

"That's bullshit," Nick said. "Bullshit."

"Just as long as we're all on the same page," Alex said.

Nick called Tori that afternoon, and asked her out for dinner after he left the office. Her heart was tripping double-time as she agreed. Finally. A chance to clear the murky air hanging between them. They drove over to Ozzie's, a fifties-style diner in Longport.

"Do you mind so much?" she asked him as they slid into a booth. "About Leigh working at my shop?"

He leaned back in his seat and expelled a long breath. "Leigh usually works in my office in the summer. But she's bored with it, so I guess it won't hurt her any to work for you instead."

Tori let herself relax. "I'm glad. She's been a big help

already." She smiled, fingering her napkin. "She's so sweet and agreeable."

Nick gave a snort of disbelief. "Leigh? Agreeable? Are we talking about the same girl?"

"She does everything I ask her to—and even thinks up extra jobs. And she's always smiling."

"She wants to get on your good side. Wait until she doesn't like something you tell her to do. The sparks'll fly then."

Tori tore a long strip off the edge of her napkin. "I don't think you're being fair to her."

"That's because you don't have kids. You have no idea. Leigh's first word to me was 'no.'"

"She was a handful, huh?"

"That and more. She was a tough baby, and even when she got older . . ." He shifted, letting his hand drop to the table. "It's been one thing after another. This teenage crap is the worst. See these gray hairs?" He jabbed a finger toward his temple. "Premature. Don't get me wrong: I love my daughter, but raising her has emptied me out. That's why I'll never do it again."

Tori froze. "Never do what?"

He didn't seem to notice that her breathing had gone shallow. He took a generous swig of his soda. "I'll never have another kid. Stick a fork in me; I'm done."

"But . . ." Tori's napkin turned to shreds in her fingers. "You're only thirty-five. Lots of men your age are just starting families."

"Good luck to them," Nick said. "Believe me, they're gonna need it."

"But . . ." Tori felt the world slipping away from underneath her, as if the tide had come in to wash away the ground she stood on. "Don't you want a son? To carry on your name? I thought that was important to most men."

"Not to this one. I'm not into that firstborn ego crap. I've got three brothers. Let one of them carry on the family name."

Their dinner arrived just then.

But Tori's appetite was gone.

She talked it over with Chelsea.

"Maybe he'll change his mind," Tori said, pacing a narrow strip of carpet in front of Chelsea's sales counter. Her stomach hurt something awful. "Maybe after we've been together a while, he'll decide another baby wouldn't be such a bad thing."

"Are you listening to yourself?" Chelsea demanded. "You're out of your mind. The man told you flat out he doesn't want any more kids. You have to respect that. It's not fair to him if you don't."

Tori didn't have any answer.

Chelsea came around the counter and hugged her. The sisterly gesture made Tori's throat ache.

"Aw, honey. I know it sucks. But you can't ignore the facts. You spent the last five years being what Colin wanted. Don't spend the next five being what Nick wants." She held Tori's gaze steadily. "You have to do what's best for you."

Tori took a deep breath. Her friend was right.

But it hurt like hell to admit it.

Nick came over that night in a good mood, bent on sweet-talking Tori right into bed.

And despite the warning bells ringing in her head, Tori let him.

The afterglow faded more quickly than it should have. Tori lay beside Nick, staring up at the ceiling. He drew lazy circles on her arm. She turned her head and looked at him.

Her expression must have given her away, because he said, "What's up?"

Tori exhaled. "There's something I need to tell you."

He pushed himself up on his elbow, his brow furrowing. "That sounds serious. What is it?"

"I'm going to have a baby."

He jerked upright. "You're pregnant?"

The anger in his dark eyes scared her. "No!" Tori sat up, pulling the sheet over her naked body. "No! I'm not."

Relief wiped his expression clear. "Then what—"

"I said I'm going to have a baby." She stared at the tent her knees made of the bedsheet. "And I am. I'm just not pregnant yet."

She could feel his gaze boring into her. "You're not making any sense."

"I'm making perfect sense." She still didn't look up. "I'm thirty. I want to be a mother, so I'm going to get pregnant. Soon."

He shifted on the mattress, and the heat of his body receded. His voice, when he spoke, was tight.

"And who, pray tell, is the father of this child going to be?"

"Don't worry," Tori said, fighting tears. "It won't be you."

He was still for a long moment.

"Then who?" he said at last. His voice was taut and scratchy.

She drew a breath. "I . . . I've decided to use a donor. A sperm donor."

His jaw dropped. "You're shitting me."

"No," she said, straightening her spine. She finally found the guts to look at him. "I'm not kidding. Lots of women do it! Chelsea—"

"Chelsea's a freaking lesbian! It's not like she had a choice."

"Straight women use donors, too! If the husband is sterile, or if there's no guy around . . ."

He just looked at her.

"I want a baby," she said limply. She could feel the tears gathering, and her eyelids worked furiously, trying to hold them back. "I want a family."

His expression softened then. He scooted closer and brushed a curl out of her eyes. "You don't need to have some stranger's child. You could adopt a baby."

Her hand, completely on its own, went to her stomach.

She was all too aware that he'd left himself out of that picture.

"I want my own baby," she whispered. "And I almost had her. Last year. I lost her."

"You lost a baby?"

"Yes." And suddenly she was angry, so angry she had trouble catching her breath. "I got pregnant. My boyfriend wanted me to get an abortion."

"Did you?"

A single tear escaped. "No! How could you think I would do that? I wanted her so badly."

He dragged a hand over his head. "Tori—"

"I miscarried. Right after Colin and I fought. He didn't want his own child! I told him I was having the baby and there was nothing he could do about it. I was so upset." She sniffed. "Turned out he didn't have to do anything about it. The next morning the contractions started. Ironic, huh?"

"Ah, honey." Nick's arm went around her, pulling her close. She let his heat seep into her. He was so solid and strong. He tipped up her chin, forcing her to look at him.

"That must've been hell."

"I didn't get pregnant on purpose." It was suddenly very important that Nick was clear on that point. "I knew Colin wasn't into kids. And I was okay with that, until I found out there was a baby growing inside me. . . ." She wiped her eyes with the back of her hand. "I thought Colin would be glad, too, once he got used to the idea."

"The guy was an asshole."

"I was with him for five years, Nick. I thought I knew him. . . ."

His arm tightened around her. Her voice trailed off, and they were both silent for a moment. When Nick finally spoke, his tone was distant.

"Thirty's not old. You've got plenty of time to have a baby."

"But I don't, not really." She told him what Dr. Janssen had said about her endometriosis, how it would lead to scarring and infertility. And how pregnancy could reverse the condition.

Nick's disbelief was clear. "There's got to be some other option."

"Surgery. Or massive amounts of hormones. I can't do either."

"Why not?"

"I was on the pill for a while. Colin wanted me to take it. But the hormones messed me up and I had to stop. The pills the gynecologist wants me to take are just souped-up versions of the ones I couldn't handle."

"Then have the surgery."

"No." She pulled the blankets more tightly around her. "I hate hospitals. My mother was in and out of them all the time when I was young. She died in one. I can't even walk into a hospital without feeling like I'm going to faint. When I had the miscarriage and had to go to the emergency room . . ." She shuddered.

"But if you need surgery—"

"I don't. I just need to get pregnant. Soon. The longer I wait, the worse my chances will be." She met his gaze. "This means everything to me, Nick. I'm going to do it. Don't try to talk me out of it."

He swore softly. "Tori. A baby's a big commitment, and an even bigger time sucker. You just started a business. How the hell do you think you're going to run your shop and take care of an infant, too, with no family to help out?"

No family. She fought back tears. "I'll manage."

"It's a bad idea."

She broke his touch on her arm. "I didn't ask your opinion."

He regarded her in silence for a moment, then swung his legs over the side of the bed and stood. He rummaged around on the floor, looking for his clothes.

"You might not want to hear it," he said, "but I'll give you my opinion anyway. A baby is not a one-person job. It's exhausting enough for two parents. What if the kid has colic?

What about when he gets sick? Are you going to work all day and stay up all night, too?"

"I'll worry about that if it happens." She watched him pull on his pants. She wanted to get to her clothes, too. But she didn't want to come out from under the blanket.

He finished dressing. "The kid will get sick, Tori. All babies do."

She sighed. "I think you should go."

He didn't move. He just stood there, looking at her for the longest time, as if she were someone he'd never seen before.

"Won't it bother you," he said slowly, "to give birth to a stranger's child?"

"No," she said, after the slightest hesitation. "It won't. In fact, I have a donor all picked out."

His eyes widened. "You're really serious about this? I mean, you've been making arrangements and you haven't even told me?"

"I'm telling you now. I went to the same clinic Chelsea used. They gave me pages of information about the donors. I almost feel like I know the one I picked out." And then, because Nick was looking at her as if she were the biggest freak show on the planet, she added, "He's nothing like you."

He crossed his arms over his chest. "Oh. Really?"

"He's a marathon runner. He has black hair and green eyes, like me, so the baby'll look like me. He's a journalist, he likes old black-and-white movies, and he votes Democrat."

Nick's jaw worked. "Sounds like a real stand-up guy."

"And," she said, "he's gay."

Nick stared. "You're planning," he said slowly, "to have a gay man's child?"

She crossed her arms, mirroring his pose. "Unless you're volunteering to be his replacement."

Oh, God. As soon as she'd said it, she wished she hadn't.

Nick's expression went from disbelieving, to shocked, to truly and royally pissed. All in the span of a heartbeat.

"Don't." His voice was harsher than Tori had ever heard it. "Don't even think of putting that on me."

"It was just a joke," she said lamely. "I didn't mean it."

She didn't know if he even heard her. He stared at her another few seconds, then shook his head and ran his hand down his face.

"We've known each other less than a month, Tori. There is no way I'd let myself be cornered into fathering the child of a woman I barely know."

His words hurt. Badly. "I don't want to corner you. Forget it. Forget I said anything."

He found his shirt and pulled it on. "I'm damn well going to try."

He gave her a long, steady look before he walked out the door.

Chapter Twenty-two

Sometimes, you don't even realize how much you want something until your brother has it first.

"There you go," Jason said to Tori early the next morning. "I set you up with an Internet account, e-mail, and everything. Leigh can show you how to use the inventory software."

She gave her new computer a dubious look. It wasn't that she didn't like computers; it was just she'd never had the money to buy one. Colin had taken care of all the e-mail and other stuff while they'd worked for Weird Zone, so Tori had never bothered to learn more than the absolute basics. She could surf the Internet and use e-mail and a word processing program, but as soon as one of those nasty error windows popped up, she was lost. Just the thought of accounting and inventory software made her palms sweat.

Her anxiety must have been obvious, because Leigh laughed. "Don't worry, Jason and I will help out if you have a problem. You can't expect to run a business without a computer."

"I suppose not."

Jason sent her his all-American grin. Tori liked Leigh's boyfriend. The minute Leigh had asked him, he'd built Tori a dirt-cheap computer, and had come over to set it up.

"I'd like to stay and help out some more," he said now, "but I'm due on the beach in fifteen minutes." He gave Leigh a quick kiss and was gone.

He was a sweet boy, easygoing and personable, and he was so obviously in love with Leigh. Leigh had told Tori about

Nick's irrational dislike of Jason, and how she'd been banned from dating him after their car accident the night of Leigh's emergency midnight call to her father. Privately, Tori thought Nick was coming down on the kids too hard. They were really a perfect couple.

Unlike Tori and Nick. After that scene last night, she didn't expect him to call today, or maybe even ever again. She tried to ignore the ache in her chest where her heart should have been.

"I like Jason," she told Leigh.

"I'm glad," she said, but her smile was a thin line.

"What's wrong?"

Leigh avoided Tori's gaze. "What makes you think there's something's wrong?"

"Wild guess," Tori said dryly. "Is there?"

She hesitated a second, then nodded. "Yeah, there is."

"Want to tell me about it?"

Leigh half turned toward a collection of magnetic affirmations displayed on a metal tower. She lined up *I release my past*, *Power is in the present moment*, and *My perfect future awaits me*, then frowned at the arrangement and scattered it.

"I love Jason," she said finally.

"Is that a problem? From what I can tell, he feels the same about you."

"Yeah, he's told me that." A pause. "He . . . he wants to make love."

No surprise there. Tori had seen the hot looks Jason sent Leigh's way. "How do you feel about that?"

Leigh slid Tori a quick glance. "You're sleeping with my dad, aren't you?"

Tori nearly choked. "You don't really expect me to answer that, do you?"

"I guess not," Leigh said, sighing. "What I really want to know is, how do you know when it's right? Sex, I mean."

Could a woman ever know? "Well," Tori said. "I, um—"

"Because I've never done it before, you know?" Leigh's

words tumbled out, as if they'd been waiting a long time to be released. "Even though my best friend, Stacey, has, with her boyfriend, and she says it's no big deal. And Jason wants to do it so much—"

"What do you want?" Tori cut in.

Leigh shut her mouth and frowned, as if she hadn't really considered that angle of the problem. "I want it, too, I guess." She colored a little. "Especially when he kisses me. It's just that . . ." She trailed off.

"Just what?"

"Just that it's not Jason's first time, you know? He's always been popular. He could have any girl he wants."

Tori tried to piece it all together. "So . . . you think if you don't sleep with him, he'll find someone else who will?"

"No," Leigh said—a bit too quickly, Tori thought. "I don't think that. I mean, if that were the case, he'd already be gone, right?"

When Tori didn't immediately answer, she rushed on. "You know, I'm just about the only girl in the junior class who hasn't done it."

"I can't believe that," Tori said. "And anyway, even if it's true, that's hardly a reason to give away your virginity."

"Maybe not. But I feel like some kind of freak. Like some fifties throwback." Her color rose. "And you know what else is twisted? My dad doesn't even see how straight arrow I am. He thinks I'm a slut."

"Leigh, I really doubt your father—"

"Dad's on my case about my clothes all the time. And don't even get me started on the belly ring. You would've thought I'd walked naked onto the beach! He thinks Jason and I have already done it. Not that it's any of his business."

Tori was floundering at this point. Leigh's breathing was short and gasping, as if she were about to cry. What was Tori supposed to say? What did Leigh need to hear from her?

"Can I ask you something?" Leigh said.

"Of course," Tori replied cautiously.

"How old were you when you did it for the first time?"

Well.

That was certainly a topic Tori didn't care to discuss. But Leigh's eyes were getting watery. She looked so forlorn, so troubled, so . . . motherless.

Tori found herself answering. "Sixteen," she said slowly. "Younger than you are now. And I can tell you, Leigh, it was a big mistake."

Leigh sniffed. "What happened?"

Now it was Tori's turn to rearrange the affirmation magnets. "When my aunt got sick, I went to live with a foster family. I was thirteen. I knew they didn't really want me—I learned pretty quickly they were after the state money that came with me. I stirred up so much trouble, they eventually decided I wasn't worth it. I didn't give the next family a chance to reject me—I was nasty to them from day one. So by the time I turned sixteen, I was already on my fourth foster family. I was the new kid in school again. I wanted so much to belong."

She got a hollowed-out feeling, remembering. "I met this senior—a football player—at a party. He was very good-looking—all the girls liked him. He was funny, too. He stuck by me all night, made sure I always had a drink in my hand. The next thing I knew, we were in one of the upstairs bedrooms and I was giving him what he was begging for. I thought that if I did, it meant I was his girlfriend."

"But you weren't," Leigh guessed.

"No. The next Monday, he hardly grunted in my direction. What was worse, he told all his friends what we'd done, and every time one of them saw me in the hall, he'd whistle and make a crude remark. I wanted to die." She tried for a smile, and failed. "I made sure I had a new foster family and a new school before the next marking period."

"Oh, Tori." Leigh touched her arm. "I'm sorry. I shouldn't have asked."

"No, it's all right. I wouldn't have told you about it if I hadn't wanted to. And I'm not saying Jason doesn't love you or that you shouldn't make love with him. That's your own choice. I'm just telling you I wish I hadn't thrown my virginity away so young. I used to dream how perfect the first time would be, with pink satin sheets and champagne. And poetry. I wanted my first lover to recite poetry in my honor." Tori forced a laugh. "You know, I never did find one who did that, even later."

Leigh didn't answer. The corners of her mouth were turned down. Her brow was furrowed, her gaze turned inward.

Suddenly, it occurred to Tori there was something else Leigh might need guidance with. Something a girl definitely wouldn't discuss with her father or grandmother.

"There's one other thing I wish I'd had my first time," Tori said.

Leigh looked up. "What's that?"

"A condom. The football player didn't use one. I lived in sheer terror until my period came. I hope, if you and Jason decide to make love, that you carry protection."

"I don't have any. But I'm sure Jason will think of it."

"You shouldn't count on it. What if things heat up and neither of you is prepared? Promise me you'll pick up a box of condoms."

Leigh grimaced. "No way. I'd die before I'd go through a checkout line with condoms."

"In that case . . . wait here." Tori left the store and went to find the box of condoms Nick had left in her bedroom.

She had a feeling she wouldn't be needing them anytime soon.

She pressed three foil squares into Leigh's palm.

"Take them," she said. "A girl can't be too prepared."

For the rest of the day, Leigh kept a close eye on the condoms.

Tori saw her check them between ringing up sales. Leigh bagged a tie-dyed T-shirt, looked in her purse, sold a book about fairies, looked in her purse, wrapped up a figurine, looked in her purse. . . .

Had Tori done the right thing, giving them to her?

She was about to say something when Leigh's cell phone rang.

"Hello?" Her brow creased. "Nonna? Where are you? *How* much? You're kidding me. . . . No, I won't call him. Look, don't do anything. Stay put. I'll be there as soon as I can."

She cut the connection and closed her eyes. "Shit."

"A problem with your great-grandmother?"

Leigh opened her eyes and looked at Tori. "Yeah. Could I borrow some cash from the register? Just for today?"

"Of course," Tori said, "but what's wrong?"

"Nonna's about to get arrested."

"You're kidding."

"I wish I were. You know how she took that chakra bracelet the other day?"

"Yes, but—"

"Well, it's this thing she does. It's like she can't help it. A compulsion or sickness or something. Usually she just steals from this old guy that's known the family forever, and my dad stops in at his store once a month and pays him off. But yesterday she 'picked up' your bracelet. And now she's snatched a man's dress shirt from a fancy boutique at the Trump Taj Mahal."

"Oh, no! And she got caught?"

"Yeah. To make matters worse, from what she just told me on the phone, it's not the first time she stole something at that shop, either. She took a necktie last week, and the manager has her on video. If she doesn't cough up cash for the tie in half an hour, he's calling the cops."

"You have to call your father."

"No," Leigh said. "No way. Nonna made me promise not to. He's been on her case about this."

"What about Rita? Or one of your uncles?"

"Nonna tried Johnny and Alex first, but neither of them is picking up. Mimi took Sophie to the mall—I doubt if she could make it over to Atlantic City in time. I'm the only one close enough, but I don't have that kind of money in my purse." She slapped the counter. "And I don't have a car, either. Could I borrow yours? Along with the cash?"

"I'll drive you," Tori said immediately, reaching under the counter for her purse.

"But what about the shop?"

"I'll put up the 'Closed' sign." She hit the release on the cash drawer. "How much do we need?"

"Two hundred and twenty dollars."

Tori's jaw nearly hit the floor. "For one tie?"

Leigh shrugged. "It's a designer store."

Twenty minutes later, Tori left a perplexed valet parking attendant frowning at her beat-up Toyota while she and Leigh sprinted into the casino lobby.

"Second floor," Leigh said, angling for the escalators.

They found Nonna reciting a recipe for ricotta cheesecake to a pencil-thin salesgirl while a paunchy store manager silently fumed. The man grunted as Tori counted out the bills for the necktie. She threw in an extra twenty, for good measure.

"Nonna, are you nuts?" Leigh raged as they left the boutique. "What ever possessed you to steal from a casino?"

"They got nice stuff there," Nonna said.

"Well, don't do it again. Please. Dad'll have a stroke." Leigh turned to Tori. "I'll get him to write you a check for the money we borrowed."

Tori thought of Johnny and his insistence that Nick would never send her a bill. And then she thought of Nick, and how angry he'd been when he'd left the day before. Their relationship was on shaky ground, and she didn't like the money she owed him hanging over her head.

"Don't bother," she told Leigh. "I owe your dad a lot of money. You can tell him that was the first payment."

"You'll never guess what," Johnny told Tori that evening.

Tori raised her brows. Nick's brother had come knocking on her door about an hour after closing time. Now he was lounging against her sales counter, eating a candy bar.

"All right," she said. "I'll bite. What?"

"I got my mother a gig at the nightclub where I work."

"Rita's a comedienne?"

He chuckled. "God forbid. No, it's a singing gig. Ma's got a sweet voice, but all she ever sang were church hymns. I hooked her up with a voice instructor I know, and bang! She's going pro." He took a bite of chocolate. "She's always wanted to, you know."

"That's wonderful! I'd love to hear her."

He chuckled. "She's kept it a secret from everyone. No one in the family knows but me. And now you."

Tori refrained from pointing out that she wasn't exactly part of the family.

"Ma's debut's next week," Johnny said. "On the Fourth of July. Get Nick to take you." He laughed. "That is, if my big brother can take the pole out of his ass. He was pretty pissed when Ma announced she was doing a show at my club."

"Really?" Tori's gaze drifted to the phone.

Johnny didn't miss it. "Expecting Nick to call?"

Tori sighed and looked back at him. "If you must know, not really."

"Trouble in paradise?"

A sudden sharpening of his tone made Tori look back at him. He was still lounging on the counter, but suddenly he didn't seem so casual.

"We had a . . . difference of opinion," she admitted.

"Let me guess," he said. "Nick's being a wet blanket about something."

She rubbed her arms. "I wouldn't exactly call it that. But he is taking a conservative view."

Johnny saluted her with his candy bar. "That's my big brother." He bit off another hunk.

Tori frowned at him. "Is that your dinner?"

"Probably. Want some?"

"No."

He finished off the bar and shot the wrapper, basketball-style, into the trash can. "So, if things are in the pits with you and Nick, what're you doing tonight?"

Tori shifted her weight. "I don't have anything planned."

"Then hang out with me. I have a gig at eleven, but we've got plenty of time to have a real dinner and maybe play a couple hands of blackjack before I have to be at the club. I've got some friends coming to the show tonight. You can sit with them, front and center."

He gave her an expectant grin, waiting for her answer. She tapped her lips with her forefinger, pretending to think it over.

"I don't know," she said. "Are you any good?"

He shot her a look. "Babe, I'm the best."

"Damn, you're lucky," Johnny said two hours later.

Tori counted her winnings before answering. "Seven hundred and sixty! This is great," she said, beaming.

"Were you counting cards?"

"Who, me? I wouldn't know where to start. I just listened to my inner voice."

"Well, do that a few more times, and the casino'll put your inner voice on their blacklist. They don't let psychics in, you know."

She blinked at him. "You think I'm psychic?"

"Sure," he said, nodding at the wad of cash. "Why not?"

"Because Nick and Alex are so logical, and Leigh is, too. I thought . . ."

"That I'm like all the other fish in my gene pool?" Johnny laughed, but the note was strained. "People think that all the time. When you're the last brother in a streak of four, you're like the invisible man."

"I never thought of it like that before."

"I guess you wouldn't," he said. "Seeing how you're an only child."

She looked at him then. Really looked. Johnny's constant joking made it hard to take him seriously. But his eyes weren't laughing now. Looking into them, she caught a glimpse of something that reminded her of Nick. And she realized that under Johnny's mask of joviality, he was just as driven, and just as stubborn, as his oldest brother.

"You're tired of it," she said. "Tired of not being seen."

"It gets old," he admitted. "That's why this *Franklinville Hospital* thing . . ." He trailed off.

"You really want that role, don't you?"

"More than anything."

"I have something that could help, maybe," she said. "I have a spell I could cast."

A smile tugged at his lips, but it wasn't a mocking one. "You're a witch, too?"

"No. But I met a few real witches while I was working for Weird Zone. One was an old Cajun woman. She gave me a bundle of candle magic spells. I have a couple left, and I think there's one that will work for you."

He looked intrigued. "What do I have to do?"

"I'll show you," Tori said. "After your gig."

It was past two by the time they got back to Tori's. Tori's sides still ached from all the laughing she'd done while Johnny was onstage. He had real talent. He was as relaxed telling jokes to strangers as he was goofing around with his family—his family minus Nick, anyway. He'd gotten more applause than the other three acts combined.

He watched with hooded eyes as Tori set the box containing the spell kits on the sales counter. "Got any love spells?"

She looked up at him. "Yes, actually."

"So why don't you cast it on Nick?"

She looked away. "Bad karma. The witch I got them from made me promise never to cast a love spell for a specific person. And to never, ever cast one for myself."

"So in other words, a spell to attract someone else's faceless dream man might be okay, but one that'll slam sense into my brother's thick head is a no-no?"

"Something like that," she said as she undid the tie on a bag. "Here's your spell. Blue is for good luck."

She slid the contents of the kit onto the counter. This time there was just one item packed with the candle—a scallop shell. She scanned the instructions. "It says to cast the spell near a large body of water, preferably an ocean."

"Well, isn't that lucky? We've got one of those right outside." Johnny tugged her hand, threading his fingers through hers. "Let's go."

The contact was unexpected, and more intimate than it should have been. Tori went still.

"Wait," she said as he pulled her toward the door. "It also says you have to put something that symbolizes your wish into the shell before the spell is cast."

He thought for a moment. "Do you have a newspaper?"

"Yes, but it's a couple days old."

"Doesn't matter."

She found a copy of the *Press* in the kitchen. Johnny turned to the page with the television schedule and ripped out the entry for *Franklinville Hospital*.

"'Will Dr. Marshall survive?'" Tori read over his shoulder.

Johnny let out a breath. "God, I hope not. The good doctor is a sanctimonious asshole. And the guy who plays him is a rotten actor. How he got the part, I'll never know."

"His face?" Tori suggested. "His body?"

"Then you've seen *FH*," Johnny said with a rueful laugh.

"Hasn't everybody? Dr. Grant Marshall is Hot with a capital H."

"Shit, you, too?" He tossed the newspaper to the floor. "Damn it, who am I fooling? I'll never get the part of Dr. Marshall's replacement. I'm too skinny, and not nearly good-looking enough. Who the hell cares if I can act?"

"Oh, come on. You're not *that* hard on the eyes. And I don't think anyone could ignore your talent. You were fantastic tonight."

"I love you, too, babe." His tone was light, but the teasing spark had faltered. "You know, Nick thinks I should quit the auditions and concentrate on my 'real' job."

Tori didn't doubt that for a minute.

Johnny put his palms on the kitchen table and leaned toward her, his expression more intense than she'd ever seen it. When he spoke, his voice actually vibrated. "Nick doesn't understand. He never did. He thinks the stand-up gig and the auditions are a distraction. But I hate the construction business. The only reason I can work for Santangelo Construction during the day is *because* of the comedy and the acting. If I didn't have that, I'd wind up in a padded cell."

"Then why work for Nick at all?"

"Because of Ma. She wanted me there. She says Nick needs family to watch his back. But you know what? It's not true. Nick doesn't need anybody. Nothing gets past him. He's a friggin' machine."

Tori opened her mouth, but didn't get a chance to reply. Johnny's color was rising. He straightened and pressed a fist to his palm, cracking his knuckles.

"I'd be lying if I said that's the only reason, though. I went to work for Nick because I've always wanted to make him proud of me. You don't know what it was like after our father died so suddenly. Ma was a mess. Dad left a lot of debts. Our house was newly built, and mortgaged to the hilt. Santangelo Construction was leveraged past its worth. But Ma couldn't handle anything more emotionally taxing than getting up in the morning and going through the motions of living. We were in real danger of losing everything; did you know that?"

"No."

He expelled a sharp breath. "I don't know how Nick held it all together. He was only two years out of high school, but he refused to declare bankruptcy. He took over Ma's finances and worked like a dog to keep the creditors at bay and straighten things out at Santangelo Construction. And in the middle of it all, Cindy up and left him. Alex did his part by getting a scholarship to the police academy, and Zach enlisted in the navy straight out of high school so we'd have one less mouth to feed. I was only nine when Dad died—

what the hell could I do? Leigh was sick and crying all the time, so I told her jokes." He made a sound in his throat. "Somehow, Nick pulled all of us through. And he was only twenty, and a single father, with a daughter who was in the hospital with asthma attacks about once every month. He grew up fast."

Tori was stunned. "My God. I didn't realize."

"By the time I was eighteen, somehow Nick had scrounged up enough money to send me to a state college. Ironic thing was, I didn't want to go. But Nick and Ma insisted, so I went. I can't tell you how pissed Nick was when I dropped out and moved to Hollywood."

"I'll bet he wasn't pleased," Tori agreed. But she didn't think Johnny heard her.

"I thought after all the school productions I'd starred in, it would be a snap to get an acting job. God, you wouldn't believe what an idiot I was." He picked up the newspaper he'd flung on the floor and tossed it back on the table. "It wasn't easy coming home with my tail between my legs after I'd run out of money."

"I can imagine it wasn't."

Johnny's head came up suddenly, as if he'd just remembered Tori was there. He gave her a wry grin. "I'm sorry; I didn't mean to bore you senseless with my emotional baggage. Your homecoming had to be rougher. At least I didn't come home for a funeral."

"It wasn't easy," Tori said. "I miss Aunt Millie. She was my only family, and I enjoyed my visits with her in the nursing home. She never made me feel guilty that I wasn't around more. I thought she'd always be here for me."

He touched her cheek with his fingertip. "I'm sorry."

They stood there for several heartbeats, gazes locked. Then Johnny seemed to remember himself. A sheepish look flitted through his eyes and his hand dropped.

"Hey," Tori said, her voice too bright. She picked up the candle and the forgotten scallop shell, and located her matches. "Where's that *Franklinville Hospital* TV listing?"

Johnny opened his fist. "Right here."

"Put it in the shell."

They walked to the beach with a good two feet of space between them. The stretch of shore was quiet except for the crash of the surf.

She thought of Nick, working through his grief at his father's death while trying to save his home and provide for his mother and siblings, and deal with his wife's desertion and his daughter's health issues. No wonder he was so driven, so serious. So cautious.

They arrived at the ocean's edge. She set the candle into the wet sand and put the shell with its scrap of newspaper next to it. Johnny built up a curved wall to act as a wind block.

"Is the tide coming in or going out?" Tori asked.

Johnny examined the shoreline. "Coming in, I think."

"Good." Bending, she lit the blue candle, murmuring a prayer as the flame caught and burned. Johnny stood next to her. He was so close she could feel the rise and fall of his breath.

"Now what?" he asked.

"We wait for a wave to extinguish the candle and take your wish out to sea."

"That's all? Aren't you going to chant bad poetry? Or maybe get naked?"

"No."

"Damn."

Laughter bubbled into her throat. Just then a wave rushed them. The surf splashed their ankles, spraying high over the sand wall Johnny had built. The flame went out. As the water receded, the scallop shell went with it, disappearing in a swirl of white froth.

"That a good sign?" Johnny asked.

"The best," Tori told him.

Chapter Twenty-three

*Sometimes, it takes a family member
to point out the obvious.*

"Tori's having a baby," Nick told Alex over cheesesteaks at Atlantic City's White House Sub Shop. Too late, he realized he should've waited for his brother to set his coffee down. The cup cracked against the tabletop, hard, sloshing burning coffee over the side.

"Ouch! Shit," Alex said, shaking droplets off his hand.

"Sorry," Nick mumbled. He yanked a napkin out of the holder and shoved it in Alex's direction.

Alex eyed him as he mopped up the mess. "You wanna run that by me again?"

"Tori's planning on getting pregnant," Nick clarified. "She was expecting a year ago, with her ex, but she lost the baby and they split. Now she wants to get pregnant again."

"And you're okay with that? I thought you didn't want any more kids."

"Apparently, I'm not going to have anything to do with it. She's decided to use an anonymous sperm donor."

Alex stared at him for a beat, openmouthed. Then, "And you're going to let her?"

Nick exhaled. "What right do I have to stop her?"

"Well, for starters, you're seeing each other. That should count for something."

Nick picked up his Coke, even though he'd already finished the bottle. "Sure, we're seeing each other. Or rather, having sex."

He grimaced. "Okay, so it's great sex—mind-blowing sex, if you have to know. But it's not like we've been talking commitment or anything." He set the bottle back down and started fiddling with the saltshaker. "Damn it, Alex, I like Tori. I like her a lot. But a baby? Now? Hell. I'm not ready to think about getting married again."

"Last I checked, marriage wasn't a requirement for fatherhood," Alex said dryly. He plucked a fresh napkin from the holder, took his pen from his breast pocket, and started doodling.

"So . . . what, you think I should play stud for Tori? Knock her up and leave her to have my kid as a single mother?"

Alex looked up. "Did I say that?"

"Damn it, Alex, no child of mine is gonna be raised anywhere but under my roof. How the hell could Tori ask that of me?"

Alex drew another series of lines on his napkin. "*Did* she ask? Before she settled on the donor plan?"

"Not in so many words, no. But she hinted. I got pissed and walked out."

Alex studied him. "You serious about her?"

"I don't know," Nick said honestly. "I've only known her a few weeks, but she's the first woman in a long time that . . . Hell. Maybe there's something there, if we give it time. Six months, a year . . ."

"Tell her that, then. Ask her to put off the pregnancy."

"I tried to, but she's got reasons for wanting a baby soon." He explained Tori's health problem. "She won't take hormones, won't have surgery. She figures pregnancy's her cure."

Alex grimaced. "You know, if Tori does get pregnant, everyone will assume the baby's yours."

"Don't you think I know that? I'll look like the world's biggest asshole. And she'll be carrying another man's child." Nick slammed the table with his palm. "God*damn* it."

Alex pushed his drawing over to his brother. Nick picked it up. Alex had drawn Nick standing between a brick wall and a large boulder.

"What are you going to do?" Alex asked.

Nick crumpled the napkin in his fist. "Not much I can do, is there?"

Leigh rushed into the shop, late for work.

"Sorry," she told Tori, breathless. "I was with Jason."

Tori stopped refolding the tie-dyed T-shirts a pack of vacationing teenagers had left in a wrinkled heap the day before. "How are things going between you two?"

Leigh avoided her gaze. "About the same. Oh," she added, pulling an envelope from her pocket. "I almost forgot. Dad left this on the kitchen table this morning. It's got your name on it."

Tori took the envelope, her heart tripping at the sight of her name in Nick's bold handwriting. She'd been hoping he'd call, but maybe it had been easier to put his feelings in writing.

No. Apparently, he had nothing to say, because the single item inside the envelope was a bank check. It was drawn on his personal account, in the amount of two hundred and forty dollars. The exact amount Tori had paid the boutique manager for Nonna's stolen necktie.

Heat rose, flushing her cheeks. "Didn't you tell your father to deduct this from what I owe him on the shop?"

"Yeah. I did. He said you didn't owe him anything."

Little red starbursts appeared in Tori's vision. "Excuse me a minute."

She escaped to the kitchen and punched in Nick's cell number. One ring, two, three . . . after the fourth, it switched over to voice mail.

Tori made a sound of exasperation and dialed his office number.

"Nick's here," Doris told her. "But he's in an important meeting right now. I'm holding all calls."

"Do you know when he'll be free?"

"I'm not sure, Tori."

Tori hesitated, then forged on. "Well, then, maybe you

could help me. I've misplaced the invoice Nick gave me for the work on my shop. Could you make up another one?"

"Oh, it would be no problem, dear, but I don't know anything about your job. Nick told me not to open an account for you. He said he'd handle it."

Tori hung up, fuming. Johnny was right. Nick seemed determined not to take money from her. In exchange for what they'd done in bed? The thought made her ill.

Maybe that was why he didn't have a problem walking out her door without a word.

"I'm going out," she announced to Leigh as she reentered the shop. With tight, angry motions, she gathered her purse and car keys from under the counter.

"Tori! Wait a minute."

She paused with her hand on the doorknob and turned. "What?"

Leigh was waving Nick's check at her. "You forgot this."

She drove all the way to Atlantic City before she realized she had no idea where Nick's office was.

It took her twenty minutes to locate a pay phone. *God.* Was she the single cell-phone-less person in America? She finally hit pay dirt at a grimy gas station, where—amazingly—the Yellow Pages were still attached to the graffitied shelf below the telephone.

A few minutes later, she pulled into the parking lot of a brick office building in an older section of town. As luck would have it, Nick was just coming out the front door, briefcase in hand.

His dark eyes widened as she got out of the car. "Tori. What are you doing here?"

"This." She marched up to him, ripped his check in half, and threw both pieces at his head.

He watched the paper flutter to the pavement. "What's going on?"

"How dare you send me a check for Nonna's tie!"

He dragged a hand through his hair. "What, is it a crime for a person to pay his bills?"

"What about my bill, Nick?" Her voice rose shrilly. "When are you going to send that? Or do you already consider yourself paid?"

He stared. "I don't know what the hell you're talking about."

"I am *not* paying for the renovations to my house with sex, Nick."

He couldn't have looked more stunned if Tori had slapped him. "You think I did all that work for sex? Oh, for chrissakes. You should talk. You're the one paying for stud service."

She was momentarily rendered speechless. Then, "You are such a jerk! I can't believe you just said that."

His expression was unreadable, but she saw his eyes flick toward her stomach. "So, have you gone and done it yet? Are you pregnant with some stranger's child?"

She couldn't look at him.

"Well? Are you?"

"Is that why you haven't called these last few days?" Her stomach cramped, and she pressed her palm there, willing it to relax. "You don't want me to have your child, but you don't want me to have anyone else's baby, either? That's hardly fair, Nick."

He exhaled, rubbing a hand over his face. "Tori, you're killing me with this, jumping into this baby thing half blind. If you'd just stop to think it over logically . . ."

A sudden, quiet stillness settled over her. Colin had said those exact same words. *If you'd just stop and think logically, Tori, you'd realize an abortion is the best thing for both of us. . . .*

It was as if all the oxygen had been sucked out of the air. Tori struggled to find her voice. "It's none of your business if I'm pregnant or not." Her hands shook as she fumbled in her purse for her checkbook.

"What do I owe you, Nick? Tell me, and I'll write you a check. Then everything will be even between us."

He stared at her. "Okay. Fine. You want to even things up? The going rate for all the work I did is ten thousand dollars."

Tori gaped at him. "I don't have that kind of money!"

He laughed, but it wasn't a pleasant sound. "Don't you think I know that? Why do you think I haven't sent a bill?"

"I can give you a thousand," she said, scribbling. "I'll pay the rest as soon as I can."

Nick sighed. "Look, Tori, I don't want your money."

"I want you to take it." She shoved the check at him. "Please."

He looked at the check, then at Tori. "You'll need it for the baby," he said quietly.

"Please, Nick. I don't want this debt hanging over me."

He stared at her, and she at him, for what seemed like forever. Until she became aware of a figure moving between the parked cars on her right.

Nick saw it, too. "Oh, Christ," he muttered. "Just what I need."

Johnny strolled up to them, fists sunk deep in the pockets of his baggy jeans. "I think you'd better stop harassing the lady, big brother."

"Stay out of this, Johnny. It's none of your business."

"Like hell it isn't." He planted himself at Tori's side, his easy movement doing little to mask the tension in his body. "You think I'm gonna stand back and let you bully Tori? Forget it."

"Bully her? How? By cutting her a break? Jesus."

Nick snatched the check out of Tori's hand and crumpled it in his fist. "Fine. You've paid me. Are you happy now?"

No. She was miserable.

She ran to her car, leaving Nick and Johnny standing together on the asphalt.

"Well, now, that was slick," Johnny said, as Tori's Toyota peeled out of the parking lot. "I shoulda been taking notes."

Nick felt like punching something, and Johnny was standing too close for comfort. "Just shut up, okay? I'm not in the mood for your jokes."

"You never are."

"You got that right."

Johnny propped his hip against a car. "So. You got Tori pregnant?"

"No."

"Oh, come on, Nick. I heard you telling her to save her money for the baby. It's déjà vu all over again for you, isn't it?"

Nick swore. "No, it's not. It's not my baby Tori wants."

The smirk abruptly vanished from Johnny's face. He pushed off from the car. "Then whose?"

"She wants to get artificially inseminated by an anonymous donor."

"No shit?" Abruptly, Johnny's smile returned. "Why? Your little guys not swimming straight?"

"Damn it, Johnny, it's not a joke. Tori's decided she wants a baby in nine months. I'm not in the position to give her one on that timetable."

"No? Well, then, maybe I'll volunteer to help her out. Sounds like a job with benefits."

Nick grabbed a fistful of Johnny's shirt. "Don't even think about it."

Johnny regarded him steadily, his blue eyes unblinking, just inches from Nick's own. He didn't struggle, didn't even glance down at Nick's fist.

"You know, this might not be the best time to mention it, big brother, but you seem a little on edge."

Nick drew a breath and unclenched his fist, releasing him. "I'd be a lot calmer if I wasn't doing your job on top of my own."

"What? I turned in the Carter bid. And finalized the sub-contracts for Lighthouse Harbor."

"Doris told me you want more time off."

"I've been called back to the *Franklinville Hospital* set. Is that a problem?"

"Hell, yes, it's a problem. You're flat out of personal days."

"I'll make up the time in the evening."

"You'll work during business hours, or not at all. Take off for New York, and you're out of a job."

For once, Johnny looked nonplussed. He rubbed the back of his neck. "Shit, Nick. Are you *firing* me?"

"I'm laying down the law. Something I should've done a long time ago."

"This is about Tori, not you and me."

"Tori has nothing to do with this. This has been coming for a long time, Johnny. Go to that audition and you're through with Santangelo Construction."

Real hurt flared in Johnny's eyes. For a split second he looked very young, and completely lost, like he had in those months after their father's sudden heart attack. *Hell*. At least Nick had been an adult when he'd lost his father. Johnny had been nine.

He hesitated. What the hell was he doing, kicking his little brother out of their father's business? He opened his mouth to take it all back, but before he could, Johnny, true to form, flipped off one of his smart-ass remarks.

"That's fly, dawg. I've been ready to cut outta here for a while now."

"Everything's a joke to you, isn't it?" Nick demanded. "When the hell are you going to grow up?"

Johnny's hands had curled into fists. "Grow up? And just what does that mean to you, Nick? I do every damn thing you ask around here. I've jumped through every one of your F-ing hoops. I may not do it nine-to-five, but the work gets done. What else do you want? Blood?"

"No. Just competence. You screwed up another change order on Bayview. It's gonna cost me."

"So sue me. You never made a mistake?"

"I've made plenty," Nick said tersely. "But unlike you, I don't expect everyone to clean up after me. You . . . you've had everything handed to you. You get a free ride to college and what do you do? Drop out. Do you know what I would have given to be in your place?"

A vein in Johnny's temple jumped. "Believe me, I know. It was the only damn thing that kept me there for two years. I wanted to make you proud. Now I see all I made you was jealous."

"Jealous?" Nick couldn't believe it. "Of you?"

"Yeah. Maybe you're still jealous. Maybe you can't stand that I have the balls to go after what I want."

"Oh, give me a—"

"Take a good look at where you are, Nick." He jerked his head at the corner of the parking lot, where trash overflowed from a Dumpster. "You used to be an artist. You dreamed of designing buildings. Skyscrapers. Museums. But you settled for this."

Nick stared at him. "If I'm such a loser, then why do you work for me?"

"Who the hell knows? Because Ma asked me to? Because you're my brother? Because I once worshiped the ground you walked on? All I ever wanted was for you to stop working long enough to see me. Who I really was." He scuffed the ground with the toe of his running shoe. "But I'm not missing this audition, Nick. Not even for you. I can't. It's my best shot to get what I've been working for all this time."

Slowly, Nick picked up his briefcase. "So you expect me to give you more time off?"

"I don't expect you to give me shit, Nick. And I'll even save you the trouble of firing me."

Johnny shoved his hands in his pockets. "I quit."

Chapter Twenty-four

Motherhood is a giant step into the great unknown.
Look before you leap.

"I'm not surprised Nick wouldn't support you when you told him about the donor," Mags said, jiggling Lily on her shoulder. "You want to have another man's baby. It's an affront to his male ego."

"It's all that testosterone," Chelsea said as she walked down the vitamin aisle at Healthy Eats, clipboard in hand, taking inventory. "It makes men territorial."

"I wasn't expecting him to be so angry," Tori said. She rubbed her bare arms. "He wants me to wait, have the surgery instead, but he says he's not interested in marriage and he definitely doesn't want any more kids. So where does that leave me?"

"He's just mad you're not shaping your life to his needs," Mags said. "But he doesn't want to shape his to yours, either."

Mags was right about that. "I've been there with Colin," Tori said. "I swore when we split that I would never again rearrange my life goals for a man." She let out a long breath. "It's just that I . . . have feelings for Nick, you know?"

Chelsea sent her a troubled look. "Maybe you should consider putting the pregnancy idea off for a bit. Until summer's over. After all, you're just getting your shop started."

"But it might take a couple months to get pregnant," Tori said. "And if I wait too long, it might not happen at all."

The three of them fell silent.

Finally, Chelsea gave Tori's arm a squeeze. "You have to go with your heart. Just remember, we're here for you, whatever you decide."

She decided to do it.

The next day, she paid the fee to Choices. In return, she received an instruction booklet, an ovulation predictor kit, an insemination syringe and—her heart beat faster each time she looked at it—a home pregnancy test kit.

A couple days later, the ovulation kit said all systems were go.

Another call to Choices, and by that night she had everything she needed to do the deed. A vial of sperm. A syringe. An instruction pamphlet. She laid the first two on the bed and read the third.

Looked at the syringe. Looked at the vial.

Felt vaguely panicked.

Read the instruction booklet again.

Relax, it advised.

Easier said than done.

She opened the cabinet where she'd stashed the last two candle magic spell kits. She'd been saving one of them for this very moment. Green was the color of fertility. The green bag held a candle of the same color, a circle of green felt, a long, sharp needle, and instructions that included a freshly peeled hard-boiled egg.

She didn't happen to have any eggs, because of the vegan thing, so she went up to the corner convenience store and bought a half dozen. Then she waited by the boiling pot, her anxiety rising with the bubbles. Even after the water had cooled and she'd lit the candle, even after she'd wrapped the egg in the green felt and secured it with the needle, even after she'd snuffed the candle and buried the egg in her tiny backyard, doubts whispered down her spine.

She returned to her bedroom and put on a CD featuring calm forest and waterfall sounds, hoping it would soothe her nerves. The CD player was the one Nick had bought her, after he'd tossed the beat-up one with the frayed electrical cord in the trash.

There was a stabbing sensation in her chest and stomach, as if Tori's heart were breaking into sharp slivers and sliding downward.

She sat abruptly on the edge of the bed, hugging herself, trying to block Nick from her mind. She tried to concentrate on the baby, the one she'd make without him. Would it be a girl? A boy? Would the child take after his anonymous father? Were there biological cousins he'd never know? Grandparents and aunts and uncles who would never cheer at any of his soccer games?

Would he ask about them? Miss them?

Would he end up, like Tori, longing for a real family?

You're jumping into this baby thing half blind, Nick had said. For the first time, Tori stopped to consider that maybe he was right. But not for the reasons he'd recited—that she didn't have enough time or money. Or that raising a child might cause heartache or sleepless nights. Those things didn't matter. She was ready and willing to brave them.

What she couldn't find her way around were the new images that had taken up residence in her imagination where her future baby resided.

The child was no longer a little girl who looked like Tori.

He was a little boy with Nick's eyes and Nick's smile.

She picked up the vial of sperm, wrapped it in a paper towel, and threw it in the trash.

She just couldn't do it.

Chapter Twenty-five

Brothers fight. Sometimes, they even draw blood.

"Johnny told me you cast a candle magic spell for him," Leigh told Tori Saturday afternoon during a rare lull in customer traffic. It was the Fourth of July, and they'd been doing a brisk business. "Do you think you could cast one for me, too?"

Tori studied her assistant. Leigh had been acting strangely the last few days—vacuuming the clean rug, dusting the dustless counters, and rearranging the merchandise with a single-mindedness that Tori could only call obsession.

She'd been talking a lot, too, in a nervous kind of way.

"I thought you don't believe in magic," Tori said.

Leigh got out a bottle of spray cleaner and started wiping down the spotless glass on the front of the sales counter. "Well, I didn't, at first. But Johnny told me about the spell you cast for him, and . . ."

Tori laughed. "And because of that you've changed your mind? Even though he hasn't even gone for his final audition yet?"

"Yes. No. I don't know. I'm just . . . well, I just thought maybe a love spell would help. Johnny said you had one."

"Let me guess. You want me to cast it on Jason."

"Yeah." Leigh abandoned the rag and sprayer on the counter. "I told him I'd meet him tonight. His family's out of town."

Tori regarded the girl seriously. "Ah. So that's why you're so jumpy."

"I'm kinda nervous." She swallowed. "Kinda? Who am I kidding? I'm petrified. But if I knew he really loved me, I think it would help me relax."

Tori touched her shoulder. "Jason loves you, Leigh. I can tell every time he looks at you."

She didn't seem convinced. "A spell might help."

"Love spells are tricky," Tori said. "It's bad karma to cast them on a specific person."

The girl's face fell. "Oh."

"But . . . I could cast a general love spell. If Jason's already in love with you—and I know he is—he'll feel it."

"Oh, Tori, would you?"

She retrieved the last of the Cajun witch's spell kits. Inside the red bag she found a small vial of rose oil and a very thick, blunt-tipped red candle.

Leigh picked up the candle, her expression a study in thoughtfulness. Making a circle with her thumb and forefinger, she tested its thickness.

Her fingertips didn't touch.

Tori blinked. With a little imagination, that candle looked like . . .

Leigh giggled. "Right. What do I do now?"

Tori refocused on the instructions. "Pour some of the oil on it."

Leigh opened the vial and drizzled some on. "Now what?"

" 'Rub it in,' " Tori read.

Leigh ran her fingers up and down the candle, lightly at first. Then, her grin widening, she anchored the base with one hand and started stroking up and down.

"Oh, my God." Tori smothered a snort of laughter.

Leigh shot her a look. "I wonder if Jason's this well endowed?"

Tori's shoulders started to shake. "You're not supposed to be thinking of Jason, remember?"

"Oh, right. I forgot." Leigh stroked faster. "How long do I have to keep this up, do you think?"

Tori consulted the instructions. "Until—"

She broke off as the candle slipped out of Leigh's fingers, skidded across the counter, and bounced on the floor.

"Um, until that happens, I guess."

Leigh burst out laughing. Tori joined her, and for a while neither of them could stop. Every time Tori thought she'd gained some control, she'd exchange glances with Leigh and they'd both start up all over again.

"Anything else?" Leigh finally managed to gasp.

Tori's sides hurt. "You have to light it. To release its, um, *energy*."

They dissolved into laughter again.

Finally, Tori bent to pick up the candle. Leigh was still giggling as she prepared to light the match.

"Here goes."

The flame sizzled, then caught and held. A scant moment later, the door to the shop opened. Tori's head snapped around. Nick's grandmother stood on the threshold.

"Nonna!" Leigh jumped up. "What're you doing here?"

Nonna peered suspiciously at the burning candle. "I came to invite Tori to our Fourth of July barbecue tonight."

"Sure," Leigh said, quickly blowing out the flame. "She'd love to come."

The barbecue at the Santangelos' was a boisterous affair, awash with chatter about Rita's upcoming singing debut at midnight that night at Johnny's club. Nonna frowned, but everyone else wished Rita luck.

Everyone except for Nick, that was, since his place at the table was empty.

"He's got a business dinner," Johnny told Tori. He manned the grill, wearing a chef's apron emblazoned with the words, STAND BACK—I'M SO HOT I'M ON FIRE!

"On the Fourth of July?" Tori asked, incredulous.

Johnny shrugged. "The man doesn't know the meaning of the word 'holiday.' The client's Canadian, in town on a working vacation, so what does he care about Independence Day? When he called last week, Nick jumped."

When the dinner was ready—hamburgers and hot dogs for the Santangelos, a veggie burger for Tori—Sophie took the seat between Tori and Leigh. "I wanna go to Atlantic City, too, Daddy," she told her father. "To see the fireworks. Uncle Johnny said he'd take me."

"So I did," Johnny said. He looked from Alex to Tori and Leigh. "What about it? Everyone game?"

"Sure thing," Alex said. Leigh shot Tori a nervous look. "Just as long as I'm back here by eleven."

An hour later Tori stood on Atlantic City's Steel Pier, surrounded by squealing children and laughter.

"Did you see?" Sophie tugged her arm. "Did you see me on the spaceship ride?"

Tori smiled down at her. "I saw."

"The Ferris wheel's next," Johnny announced, materializing with two paper cones topped with fluffy balls of cotton candy. "Then I'll win some prizes for the ladies."

He wasn't joking. Within the hour, Sophie was hugging a five-foot purple alligator, Leigh was the proud owner of a glow-in-the-dark alien, and Tori had the fuzzy stem of a giant smiley-face flower in hand.

"Is there any game you can't win?" she asked Johnny, impressed.

"Nah, can't think of any."

Tori returned his cheeky grin. This was fun. Twilight and the fireworks were still an hour or so off. The Atlantic City Boardwalk was alive with tourists, either milling about on foot or riding in hand-pushed rolling chaises. On the pier, rides spun, kids laughed, and hot dogs and popcorn scented the air.

Families were everywhere. And wonder of wonders, Tori felt like she was actually part of one. Sophie clung to her hand while Alex walked a few steps behind, scanning the crowd. Johnny's jokes streamed past her ear. Leigh had hooked her arm through Tori's as if they were sisters.

Suddenly Sophie stopped and turned to her father. "Daddy?"

"Yes, honey?"

"I gotta go potty."

Alex groaned.

"I'll take her to the ladies' room," Leigh said with a laugh. She grabbed Sophie's hand. "We'll meet you guys back here."

"I'll go get some caramel corn in the meantime," Alex said. He loped off in the other direction, leaving Tori and Johnny alone.

Johnny watched them go. "They'll be a while. Want to walk up the Boardwalk a bit?"

"All right."

They left the amusement pier to stroll on the Boardwalk between the bright casinos and the dark sea. For a long while, Johnny remained uncharacteristically silent.

"Something wrong?" Tori asked.

He hesitated, then sighed. "I guess I'm not going to be able to keep it a secret from everyone for long. I quit my day job. Right after I stumbled on your fight with Nick."

"You quit Santangelo Construction?" Tori came to halt, forcing him to stop and turn back. "I certainly hope it wasn't because of me."

"No. Not really. It's been coming for a while. Nick and I just don't get along."

He was bleaker than Tori had ever seen him. "I'm sorry."

"Don't be. I hated that job. I probably never should have taken it in the first place." He studied her, his eyes grave. "Tori, I wanted to talk to you about something. Nick told me you're planning to have a baby."

"Johnny—"

"And I wanted to tell you I think that if that's what you want, then you should go for it. I've seen you with Sophie. You'd make a great mom."

Her belly twinged. But she wasn't sorry she'd chickened out at the last minute. It hadn't felt right to go ahead with the insemination. Not when she was so obsessed with Nick. But where were she and Nick now? Nowhere.

"Please," she said. "Could we talk about something else?"

He searched her face, and for a moment she thought he was going to pursue the subject. Then his expression morphed, and he was back to being Johnny the comic.

"Okay. Enough about you, then. Let's talk about me."

She chuckled. "All right. What about you?"

They started walking again. "The *Franklinville Hospital* screen test is coming up and I'm nervous as hell."

"I thought actors were supposed to be nervous. Doesn't it give you an edge or something?"

He darted a glance in her direction. "That's a crock." Then, "It's a love scene, you know."

"What is?"

"The screen test. It's a scene between a new character, a street-tough surgeon named Gavin Hunter, and Macey Lark, the reporter."

"Macey Lark? I've seen her on the show. She's gorgeous."

"And tough. She's investigating Hunter and threatening to go public with the skeletons in his closet. But she's hot for him, too, which is a problem."

"I'll bet."

He moved closer. "He wants her just as badly. In fact, Hunter can't seem to keep his hands off Macey. And she doesn't mind at all."

Tori snorted.

"The scene for the screen test is set at the hospital charity ball."

Without warning, Johnny swung around and caught Tori about the waist, twirling her in a circle. Tori grabbed his shoulders and shrieked. The smiley-faced flower tumbled out of her hand.

"Johnny! What are you doing?"

In lieu of an answer, he waltzed her across the Boardwalk, scattering the crowd. "Okay, so picture this. Dr. Hunter's at the ball. He sees Macey across the room, talking to one of the hospital's biggest benefactors. Hunter's afraid of what Macey might let drop to Mr. Moneybags, so he interrupts their potentially damning conversation and drags her onto the dance floor."

"How resourceful." Tori shrieked as Johnny dipped her.

He pulled her upright and grinned. "Hold on tight."

He twirled her dizzily past an older couple, who turned to stare as they flashed by.

"Dr. Hunter maneuvers Macey into a dark corner of the ballroom," Johnny said. "No dark corners here on the Boardwalk, so we'll have to improvise."

He danced them to the top of the steps leading down to the beach, upon which Johnny scooped Tori into his arms and ran down the stairs.

"You're nuts!" She clung to his neck.

"Funny, that's just what Macey tells Hunter. How did you know?"

A laugh bubbled up in her throat. "Put me down."

He waggled his brows. "My pleasure." Then he released her with excruciating slowness, sliding her down the length of his body until her feet touched the sand.

"Johnny . . ."

"Okay, Tori, work with me here. You're Macey; I'm Hunter. The scene goes like this: You accuse me of murder. I tell you to keep your nose out of things you don't understand. You threaten to splash my story all over the front page of the *Franklinville Gazette*. Ready?"

"What? You want me to act this out with you? I don't know what to say!"

"Doesn't matter. Just ad-lib. I'll fill in the rest."

"I can't—"

His expression morphed from playfulness to anger. "Macey, I'm warning you: Don't do this."

Tori blinked. In less time than it took a heart to pulse a single beat, Johnny Santangelo had vanished. In his place was a man who was grim and dangerous, with haunted blue eyes and tension radiating from his lean body.

Dr. Gavin Hunter, a man with a secret to protect.

"Go to the press," Hunter growled, "and you'll regret it."

"I . . ." Tori floundered for a response. "Um . . . I'll regret it more if I stay silent."

Johnny stepped closer, forcing her to tilt her head back to look up at him. "You think I killed Frank Dermott, don't you?"

"I've . . . I've seen the evidence."

"Evidence can be faked."

"Was it faked? I'm not so sure about that."

He scowled. "It's not what you think."

"But, Johnny—"

"Gavin," he corrected, breaking character to give her a quick grin.

"Oh. Right. Sorry." She drew a breath and started over. "But, Gavin, I saw the police report with my own eyes. I saw the evidence. It's an open-and-shut case, unless . . . unless you can give me something to go on. Something to make me believe in you."

A breeze fluttered past, blowing a curl into Macey's—or Tori's—face. Hunter—or was it Johnny?—tucked it behind her ear. His fingers lingered on her cheek. Traced a path to her lips.

"Macey." His voice was low and rough as he cradled her head in his hands. "Facts don't mean anything. You can have all the facts in the world, and still not see the truth. And the truth is this. . . ."

His gaze dropped to her lips.

And then he kissed her.

Nick pushed through the revolving door, glad to exchange the stale atmosphere of the air-conditioned casino for the blast of humid sea air that greeted him on the Boardwalk. His dinner meeting with his potential client had taken longer than he'd expected, and he'd had a hell of a time concentrating on the business at hand.

All he could think of these days was Tori.

The Boardwalk was packed—another hour or so and fireworks would burst over the Steel Pier. He threaded his way through the crowd, working his way toward the railing on the ocean side of the Boardwalk. When he reached it he stood for a moment, just staring over the beach at the darkening ocean.

What was Tori doing tonight? Was she spending the Fourth with her friends? Or sitting home, alone and lonely? More important, was she already pregnant? He counted back to the night he'd found her curled up in bed, her face drawn with pain. A little more than two weeks ago.

Was it already too late to stop her? Maybe not. Maybe he should head over to her place. Try to talk things out. Maybe if he laid all his cards on the table, as Alex had suggested, he could make her listen to reason. Maybe . . .

And then he saw her.

She wasn't home at all. Or with Chelsea and Mags. She was right there below him, on the beach, standing in the shadow of the access stair. She wasn't facing him, but he had no doubt it was her. She was wearing a hot-pink halter dress he'd seen before. A bright streak of color against the sand.

Then he recognized the man she was with.

Johnny. ·

Nick went still. Tori's conversation with his brother looked intense. Too intense. Johnny was leaning close. Too close. Nick stared as his brother framed Tori's face in his hands.

And then he kissed her.

Johnny's lips covered Tori's. His fingers sifted through her hair, coaxing her closer. Her feet slipped in the soft sand. She lost her balance and pitched against his chest.

Oh, my God.

What was happening here? Dr. Gavin Hunter kissing reporter Macey Lark? Or Johnny Santangelo kissing Tori Morgan?

Which did she want it to be?

She liked Johnny. A lot. She appreciated his good humor and honesty, and his ability to share freely what was in his heart. He was sensitive and artistic. Spontaneous. He liked late-night walks on the beach, was willing to believe in magic, and he could charm the salt out of the Atlantic.

He might've been Tori's perfect man, except for one tiny detail.

He wasn't Nick.

There. She'd finally admitted it. She was in love with Nick Santangelo. Hopelessly, ridiculously in love. She didn't want to be—she'd known from the first it would be a bad idea—but there it was.

She drew back gently, breaking the kiss. Johnny's arms relaxed, but he didn't release her completely. She caught a glimpse of vulnerability in his eyes before the mischievous glint returned.

"How'd I do? Think I'll get the part?"

"I'm sure of it," Tori said weakly. "They'd be crazy not to—"

"Goddamn it, get your hands off her."

She froze, heart pounding into her throat. She met Johnny's eyes.

"Nick," she whispered, not turning.

Johnny's expression hardened as his gaze shifted to a point behind her. His hands stayed exactly where they were, on Tori's bare shoulders.

"Yo, bro. 'Sup?"

Tori turned slowly. And there Nick was, not three strides away, glaring down at her. His frown was so intense his eyebrows were nearly a single dark slash over his angry eyes. She took in his navy blue business suit. She'd never seen him dressed so formally. His shirt was white, his necktie dark and unimaginative. Of course.

He looked wonderful.

Johnny still had one hand on her shoulder. Nick's arm shot out, colliding with Johnny's chest. "Get away from her. Now. She doesn't need to be mauled by the likes of you."

Johnny stood his ground. "What Tori and I do is none of your business."

"Like hell it isn't." Nick took a menacing step and caught a fistful of Johnny's Hawaiian shirt. His left arm drew back, fingers clenched.

Tori made a grab for his forearm. "Don't you dare hit him!"

"Damn it, Tori." Snarling, he shook her off. "This is between me and Johnny."

"No! He's your brother! I won't let you hurt him!"

"Hey, I'm not too proud to accept help from a girl. I've got a pretty face to protect." Johnny smirked, but his stance had widened, and his eyes were deadly serious. The muscles in his forearms flexed, his hands fisting. "Hold him for me, Tori, why don't you, while I beat some sense into him."

And then, without waiting for assistance, Johnny let loose a wicked right hook.

His fist connected with Nick's jaw. There was the sickening sound of knuckles smacking flesh.

"Umph . . ." Nick's head whipped to the left as the air vacated his lungs. He took a stumbling step back.

Tori stared, stunned beyond speech, her own breathing completely stalled.

Nick recovered quickly, regaining his balance in the soft sand. Johnny stood, chest heaving, hands fisted at his sides, eyes wary.

Slowly, Nick brought his hand to his lower lip and touched blood. He stared in disbelief at the crimson smudge on his fingers.

Then he seemed to snap. "You little shit . . ."

His arm went back. Tori snapped from her shocked daze. "No!" she screamed, springing forward. She leaped at Nick's arm and hung on. "Don't you dare hit him back!"

"Let him go, Tori. I'm ready for him." Johnny's fists flexed.

"Shut up," Tori told Johnny. "Just shut up. I can't believe this—the two of you brawling on the beach like teenagers. Cut it out now or . . . or . . . or I'll tell Rita! And Nonna, too!"

Nick swore. "Fine." He jerked his arm down so abruptly

that Tori, who was still holding on, lost her grip on his coat sleeve.

She stumbled, and Nick caught her.

She smelled alcohol on his breath. "You've been drinking."

"Not nearly enough for this kind of shit." His eyes bored into her as his arm tightened around her waist. "What the hell are you doing, Tori, kissing that lowlife?"

She tried to disentangle herself from his embrace, and failed. "I'll kiss who I want."

"Like hell you will."

Johnny snorted, arms crossed over his chest, regarding his brother with some disgust. "Did I stumble onto the set of 10,000 B.C.? Did I miss the part where Tori went up for sale? Back off, Nick. You don't own her."

"She's got better things to do than slum in public with you."

"Like what? Sit by the phone and wait for *you* to call?"

Nick's jaw worked. Tori had a clear view of the vein bulging at his right temple.

He let her go and took a step back. Tori stood, locked in place by his eyes. There were so many emotions there. She couldn't even begin to sort them out. But she did see fear, and a good measure of lust.

Something deep inside her heart clenched.

"Come on, Tori." Johnny grabbed her elbow. "We've gotta find the others before the fireworks start."

The fireworks had already started, as far as she was concerned.

"You go ahead." She rooted around in her purse and found a tissue. Going up on tiptoe, she blotted the blood from Nick's lip. "Nick'll drive me home . . . won't you?"

"Yeah," he said thickly. "I will."

Johnny blew out a long breath. Tori could see him moving at the edge of her vision. "Damn it, Tori. I hope you know what you're doing."

She didn't, she realized. She didn't have a clue.

She and Nick left the Boardwalk, fighting the fireworks crowd. Nick took her hand as he shouldered his way through the throng, not speaking. He retrieved his truck from the casino valet, tossed his suit coat and tie behind the seat, and pulled onto Pacific Avenue. All still in silence.

They were halfway home when he flexed his hand on the steering wheel and sighed. "I was way out of line back there."

She turned in her seat, facing him. "It wasn't a real kiss, you know."

His jaw locked. "Looked real enough to me."

"We were practicing a scene for Johnny's screen test."

"Jesus, Tori. Please don't tell me you really believe that."

She didn't answer.

"Johnny's no good for you. He's too young. Unstable. He's got a week-to-week lease and no money in the bank. He falls in love with a different woman every couple months."

"At least he talks to me. Unlike some people."

A few heartbeats passed during which the temperature in the truck seemed to dip fifteen degrees. Finally, Nick answered. "I'm sorry about that."

"Excuse me?" Tori put a hand to her ear. "What did you say?"

Nick shot her a look. "Nothing."

"Was that an apology? Because if it was, please repeat it. It's been so long since I've had the opportunity to faint dead away."

"Very funny," Nick muttered, his eyes fixed on the road.

She stared at his profile, her chest tight and aching. She hated him like this, so cold and distant. She wanted to see his eyes spark with laughter. She wanted his slow, sexy smile.

She stared out the passenger window, blinking hard. The heavy, sodden silence hung between them as they approached her street.

But to Tori's surprise, Nick didn't drive to her house. Instead, he made a hard left and drove to the beach. The truck lurched to a stop at the seawall.

Tori braced her arm on the dashboard. "This is a no-parking zone."

"Too bad."

Nick's hands still gripped the steering wheel. He stared straight ahead, though the road had come to an end.

"Did you do it yet?" he asked quietly.

She bit her lip. "Do what?"

The streetlight cast his face in harsh angles. "Don't jerk me around, Tori. You know what I'm talking about."

She swallowed. "No," she said. "I didn't do it."

Nick's grip relaxed, but only slightly. "Why not? Isn't it about the right time of the month?"

Tori shifted in her seat. *I didn't do it because I love you* didn't seem quite the thing to say.

"Yes, it's the right time of the month. But the more I thought about it, the more I thought it seemed too . . ."—she cast around for the right word—"impersonal," she finished lamely.

"So." His voice was deadly quiet. "You've decided Johnny is less, what . . . *impersonal?*"

She sat up straighter. "Johnny? What are you talking about?"

"Johnny has no idea what it means to be a father, you know. None at all. He certainly won't be the kind of father your child deserves." His hands flexed again on the steering wheel. He shot her a grim look. "Stay away from him, Tori. You'll only get hurt."

Her jaw had gone slack. "You thought . . . You think . . . You think I want to get pregnant with *Johnny?*"

"Don't you?"

"Of course not! We're just friends."

"Friends." He laughed harshly. "Friends who put their tongues down each other's throats. Either you're an idiot or you think I am."

"God," she spit out. "You really are a jerk sometimes."

"So you've said."

She made a sound of frustration. "Johnny and I are just friends. Why can't you believe that?"

He turned fully toward her then, one arm draped over the steering wheel, his dark gaze searching. Heated.

"I don't believe it because I can't imagine any guy being just friends with a woman like you. You and I could never be 'just friends,' Tori. Shit. When we're together, all I can think of is how long it will be before I can get inside you again."

Her body responded violently to the crude declaration. Her nipples tingled; her womb clenched. Her thighs grew moist. She braced her arm on the dashboard, trying desperately to drag in enough oxygen to inflate her lungs.

He reached with his right hand to stroke her cheek. Then he slid his fingers around her neck and into her hair. His touch was like a velvet flame. She wanted to get lost in it and burn up.

"Ah, Tori. You make me lose my mind."

"Is that so bad?" she whispered.

"Oh, yeah." His grip tightened in her hair, anchoring her head in his grasp. "It's bad. If you had the sense God gave a rock, you'd see it."

He tugged her close, until his lips hovered a bare half inch from hers. She smelled wine on his breath, mingling with the spice of his aftershave. "I'm not ready for this," he said. "For you. For us. I wanted to go slow. But you? You insist on a fast track to disaster."

"Nick, I—"

"You want to mix everything up. A baby first. Then marriage. Then love. You want everything ass-backward." He drew back, releasing her, a new, disturbing energy crackling around him. A spurt of panic rushed through her.

He got out of the truck and slammed the door. Rounded the hood. Wrenching the passenger door open, he closed his fingers around Tori's wrist. "Come on."

He yanked her down from the cab before she had a chance to reply. He slammed the door shut behind her and started walking.

"Nick, wait." His grip on her wrist was unrelenting. She

stumbled, trying to keep up with him. Up the seawall steps, then down, to the beach. Then out across the soft sand.

She lost one sandal. Desperately, she kicked off its mate. He didn't seem to notice.

"Damn it, Nick, stop! What do you think you're doing?"

He stopped abruptly and turned. He didn't release her wrist. She gasped, catching her breath.

Then she looked up at him.

And immediately wished she hadn't. She was only just beginning to realize how very angry he was.

"What am I doing?" He repeated her words slowly, his voice growing more intense with each syllable. "Why, I'm getting ready to have sex with you. Right here on the beach. That's what you wanted so badly before, isn't it?"

His grip burned hot on her wrist. "Well, yes, but—"

"You wanted a guy who doesn't care about the rules, right? One who doesn't give a shit about what's practical, what's safe. What's right."

Bending suddenly, he slid an arm behind her knees and picked her up. She cried out and flung her arms around his neck. He strode toward the ocean, his arms tightening with each step. His breath came harsh and hot on her cheek. He stopped just short of the water's edge. Her feet touched the sand.

With a groan, he anchored her head in his hands. "Tori . . ."

She had one brief second in which to read his intent before his mouth covered hers. His lips were demanding, almost brutal. He kissed her, robbing her of breath, of will, of any notion of resistance.

Her arms snaked around his neck and held on.

Just as she surrendered, he tore himself away. "Is this what you want, Tori? Is this who you want me to be?"

He was hard. She could feel him through his trousers and her sundress, hot and demanding against her belly. There was a desperation in his voice she'd never heard before. A vulnerable note that struck a chord deep inside her. Because she knew how painful it was when you weren't the person—the daughter, the lover—that someone else wanted. And she couldn't believe she'd done that to him.

"Nick . . . Nick, I—"

"No. Don't talk." He kissed her again, more gently this time, some of his control returning.

"You don't have to—"

"Shh." The hot wash of his breath bathed her temple. He smoothed his hands up her back. "Let me make love to you, Tori."

"Yes." She melted into him, her lower body rubbing against his arousal. His fingers were already unlacing her halter.

"Move your hips like that again," he breathed. "I like it."

The top of her sundress fell away. He thumbed her bare nipples, bending to kiss her mouth at the same time. She groaned, rocking her hips against his erection.

"That's it." He hardened impossibly. His arms tightened around her. She felt herself falling, the ground moving upward to meet her, and then she felt her shoulder blades press into the cool, damp sand.

Nick loomed over her, his eyes intense, one hand easing her skirt up over her thighs.

"You'll ruin your good clothes." She gasped as he found the sweet spot between her thighs.

"Screw the clothes."

He leaned over her; the tip of his tongue found her ear. A tidal wave of weakness washed through her and she shuddered, reaching for him. He levered himself up on his elbows, watching as she undid the slippery buttons on his dress shirt with trembling fingers. The smooth fabric parted. She spread her fingers on his bare chest. His heart pounded under her palms.

The last breath of an ocean breaker slid close, but didn't touch them. Nick shoved her halter top to her waist and bent his head to one breast. He caught her nipple with his teeth, biting gently. His hand slid up the outside of her thigh, lifting her skirt to her waist.

"You always wear these flimsy dresses. Is it because you want to drive me crazy? You've done it, you know. I'm officially insane."

He stroked her through her panties. Then he groaned. "God. You're so wet for me."

"Yes."

"Good."

He worked her panties free, losing them in the sand. A breeze whispered across her moist skin, making her shiver. He nudged her legs apart, lifting her knees.

His breath hitched. The ocean roared in her ears.

"You're so beautiful like this." His voice was ragged and full of wonder. "So wild. So open."

She gazed up him. His face, so handsome, so harsh, was framed by silver night clouds. The sand was cold on her back, but male heat bathed her stomach and thighs. Nick looked at her, his expression almost reverent. As though she were the moon, the stars, and the heavens, all rolled into one.

She clung to the moment. It was everything she'd wanted, everything she'd imagined. Her fingers fumbled at his belt buckle, tugged at his zipper. She slipped her hand into his boxers and stroked him. He was heavy and hot, hard and soft, all at once.

He guided her hand away. His hot mouth opened on her breast; his hands swept over her bare skin. He teased her until her breath came in gasps, stroking his fingers between her legs, his tongue licking into her mouth.

She raised her hips in invitation. He ran his palms over her bottom, tilting her hips. He entered on one strong stroke. She felt him deep inside, deeper than she'd ever felt him before. Her body clenched around him, possessing him. Claiming him as hers.

He flexed his hips, making her groan. "This really turns you on, doesn't it?"

"What?"

"Doing it in the open. Where anyone could see us. Hell, someone could be watching right now. Do you like thinking about that? About someone watching?" He cradled her head in his palms and took her mouth as he drove himself inside her.

God help her, she did like it. She tried to tell him, but all she could manage was a gasp as he plunged deep.

"I don't," he said.

"Wh-what?"

He rocked back and forward, stealing her breath again.

"I don't like it. I hate it. I hate cheapening what we have by rutting in the sand like horny teenagers. I hate how I lose my mind when I'm with you. Hate that you make me want to do things like this." He pulled out almost completely, then caught her hips in a painful grip and slammed back in. It felt so good she wanted to sob.

But his words . . . his words didn't feel good at all.

"I don't want to be this way with you, Tori. So . . . raw and desperate. It just hurts too goddamn much."

A wave caught them, drenching Tori's skirt. Nick's body pressed her down into the wet sand. He moved inside her again. The pleasure rose.

"Nick . . . Oh, God . . ."

"Yes," he hissed, his voice low and intense, his body moving more quickly, more deeply inside her. "Say my name, Tori. Scream for me."

Another wave skittered across the sand, splashing their joined torsos. Nick cradled her in his arms, shielding her from the worst of the water, never once losing his rhythm. Her hips lifted off the ground with each thrust. Sand scraped her back.

Another wave hit. An answering swell surged inside her, lifting her, pushing her high, then higher still. She wrapped her legs around Nick's waist, her inner muscles rippling. But the big payoff wouldn't come. The edge just hung there, out of reach.

She moaned, reaching for the fall with all that she was. It was no use. Nick was deep inside her, and it felt incredible. But it wasn't enough.

He wasn't close enough.

"I love you," she cried on a gasp. "Do you hear me? I love you."

"Tori . . ." He groaned, gripping her bottom and slamming into her body so savagely that for a moment she couldn't breathe. He bit her neck, sending a spark of pain into the surging pleasure.

"Come for me, Tori. Come *with* me."

His plea sent her over. She crashed and broke in a free fall, clinging to him. He went rigid, groaning his own release. She felt the hot pulse of his seed shooting deep inside her.

And that was when she realized they hadn't used a condom.

The wave of pleasure crashed, rolled, receded. Nick lowered himself to the sand beside her, his lips pressing the hollow of her neck, his breath coming in gasps. She lay still, her hand cradling his head, her heart nearly pounding out of her body. Her senses were spinning, as if she'd stepped off a whirling boardwalk ride. She was happy, shaken, and trying to catch her breath.

All too soon he levered himself off her. He stood and offered her a hand up. His dress shirt was plastered to his torso, and his trousers were covered with sticky wet sand.

A cool breeze stirred the air, and she shivered.

"Shit," Nick said. "We're freaking soaked."

Chapter Twenty-six

A little family planning is always a good idea.

Leigh checked the condoms in her jacket pocket before leaving the house. She'd taken one, then at the last minute went back to add a second.

Who knew? Better to be prepared than sorry.

Jason, looking very hot in gray sweatpants and a Beach Patrol T-shirt, was waiting by the dunes.

"I didn't even have to sneak out," she told him. "No one's home. We were all at the Boardwalk, but we couldn't find Johnny and Tori before the fireworks started; then Johnny called and said they'd already left. I think they were headed to Johnny's club to hear Mimi sing. So Alex brought me home. He took Sophie to his place for the night."

"What about your dad?"

"I have no idea where he is."

"So it's all good." Jason slung his arm over her shoulders and kissed the top of her head.

They cut across the beach toward his street. But he didn't kiss her again until they were in his kitchen, behind the closed door. His lips touched hers once, twice, then a third time.

"I can't believe you're finally here."

A shiver of excitement raced through her. At least, Leigh hoped it was excitement. What else could it be? She loved Jason. And he loved her.

"I can hardly believe it myself."

"Yeah. I thought . . ."

"What?"

"Never mind. You're here now. That's all that matters."

He pulled her close. The crazy fire swept over her, the one only he could light, the one that made her forget all her doubts. His lips touched her cheeks, her nose, her eyelids. His hands framed her face, his fingers sifting through her hair. His mouth slanted over hers, his tongue sliding along the sensitive inner lining of her lower lip. She sighed and let him in.

She wrapped her arms around his neck and pressed her body against him the way she knew he liked. She was rewarded with a sexy sound from the back of his throat, something between a moan and a growl. His arms tightened around her as he slid his tongue in and out of her mouth in an imitation of what they'd soon be doing with their bodies.

She stiffened slightly, thinking about it.

He pulled back, breathing heavily, his forehead pressed against hers. "Are you sure you're okay with this? Because if you're not, tell me now. I won't be able to take much more. I want you so bad."

"I want you, too," she said quickly.

"God, I'm glad." He hugged her close, and she felt his smile against her temple. "I love you, Leigh. Let me show you how much."

He caught her hand and moved it to his stomach, then lower, slipping it beneath the elastic waistband of his sweats. He closed her fingers on his erection, holding her there.

Oh, God. It was hot in her palm, and very hard. In fact, it was harder than she'd imagined, and . . . it was *pulsing*. The sensation unnerved her.

He slid her hand along his shaft. She tried to imagine opening up her body and letting it in. Would it hurt? Stacey said it had, the first time.

She tried to take her hand away, but she didn't pull very hard and he didn't seem to notice.

"God, that feels good," he said.

"Jason . . ."

He gave her a lopsided smile. "Nervous?"

"I guess."

His arms went around her. "Don't be."

"But . . . it might hurt," she said in a small voice.

"Nah," he said. "It won't. I won't let it. Come on."

He laced his fingers in hers and tugged her toward the stairs.

"We didn't use a condom."

Tori threw out the comment as casually as she could, while she retied her halter straps behind her neck.

Nick gasped in a breath.

It was as if he'd been sucker punched. He actually staggered a step backward. At the same exact instant, Tori's stomach cramped.

"Fuck." He dragged a hand down his face. "*Fuck.*"

And that about summed it up, Tori thought savagely. Suddenly, what they'd done on the beach seemed cheap. Just like Nick had said.

She licked her lips, which had gone dry. "I guess that means forgetting the condom was an accident?"

"Hell, yes, it was an accident! Jesus. Do you think I'd—" He cut himself off, his eyes widening. "You did, didn't you? You thought I didn't use a condom on purpose. You thought I'd decided to give in and get you pregnant."

She started walking up the beach. He followed. In the distance, an explosion of fireworks burst over the brightly lit Atlantic City skyline.

"No," Tori said, painfully aware of Nick's grim expression. "I didn't think you wanted to get me pregnant. That would be the absolute last thing I would think."

He grabbed her arm. "You should've said something. When you realized we weren't protected."

She shook him off. "I was caught up in the moment." She laughed, but the sound was ugly. "Just like you."

She picked up her pace.

"Tori. Come back here."

She ignored him and ran for the street. At least, she thought she was running that way. It was hard to see. Her vision had suddenly blurred.

"Tori, stop. We have to talk about this."

"Talk?" She whirled around to face him. "Now you want to talk?"

His jaw locked. "Yeah. I do." He stared at her for a long moment. "I want you to know that if you're pr—" He just about choked on the word. "If you're pregnant, I'll stick by you. I won't abandon my child."

The glare of the street lamp washed out his complexion. He looked exhausted, Tori thought. Exhausted and depressed.

"But you don't want another child. Ever. You told me that."

Seconds ticked by. "Yes," he said quietly. "I did say that. At least, I don't think I want one. And certainly not like this, not when . . ." He rubbed the back of his neck. "Look. What I'm trying to say is, call me old-fashioned, but I believe a baby's parents should be married before it's conceived. Otherwise, it's a big mistake to bring a child into the world."

"And you wouldn't be caught dead marrying me. Is that what you're trying to say?"

"No, damn it, it's not. Stop putting words into my mouth."

But he'd hesitated a moment too long before saying it.

Tori's heart dropped like a stone in the ocean.

"I know you don't want to marry me." She hugged herself, trying to stop her shivering. She could still smell him on her skin, could almost still feel him inside her.

"And you know what?" she continued. "I'm glad. We'd be miserable together. In fact, I wouldn't marry you if you begged me."

He just stood there, eyes hard and angry, arms crossed. Looking at her, but saying nothing.

She gathered the scraps of her pride and started walking home.

He didn't follow.

Leigh was just about naked.

Her shirt and bra had disappeared almost as soon as they'd entered Jason's bedroom. Her shorts had been a more recent addition to the clutter on his floor. But he wasn't rushing her. Oh, no.

They'd started out on the beanbag chair in the corner. That had been fine. After all, they'd made out there before, plenty of times, though never with the house empty. Jason had gone so slow, been so sweet and gentle, that it'd been Leigh who'd finally reached behind her back and unhooked her bra.

Things went quicker after that.

Now she lay on Jason's double bed wearing nothing but a lacy thong. Her breath quickened as he stripped off his T-shirt, the movement causing his pecs to ripple. Leigh had seen his bare chest loads of times, of course, but somehow, here in his bedroom, in his *bed*, the sight of him hit her harder.

He leaned over her, his gaze dropping to her breasts. The tight smile on his face looked more like pain than anything else. "You're like a dream, Leigh. Like a centerfold."

She gave a nervous laugh. "That's supposed to be romantic?"

He flashed her a grin. "Sorry." He turned away to put on a CD. He was back in a heartbeat. He caught her hand, and then, like some character from a book, kissed her fingers. One by one. He caught her gaze over the back of her hand, his beautiful eyes flaring dark.

He stood and pushed his gym pants over his hips. She sucked in a breath—he'd gone commando under his sweats! She tried not to ogle, but her eyes dropped anyway.

She couldn't *not* look at him.

She stared. Jason's penis was huge and red and ugly, with

a bulging purple vein running down one side. She couldn't take her eyes off it. Suddenly, a scrap of lace and dental floss seemed a pretty flimsy barrier between her virginity and Mr. Red.

The thought made her giggle.

Jason took a step toward the bed. Mr. Red bobbed.

It looked way too big to fit.

Not a comforting thought. But, really, it couldn't be true. When had she ever heard of a guy's thing not fitting?

Never, that was when.

She lowered her lashes and made another surreptitious appraisal of Jason's package. When you got right down to it, a penis was a truly ridiculous-looking appendage. A baseball bat with a misshapen knob on top.

It was just the same color as Tori's love spell candle.

The giggles hit again.

Jason's expression cooled a bit. He looked less like a lover and more like a confused puppy. A naked confused puppy.

It was too much. Leigh struggled to keep the laughter down, she really did, but she truly couldn't help it. She was too wound up, too nervous. She giggled again, then laughed outright.

Jason frowned. "What's so funny?"

Leigh clamped her hand over her mouth, biting down on her bottom lip so hard she was sure she tasted blood. Jason looked really annoyed, and she couldn't blame him. She had to stop laughing. She really had to.

She couldn't.

"Shit," he said. "What's the matter with you?"

"Nothing," she gasped.

"It's not nothing."

"I'm sorry." She struggled to keep another bubble of laughter from bursting.

"I thought you wanted this, Leigh." His voice quavered a bit.

Leigh's laughter ebbed. "I do. You know I do."

And she did. She really did. The trouble was, she wasn't sure if she wanted it right here, right now.

But she didn't know how to tell that to Jason.

The mattress dipped under his weight. He rolled toward her, pulling her into his arms. Her breasts rubbed against the blond curls on his chest. His legs slid between hers.

Every part of her touched every part of him. Skin-to-skin. She could smell his deodorant, even taste the sweat on his skin; they were that close.

Too close.

He nuzzled her breast. Kissed her nipple. She grabbed fist-fuls of his quilt to keep herself from pushing him away. What was wrong with her? She was acting like a little girl. After all, her virginity was no big deal. It was a liability, actually. Something to get out of the way.

All her friends had done it. Even Stacey. There was nothing to it. All she had to do was lie back and let Jason do his thing. It wasn't *his* first time. He knew what he was doing.

He left her breast to kiss her lips again. Leigh concentrated on that. It was nice. Familiar. She loosened her death grip on the quilt, forcing herself to skim her hands up Jason's chest. She linked them at the back of his neck.

His full weight came down on her. He kissed her neck, her shoulder. He was breathing harder now, his skin shiny with sweat. Mr. Red was prodding her thigh.

She tried not to think about that. At least, not yet. She thought about Jason's mouth, his lips. He was a fantastic kisser, and he was really getting into things. He threaded both hands through her hair and held her head steady while he explored her mouth with his tongue.

She sighed and relaxed a little. It felt good. Her apprehension receded. She could do this. He left her mouth and kissed his way down her neck to her breasts. He caught one nipple in his mouth and suckled gently.

She gasped and arched a little ways off the bed. This was good, too. Very good. She cradled his head against her breast, feeling sexy and womanly. And there was an added bonus. In order to reach her breast with his mouth, he'd had to scoot down her body. Mr. Red was no longer jabbing her thigh like a blunt-tipped fireplace poker.

He nuzzled her cleavage and dipped his fingers inside her thong.

She tensed. "Jason—"

"Shhh . . ." He eased the thong over her hips. Over her thighs. Over her calves.

Oh, God. Now she was completely naked, and Jason was looking at her with an expression she'd last seen on a trip to the zoo—in the wolf habitat. He lowered himself on top of her again, kissing her, touching her everywhere.

"I want you so much, Leigh." He covered her mouth and kissed her again, harder, deeper. Mr. Red was back, harder and hotter than before. If that were even possible.

"I love you, Leigh. You know that, don't you?"

She couldn't breathe.

She remembered the condoms.

"Jason?"

"Hmmm . . . ?"

"I . . . I don't want to get pregnant. I *can't* get pregnant. My dad would freak. We have to use a . . ." She couldn't bring herself to say it. *Oh, God.* Why hadn't she brought this up when they both had all their clothes on?

"Condom," he said, pulling back a little.

"Do you have one? Because if you don't, I have a couple in my jacket."

"You brought condoms?" His eyes registered surprise and more than a little amusement. "You didn't need to. I've got some."

"Oh."

"Leigh. I told you not to worry, didn't I?"

"Yeah," she said, feeling foolish. "You did."

He leaned across her and yanked open the drawer of his nightstand. He fumbled in the clutter and emerged with a square packet. Sitting back on his heels, he ripped it open and rolled it on.

Mr. Red became Mr. White.

Leigh supposed she should have felt relieved, but somehow she didn't. Jason's equipment seemed even more menacing now that it was sheathed. He crawled back to her on all fours like a big, deadly cat.

She stared up at the ceiling and saw a New Jersey Nets poster.

And that was when she knew she couldn't go through with it.

She didn't want this. She loved Jason, and he loved her, but this didn't feel right. It wasn't enough. She wanted something different.

She wanted pink satin sheets and champagne, in a fancy hotel room.

Not a blue cotton quilt in a teenage boy's bedroom.

She wanted to wake up in the morning to room service and breakfast in bed. Not to sneak back into her house in the dead of the night. She wanted a fourposter bed with a frilly canopy. Not the New Jersey Nets.

She wanted to be a woman making love to a man.

Not a girl fooling around with her boyfriend.

Jason slid his knee between her legs and parted them. He kissed her, their tongues touching. His arousal prodded her, poised at the entrance to her body.

She braced her hands on his shoulders. "Jason."

"Easy. It won't hurt. I promise." He flexed his hips. "No!" Leigh wriggled, trying to stall his forward progress. "No, Jason, stop. I don't want this."

"You're just scared. Relax. It'll be good."

"No." But the word was absorbed by Jason's kiss. She twisted her head and shoved as hard as she could on his shoulders. "No," she said, louder. "No."

When he tried to kiss her again, something snapped. She thrashed, pounding him with her fists.

"Shit." He caught her wrists in his hands. "Leigh, baby, stop it! What's gotten into you? What's wrong?"

She couldn't look at him. "I told you, I don't want this, Jason."

He levered himself up. "You gotta be kidding me. You said you did. I thought you wanted this as much as I do."

She could hardly look him in the eye. "I . . . I haven't been honest. I don't want it. Not really. At least, not . . . now. It's . . . it's too soon for me. I'm not ready."

His eyes showed his hurt. And his anger. "Hell of a time to let me in on it."

"Jason, I'm—"

He shoved himself off the bed and rolled the condom off his wilting erection. "I asked you down in the kitchen. I told you, if you weren't ready, just to tell me."

"I know, Jason, and I'm so—"

His palm slapped the dresser. "Don't say it, Leigh. Just don't. I don't think I can stand an apology right now." He flung the unused condom in the trash. "Shit."

He stood with his back to her, arms braced on his dresser, head bowed. He didn't move for the longest time.

Leigh's stomach did a nauseating dive. "I didn't mean to hurt you. I . . . I shouldn't have let things go this far. I should have told you how I felt."

"Yeah. You should have. You should have trusted me. But you don't trust me, do you?"

He pulled on his sweats and shirt without looking at her. When he was dressed, he found her clothes and dropped them at the foot of the bed. She felt very small, lost on his big bed.

"Jason—"

"Get dressed, Leigh." He headed for the door. "I'll walk you home."

Three a.m. was a hell of a time to be walking the beach.

Nick came to a halt at the water's edge. He stood for a time, looking out to the horizon. He could just spot the thin line where the gray of the ocean met the lighter gray of the sky. A steady wind blew into his face, smelling of damp and brine. No sense going to bed. He had to be up for work in two hours.

God. Had he gotten Tori pregnant tonight?

He imagined her stomach, round with his child. He thought about how it would be to feel the baby kick against his palm. The past seventeen years flashed through his mind—every good and bad moment of Leigh's life, it seemed, played in one exhilarating, frightening rush. His throat tightened; his heart sped up. He forced a deep breath and swallowed.

He was scared shitless.

Because Tori might be pregnant, and if she was, the roller coaster would start all over again, and he'd be on it. And just like before, Nick's relationship with his child's mother wouldn't be solid.

As if it could ever be. Truth was, he sucked at relationships. If he could gather every woman he'd ever slept with together in one room, he had no doubt that every single one of them would agree that their breakup was his fault.

He couldn't handle the emotions, the upheaval, the tears. He'd withdrawn from Cindy emotionally even before Leigh arrived, using every excuse to bury himself in his work. He'd been playing the same game ever since, and truth be told, in all those years of meaningless sex, no woman had ever made him want to change his ways.

Until Tori.

He picked a pebble off the beach and threw it into the ocean as far as he could. He didn't see it land, didn't hear the splash. When had being with Tori stopped being about sex? He hadn't seen the change coming, hadn't noticed when it happened. But now that it had, he recognized what he felt for her as something beautiful and fragile. Something he wanted to nurture and watch grow.

But Tori kept forcing his hand.

A baby. *Jesus.* It was too soon.

Even so, it hurt that Tori hadn't wanted *his* baby. That she hadn't been willing to wait until they could figure out what was happening between them. No, she wanted to be a mother right away, and it seemed any man's child would do.

The end run of a wave surged past him. It sucked sand from beneath his bare feet as it retreated. He felt like going with it, flinging himself into the sea and swimming until he was exhausted. But he didn't, of course. That would be irresponsible, and he was never that.

He turned and trudged across the sand, heading home.

At the edge of the dune, he caught the glimpse of a shadow moving on his porch, beyond the seawall. He came to a halt, watching as a dark form caught hold of what looked like a rope dangling from Leigh's balcony. The figure hoisted itself up onto the stone pier supporting the second floor.

"Hey!" He started to run.

The intruder froze. Reaching the edge of the beach, Nick heaved himself over the seawall. The figure came to life, grabbing for Leigh's porch rail.

He threw himself after it. "Stop!" His hand closed on the intruder's ankle. "Stop, or I swear, I will pull you down and break every bone in your body."

"Daddy, don't! It's me."

"Leigh?" He nearly fell over.

"Yeah."

He jumped down to the patio. Leigh clung to the pier, one hand gripping the stone, the other wrapped around a rope hanging from her balcony rail. What in God's name was she doing?

Then it hit him.

She'd sneaked out, and now she was sneaking back in. And there was only one place—one *person*—she could've gone to.

He saw red. "Get down here."

"Dad—"

"Now, Leigh."

She scrambled down, eyes on the ground.

"Look at me."

She turned sullen eyes on him, her arms hugging her waist.

"You were with Jason." He wondered how the hell his voice could sound so deadly calm.

Her chin lifted. "So what if I was?"

He felt like punching something. "God*damn* it, Leigh. I told you to stay away from that kid. Now you're screwing him behind my back?"

"Would you prefer to watch?"

Nick stared at her, stunned past all belief. *This* was his little girl? With a mouth like that? Rage slammed him like a rogue wave.

"Get out of my sight," he bit out. "Get into the house this minute, young lady, if you know what's good for you."

Leigh hesitated, opening her mouth as if to reply.

"Not a word," he raged. "Not one. I'm warning you, Leigh."

His daughter's eyes widened in real fear. She turned and fled.

Nick followed much, much later.

Chapter Twenty-seven

*No father wants to contemplate the loss
of his daughter's virginity.*

"You missed a great show last night," Johnny said, plucking a "Scorpio" scroll from the astrology display. He picked at the tape holding it closed with his thumbnail. "You really shoulda heard Ma sing."

It wasn't even six a.m. yet. Tori had been gritty-eyed and grumpy when she'd answered the doorbell. She was sure her eyes were rimmed red from all the crying she'd done in lieu of sleeping.

Johnny had taken one look at her, frowned, and had promptly launched into a stream of upbeat banter. It did nothing to improve her mood. The jittery energy coming off him told her he hadn't been to bed, either. She hoped his night had gone better than hers.

He flicked his wrist, unraveling the horoscope scroll like a streamer.

"Those are for paying customers, you know," she told him.

"I'm good for it." He fished out his wallet and slapped a five on the counter. "Keep the change."

She slid the bill back to him. "Did you sleep at all last night?"

He shook his head. "Nah. Did you?"

"No."

His eyes dropped to his horoscope, and for a moment, he looked as if he were reading it. "So," he said at length.

"What happened between you and my ever-so-charming big brother after he whisked you away last night?"

Tori didn't want to go there. "Not much. Tell me more about Rita's debut."

Johnny shot her a hard look, but didn't call her on her transparent change of subject. "Ma was incredible. She can hit a high C like no one's business. The audience loved her."

"That's wonderful. Was anyone else from the family there?"

He grinned. "Just Nonna. After Alex picked up Sophie and drove Leigh home, I went around to Nonna's and talked her into being my date. Guess what? After all the complaining, she got a real charge out of Ma's set. Hollered louder than anyone when it was over."

Tori smiled, picturing it. "I wish I could've been there."

Johnny caught her gaze. "You could've been. You know, when I drove by Nick's this morning and saw his truck in the driveway, I was surprised. I thought he'd've spent the night here with you."

"Well, he didn't."

"Hey." He abandoned the horoscope and picked up her hand. "Are you sure you're okay? What did you and Nick . . . Well, no, wait. On second thought, spare me the details of what you and Nick did or didn't do. Unless I need to hunt him down and kill him."

"You don't," Tori told him, tugging her hand out of his grip.

He was silent for a moment. Then, "Bullshit. At the minimum, I should beat the living crap out of him. You want to talk about it?"

Tori sighed. Why was it that Johnny always knew when to push, and Nick never did? Better yet, why was it that Johnny seemed so in tune with her moods, when Nick was the one who tied her heart in knots?

Easy answer. She didn't love Johnny. She loved Nick.

But, damn it, she needed someone to talk to.

"All right. You win. I guess I'm just . . . confused."

"A little more than confused, I'd say. But that's a start. What exactly don't you understand?"

"Well, for one thing," she began, "that kiss you gave me last night. Was it real?"

Johnny abruptly rediscovered the horoscope scroll. "What do you think?"

"If I knew, I wouldn't ask."

He drew a breath, then caught her eye and grinned. His hand went to his heart. "Macey Lark, you wound me. Dr. Gavin Hunter must not be much of a kisser."

She smiled. "Oh, he isn't half-bad."

"That's a relief." His tone was carefully light.

She met his gaze. "It's just that Macey's in love with someone else."

Johnny's blue eyes were soft. "Hunter knows that. He just wishes he could've kicked some sense into the stubborn ass's head for you."

"Thanks," Tori said. Silence fell. When it started getting awkward, she asked, "When's your screen test?"

"Next week. And if that goes okay, they'll call me back for a final. Since my day job's history, I'm giving Ma my slot at the club and blowing town. I'll be staying with friends in Manhattan for a while."

He paused, and the silence settled around them again. When she didn't reply, he let out a long breath. "Nick cares a lot about you, Tori."

She tried for a laugh. "I don't know about that. He's in lust with me; that's all."

"No, it's more than that. After what I saw last night, I'd run over to the Borgata and put money on it. I've never seen my brother so tied up in knots over a woman."

She sighed. "All we do is fight."

"It's the baby thing," Johnny said. "It's thrown him." He hesitated. "Did he tell you Leigh almost died when she was a baby?"

She looked up, startled. "He said something about Leigh

being a difficult baby, but I thought he was just talking about colic."

"It was a lot more than that. It's a miracle she's still alive."

"I had no idea."

"Nick never talks about it," Johnny said. "I don't remember too many details about Leigh's birth—I was only seven at the time. She came six weeks too early. She was in the hospital for a couple months. After she finally came home, she had this problem where she'd just stop breathing. She had to sleep wired to an alarm for more than a year. The thing used to go off two, three times a night."

"Oh, God."

"Once it was really bad. She was turning blue. Nick couldn't get her breathing again and Ma called the ambulance. After they got her stabilized, Nick just lost it. He threw up, and then broke down sobbing. I'd never seen him cry before—I thought he was invincible. That image never left me. He's human, Tori. He's stubborn and can be an ass, but gets scared shitless sometimes, too. Just like the rest of us."

Her own eyes filled with tears as she thought about it. She couldn't begin to imagine how Nick must have felt that night.

Johnny straightened away from the counter and paced a few steps toward the door. "When Leigh got older, she developed asthma. She's mostly outgrown it now, but she was in the emergency room plenty of times when she was younger. She still carries an inhaler everywhere." He stopped, drew a breath. "It's why Nick's so hard on her. He just wants to protect her."

"I didn't realize."

Johnny turned, his eyes seeking hers. "Leigh's put Nick through hell over the years. If he doesn't want another child, well, that's why. He doesn't think he can handle it."

Tori's hand stole to her stomach.

No condom, and it was the fertile time of her cycle.

Nick might not have a choice.

Nick came awake with a start, heart pounding inside his ribs. He'd fallen asleep sprawled on top of his comforter—even though he hadn't meant to doze, didn't even remember lying down.

He'd dreamed of Leigh, her infant body limp in his hands, her lips turning blue before his eyes. The shrill bleat of the sleep apnea alarm still rang in his ear.

He sat up, trying to shake the past from his head. His hands were actually trembling. His stomach felt sick.

He glanced at the clock and saw it was past seven. *Damn.* He had a job site meeting at seven thirty. Shoving himself off the bed, he stripped and dressed without even taking a shower. He'd grab coffee on the way in. With any luck, he'd make it on time.

As he descended the stairs, Leigh's voice drifted up from the foyer. An adolescent male voice answered her.

Nick halted in midstep.

Jason.

The idiot must have a freaking death wish.

". . . sorry," Jason was saying. "I just wanted you to know."

"You shouldn't be here," Leigh returned in a low voice. "My dad—"

"Leigh, give me a minute. I was a jerk last night. I'm sorry."

Leigh's reply was tight. "You didn't say a word the whole time we walked home."

"I know, and I'm sorry. But don't cut me off now. I need to—"

"I'm not cutting you off. My dad caught me climbing up the balcony after you left. I thought he was going to have a stroke! If he sees you now, he'll—"

"Beat you to a bloody pulp," Nick said as he descended the last steps into the foyer. "Or maybe I'll just beat you senseless. You're not welcome here, MacAllister. Get out."

Jason met his gaze unflinchingly. He was so tall, his eyes were on a level with Nick's. "Mr. Santangelo, I—"

Nick advanced. Jason, wisely, took a step back.

"Leigh's forbidden to see you," Nick said, trying to keep his voice even, but not quite succeeding. "But somehow, you can't get that through your thick skull. Can't keep your pants zipped. Well, think of *this* the next time you get a hard-on: Touch my daughter again and I will take you apart piece by piece."

"Daddy!"

Real fear registered in Jason's eyes, but to Nick's amazement, the kid held his ground.

"You don't understand, sir. Leigh and I—"

Nick wrenched the front door open. "Get out, MacAllister. Get out now, or so help me God, I won't care what I do to you."

Jason stumbled backward so fast he nearly fell down the damn front steps. *That kid screwed my daughter*, Nick thought savagely. *My daughter.* He felt like pounding Jason's face into the sidewalk.

Somehow, he managed to keep from laying a hand on him.

He slammed the door shut and turned to face Leigh. Her blue eyes were blazing with fury. Well, too bad. She wasn't the only one royally pissed.

"I can't believe you talked to Jason like that!"

"You're on shaky ground, young lady. I suggest you don't make things worse for yourself."

"Worse? How could I possibly make things worse? I'm the daughter of a raving lunatic!"

"And I'm the father of a little slut. How long have you been sneaking out to screw Jason? A month? Two months?"

"Oh!" Leigh's fingers curled into fists, her whole body shaking. Her blonde hair whipped around her face as she shook her head. "Why do I even bother talking to you? You never listen."

"I'm listening now," Nick said evenly. "Tell me. How long?"

Her chin lifted. "Oh, probably just about as long as you've been screwing Tori."

There was a long, thick silence.

Nick's face went hot. "You leave Tori out of this. She's a grown woman. You're not."

"So you keep telling me."

"At least tell me Jason used a condom. A baby is the last thing you need. A pregnancy at your age will screw up your whole life."

There was another beat of dead silence; then pain blossomed in Leigh's eyes.

"Yeah. You should know all about that, huh?"

Ah, shit. Nick dragged his hand over his head. "I wasn't talking about you. You know that."

"I do? Could've fooled me. I know I was your big screwup. I *know* you didn't want me. But you can relax. I'm smarter than Mom was. I carry my own condoms."

"You do?" Nick was stunned.

"Yeah. In my purse. I never know when I might need one."

"Shit."

She tilted her head, her heavy blonde hair brushing her shoulders, and for a moment Nick saw Cindy, looking just like this on the morning she'd left him. He shut his eyes.

"You want to know where I got them?" he heard her say. "From Tori, that's where. She gave them to me."

He opened his eyes and sucked in a breath.

"*Tori* gave you *condoms?*"

"Yeah. She told me I needed to be prepared, because guys screw first and think later." She crossed her arms and waited a beat. "But I guess you know all about that, huh, Dad?"

Jesus. How could Nick possibly come up with an answer for that?

He was guilty as charged.

"You gave my daughter condoms," Nick shouted. "*Condoms,* for chrissakes."

"Nick." If Tori had thought Nick had been angry the night before, it was nothing compared to how enraged he was now. She found herself wishing Johnny hadn't left fifteen minutes before.

"Good morning to you, too. Do you want to come in? Or would you rather wake my neighbors?"

"Are you saying you didn't do it?" he demanded, striding into the shop. He pivoted to face her. "Are you saying my daughter is a liar?"

"No," Tori replied quietly. "I'm not saying that."

He paced the cramped space in front of her counter, like a wounded panther trapped in a cage.

"I caught her sneaking into the house last night. She'd been with Jason." He scowled in Tori's direction. "She said she talked to you about sex. She said you gave her condoms. God*damn* it, Tori. Is it true?"

"Yes, but—"

Nick swore. "How dare you tell my daughter to have sex with her boyfriend."

"I didn't tell her that! Not in so many words. I just talked to her. She came to me for advice."

"For what? Which position to do it in?"

"Don't be crude," Tori said sharply. "Leigh was trying to decide whether she should do it at all. I told her to trust her heart."

"What kind of crap is that to tell a teenager? You should've told her to keep her goddamn knees pressed together."

Tori drew a breath. "Leigh's seventeen, Nick. She'll be eighteen before the year's out. She's not a child anymore."

"She's not *your* child, you mean."

He started pacing again. "You had no right to interfere, Tori. Do you know what it does to me, thinking of Leigh taking off her clothes for that kid? He's a jock out for whatever he can get. If he gets her pregnant, she'll be paying for it for years."

"Which is exactly why I gave her the condoms."

"She wouldn't need condoms if she'd just stay away from him. He's leaving for college in a couple months. She doesn't need to be pining over him once he's gone. Letting him go would've been a hell of a lot easier if she hadn't slept with him."

"A lot of things are easier if you don't get close to someone."

He exhaled. "Tori—"

But he didn't have time to finish the sentence, because just then Tori got her third early-morning visitor.

Leigh.

Nick's daughter faltered briefly in the doorway as her father swung around to confront her. Then she marched into the shop, chin lifted. Nick's face flushed purple. Tori thought he was going to explode.

"What are you doing here, Leigh?"

"I work here, remember?"

"Oh, no," Nick said. "Don't even *try* to go there. You do not work here. Not anymore."

"You can't tell me what to do!"

"I certainly can. If I have to lock you in your room to make you obey me, I will."

"That is so wrong! You just can't—"

"Leigh," Tori said quietly. She moved to the girl's side and laid a hand on her arm.

Leigh looked at her, probably for the first time since entering the store.

"Do what your father says."

She gave a disbelieving gasp. "You agree with this fascist?"

"No. Not completely. But he's your father. You have to do what he says."

"So you're firing me? Because he *told* you to?"

Tori glanced at Nick. His grim expression and rigid stance told her he wouldn't budge an inch on this. And things would only be worse for Leigh if she tried to defy him.

She sighed. "Yes, I suppose I am."

Leigh drew a ragged breath. "Fine. Just fine."

She whirled around and stomped out the door.

Silence ensued. It continued for the longest time, stretching and settling all around like a thick, putrid fog. Tori eyed Nick. He'd gone unnaturally still, his eyes flat. It was as if he'd drawn so far into himself that he didn't even see her anymore.

"We should talk," she ventured.

He dragged a hand down the side of his face and looked at her. He blinked and gave a small shake of his head, as if coming out of a dream. Or a nightmare.

"Talk? What the hell about?"

"Leigh. I think . . . Don't get me wrong; I know you want to protect her. I know you love her so much you'd lay down your life for her. But did you ever stop to consider that you might be coming down on her a little too hard?"

"And you're qualified to tell me that because . . . ?"

"Because I care about her. And you." She took a deep breath. "I love you, Nick."

He stared at her. "You love me. That's a joke. How could you love me? You don't even know me."

"I think I do."

"No. If you did, the last thing you'd do is give my daughter condoms behind my back. Why didn't you come to me with this? Tell me what Leigh was planning?"

She bristled. "And betray her confidence? I couldn't do that."

"No, you just encouraged her. Tucked condoms into her purse, for chrissakes." His head snapped up, eyes widening. "Shit. Don't tell me they were the condoms I bought for us!"

She flushed crimson. "I only wanted to protect her, Nick."

"Damn it, Tori, that's my job. And I'll do it the way I see fit. I don't need your interference."

"You're overreacting. I know Leigh almost died as a baby, and you're scared to death something will happen to her, but—"

He paled. "Who told you that?"

"Johnny."

He was silent for a long moment. Then, "The two of you discussed me?"

Tori bit her lip. "He told me some things, yes."

His jaw worked. "He had no right to."

She put out her hand, but he was so distant, so out of reach. "Nick, Leigh's not a fragile little girl anymore. She's a young woman. She needs some space to figure things out on her own."

"So what are you suggesting? That I turn my back and let her screw her boyfriend in her bedroom?"

"No. Of course not. I—"

"Tori, Leigh has been the most important part of my life for almost eighteen years. I'm her *father*. Do you have any idea what that means?" He gave a short laugh. "But what am I thinking? How could you know? You think fatherhood's a five-minute job."

"Nick, I—"

But he was already moving toward the door.

Chapter Twenty-eight

*Whatever you do, try not to get married
for the wrong reasons.*

Tori didn't see Nick for a while after that sorry scene. She didn't see Leigh, either, or any of the Santangelos. Johnny called twice from New York, but both times there had been a party going on in the background, and they didn't talk long. He told her he was meeting with his agent and prepping for his screen test with some of his actor friends. Tori wished him luck and kept her problems to herself.

It was the height of the summer season. The sun was hot, the beach crowded, and Destiny's Gate was making money hand over fist.

And Tori was miserable. She was out of candle magic kits, too, and none of the tarot readings she tried provided any insight. She was just going to have to get through this without magic.

She was thankful she had Chelsea and Mags. They tried hard to talk her out of her funk.

"There are plenty of other fish in the sea," Mags said. "And anyway, you said yourself you and Nick were too different to last."

"She doesn't need to hear that right now," Chelsea said, frowning at her partner. "God, you can be so insensitive sometimes."

Mags shrugged. "I'm just stating the obvious."

Tori let Lily pull on her necklace. Her arms tightened

around the little girl's wiggling body. She was so sweet, so innocent. Tori's throat clogged.

"Now see what you've done," Chelsea muttered to Mags. "You've made Tori cry."

Tori shook her head, but succeeded only in dislodging a few tears from her eyes. She nuzzled Lily's hair, trying to hide them.

"I'm not crying," she said. But it was a lie. For the last few days she'd been sobbing nonstop. Probably PMS. She was expecting her period any day now.

Except days passed, then a week, and it didn't come.

It didn't come, and she dared to hope.

Nick showed up a few days later. It was late afternoon, and Tori was closing early. South Jersey was suffering from a wicked heat wave, and the shop was unbearable, even with three fans blowing.

The first thing Nick said when he stepped through the door was, "You need air-conditioning."

Her heart lurched. He looked so good, so impossibly handsome, so heart-stoppingly sexy. He must have been spending some time outside lately, because his face was sunburned.

"And you need sunscreen," she replied.

"I know, I know." He rubbed the back of his neck, then winced. "I keep forgetting. We just broke ground on a new job, and I've been out on the site a lot."

They stood there a few seconds longer, just looking at each other. She noticed the tired lines around his eyes, and the unfamiliar way his shoulders hunched.

"Why are you here? Is something wrong? Is Leigh—"

"Leigh's fine." He advanced farther into the shop. He was too big for the place; his elbow knocked into a wind chime. The tingling bells faded before he spoke again.

"I came to see how you were."

"I'm fine." Tori's fingers gripped the sharp edge of the counter. Suddenly, she knew why he'd come. And it didn't have anything to do with her.

His gaze dropped to her stomach. "Are you . . ."

"It's a few days too early to tell."

He met her gaze. "You'll call me if you are, won't you?"

She didn't answer.

He paced nearer, closing the distance between them until only the glass sales counter separated them. "If you're carrying my child, Tori, I want to be part of his life."

"Even if you didn't want him in the first place?"

"Yes." He hesitated. "And . . . I've done some thinking. If you're pregnant, I'll marry you. If that's what you want, I mean."

Her heart nearly left her body. *I'll marry you.* She'd longed for those words, but not like this. Never like this.

"You're proposing?" She felt very far away, as if she weren't there at all.

Nick shoved his fists into his pockets. "If you're pregnant, we should do the right thing. A child should have parents who're married." He rocked backward on his heels. "When he's first born, at the very least."

"So." The syllable echoed oddly over the rushing sound in her ears. "Let me get this straight. You want to marry me so your child won't be . . . what? Illegitimate?"

"That's right."

"And then we can divorce afterward?"

"I didn't say that. I . . . care about you, Tori. I think we could make a go of it." He grimaced. "I'd like to try, anyway."

"But only if I'm pregnant."

He swore under his breath. "I'm making a mess of this."

"Yes, you are." The rushing noise mounted to a roar as rage kicked in. "What makes you think a proposal from you is such a great deal for me? What makes you think I'll say yes? This is the twenty-first century, Nick. There is no way I'm going to marry a man just because he forgot to wear a condom."

"Tori, look, I—"

"If you're smart, you'll leave. Now. Without saying another word."

She flung her anger at him; it became almost a visible barrier between them. She wanted him to knock it down. She wanted him to reach past her hurt and her rage and drag her into his arms. She wanted him to kiss her, to tell her his proposal wasn't just about the baby. She wanted him to say that he loved her, that he couldn't live without her, that he would die if she didn't say yes.

He didn't say any of those things. He just clenched his jaw so tight she thought it would snap. And then he walked out the door. Again.

She got her period the next day.

Chapter Twenty-nine

Life can get lonely, with or without a family.

Nick shook hands with the Atlantic City building inspector. Thank God almighty, Bayview was a wrap. He wouldn't miss this job—hell, he'd be thrilled just to break even when the accounting was done. Excusing himself, he stepped into the job trailer to check his voice mail.

There was a message from Tori.

His gut clenched. It had been two days since he'd seen her. She must know by now whether or not she was carrying his child.

His child.

A baby he didn't want. He was sure of that, but despite his certainty, images blossomed in his mind, and they weren't all horrific. In one, Tori cradled a newborn, the child suckling at her breast. Breast-feeding had been something Cindy'd flatly refused to do, no matter how much Nonna and Rita had coaxed her. But Nick was sure Tori would want to nurse their baby.

In another flash he saw himself on the beach, building an enormous sand castle. Leigh used to love that. He covered tiny toddler legs with wet sand, heard the giggles, felt a sloppy kiss on his cheek. He'd worked so much when Leigh was a baby that memories like those were scarce. If Tori were pregnant, things would be different. Despite the fiasco this Bayview job had turned out to be, his business was a lot more stable now. He could make time. He could make sure he and his new son or daughter had more of those moments.

"Yo, Nick," a voice said.

He started, coming back to his surroundings, phone still cradled in his hand. He looked up at his job super.

"Yeah, Joe?"

"Southerland's here. He wants to go over the punch list. Says there are a couple of things we gotta take care of."

"Tell him I'll be there in five."

"Will do."

The trailer door banged closed. Nick punched in the code for his voice mail, his heart pounding as he waited for Tori's message to come over the line.

"Nick? This is Tori. I, um . . ." A pause. "I just wanted you to know—there's not a baby. I got my period yesterday." Another pause. "Don't, um . . . don't bother calling back, okay?"

He snapped the phone shut, but couldn't seem to stop staring at it. Tori wasn't pregnant. *Hallelujah.*

He waited for relief to flood through him.

It didn't come.

Instead, he was awash with regrets.

Tori cried enough tears to fill one of Nick's five-gallon spackle buckets. She closed the shop and spent three days in bed, sweating in the awful heat, nearly bent double from the cramps. She wasn't pregnant with Nick's child.

Every time she thought about it, she started crying again.

Finally, on day four, she pulled herself together and got out of bed. She had to accept the fact that her time with Nick had just been a small detour on her life road. She needed to get back on track. But how?

She'd soured on the whole sperm donor idea. It was a great choice for some people, she supposed. Like Chelsea and Mags, or hetero couples who needed help conceiving. But for her, it just didn't feel right anymore. So she stiffened her spine and went back to Dr. Janssen.

They had a serious talk. The thought of surgery made

Tori feel light-headed and queasy, but she was determined to go through with it. It was her best option for preserving her fertility for the future. Someday, if she met the right man to be a real father for her child, she would think again about becoming a mother. But for now, she had to put her energy into getting over Nick.

The heat wave broke that night, a black storm blowing in from the north. The nor'easter poured buckets, and the next day was windy and unseasonably cool for August. Another storm threatened. Beachgoers headed inland, to the malls and movie theaters, leaving Tori pacing an empty shop.

Finally, at quarter to six, she gave up and turned the sign in the window from OPEN to CLOSED.

She walked down to the beach. The wind was brisk and steady. It whipped stinging sand like pepper shot across her calves. Tufts of yellow sea foam formed a jagged line along the shore. She walked into the wind, picking her way through the detritus coughed up by the sea. A frayed plastic rope, a piece of splintered driftwood. A tangled fishing line.

She should've walked in the other direction. Or better yet, stayed off the beach entirely. But she couldn't seem to help herself. The footprints she made in the sand led directly to the beach in front of Nick's house.

She blinked as she saw Leigh and Sophie at the water's edge. Leigh was staring out to sea, hands slung into the pockets of a red-and-white Beach Patrol windbreaker that was much too large for her. Jason's, Tori thought. Sophie, a red plastic bucket in hand, scrambled back and forth near the water, head bent as she searched among the scattered shells for treasure.

"Hey," Leigh said when she saw Tori. Jason's jacket nearly swallowed her whole.

"Leigh. How've you been?"

"Okay, I guess."

"Tori!" Sophie sped toward her, brown curls flying in the wind, her pink Lucy-the-elephant sweatshirt a blur. "Tori, guess what? I get to sleep at Leigh's house tonight!"

Tori smiled down at her. "That's great, sweetie."

Sophie grinned, then turned and scampered back to the ocean. Tori turned to Leigh. "Have you been working at your dad's office?"

"No. I haven't seen much of him at all since—" She cut herself off and sighed. "Since that last day at your shop. He practically lives at the office now."

"I guess he's busy with work."

"Yeah. He always is."

Sophie ran back to them. "Look, Tori! I found a starfish."

Leigh peered into the plastic bucket. "Hey, you did."

Tori crouched down beside her. "It's beautiful."

"I named him Starrie," Sophie said. "Can I keep him?"

"No," Leigh told her. "He's still alive. You have to throw him back."

Sophie's bottom lip bulged. "But I wanna keep Starrie. He can be my pet."

"He won't like that," Tori said. "He belongs in the ocean. He'll only die if you try to keep him." She laid a hand on Sophie's skinny shoulder. "Think how sad you'd be then."

Sophie pouted. "But if I throw Starrie back, I'll be sad *now.*"

Leigh and Tori exchanged glances.

Leigh hunkered down beside Tori and Sophie. "But what about Starrie's family? His mom and dad are probably looking for him."

Sophie's brown eyes widened. "You think so?"

"Yes," Tori put in. "His brothers and sisters are probably looking for him, too."

"And his Nonna?"

"Yep," Leigh said. "You wouldn't want to make Starrie's whole family sad, would you?"

Sophie tilted her head, her forehead creased in a frown. "I guess not," she said with a sigh. She headed back toward the ocean, her feet dragging now, her bucket slapping her leg. She paused before she reached the water, though, captivated by some new treasure.

"Thanks," Leigh said as they both stood. "She would've been screaming after I pitched Starrie back in."

Tori's gaze lingered on Sophie's tangled curls. "I miss her."

"She's been asking about you, too."

The wind gusted, raising goose bumps on her bare arms. She shivered, hugging herself. She should've worn a windbreaker, like Leigh.

"I miss you, too," Leigh said softly. "Let me come back to work for you."

"I don't think your father would go for that."

She hunched against the wind. "I don't care."

"That's not true. You love him."

"So do you, Tori. And . . . I know he cares about you. I ruined it for you."

"Oh, Leigh." She saw tears on the girl's face and she knew they weren't from the wind. "What happened between your father and me wasn't your fault."

"Yes, it was. He wouldn't have been so angry with you if I hadn't lied to him."

"Lied? About what?"

Leigh looked at her toes. "I told him Jason and I had . . . you know, done it. With one of the condoms you'd given me. But it wasn't true. We were going to, but at the last minute I remembered what you told me."

Tori's face must have been a complete blank. What had she told Leigh? She couldn't remember, exactly.

Leigh took a gulp of air and forged on. "You know, about the pink satin sheets and champagne?"

Tori blinked. "And you remembered that?"

"Yeah. I did. And you know what, Tori? I decided I want that, too. That's why I told Jason I wanted to wait. He was disappointed at first, but now we're okay."

"I'm glad you were honest with him."

"Yeah."

"Are you still sneaking out to see him?" Tori asked. "Or has your dad eased up on the two of you?"

She bit her lip. "Dad will never ease up. Not after I told him I'd slept with Jason. I don't even know why I said that—I just got so mad when he assumed we were doing it. Now he won't even listen to me when I try to tell him the truth."

She swiped a hand across her eyes. "So you see? It's all my fault you two split up."

Tori gave her a hug. "It's not. Nick and I have plenty of differences that have nothing to do with you. Please don't blame yourself."

She drew back, but Leigh didn't' meet her eyes. She looked toward the ocean instead.

And cried out, "Oh, my God. Sophie!"

Tori's eyes snapped to the sea. Sophie, still clutching her red bucket, stood chest-deep in the rough surf.

Leigh took off at a sprint. "Sophie! Get back here!"

The little girl turned and waved. "I'm sending Starrie home!"

Leigh shouted as a large swell rose behind Sophie; Tori sprang into motion, running toward the water. Leigh plunged in. Tori was right behind her. The leading edge of the swell became a line of writhing foam, poised to break over Sophie's head.

"Sophie!" Leigh screamed. "Behind you. Watch out! Hold your breath!"

Sophie turned and shrieked. The breaker crashed, consuming her in froth. The red bucket shot to the surface, bounced once, and disappeared.

"Oh, God." Leigh dove into the spot where Sophie had been.

Tori stood waist-high in the water, her skirt wrapped around her legs like seaweed. Frantically, she tracked the churning sea.

Nothing.

"Sophie!" she yelled.

Leigh surfaced, sputtering. "God, there's a wicked undertow. Do you see her?"

"No."

The single word was all Tori could manage. Panic clogged her throat. The ocean was a dark, dirty maelstrom. "I— Wait." She spotted Sophie's head, bobbing a good twenty yards out to sea.

"There!" she shouted, pointing.

"I'll go after her." Leigh gasped. "You go for help."

"No." Tori clawed at her skirt, ripping it off. "I'm a strong swimmer. I'll go."

The ocean swelled, blocking Sophie from sight.

"But—" Leigh began.

"Go!" Sucking a lungful of air, Tori flung herself in Sophie's direction.

She caught sight of Sophie's head bobbing on a wave. Her little arms thrashed. Tori stroked hard, praying Leigh would bring help in time. Her arms were burning with exhaustion by the time she reached Sophie. She grabbed the girl's waterlogged sweatshirt.

"Sophie! Hold on to me."

She heaved Sophie upward, dunking herself in the process. Before she could break the surface, Sophie had climbed up her body, wrapping her in a choke hold.

Tori slipped under, taking Sophie with her.

She struggled to pry the girl's thin arms from her neck as she kicked upward. She broke the surface, gasping. Immediately, Sophie locked her arms around Tori's neck.

"No! Don't let me go!"

Tori managed to cough up a mouthful of water before the ocean heaved again. Sophie screamed, battling to climb up on her shoulders.

"Sophie! Stay still! I can't hold you if you're moving."

Another wave sloshed, driving them both under. By the time Tori got them to the surface again, Sophie was choking.

She thrust the child skyward. "Breathe, Sophie. *Breathe.*"

Sophie coughed and drew a whooshing breath.

"That's it, sweetie. Now just . . . relax and let me carry you. I promise I won't let go."

Tori looked toward shore. It seemed impossibly far away. While she'd been struggling with Sophie, the rip current had sucked them farther out to sea. Already, she was exhausted. She'd never be able to swim all the way back to the shore. She only hoped she'd be able to keep them both afloat until help arrived.

Then a wave lifted them, and Tori realized she had a more pressing problem.

The current was driving them toward the rock jetty.

Chapter Thirty

A family in crisis pulls together.

Nick was retrieving his briefcase from his truck when Leigh stumbled over the beach access stairs, drenched and gasping.

"Dad!"

He met her in the middle of the street. "What? What is it?"

She doubled over, coughing. "Sophie. She waded in too far . . . got caught by the undertow. Tori went in . . . after her. . . ."

He shoved his cell phone at her. "Call nine-one-one."

He took the steps three at a time and hit the beach running.

The Atlantic stretched wide, a gray ribbon of snarling surf. The sky hung low and heavy. Huge raindrops fell, peppering the sand with tiny craters. Nick scanned the waves, his stomach in a free fall.

He couldn't see them.

He skidded to a stop at the shore, his heart tripping like a jackhammer as his eyes scoured the water's surface. Then, thank God almighty, he spotted them.

They were close to the rock jetty and drifting closer, two heads bobbing like corks in the rough sea. A rising swell sloshed them, drove them under. Nick tore off his work boots, kicked off his pants, and dove through the breakers. He threw himself at Tori, stroking hard, keeping his head above water, unwilling to let her out of his sight. *Jesus*. If she went under . . .

He never should've let things end between them. He should've gone to her after he'd gotten that last voice mail. But it had hurt, damn it, that she'd not even bothered to tell him about the baby in person. Her voice had been so cold. Distant.

Don't bother calling back, she'd said. He'd heard it as, *I don't want you to call*. And who could blame her? He'd let her down.

He only hoped he wasn't about to do it again.

Nick was there, in the water.

At first, Tori didn't believe her eyes. She thought maybe it was a hallucination, her most desperate wish sprung to life.

"Tori!"

But no. He was real.

He stroked hard, closing the distance between them. Hauling her close, he cradled her body against his hard chest, kicking viciously to keep Sophie's head above water.

"Nick—" A wave sloshed and Tori sputtered.

He wrapped his right arm under Tori's arms and across her chest. She clutched Sophie in front of her. Stroking hard with his left arm, he set an oblique course for shore, away from the rocks, at a cross-angle to the current.

"How long has she been out?" he gasped.

"Since that last big wave hit . . ."

"Only a few seconds, then."

"Yes."

Tori slipped in his arms. He muttered a curse as he renewed his hold. But he'd stopped stroking to do it, and they'd lost the progress they'd made.

Her arms felt like they wanted to detach from her body. Her grip on Sophie was weakening. "Nick. I can't hold her anymore. I almost let her go before. . . . She struggled so much. . . ."

Nick tightened his grip. "Just hold on a little while longer. You can do it, Tori."

"She can't die, Nick."

"She won't."

"Watch out!"

They rose with a steep swell of the ocean, then dropped, roller-coaster style, into the valley behind it. The rock jetty, which had been receding, seemed to draw closer again.

"Shit," Nick spit out. "Okay. Look. This is what we're going to do." He shifted onto his back, wrapping both his arms around her. "Lean into me. Let yourself go horizontal. Then kick like hell. Can you do it?"

"I think so."

But she couldn't. She twisted in his arms. "No. Take her, Nick."

"What?"

"Take Sophie in without me."

"Are you nuts?"

"You have to."

His voice was raw. "No. We're going in together."

Another wave sloshed over them.

"Leave me," she gasped. "I'm slowing you down. I can keep myself afloat until help comes."

"Forget it."

Her voice rose to a frightened pitch. "I . . . I don't know if Sophie's breathing, Nick. What if . . . what if we can't get her out in time?"

If Sophie died, she knew Nick would never forgive himself. He'd never be able to look his brother in the eye. Sophie was part of them. Part of their family.

Tori wasn't.

"Take her." She shoved Sophie into his arms. Then, with a half twist, she kicked backward, out of his reach.

Their eyes met. His were dark thunderclouds, stark with fear.

"Fuck. I don't want to do this, Tori."

"Come back for me."

He stared.

"I will," he said. "I swear it."

Then he turned with Sophie and swam for shore.

"Where?"

Jason's bare feet pounded the wooden stairs leading to the beach. Leigh ran after him. She'd called him second, after 911, but he'd shown up first. Somehow, she'd known he would.

"There," she yelled, pointing as they rounded the dunes. "Near the jetty."

Two figures, yards apart. Tori was one, dangerously near the rocks. Her father was another—did he have Sophie in his arms? Jason sprinted toward the ocean. Leigh pumped her legs as hard as she could, but no way could she keep up with him.

He plunged into the surf. Leigh skidded to a stop at the waterline and fell to her knees. Waves, fueled by a stiff wind, crashed at a sharp angle to the shore. Jason sliced across them, his powerful torso blocking the spray of the breakers.

All Leigh could do was watch.

MacAllister had gone in after Tori.

The kid's progress was a blur on the edge of Nick's vision as he stumbled out of the waves, Sophie's body limp in his arms. Rain pelted him; wind tore at his shirt. He fought the urge to drop to his knees and vomit.

Leigh ran to him, grabbed at his arm. "Is she . . . ?"

"She's not gone. Not if I can help it." Gasping for air, he lowered Sophie to the sand and checked her breathing.

None.

In the distance, a siren wailed. *Finally.* "Run back and meet the EMTs. Get them out here fast."

She nodded and took off.

He pressed a finger to Sophie's neck. Pulse weak. Her lips were blue. She still wasn't breathing.

He had a sudden flash of Leigh, much younger than Sophie, lying limp in his arms in just the same way. He swallowed hard. He hadn't lost Leigh then; he wouldn't lose Sophie now.

His focus shrank. Time slowed. He blew a series of short breaths into Sophie's mouth. Her small chest expanded. He turned his head, listening.

"Come on, baby," he muttered. "Don't do this to me."

He gave her his breath again, forcing himself to keep an even rhythm, counting off the seconds in between. Wind whipped sand into his eyes, bringing tears. Or had they been there already? He didn't know. He wanted to look up, check Jason's progress, make sure he'd reached Tori, but he didn't dare lose his focus. He gave a breath, counted to three, gave another.

And then he felt Tori beside him, dropping onto the sand. She gasped, wheezing, as she filled her lungs. A wave of dizzying relief flooded him. Tori was alive. Thank God for that.

"Come on, Sophie," he muttered, more urgently now. Blue had crept from her lips to her skin. "Breathe, damn it."

Tears blurred his vision. Beside him, Tori was shaking. Crying. He lowered his head, giving Sophie another breath.

And she gasped. A tiny sound, but the sweetest one Nick had ever heard.

Jason dropped to his knees beside him. "Let me take over."

Nick met the kid's gaze And he realized for the first time that Jason didn't have the eyes of an adolescent. He had a man's eyes, grave and intent.

Nick nodded once and moved aside.

He reached for Tori. She was doubled over, shivering violently. He pulled her into his arms, wrapping around her like a blanket, willing whatever warmth he had left into her body.

Sophie rasped another breath. Then another.

A violent shudder shook through Tori and into Nick's body. "I'm so cold," she whispered.

"You're going into shock. Where the hell are the paramedics?"

"There," Tori said, trying to point toward the street. "They're coming."

It was the last thing she said before she passed out in his arms.

Chapter Thirty-one

You can't hide your heart forever.
Not from a family that loves you.

A soft kiss brushed Tori's forehead.

She opened her eyes. A man's face swam into focus, cast in shadow by the dim night-light illuminating Tori's hospital room.

She struggled to a sitting position. Had he come at last?

"Nick?"

"Nah. Only me."

Her expectant breath left in a rush. "Johnny."

"In the flesh."

He grinned as he flipped on the overhead light. "Try not to look so excited. I thought you'd be happy to see another pesky Santangelo."

Tori blinked against the sudden glare. "Of course I am."

And she was. She'd been surrounded by Santangelos all evening, until the nurse had kicked them out at eleven, but a million lifetimes would pass before she'd ever think of all their love and concern as a nuisance.

"It's just that I thought Nick had . . ." She turned her head toward the window.

"Don't tell me my idiot brother hasn't been in here to see you yet?"

"I guess he came to the hospital with me and Sophie, but he hasn't been to see me since I woke up."

"Leigh said he was a madman when they brought you in. Paced a rut in the waiting room carpet."

Rita had told Tori the same thing. "Then why isn't he here now?"

"I don't know." Johnny tried for another grin. "Want me to find him and beat him up?"

Tori couldn't suppress a smile. "No offense, Johnny, but I'm not sure you could take him."

"I'll have Alex do it, then. He's a professional. Or I could get our third-grade teacher, Sister Mary Frances, out of retirement at the old nuns' home. She was always real good with a ruler. . . ."

Tori tried to laugh, but it came out more like a wheeze. "Thanks, but no thanks. How'd you get in here, anyway?" She squinted at the clock. Three a.m. "It's way past visiting hours."

"It wasn't hard." He spread his arms, inviting Tori to really look at him. He wore a white lab coat over green hospital scrubs. A stethoscope dangled from his neck.

"You sneaked in dressed like a doctor?"

"Not just any doctor." He tapped his nametag.

"'Dr. Gavin Hunter,'" Tori read. "'Franklinville General Hospital.'" Her eyes widened. "Oh, my God! Does this mean you got the part?"

"Affirmative, sweetie. You're looking at *FH*'s newest bad-boy surgeon."

"Oh, Johnny, that's wonderful!" She gave him a hug, ignoring the bedrail between them. "When do you start filming?"

"Monday."

"What about the earrings and the stubble?" she asked, touching his chin. "I can't imagine any surgeon looking as wild as you do."

"Hunter does. He's got a reputation, apparently."

Tori laughed. "I can't wait to see him in action."

Johnny lowered the bedrail and sat, his weight dipping the mattress. His eyes turned grave. "I know you must've heard this about a thousand times, but I have to say it, too. Thank you for saving Sophie."

Tori picked at a rip on the edge of the hospital blanket. "It was my fault she got in trouble in the first place. If I hadn't distracted Leigh . . ."

"Don't play that game, Tori. There's never a winner. Just be glad it turned out the way it did."

She sighed. "I guess you're right."

He chucked her under the chin. "As always. They're gonna build a shrine to me someday, you know."

Tori tried for a smile and failed. A tear escaped instead.

"Cut that out," he chided. "You'll be making me cry next. Think about getting out of this place—that should cheer you up. When are they springing you?"

"Later this morning. Around eleven. After the doctor checks me over."

"Who's minding the shop tomorrow?"

"Leigh and Rita. They've been so—"

Just then, a nurse bustled into the room. She took one look at Johnny and her brows collided.

Johnny raised his palms. "Don't call the cops; I'm on my way out." He turned to Tori before he ducked through the door.

"I'll be back at eleven. I'll drive you home."

Home.

Where was that?

Nick blinked at his computer screen, but the numbers kept moving. He'd been up all night, riding a wave of raw terror he couldn't outswim. Once he'd found out Tori and Sophie were going to be okay, he'd gone home and thrown up. Afterward, knowing he'd never sleep, he pulled on dry clothes and headed to the office.

It was only a few miles, but he'd had to pull over when the tears started coming too hard and too fast.

He'd almost lost them both.

He'd almost lost Tori.

God, it hurt to love someone this much.

He dozed, head on his desk, for an hour, maybe two.

Woke up to run some bid numbers. Around four he dictated some correspondence into his handheld recorder for Doris to type up later.

Little by little, the terror receded.

His head came up when Alex walked in at six a.m., looking as haggard and worn as Nick felt.

"I thought you might be here," his brother said, lowering his big frame into the chair facing Nick's desk. "I didn't get a chance to thank you last night. For saving Sophie. God. I owe you my life. I don't know what I would've done if I'd lost her."

Nick ran a hand over his face, panic clawing to the surface again.

"You would've done the same for Leigh. And besides, it was Tori who kept Sophie afloat."

"I know. I'm going to fill her house with flowers. Is she coming home today? I was with Sophie all night and didn't get to stop by her room."

"I don't know," Nick said, not meeting his brother's gaze. "I didn't see Tori, either."

"You didn't? Why not?"

Nick picked up a pen, fiddled with the cap. "I . . . I just couldn't," he confessed. "I was a wreck. If I'd been there when she woke up, I would've lost it."

He looked up to find Alex watching him, a slightly bemused expression on his face.

Nick frowned at him. "What?"

"You really are in love with her, aren't you?"

"Yeah," said Nick, rubbing the back of his neck. "I really am."

Nonna arrived at six twenty, a bare minute after Alex had left. They must have passed in the reception area.

Nonna stepped firmly through Nick's office door, handbag clutched to her chest. Nick got to his feet.

"Nonna. What're you doing here?"

"Nicky, you look like five miles of bad road."

"I love you, too, Nonna." He frowned when Rita didn't appear in the doorway. "Didn't Ma bring you over?"

Nonna waved a blue-veined hand. "Nah. I walked."

"Walked? From Bellevue Avenue?"

She settled her handbag on Nick's desk. "Of course from Bellevue Avenue. Where else would I walk from? It ain't that far."

"Only two freaking miles, Nonna. Why are you here?"

She looked him over. "You know, Nicky, your manners could be better."

He sighed.

She took the chair that Alex had vacated. "I came to talk about your girlfriend."

"I'd rather not," Nick said, going around the desk. "Come on; I'll take you home." He picked up her handbag. The thing weighed a freaking ton. "Jeez, Nonna, what've you got in here, bricks?"

"Nah. Just a few things I picked up."

He wanted to throttle her. "Didn't the necktie fiasco teach you anything? You gotta stop with the shoplifting already."

"Who said anything about shoplifting?"

He watched her rummage through the bag, extracting items one by one. Hair spray. Breath mints. A lacy red bra, C-cup, with the price tag still attached.

Nick swore under his breath.

"Watch that mouth," Nonna said without looking up. "It'll get you in trouble one of these days. Ah. Here it is." She held up a battered cardboard jeweler's box wound with yellowed cellophane tape.

At least it didn't look like stolen goods. "What is it?"

She placed it on his desk. "Open it and see."

Bemused, he peeled away the ancient tape. Inside, the box was stuffed with old cotton balls. He pulled them out one by one. And stared at what lay underneath.

A simple, worn band of gold. One he remembered seeing on Nonna's left hand all the years of his childhood.

His throat suddenly thickened. "I can't take this."

Nonna snorted. "It's not for you. It's for Tori."

"But this is your wedding ring."

"Not mine anymore. It belongs to your fiancée."

"Tori and I aren't engaged." But his fingers tightened on the box.

"You will be," Nonna said smugly. "Remember I told you I was gonna light a two-dollar candle for you at St. Michael's and pray for you to find a wife? Well, I lit *three* two-dollar candles."

"Nonna, I don't care if you lit enough two-dollar candles to burn the whole freaking church down. Tori and I . . ." He let out a breath. "I've treated her badly. I'm not sure she even wants to talk to me anymore."

"Then you go talk to her, Nicky. Don't let her get away. She's good for you. She makes you feel things."

"And what's so great about that?" he muttered. He picked up the ring, examining it more closely.

"Look inside," Nonna said.

He tilted it into the light. The inscription was in Italian, in spidery letters.

Mia vita nelle tue mani.
My life in your hands.

His head came up, a thought striking hard. "Why didn't you give me this for Cindy?"

"That wife of yours?" Nonna snorted. "Good wine don't come from bad grapes, Nicky. I knew that girl was no good. I told your mother your marrying her would be a mistake."

"I never knew that."

"Would you have listened if I told you?"

He shook his head. "No. Cindy was carrying my child."

"That's right. And you wanted that baby, Nicky. More than anything."

And he had, he realized, stunned. He'd wanted Leigh

more than he'd wanted Cindy, more than he'd wanted college, more than he'd wanted a glamorous career as a big-city architect. Leigh's birth hadn't ruined his life. It had given him purpose, and made him the man he was today. It was the fear of losing her that had torn him apart.

"You can't hide your heart forever, Nicky. Not from a family that loves you. You have to show them your tears."

She stood and started repacking her handbag. The ring glinted in Nick's palm.

You have to show them your tears.

His fingers closed, the ring pressing a circle into his palm.

"Wait, Nonna. I'll drive you home. I'm going in that direction anyway."

Stopped at a traffic light after dropping Nonna at home, Nick punched Johnny's number on his cell. Johnny answered just as the light turned green.

"Yo."

"Johnny, it's Nick."

"Nick?" A pause. "Dude. What d'ya need?"

Nick swallowed. "Ma told me you got the soap part."

"Yeah. Yeah, I did."

"Congratulations." He paused. "I'm proud of you, you know."

Dead silence. Then, "You are?"

Johnny's voice was uncertain, the way it had been when he was younger, and Nick was the closest thing he'd had to a father.

"Yeah, I am. When's the show air, anyway?"

"Weekday afternoons at one. But don't tell me you're actually going to watch it."

"Are you kidding? My little brother's on freaking television. I wouldn't miss it for the world."

Several more beats of silence passed.

"Thanks," Johnny said. His voice was strangely hoarse. Then, "Nick? Can I ask you something?"

"What?"

"What're you doing this morning at eleven?"

"Dad! What are you doing here?"

Leigh tried to step in front of Jason, which was ridiculous, really. It wasn't as if her father could miss him. Behind her, Jason gave a soft snort. He placed his hands on her shoulders and eased her aside.

Her dad's eyes flicked toward Jason, then back to her. "I thought Mimi was going to help you with Tori's shop this morning."

"She was," Leigh stammered. "She is. She just stopped over at the hospital to bring Tori some clothes to go home in. And anyway, we're not even open yet."

Her dad looked at Jason and frowned. "Shouldn't you be on the beach by now?"

"It's my day off, Mr. Santangelo."

One of those awkward pauses followed. The kind that went on and on until it got so big and heavy no one could push it out of the way.

Her dad began to speak, then cleared his throat. He looked around the shop, back toward the door, up at the crystals hanging from the ceiling. Everywhere, it seemed, but at her and Jason. It was almost as if he were . . . nervous?

No. He couldn't be.

He drew a breath. "Leigh. I have something for you."

He took a key out of his pocket and dropped it on the counter.

She squealed. "My car? It's done? I can drive it again?"

"Yeah. *You* can drive it." He sent a pointed glance toward Jason. "No one else."

She flung her arms around him. "This is amazing! No one else, I promise!"

He kissed the top of her head, just like he used to when she was little, and it felt so good that she gave him an extra hug. She felt him smile against her hair before he let her go.

She nearly lost it when he held out his hand to Jason.

"I want to thank you for what you did yesterday. Tori ouldn't have made it if you hadn't been there."

Jason met her dad's eyes squarely as he shook his hand. eigh saw something private pass between them, a man-to- an kind of thing.

"Anyone would have gone in after Tori, Mr. Santangelo."

"Maybe. But not everyone would've gotten her back out gain. Not in that surf." He paused, clearing his throat. ook, Jason, why don't you come by the house for dinner night? Nonna's making pizza."

"I'd be glad to, sir."

Leigh shook her head, not quite believing her ears. "Does is mean you've changed your mind about Jason?" she asked er dad. "You're not going to stop me from seeing him?"

"Have I actually been doing that?" he replied dryly.

She ducked her head. "I never wanted to go behind your ack."

"I know. I didn't make it easy on you."

There was something sad in his eyes, something she ouldn't stand. She knew what it was.

"There's another thing I lied to you about," she said iickly, before she could lose her nerve.

His expression turned wary. "What now?"

She drew a breath. "Jason and I . . . we didn't . . . we aven't . . ." *Oh, God.* She was never going to be able to get out.

Jason came to her rescue. "What Leigh's trying to say is iat she and I haven't . . ." He blushed. Actually *blushed.* We haven't been, um, intimate. She . . . *we've* decided to ait."

She dared a peek at her dad. He had the oddest expression i his face. Surprise—yeah, she figured that—but something se, too. Something that looked like . . . respect.

His gaze shifted to Jason. "Leigh cares a lot about you. nd I'm beginning to realize that I've been wrong, keeping ›u two apart. I'd like to get to know you better."

"I'd like that, too, sir." Jason's voice was low, and more serious than Leigh had ever heard it. It made her heart do a little flip in her chest.

"Good. Now, Jason, can I ask you a favor?"

"Sure," Jason said. "What is it?"

"Do you think you could watch the shop alone for an hour? I need my daughter's advice."

Chapter Thirty-two

Each new branch on the family tree only makes it stronger.

Tori *hated* hospitals.

One night of muted walls and dinging call bells was more than enough to last her for a lifetime. She couldn't wait to leave. She pulled on the tie-dye yoga pants and yellow smiley-face tee that Rita had dropped off. Then she sneaked out of her room to visit Sophie on the floor below.

Sophie was staying in the hospital another day, just to make sure everything was all right. Sophie's mother, Alex's ex, was asleep sitting up in the chair beside the bed. Tori hugged Sophie tight and sent up a prayer of thanks that she was alive and well.

Back in her own room, a doctor checked Tori over, then signed her release papers. Eleven o'clock approached. If Johnny wasn't late—which he almost always was—he'd be here any minute to take her home.

She looked at the phone, hoping it would ring before she left. Hoping Nick would call. She couldn't puzzle it out. If he'd been so worried about her last night, as everyone had said, why hadn't he even stopped in to see her?

She missed him so much. She wanted to touch him, tell him she loved him, tell him it didn't matter if they ever had a baby together. She'd lost her heart to him, and she had a feeling she wasn't going to be getting it back.

Sighing, she stuffed the last of her belongings into her neon orange tote bag.

The door creaked just as the digital clock on the night stand blinked eleven. Amazing. Johnny was right on time. She pasted a smile on her face and turned to greet him.

But it wasn't Johnny in the doorway.

It was Nick.

Nick, looking tired and rumpled in torn jeans and ripped T-shirt, a day's worth of beard on his chin. He looked so handsome, her heart nearly stopped.

"I . . . I was expecting Johnny," she stammered.

"I know. He's not coming."

"Oh."

He moved closer. "This all you got?" He lifted Tori's Day Glo orange tote, looked at it, and winced. "What are you going hunting after this?"

"No," she said with a small laugh. "Just home."

Her eyes teared up. She didn't want him to see, so she brushed past him and out the door. The nurse came at her with a wheelchair, but she waved it away and all but ran to the elevator.

Nick followed, frowning. In the parking lot he helped her into his truck with a hand at her elbow. His touch was warm, and he kept shooting her quick glances that she couldn't read. A couple of times, he started to speak, then stopped, letting out a long breath and clenching his jaw.

As they drove, the town whizzed past in a jumbled blur until Nick missed the turn onto her street.

Tori sat up. "You're going the wrong way."

He sent her another one of his quick glances. "No, I'm not."

"But my house is back there."

"Yeah," he said. "I know."

He made a smooth turn off Atlantic. He pulled into his driveway, parked, and rounded the hood to open her door all before she remembered to take a breath.

He scooped her off the passenger seat and into his arms.

"What . . . what are you doing?"

He held her tight, his lips touching a quick kiss to her forehead. "You'll see."

He carried her into the house and straight up two dizzying flights of spiral stairs. Shoving a door with his hip, he moved inside a large room and set Tori's feet down on a pale Berber carpet.

Her gaze traveled the room. She was in a bedroom, and it was obviously Nick's. The furnishings were sparse, masculine. The walls were white. The carpet was the color of sand.

The whole setup desperately needed some color.

Then again, maybe it didn't. Maybe she liked it just the way it was.

"You know," he said, "I've never brought a woman up here."

Her heart seized. "Didn't your wife live here with you?"

"Our room was downstairs back then. Ma and Pop had this room. A couple years ago, Ma insisted I take it. Said she was sick of climbing the extra flight of stairs."

Tori ventured a few steps into Nick's private sanctuary. A king-size bed commanded the center of the room. It was spread with a truly hideous beige-on-black comforter.

One corner was turned down, revealing . . .

She turned and gaped at him. "You have pink satin sheets?"

He nodded toward his dresser, where a bottle peeked from an ice bucket. "And champagne. Dom Pérignon."

She sat down—hard—on the bed. Her trembling fingers brushed the pink satin pillowcase.

"Is this . . . Did you buy them for me?"

"The champagne, I had in the house. Leigh bought the sheets this morning. She said you had to have them."

She splayed her fingers on the pillow. "What else did she say?"

"Enough," Nick said quietly. "Enough to make me realize I went about seducing you the wrong way."

"There was nothing wrong with the way you seduced me. I wouldn't trade a minute of it." She studied him. "So . . . does this mean you and Leigh are back on speaking terms?"

"Yeah, we are. In fact, I'm on speaking terms with Jason, too. He's not such a bad kid."

"She hasn't slept with him, you know."

"I know." He grimaced and dragged a hand down his face. "Not yet, anyway."

"Leigh's careful. Like you. She'll wait until it's right."

"I know that, too." He let out a sigh. "I can't keep her young forever."

"No. But . . . I shouldn't have given her those condoms knowing how you felt about Jason. I'm sorry I interfered."

"Don't be. I'm surrounded by interfering women. Maybe I should even listen to them once in a while."

A smile tugged at her lips. "Maybe you should."

He took a step closer. Then—and her eyes widened when he did it—he went down on one knee.

He took both her hands in his, and brushed his lips over the backs of her fingers. "Do you think I could persuade you to interfere in my life on a permanent basis?"

Her heart gave a little jump. "How permanent?"

His eyes didn't leave her face. "Marry me, Tori."

She stared. "But . . . you don't want a wife. You don't want another child."

His grip tightened. "I know I said that, but the truth is . . . I do want those things. I'm just scared. I'm scared to death. When you were in that water and I knew I couldn't save you . . ." He met her gaze, not hiding the wash of moisture in his eyes. "I'm sorry I wasn't there when you woke up last night. Do you want to know why I stayed away?"

She nodded.

"I was here, throwing up. Crying like a baby. Loving you the way I do, knowing how much I'd love our child . . . it frightens me that much, Tori."

"Oh, Nick." She drew him into a hug. He pressed his cheek to her breast, his arms wrapping tight around her torso.

"I know you want a baby soon," he said. "But I gotta tell you, I don't think I can handle it right away. I want some time for us, alone, first. A year, maybe?"

"You can have it. You were right to want to take things more slowly. I went to my doctor last week. I told her I'd have the surgery."

He lifted his head and looked up at her. "Really? You'd do that?"

She nodded. "It's already scheduled. For the first week in September."

"I'll be there," he said. "We all will. You won't be alone for a minute." He kissed her, drawing out the sweetness. Then he pulled back, his gaze serious.

"I want you to marry me, Tori, but before you give me an answer, you should know up front what you're in for. I can be hell to live with. I'm too serious, and I have a quick temper. You'll hate it. I'll get crabby and yell at you, and then when you want to talk about it, I'll run to the office."

She smoothed the hair from his face. He turned his head and kissed her palm. "But, please, if you marry me, keep after me, Tori. Make me face myself. Make me talk. Because I'm telling you right now, I won't ever let you leave me the way I let Cindy go."

"I'll never want to leave you."

His eyes flared dark. His lips curved in the slow, sexy smile she loved. His gaze dropped to her breasts. He moved over her, urging her legs apart with his knee.

A hot, restless ache lapped at her belly.

"I love you," she said.

"A lot of people fall in love. Then they fall out again just as easily. I love you, too, Tori, but we'll need something more than love when the storms come. We'll need a commitment, and a promise. Promise to be my wife, Tori, and I'll promise never to give up on us. Never."

"Oh, Nick. Of course I'll be your wife. There's nothing I want more."

He kissed her. At the same time, he smoothly reached

past her to yank down the comforter. He tumbled her onto the pink satin sheets. His hands were already slipping under her shirt.

Before long, they were both naked.

"Wait," Nick said suddenly, pushing himself up and off the bed. "I almost forgot. The champagne."

She admired his butt as he strode across the room and popped the cork. He returned with two flutes and handed her one.

She took a sip, sinking back onto satin pillows and twirling the glass. "Champagne and pink satin sheets." She smiled. "Two out of three items on my ultimate fantasy list. Does this mean I'm going to get the poetry, too?"

Nick plucked the flute from her fingers and set it on the nightstand. He rose over her, pressing her down into the slippery, pink sea.

"Anything you want." He waited a beat. "But I gotta warn you, I only know one love poem."

She squinted up at him. "What is it?"

He gave her his slowest, sexiest smile.

" 'There once was a girl from Nantucket . . .' "

Chapter Thirty-three

> *Privacy? Privacy? What is that?*
> *The word is not part of family vocabulary.*

Later that afternoon, Nick's cell phone rang. *Jesus.* He'd forgotten to turn the damn thing off. It was somewhere on the floor with his clothes. He rolled over, checked the clock on the nightstand, and groaned.

"Six p.m.," he told Tori, who was just stirring. "We slept all afternoon."

"Not *all* afternoon," she said with a satisfied smirk.

The Notre Dame fight song continued. Nick grumbled a curse and went to fish the phone out of his pants. Out of habit, he flipped it open.

"Santangelo here."

"Yo, bro, Johnny here. News flash: It's dinnertime. You and Tori might be able to live on love alone, but the rest of us are starving, and Nonna won't cut the pizza without you. Get your horny butts down here."

A round of laughter sounded in the background—Rita, he thought, and Alex and Leigh, and—goddamn it—Jason.

"Johnny, are you calling me from the kitchen?"

"The dining room, but what's it matter? Be glad I'm not pounding on your door." His brother laughed. "Or better yet, standing there watching."

"Go screw yourself," Nick said without heat.

"Tell Nicky the pizza's getting cold," he heard Rita say in the background.

"Nick, Ma says—"

"I heard her." He snapped the phone closed and gave a rueful laugh. "Hell."

Tori sat up and stretched. "What's the matter?"

"The whole family's downstairs. They want us to get out of bed and come to dinner."

"Well . . ." Tori said, scooting across the pink satin. For a moment Nick was distracted by the sight of her bare bottom. "Let's not keep them waiting."

He watched her bend over to pick up her clothes, and he instantly went hard again.

"Are you absolutely sure you want to be part of this family? You don't know what you're getting into. No privacy, no respect. People telling you what to do every minute."

Her head emerged from her T-shirt. "It sounds wonderful."

"It's not. It's a pain in the goddamn ass."

Her green eyes danced. "I think I can suffer through it."

She padded over and wrapped her arms around his waist. He tossed the phone on the bed and pulled her close, his annoyance drifting away. Now that he'd shared his worst fears with her, they didn't seem quite so overwhelming.

Marriage, a baby or two . . . Letting himself take each moment as it came might be easier than he'd thought. Because every moment with Tori was worth a lifetime.

"You know," she said suddenly, "almost all my candle magic spells have worked."

He groaned. "Please. Don't start with that magic BS again."

"It's true! I lit that first spell for the shop, but what I was really wishing for underneath was a family. Not only did you finish my shop, but now I have the best family in the world too."

Nick fought the urge to look toward heaven. "You will never convince me that your lighting that white candle had anything to do with what's happened between us."

"The other spells worked, too," she continued, as if he hadn't said a word. She started ticking them off on her finers. "I lit a candle for success, and the shop's doing great. The good-luck spell went to Johnny, and he got his soap role. The spell for clarity led me to make the right decision about the donor. The love spell brought Leigh and Jason together, and the black candle banished all the negativity from my life."

"Tori—"

"In fact, there's only one candle magic spell left unfulfilled. The fertility spell." She sent him a smug smile, her gaze traveling slowly down his naked body. "And somehow, I have a feeling that's only a matter of time."

Nick shook his head, laughing. "Jesus. You're as bad as Nonna with this candle-lighting thing."

"Nonna? What does she have to do with it?"

"She told me she lit three two-dollar candles at St. Michael's and prayed I'd find a wife."

Tori started grinning. "And now we're engaged. You really think that's a coincidence?"

"I damn well know it is."

"Ha." She went up on her tiptoes and linked her arms round his neck. "Believe what you want. I know magic brought us together. I love you," she added. "Now and always. Magically."

"You're freaking nuts, you know that?"

He tucked a stray curl behind her ear. He shook his head, chuckling as he lowered his mouth for a kiss. Ah, well, he thought, let Tori believe in magic if it made her happy. He had to admit, there was definitely something magical about what he felt for his enchanting wife-to-be.

"You know," he said, "magic or not, I lucked out. Only a woman as crazy as you would want to marry both me *and* my family."

Nick's cell phone started ringing again.

He didn't answer it. He was too busy kissing the woman he loved.